Allegiance of Honor

Allegiance of Honor

NALINI SINGH

BERKLEY BOOKS, NEW YORK

BERKLEY

An imprint of Penguin Random House LLC
375 Hudson Street, New York, New York 10014

This book is an original publication of Penguin Random House LLC.

Library of Congress Cataloging-in-Publication Data

Names: Singh, Nalini, 1977–author.
Title: Allegiance of honor / Nalini Singh.
Description: First Edition. | New York : Berkley Books, 2016. | Series: Psy-changeling novel
Identifiers: LCCN 2015050507 (print) | LCCN 2016006696 (ebook) | ISBN 9781101987766 (hardback) | ISBN 9781101987773 ()
Subjects: | BISAC: FICTION / Romance / Paranormal. | FICTION / Fantasy / Paranormal. | GSAFD: Romantic suspense fiction. | Fantasy fiction.
Classification: LCC PR9639.4.S566 A77 2016 (print) | LCC PR9639.4.S566 (ebook) | DDC 823/.92—dc23
LC record available at http://lccn.loc.gov/2015050507

FIRST EDITION: June 2016

PRINTED IN THE UNITED STATES OF AMERICA

10 9 8 7 6 5 4 3 2 1

Cover art by Rita Frangie.

Penguin
Random
House

CAST OF CHARACTERS

In Alphabetical Order by First Name
Key: SD = SnowDancer Wolves, DR = DarkRiver Leopards, BC = BlackSea Changelings, RF = RainFire Leopards

Abbot Arrow, teleport-capable telekinetic (Tk), married and psychically bonded to Jaya

Aden Kai Arrow, telepath (Tp), psychically bonded to Zaira

Adria SD Senior Soldier, in permanent relationship with Riaz

Amara Aleine Psy member of DR, former Council scientist, twin of Ashaya, mentally unstable

Andrew "Drew" Kincaid SD Tracker, mated to Indigo, brother of Riley and Brenna

Aneca Rat changeling, child

Annie Quinn Human member of DR, mated and married to Zach

Anthony Kyriakus Former Psy Councilor, part of the Ruling Coalition, head of PsyClan NightStar, father of Faith, Tanique, and Marine (deceased)

Ashaya Aleine Psy member of DR, former Council scientist, mated to Dorian, mother of Keenan, twin of Amara

Ava SD, mated to Spencer, mother of Ben

Bastien Smith DR, mated to Kirby, in charge of DR's financial assets, brother of Mercy, Sage, and Grey

Ben SD pup, son of Ava and Spencer

Bowen "Bo" Knight Human Alliance Security Chief (and effective leader), brother of Lily

Brenna Kincaid SD Tech, mated to Judd, sister of Riley and Andrew

Carolina Arrow child

Clara Alvarez Manager of Haven, former Justice Psy (J)

Clay DR Sentinel, mated to Talin, adopted children: Noor and Jon

Cooper SD Lieutenant, mated to Grace

Council (or Psy Council) Former ruling council of the Psy race; no longer extant

Cruz Forgotten child

Desiree (Dezi) DR Senior Soldier

Devraj "Dev" Santos Leader of the Forgotten, married and psychically bonded to Katya, guardian of Cruz

Dorian DR Sentinel, mated to Ashaya, father to Keenan

Elias (Eli) SD Senior Soldier, mated to Yuki, father of Sakura

Emmett DR Senior Soldier, mated and married to Ria

Ena Mercant Psy, matriarch of Mercant family group

Evie Riviere SD, sister of Indigo

Faith NightStar Psy member of DR, cardinal foreseer (F), mated to Vaughn, daughter of Anthony, sister of Tanique, cousin to Sahara

Forgotten Psy who defected from the PsyNet at the dawn of Silence and intermingled with the human and changeling populations

Grace SD Tech, mated to Cooper

Hawke SD Alpha, mated to Sienna

Indigo Riviere SD Lieutenant, mated to Andrew, sister of Evie

Ivy Jane Zen President of the Empathic Collective, married and psychically bonded to Vasic

Jamie DR Senior Soldier

Jason DR medic-in-training

Jaya Empath, married and psychically bonded to Abbot

Jojo RF cub

Jonquil "Jon" Duchslaya Forgotten teen, member of DR, adopted by Clay and Talin

Judd Lauren SD Lieutenant, Psy, mated to Brenna, brother of Walker; uncle of Sienna, Toby, and Marlee

Julian DR cub, twin of Roman, son of Nathan and Tamsyn

Kaleb Krychek Cardinal (Tk), part of the Ruling Coalition, psychically bonded to Sahara

Katya Haas Psy, former assistant to Ashaya Aleine, married and psychically bonded to Devraj Santos, guardian of Cruz

Keenan Aleine Psy member of DR, child

Kirby DR, mated to Bastien, lynx changeling

Kit DR Soldier, brother of Rina

Lara SD Healer, mated to Walker, raising Marlee and Toby with Walker

Leila Savea BC, marine biologist

Leon Kyriakus M-Psy, father of Sahara

Lily Human Alliance, sister of Bowen

Lucas Hunter DR Alpha, mated to Sascha, father of Naya

Malachai BC, Lieutenant

Marlee Psy member of SD, daughter of Walker, cousin to Sienna and Toby

Max Shannon Human, Security Chief for Nikita Duncan, married to Sophia

Mercy Smith DR Sentinel, mated to Riley, sister of Bastien, Sage, and Grey

Miane Levèque BC Alpha

Ming LeBon Former Psy Councilor, military mastermind, cardinal telepath (Tp)

Nathan "Nate" Ryder DR Senior Sentinel, mated to Tamsyn, father of Roman and Julian

Naya Hunter DR cub, daughter of Sascha and Lucas

Nikita Duncan Former Psy Councilor, part of the Ruling Coalition, mother of Sascha

Noor Hassan Forgotten member of DR, adopted by Clay and Talin

Pax Marshall Psy, Head of the Marshall Group

Remi RF Alpha

Ria Human member of DR, mated and married to Emmett, executive admin assistant to Lucas

Riaz SD Lieutenant, in permanent relationship with Adria

Riley Kincaid SD Senior Lieutenant, mated to Mercy, brother of Andrew and Brenna

Rina DR Soldier, sister of Kit

Roman DR cub, twin of Julian, son of Nathan and Tamsyn

Ruling Coalition Formed after the fall of Silence and of the Psy Council; composed of Kaleb Krychek, Nikita Duncan, Anthony Kyriakus, Ivy Jane Zen for the Empathic Collective, and Aden Kai for the Arrow Squad

Sahara Kyriakus Psy (uncategorized designation), psychically bonded to Kaleb, daughter of Leon, niece of Anthony Kyriakus, cousin to Faith

Sakura SD pup

Samuel Rain Psy, genius, robotics engineer who developed experimental biofusion

Sascha Duncan Psy member of DR, cardinal empath, mated to Lucas, mother of Naya, daughter of Nikita

Sienna Psy member of SD, cardinal X, mated to Hawke, sister of Toby, niece of Judd and Walker

Silver Mercant Psy, senior aide to Kaleb Krychek, in charge of worldwide rapid response emergency network that spans all three races

Sophia Russo Former Justice Psy (J), married to Max Shannon, senior aide to Nikita

Stefan (Tk), Commander of the deep-sea station Alaris

Talin (Tally) Human member of DR, mated to Clay, adopted children: Noor and Jon

Tamsyn "Tammy" Ryder DR Healer, mated to Nathan, mother of Roman and Julian

Tanique Gray Psychometric, son of Anthony, brother of Faith

Tavish Arrow child

Teijan Rat Alpha

Toby Lauren Psy member of SD, brother of Sienna, nephew of Judd and Walker, cousin to Marlee

Vasic Zen Arrow, teleporter (Tk-V), married and psychically bonded to Ivy Jane, great-grandson of Zie Zen

Vaughn DR Sentinel, mated to Faith, jaguar changeling

Walker Lauren Psy member of SD, teacher, mated to Lara, father of Marlee, brother of Judd, uncle of Sienna and Toby

Xavier Perez Human, priest, friend of Judd and Kaleb

Yuki SD, lawyer, mated to Elias, mother of Sakura

Yuri Arrow, telepath

Zach DR Soldier, mated and married to Annie

Zaira Neve Arrow, telepath (combat), psychically bonded to Aden

Zane Second in command of the Rats

Zie Zen Psy elder, great-grandfather of Vasic

AUTHOR'S NOTE

Dear Readers,

Thank you for coming with me on this journey into the Psy-Changeling world. It's been a wild and unpredictable ride, hasn't it? I've had so much fun, and with every new story, I've fallen more and more in love with this world and the characters who live in it.

Shards of Hope closed what I think of as the first arc, or season one, of the series, while also opening season two. Before we dive fully into the next arc, however, I want to take a look back and see how far the world and its characters have come since *Slave to Sensation*.

Not only that, but I want to explore the myriad connections that bind these disparate characters together. In writing this book, the hardest thing was not how to bring characters in so everyone had a chance to shine, but *where*—because there is never simply one connection. Each and every character is linked to multiple others through bonds of pack, of friendship, of blood, of loyalty, and of course, of love.

So this book, while continuing the Psy-Changeling storyline—because nothing is ever static in this world—is also a walk through the interconnected lives of many of the characters who've become important to us over the past books and novellas. With a cast this sprawling, not everyone gets a mention or page time in each book (imagine how long the books would be if that happened!), but in this story, we get an update on a whole lot of people.

Even then, not everything I wanted to add made it into this book, so I'll be sharing more than one deleted scene in my newsletter over the coming months. You can subscribe to the newsletter for free at my website: nalinisingh.com.

I hope you enjoy *Allegiance of Honor*—and here's to the next book and season two of the Psy-Changeling series.

~ Nalini

Tesseract

NO ONE COULD'VE predicted this moment in time.

And, as the clock ticks onward in 2082, no one knows what is to come. The world has changed in countless ways since the day a cardinal empath sat across from a changeling alpha, the empath trying to hide her emotions, the alpha trying to see under her skin.

There has been war, destruction, piercing love.

Loyalties have been tested.

A way of life overturned.

Blood has run red as those who would hold on to power cut down innocent lives.

Soldiers have died.

Children have been born.

Bonds have formed.

Hearts have entwined.

Old enmities have been forgotten and there is a fragile peace . . . and the world stands at a critical crossroads.

Will the bonds hold?

Or will chaos reign?

PART 1

Chapter 1

LUCAS HUNTER, ALPHA of the DarkRiver leopards, ended the comm call with a touch of his index finger against the screen. The outwardly calm action belied his current state of mind: his jaw was a grim line, his claws shoving at the insides of his skin as the black panther within snarled.

He was still battling the urge to release that snarl when one of his sentinels stuck his head into the room. That room was Lucas's private office at the pack's Chinatown HQ, from where they ran their myriad business enterprises. Pitch-black hair and dark green eyes vivid against the deep brown of his skin, his shoulders solid, Clay was officially the Chief Construction Supervisor at DarkRiver Construction, but before that, he was one of the most trusted members of the pack, a man Lucas knew would always have his back.

Today, the sentinel was dressed as if he planned to go to a site, his pants of a tough black material appropriate for the outdoor environment and his T-shirt wild green with DarkRiver Construction in white on the back. But when he spoke, he said, "Jon and his friends found something down by the piers."

Lucas scowled, not in the mood for juvenile high jinks today. "Why aren't they in school?"

"Half day off. Some big citywide teachers meeting." Clay's right T-shirt sleeve lifted as he braced his hand against the doorjamb, revealing the slashing lines of the tattoo that echoed the hunter marks on the right side of Lucas's face. Lucas had been born with those jagged, primal marks that identified him as a changeling hunter, born with the ability to track down and execute changelings who'd gone rogue, submerging totally into the animal side of their nature.

Unlike wild animals, however, rogue changelings couldn't be left to roam, because despite their animal skin, they *weren't* animals. Rogues always came after the people they had loved when whole, as if part of them remembered who they'd once been and envied their packmates and lovers for still living that life. Lucas hadn't had to execute a rogue for over seven years, and he hoped that record held for another seven and another and another.

No alpha wanted to kill his people.

Clay's tattoo denoted something far different; like the rest of DarkRiver's sentinels, he'd had the mark inked as a silent symbol of his loyalty to Lucas. That loyalty was a truth Lucas never took for granted. An alpha who didn't value the respect of such strong men and women shouldn't be alpha.

"Anyway, I'm heading over to see what's up," Clay said now. "Kid sounds worried."

"I'll come with you." Lucas walked around his desk, shrugging his shoulders back to loosen muscles that had bunched up at the start of the comm call and stayed that way. "Could do with the fresh air. You want to walk?" It wasn't far to the waterfront.

Clay glanced at the heavy black watch strapped to his left wrist. "Better drive. I have to be at a work site within the hour."

"I'll walk back so you can head to the site straight after we speak to the boys." Sliding out his phone, Lucas sent a message as they walked out of the building and hopped in a pack vehicle.

The reply that made his phone buzz thirty seconds later helped with his feral tension. As did the emotions that kissed him through his mating bond with Sascha. Nothing calmed his panther as quickly as her touch. And though she was a woman who could heal emotional wounds, her empathic gift a treasured one, he knew she wasn't trying to manipulate or influence him. It was Sascha's love itself that settled him, along with the knowledge that she and their child were safe and sound.

Beside him, Clay stayed silent until after they'd pulled away from the

HQ. That silence held no dark emotional undertones as it once had—the big, heavily muscled sentinel was simply quiet.

"A pool of silence," Lucas's mate had said not long ago, the white stars on black of her cardinal gaze lit with the sparks of color that appeared only in the eyes of empaths. "But it's not emptiness. Clay's just so calm, so centered, and so very, *very* content that I feel an untainted peace when I'm near him."

Clay hadn't always been that way. He'd come into DarkRiver as a strong but undisciplined eighteen-year-old who'd never before been part of a pack, who'd never even known another changeling leopard his entire existence. More than that, he'd spent years in juvenile detention. It had left him angry and lost and aggressive, a big, dangerous cat who'd had no idea how to handle either his strength or the fury riding him.

It was Nathan, DarkRiver's most senior sentinel, who'd found that lost boy and hauled him into DarkRiver. But it was Clay who'd done the hard work to become a sentinel himself, earning his place at Lucas's side. Emotionally, he'd still been broken for a long time, his duties to Dark-River and his loyalty to Lucas and the other sentinels the only things that kept him from surrendering to his demons.

Then had come Talin.

In mating with her, then adopting Jon and Noor, Clay had truly left behind the loneliness and pain of his past.

"Trinity Accord?" The sentinel glanced at Lucas before returning his attention to the road.

Putting down the passenger-side window, Lucas tapped his fingers on the edge of the door. "Yes and no."

The world-spanning and groundbreaking cooperation agreement had gone from idea to fruition in an impossibly short period of time, thanks to the existence of the Consortium. The shadowy group's aim of destabilizing the world in order to take advantage of the ensuing chaos had ended up having the opposite effect when the various disparate parties began to talk and realized they had a common enemy. Unfortunately, while

Trinity was a critical asset in the fight for a stable world, the speed with which it had been cobbled together had resulted in more than one critical hole.

The fact that the rush had been unavoidable didn't mean the resulting issues weren't still a pain in the ass. Especially since, with the ink barely dry on the names of the first signatories, Trinity had no administrative structure, which meant everything was being handled on an ad hoc basis.

But that wasn't what had a growl building in the back of Lucas's throat, his panther bristling with aggressive protectiveness once again as the comm call came to the forefront of his mind. "Aden called to pass on some intel," he said, referring to the leader of the Arrow Squad. Assassins and black ops soldiers without compare, the deadly bogeymen of the Psy race had of late become quiet heroes.

It was Aden who'd set Trinity in motion.

Clay shot him another quick look. "Your claws are out."

"Fuck." Lucas retracted them with conscious effort of will, then shoved his hair out of his eyes; the black strands reached his nape at the moment. He'd have had it cut shorter except that Sascha loved running her fingers through it. He might wear a human skin at times, but he was also very much a cat—he wasn't about to do anything to lower his chances of being petted.

Unfortunately, it wasn't such pleasurable thoughts on his mind right then.

"Aden's people picked up chatter about Naya in the back channels of the PsyNet." Sascha had explained the psychic network that connected all Psy on the planet, except for the renegades, as a giant repository of knowledge. It was fluid and so big that no one could ever know every part of it.

The Arrows, however, walked its darkest alleys. Heroes or not, someone still had to hunt the monsters that prowled the PsyNet, the twisted minds that wanted only to murder and to hurt. Because despite over a century of cold emotionlessness that had been meant to erase mental instability and turn them into a race without flaws, the Psy still had an abnormally high number of serial killers. The Arrows alone had the strength and the skill to take down those vicious monsters.

"Why are strangers talking about your cub?" Clay's question was a growl. "Naya is none of their fucking business."

"Exactly." Lucas's protective urges had never been anything but violent. Part of it was simply who he was—he'd been born with the potential to be alpha and that included a powerful protective drive.

In his case, that drive had been honed to a razor's edge by the horror of the childhood attack that had left his mother dead and his father critically injured, Lucas a prisoner of an enemy pack. Young and weak and heartbroken from watching his mother die in front of him, he'd fought desperately to escape his bonds, save his father. He'd failed.

That boy, however, hadn't existed for a long time. Lucas was a man now. An alpha christened in blood. Anyone touched a hair on the head of *any* of the people under his protection, and he'd rip their arms off. That was just for starters. "Aden didn't have too many details," he told Clay, "says the speakers didn't specifically reference Naya by name, but their mention of a Psy-Changeling child with a leopard father makes that a moot point."

At this instant in time, there was only *one* child in the world who had a Psy parent and a changeling parent: Nadiya Shayla Hunter. Naya. Lucas and Sascha's fierce, intelligent, mischievous daughter who was a couple of weeks away from turning one.

Less than a year of life and she'd already changed Lucas on a fundamental level.

He understood now why his father had passed in peace. Carlo Hunter had fought alongside his beloved mate, Shayla, to protect their son, then fought the agonizing pain of losing her and the effects of brutal torture long enough for pack to come. But despite his massive injuries, he'd left this world in peace. Death meant nothing when his child was safe.

"You think it might just be curiosity?" Clay asked. The sentinel was clearly fighting to keep his breathing even, his hands flexing and unflexing on the steering wheel. "Now that Silence has fallen and the Psy are free to feel emotions, have relationships, they have to be wondering about the future. Naya's a living, breathing symbol of that future."

"No." Even had it been curiosity, Lucas still wouldn't have liked that his daughter was being talked about by strangers, a dangerous percentage of whom were virulently against the fall of Silence and the "dilution" of Psy "perfection," but this was far worse. "Aden said his people heard mentions of 'purity' in the chatter." Not everyone liked change, especially when that change challenged their worldview of their own race as superior.

"Fuck." Clay's voice was harsh. "I thought Pure Psy was dead."

"They are." The violent pro-Silence group had been hunted out of existence. "But their ideas are still floating around being absorbed by fanatical, ugly minds. No proof, but the Consortium's probably stirring that rancid stew." What better way to destabilize the world than to slyly encourage hatred among the races?

It was, after all, a tactic they'd already attempted on a bigger scale.

"It had to happen," Clay said unexpectedly. "With the Es suddenly becoming so powerful, there's got to be a hell of a lot of resentment simmering in the minds of folks that previously considered themselves top dogs. Suddenly, all these 'inferior' Psy are being held up as heroes."

Lucas nodded. His own gifted mate had once called herself flawed, been taught to see herself that way. "Aden's people only caught fragments, but there was definite mention of the fact that Naya's mother is an E—and discussion of how to get to them both." Fists clenching, he forced himself to think. "I'm going to review every security protocol around Naya and Sascha."

He knew he'd have Sascha's full support; his mate might chafe at some of the security precautions she had to take as a result of being one half of DarkRiver's alpha pair, but she was completely onboard with any safety measures when it came to their cub. If anything, Sascha was even more protective than Lucas—he often had to remind her that Naya was a leopard changeling, needed more freedom than a human or Psy child of the same age. Cats didn't like being caged. Not even little cats with fragile bones and baby-soft hands.

Remember that, he ordered himself. *Don't allow the enemy to force you into a position where you're the cause of hurt to your own child.*

SASCHA kept a firm hold on her worry after Lucas's message alerting her to dangerous talk in the PsyNet about Naya. It was difficult when she knew exactly the kinds of treacherous minds that hid in the dark corners of the Net and how violently some of those minds despised the primal nature of the changeling race.

To them, Sascha and Lucas's precious child would be an abomination.

Fury churned in her gut.

"Mama!"

Wrenching her anger under control with a harsh effort of will, Sascha tightened her grip on Naya's hands where her baby walked in front of her. Her and Lucas's green-eyed little girl had good balance for her age and a stubborn determination to walk, but she was still little and the forest floor wasn't exactly even, so Sascha was helping keep her upright.

Not that Naya hadn't made a break for it once already.

For the moment, however, her tiny fingers held on firmly to Sascha's hands, her skin soft and the color a golden honey brown. A meld of Sascha's dark honey and Lucas's muted gold. Anglo-Indian, Japanese, Irish, Italian, more, Naya had a beautifully complicated genetic inheritance.

"Naya!" she responded in the same delighted tone, causing her daughter to laugh that big laugh of hers.

Having driven from the aerie, she, Naya, Julian, and Roman were walking the final meters to a border section of DarkRiver's Yosemite territory; the land had been designated a play area for the regular gatherings DarkRiver cubs had begun to have with Arrow children. The sessions had initially been meant to teach the Arrow children how to play when, prior to Aden taking control of the squad, they'd had their innocence suffocated by training that sought to turn them into pitiless assassins and nothing more.

It had very quickly morphed into a fascinating exchange: The changeling and human children taught Arrow young to laugh and to have fun, while the baby Arrows made their wilder playmates stop and think more often than they otherwise might have done. But the best things were the friendships that had begun to form, with the children talking to one another via the comm between sessions.

The pack had put up climbing frames as well as swings in the area, though there was also an open field for unstructured play. Not many nonpack humans lived out this way, but the rare ones who did knew they were welcome to use the equipment and to join in the playgroup.

"Boys."

Julian and Roman froze where they were scampering up ahead, two little statues in jeans and T-shirts. Sascha's lips twitched. It had taken her time to learn that tone, but it was very effective at getting her favorite dose of double trouble to pay attention.

Tamsyn's boys had been the first changeling children Sascha ever met, and she adored them to pieces, was guilty of spoiling them—but she'd also learned to discipline them as they grew. Not because they were naughty in a bad way, but because both were strong personalities and needed to understand that right now, Sascha was the boss when they were with her.

The rules of pack hierarchy existed for a reason, and for DarkRiver cubs, it existed to give them a firm foundation on which to stand. No confusion, no fear. Just a safe place where they could flex their own strength and grow into their personalities.

Oddly, the tone also seemed to work on the boys' pet cat, Ferocious, who—thanks to Roman and Julian's fierce defense of their pet—tended to think of herself as a great big leopard, too. Today, however, Ferocious was at home, so Sascha had to handle only the twins, both of whom were now in their first year of school.

Reaching the two adorable "statues," Naya still holding on to her hands, Sascha said, "You can move now, but stay close." These play sessions would only work long-term if everyone felt safe.

Arrows were Arrows because they'd been born with lethal psychic abilities.

The adult Arrows who helped supervise these sessions extended their own impenetrable shields to encompass the minds of Arrow young, so the kids couldn't strike out by accident and felt free to play without worry of losing control over their deadly powers. Regardless of that, Sascha also always added a layer of protection over the minds of any human or changeling children in the playgroup.

Unlike most humans, changelings had strong natural shields, but there was no point in taking chances.

Ashaya usually attended, too, and between them they could cover the entire group. The rare times the scientist didn't make it, Faith stepped in. Unlike Sascha and Ashaya, the foreseer didn't have a child, but she loved playing with the children and was always happy to help out. And since Faith could create hyper-realistic illusions that fascinated the kids, she was a popular visitor.

Today, Sascha reached the play area to find both women in attendance. The rich brown of Ashaya's skin glowed in the sunlight, her gorgeously wild curls tightly contained in a braid. Those curls were dark brown at first glance but contained so many shades within, from pure black to threads of gold. The other woman was wearing jeans and an oversize UC Berkeley sweatshirt that looked like it must be her mate's.

Beside her, Faith high-fived Keenan before Ashaya's six-and-a-half-year-old ran off to play. While the Arrows hadn't yet arrived, several other DarkRiver cubs, as well as two of their nonpack human friends, were already scrambling over the climbing frames. Today's morning-only school day would allow for a longer play session, and the children were clearly delighted at the idea. The Arrows had their own school but had been happy to mirror the half-day break.

"Can we go play, Sascha darling?" Julian asked, his impish expression hitting her right in the heart.

"Yes, you can, Mr. Ryder."

Her solemn response made the twins laugh so hard their eyes turned the green-gold of their leopards, before Julian held out a hand to Naya while Roman did the same on her other side. "Come on, Naya!"

Naya grabbed both boys' hands at the same time in an impressive feat of toddler coordination and off they went. "For two such energetic boys," Sascha said to Faith and Ashaya, "they're incredibly patient with her." As she watched, the twins lifted Naya onto a toddler-appropriate swing and made sure she was secure.

Naya happily kicked her legs.

"They are," Ashaya agreed with a smile, while continuing to keep an eye on the children. "Part of it is personality, but it's also a testament to how they're being raised and how DarkRiver as a pack raises its children." She frowned as a little human girl almost slipped—only to be hauled to safety by a quick-thinking cub.

"Maureen had to take her baby to the doctor," Ashaya said, referring to one of DarkRiver's human neighbors. "She asked us to watch her two girls."

Sascha had already automatically extended her shields to back up Faith and Ashaya, taking special care to protect the human children. Their minds were even more vulnerable than those of changeling young. "I have them."

"I love this." Dressed in a thin V-necked sweater in royal blue that set off the dark red of her hair and looked beautiful against her creamy skin, Faith perched herself on a bench the kids used as an obstacle to jump or clamber over, as a clubhouse for playing under, for whatever else their imaginations made of it. "There's so much promise here, so much light."

Ashaya's pale blue-gray eyes met Faith's cardinal starlight. "I know exactly what you mean. The children have no concept of race or war or different political ideologies. They just know a good friend from a bad one."

A car engine sounded, faint but unexpected enough that Sascha instinctively looked that way. Of course she couldn't see anything through the trees, but she felt a telepathic knock soon afterward. The mind was a familiar one, all cool control and power: Judd Lauren, former Arrow, powerful telekinetic and current SnowDancer lieutenant.

Wondering why he'd driven down from the wolf den high in the Sierra Nevada mountain range, Sascha responded to his telepathic touch with a question. *Did you come to see how we run a session?* The SnowDancers had mostly been involved with older Arrow teenagers to date, but she knew they'd been discussing a playgroup.

I've got Marlee with me, the lieutenant answered. *She's curious if there are any Psy kids her age she could play telepathic games with. Toby plays with her but she knows he lets her win.*

Sascha couldn't help her smile at the mention of Marlee's brother and Judd's nephew, a sweet just-turned-thirteen-year-old boy with a slight empathic gift and a generous heart. *Most in this group are younger but I have a contact number for Vasic. Let me see if he knows a child who'd enjoy having a non-Arrow telepathic playmate.*

She and Vasic had finished their conversation by the time Judd arrived with Marlee. The ten-year-old's strawberry-blonde hair was in a single braid to one side of her head; she was dressed in black canvas pants suitable for the outdoors along with a light blue T-shirt with the image of a cheerful yellow and white daisy in front.

Face lighting up at seeing Sascha, Judd's niece ran over to hug her.

Sascha's work helping Toby handle the empathic component of his abilities meant she was a far more regular visitor to the wolf den than most of her packmates. She felt as if she knew all the SnowDancer children. "Hello, sweetheart." She squeezed this child close. "You know Faith and Ashaya, don't you?"

"Hi," Marlee said with a smile, though she stayed tucked against Sascha.

"Marlee!" It was Keenan, calling from his perch on top of the climbing frame.

Marlee skipped over to talk to the younger boy. Like all children who grew up in a pack, she was used to having friends across age lines. As she grew older, she'd be expected to babysit the pups or to help any elders who requested it, so that pack bonds would continue to form between young and old.

It was oddly similar to how Psy family groups functioned, at least in terms of the continuity between generations. According to Sascha's education records, her maternal grandmother, Reina Duncan, had played a role in overseeing her development when Sascha was younger.

That oversight had been from a distance, in Reina's position as head of the Duncan family. It had also stopped long before Reina's death—when Nikita became the power behind the throne. In truth, Sascha wasn't certain her mother hadn't manipulated things right from the start, but Reina's was the signature on her earliest school and conditioning records.

It wasn't family as changelings knew it, but it was family nonetheless.

She was thinking about the other similarities that existed between the races when Vasic began to 'port in the Arrow children, including a girl and a boy around Marlee's age. Except for the latter three, who—watched over by Judd—cautiously settled beside a tree to play psychic games Sascha knew were designed to heighten telepathic agility and skill, the children had all played together previously.

As a result, it took no time for them to join in the games already in progress.

The squad currently had no child as young as Naya, and her usual two-year-old pack playmate had a checkup with their healer today. But Sascha's baby was never alone. The kids took turns pushing her, and a sweet three-year-old child Arrow with chubby red cheeks and light brown curls scrambled into a neighboring swing with Vasic's help, then seemed to fall into an earnest conversation with Naya.

Sascha could feel her cub's happiness. Naya soon tried to reach out to her new friend using her telepathic abilities, but Sascha gently reminded her to ask permission first, then showed her how. Even as she did that, she was monitoring the other children under their care for any signs of distress. Not just in terms of an accidental psychic hurt, but because she was an empath, she could no more stop watching out for their emotional well-being than she could for their physical health.

It was ten minutes later that she became aware of a kerfuffle in the football game in progress on the field next to the play equipment.

A cub in leopard form had apparently nipped the butt of an Arrow child, who must've struck out psychically, from the way that Arrow child suddenly stilled and looked pale-faced toward the young Arrow who must've contained the strike before it did any damage.

Abbot's blue-eyed gaze met Sascha's and Ashaya's in turn. *What do I do now?* he seemed to ask.

"I've got this." Ashaya strode over to the two miscreants and pointed to a spot under a tree.

Both children trudged over, heads down. Ashaya made them sit there, away from the games, with only each other for company, for fifteen minutes.

Then she made the cub say sorry for biting—after asking him to shift so the Arrow child could understand him.

"That's okay," the Arrow boy said with a generosity that immediately caused the DarkRiver cub to smile. "I should've thought before I acted. That's what the teacher says to do. I could've hurt you."

"I'm not supposed to bite," the cub confided in a shamefaced whisper. "My teeth are really strong."

The Arrow boy nodded, clearly seeing the parallel.

"Good boys." Ashaya hugged them both before setting them free to join in the play—which they did together.

Meanwhile, Naya was having fun telepathing her vocal new friend, while Faith and Vasic pushed them on the swings. The teleporter, who'd lost his left arm after a failed biofusion experiment, appeared to be testing a new prosthetic. Its gleaming metal finish fascinated the children, with Vasic often hunkering down so they could touch small hands to the metal, patting at it curiously and asking him questions.

How many is that now? Sascha asked when he bent down for a curious cub, aware the brilliant engineer behind the prosthetic was obsessed with finding one that worked with Vasic's damaged systems.

This one doesn't count—it's a piece Samuel uses to test different components, the teleporter told her as he rose back to his feet and continued to push Naya, who was nowhere near tired of the motion yet. *This time, he's checking a computronic mechanism that he hoped would fix a heat buildup issue.*

Is it doing what it should?

A shake of Vasic's head, his handsome face expressionless but not cold. *I can already feel the heat levels rising at the point of the join. In fact, can you and the others handle shields while I leave to remove it?*

Of course. With Judd, Faith, Ashaya, Sascha, and Abbot, they had plenty of psychic power at their command.

Vasic had only been gone about a minute, and Sascha was giving a thirsty child a cup of water from the supplies Faith had brought with her, when she caught sight of Roman about to fly off the top of a climbing frame.

"No." She knew he was going to hit wrong, would probably break his arm . . . but he shifted midfall, landing in a roll that knocked the air out of his feline body but didn't otherwise do any damage.

Heart thudding, Sascha stopped herself from rushing over. Leopard cubs needed independence, she reminded herself for the thousandth time. But she watched him until she was sure he truly hadn't hurt himself—a fact that became obvious when he sauntered off, tail proudly up and a smug expression on his gorgeous little face.

That's when she noticed that Naya's attention was riveted on the older cub.

She managed to contain her groan until the child who'd come over for a drink ran back to join his playmates. "Naya's going to start jumping off high perches soon, isn't she?"

Ashaya patted her hand. "She'll survive. Keenan's fine and he's not a cat. In the interests of transparency, he did fracture his arm the first time his leopard friends tried to teach him the tree road, but it was a one-off."

"That's not very reassuring," Sascha said darkly.

Laughing with a warmth that belied the years she'd spent trapped in chill Silence, the other woman pushed up the sleeves of her sweatshirt, the temperature in the forest relatively cool despite how close they were to summer. "I'm looking forward to seeing what tricks a Psy-Changeling child will come up with."

A Psy-Changeling child.

Yes, Naya was that. Unique . . . and hunted because of it.

Chapter 2

HAVING BEEN CAUGHT in a sudden traffic jam caused by a delivery truck that had spilled its load across the road, Lucas and Clay were still ten minutes out from reaching the piers. It was frustrating when the point of taking the car had been to speed things up, but Jon and his friends had promised to stay exactly where they were until the two of them arrived.

"Can you talk to Teijan?" Lucas asked as he picked up the sharp scent of brine, the water close now. "Brief the Rats to keep their ear to the ground for *any* mentions of Naya outside DarkRiver and SnowDancer. Even things that seem benign."

The Rats, only four of whom were actually changeling—three adults and one child—chose to live in the disused subway tunnels beneath San Francisco, but they had the ability to blend into the woodwork in every part of the city. It made them a highly effective spy network—and while that network didn't work *for* DarkRiver, the pack had an agreement with the Rats that meant Teijan would pass on any important information.

In return for that loyalty, DarkRiver permitted the far less powerful pack to live in its territory without fear when, as the dominant predators in the region, DarkRiver would've been justified in forcing the Rats out. With brutal violence, if need be. A harsh law, but it kept peace between the predators.

As it was, Teijan and his Rats had pledged loyalty to DarkRiver, and the intelligence that flowed to DarkRiver from the smaller group was invaluable. If any of that intel resulted in business deals, DarkRiver passed on a percentage of the income. Over time, the businesslike arrangement had changed into something that wasn't an alliance . . . but was perhaps as close to it as could happen between two groups with such a wide power differential.

Instead of cowering in their tunnels, the Rats had fought for the city when San Francisco was attacked.

Lucas would never forget that.

"Consider it done." Clay slowed the car to permit a pedestrian who'd miscalculated the light change to cross safely onto the sidewalk. "You want to feel out some of your Trinity contacts, too? Ask them to keep an ear open?"

Lucas scowled, his arm braced on the window frame and his eyes taking in the vibrant life of San Francisco. "I'll think about it, but right now, I only truly trust a tiny minority of those who've signed the accord." All were people he'd known and trusted *prior* to the formation of the ambitious cooperation agreement.

Lucas wanted the Trinity Accord to succeed, probably more than any other individual in the world aside from Sascha, but at this point, it was far too new and untested. "Trinity has two major issues," he said to Clay. "The first is how to confirm the sincerity of those who sign it and want to be part of any Trinity-wide discussions. Consortium plants as well as others who have their own reasons to want the accord to fail are a certainty."

Peace wasn't good for everyone, including those who manufactured weapons and made their money off the misery of others. Post-Trinity, people had stopped blowing one another up, and, inside the Net, the civil war was apparently at a truce that was holding. The pro-Silence faction hadn't disappeared, but according to those who understood the complex political situation in the Net, the rise of the empaths had shaken it to its core.

Designation E had been crushed under Silence, their ability to sense emotions and heal wounds of the heart and the mind considered unnecessary in a race that had outlawed emotion and that punished any deviation from the status quo with vicious psychic brainwipes. Yet this past winter, the empaths had categorically proven that they were very much necessary.

Without the Es, the PsyNet would've collapsed—would *still* collapse should they be taken out of the equation.

And without the biofeedback provided by the PsyNet, those of the Psy race would die horrifically painful deaths in a matter of seconds.

It left the most well-known pro-Silence groups in a quandary: How could they re-create a society without emotion when a vast majority of the linchpin members of that society were empaths, emotion their lifeblood? As a result, they'd stopped their vocal protests while they debated the issue; even the unstable fringe elements had halted their spate of bombings and shootings, though no one could predict how long that would last.

Of course, the Trinity Accord wasn't behind either of those outcomes, but it *was* currently the focus of the world's attention. Including that of the malcontents from all three races—everyone was waiting to see what came next, whether Trinity would become a powerhouse or fall flat.

However, it wasn't just the weapons makers who had to be unhappy with Trinity's flow-on effects. There were no doubt business owners—Psy, human, and changeling—pissed off because Trinity had facilitated an explosion of cross-racial business networks. Great for the clever operators who were good at what they did. Not so good for those who'd been coasting by with substandard work because the competition wasn't as accessible to their clients.

Even powerful families with links to large medical corporations had to be looked at with a suspicious eye, because in times of peace, certain types of medicine were either no longer needed—or no longer profitable. "It's a crapshoot as to who's sincere and who's not," Lucas added. "That's going to be a long-term issue."

Clay's hand moved smoothly on the manual controls. "Ming LeBon really requested to sign the accord?"

"Just to screw things up even more." Lucas didn't bother to contain his growl this time. "Hawke might have held off on killing the son of a bitch, but SnowDancer will pull out of Trinity the instant he's permitted to sign, and so will we." The wolf pack and DarkRiver were blood allies and Ming LeBon had threatened the life of Hawke's mate among his other murderous crimes.

"The Forgotten will also leave." Founded by rebels who'd defected from the PsyNet at the dawn of Silence over a hundred years earlier, the Forgotten—who'd intermarried with humans and mated with changelings—were beginning to show unique new abilities unseen in the "pure-blooded" Psy population.

Ming Lebon wanted access to those abilities, had been behind the abductions and deaths of a number of Forgotten children.

"Arrows will go, too," Clay pointed out.

"No question." Ming had been the squad's leader for a long time, but from what Lucas had picked up, the ex-Psy Councilor had treated the men and women under his command as disposable pawns, signing kill orders for "malfunctioning" Arrows and using the squad as his personal death army.

Aden might've initiated the accord, but Lucas had the feeling the other man—and his squad—would rather rebuild alliances from scratch than be linked to Ming LeBon again in any way, even through the gossamer-thin bonds of Trinity. "And," he added, "the second DarkRiver and Snow-Dancer leave, we take a large number of packs with us." People who might not be allies but who were friends or who trusted the two packs to assist them should they have need, far more than they did strangers in a nascent accord.

There was an unexpected smile in Clay's voice when he spoke again. "Maybe proof of membership in the 'Ming LeBon Should Die' club should be a prerequisite for signing the accord."

"Funny." Eyes focused straight ahead but mind on this mess of a situation, Lucas shook his head. "The problem is that certain minority members want Ming to be part of Trinity—and fuck, I see their point." The ex-Councilor was currently the reigning power in a significant portion of Europe. "It might be better to have him in the fold so we could monitor him a little more closely."

Clay growled. "He'd still be poison."

"Yes." Lucas had the ability to see the other side's point, his disciplined temper the reason he'd been nominated to speak for so many changeling packs on anything to do with Trinity, but he wasn't *ever* going to agree on the Ming issue. "I wouldn't trust any discussion in which he had a part; we'd always be waiting for him to stab everyone in the back—Ming only cares about Ming."

Eyes narrowed at the thought of the ex-Councilor, Lucas was stretching out his denim-clad legs when a couple of men on the sidewalk caught his eye. "Jamie looks like he's over his jetlag." The senior soldier had flown home straight from the Solomon Islands, the distant country the last stop on his roaming of the world.

Nearly every cat roamed at some point in his or her life. Some for weeks, others for months, a rare few for years. It was part of their nature, part of what made them as feline as they were human. That time exploring the world helped them grow, helped them settle into their skin. Almost all returned home, however, their humanity tempering the more solitary inclinations of the leopard within.

In the thirteen years he'd been alpha, Lucas had lost only three of those who roamed. One in an accident that could've happened anywhere in the world, two others in much happier circumstances: they'd found their mates in different corners of the globe, decided to stay. In doing so, those two had connected DarkRiver to a pack in India and one in Botswana.

"I saw him this morning," Clay replied. "He's asked Nate to put him back on full active duty, and he's back to his tech position at CTX."

"Tech" was a broad shorthand term used by any number of specialists. In point of fact, Jamie was a highly qualified sound and holo-imaging specialist. First, though, he was a DarkRiver dominant and trusted senior soldier on the cusp of becoming a sentinel. Walking beside him had been a younger packmate who held incredible promise.

Lucas didn't think it was chance that Kit was talking to Jamie.

"The Ming situation." Clay bared his teeth at a double-parked car in front of them, before managing to swing around it. "Is it going to be majority rules?"

"Trinity has no official voting system." One of those things that had been skipped over in the rush to create a united front against the Consortium. "Those of us Aden pulled in right at the start, we didn't consider that we might want to keep people *out* of the Trinity network. Discussions were all about how to convince people to have faith in it."

Lucas often wondered why the hell he'd volunteered to be the first point of contact for overall Trinity business for more than twenty-five packs and counting . . . and then he'd remember Naya. His and Sascha's smart, funny cub who'd smacked big kisses on his face today before he left the aerie, and who collapsed into giggles when he tickled her. Half Psy, half changeling, all mischief—and as Aden's intel had put into sharp focus today, a threat to those who abhorred change and wanted to freeze the world in time.

His gut tensed again, claws shoving at his skin. He'd permit no one to dim her light.

He also wanted her to grow up in a united world, not a divided one. Naya should never have to choose between the two sides of her heritage.

Lucas would fight to his last breath to make that happen.

"What's the second problem?" Clay brought the car to a stop in front of an Embarcadero warehouse owned by DarkRiver. "You said two."

"Let's walk and talk," Lucas said. "You might still make the site in time."

Stepping out into the salt-laced air of the waterfront after putting up the passenger-side window, Lucas shut the door, then joined Clay as the other man headed in the direction where the boys were waiting. The sun rained down on them out of a cloudless blue sky, the winds light. Lucas could hear the faint buzz of voices in the distance, feel the vibration of the vehicles on the road, smell the saltwater taffy made fresh in a nearby boutique candy shop.

The sunshine made the panther within Lucas stretch out into a lazy sprawl; he had to resist the sudden temptation to shift and sun himself on the pier. That was *not* alpha behavior—on the other hand, it would be amusing to see people's reaction to a black panther in their midst, especially if he walked into a butcher's and pointed to a prime cut of meat.

Changeling cats being bigger than their wild counterparts, he'd make quite an impression.

"Gotta love this sun," Clay said right then. "Makes me want to curl up and go boneless like that tabby over there."

Grinning, Lucas told the sentinel what he'd been thinking. Clay's smile was slow, deep. "Let's do it for Halloween. Give the tourists a shock. We can chase the ones who are mean to the shopkeepers."

Deeply amused in a way only a feline could be, Lucas skirted a tiny yapping dog on a leash that thought it was a mastiff. A single hard glance from Lucas would've shut him down, but why spoil a tiny dog's dreams of glory?

"Second issue is connected to the voting situation," he said as they walked. "It all arises from the lack of a governing charter or constitution." Something that was deeply necessary to the success of such a diverse body, one with members scattered across the world.

Right now the accord was an agreement to communicate, and they had vehicles in place for that. But to become a truly stabilizing force that would lead to the United Earth Federation, it needed to become far more cohesive. Especially since trust remained a huge, complicated question for the entire membership.

"There are the boys."

Lucas nodded, having already caught their scent, recognized them as pack. Shoulders tensed and legs bouncing nervously on sneakered feet, the four teenagers were huddled in a small group, their faces unusually solemn.

Spotting Clay and Lucas, Jon said something and the boys jogged across to meet them in the middle of the pier. The four sixteen-year-olds were dressed as boys their age currently dressed—white T-shirts under open shirts of various hues and types, atop baggy board shorts that reached past their knees, and brightly colored sneakers they'd all personalized.

However, though they were wearing shorts meant for the surf, they were carrying hoverboards. All in all, an ordinary sight.

"We were hanging out when we saw it," Jon said, his extraordinarily beautiful face shadowed under the bill of a battered gray cap and his distinctive violet eyes hidden by hazel contacts.

Certain dangerous people knew the teenager existed and was part of DarkRiver, but there was no reason he had to make himself a high visibility target. Right now, he looked like a thousand other boys in the city. He wasn't. Jon was one of the Forgotten, part of the young generation that was displaying striking new psychic abilities.

DarkRiver had promised to back the boy should he want to ditch the contacts, stop dyeing his white-gold hair, but Jon had decided it was safer for his buddies and his little sister if he stayed under the radar until he was older and stronger. "Stops people from staring at me, too," he'd said to Lucas, rubbing the place on his neck where he'd once had a Crawlers gang tattoo. "I just want to be one of the juveniles, you know?"

Lucas understood, even better than Jon likely realized. Clay, Talin, Noor, and DarkRiver were the first real family Jon had ever had, the first time he had people around him on whom he could rely no matter what. He hated being reminded that he was in any way different from his packmates.

"Is the thing you saw in the water or caught under the pier?" Clay asked the boy he'd adopted. It could've proved problematic, given Jon's past, but of all the men in DarkRiver, it was Clay who best understood what it was to be a lost boy.

He and Jon had connected like two puzzle pieces.

Now, the boy shook his head, while around him, the other teenagers looked anywhere but at their alpha or Clay. "We were goofing off and it looked interesting, so, um"—his golden skin pinked—"these guys hung me off the pier by my ankles and I plucked it out."

His panther impressed by the group's ingenuity and huffing in laughter at their very cublike behavior right then, Lucas took the small bottle one of the other teens held out. He could see why it had caught their attention. The bottle was crafted of lime green glass and partially covered by barnacles. Bobbing on the water under the piercing sunlight, it would've sparkled like a jewel. "You boys opened it?"

Again, Jon was the one who spoke. Definitely a dominant and one

Lucas was certain would grow up to become a cornerstone member of the pack. Lucas wouldn't hesitate to leave Naya in Jon's care; that said everything about his trust and faith in the boy.

"Yes, sir." Jon's voice was as clear as a bell. "We saw the stopper and were joking about finding a message in a bottle. And then . . ." Lifting a hand, he passed a thin, curling piece of paper to Clay. "I didn't want to try and put it back, maybe tear it."

"You did the right thing." Unrolling it with care, Clay held the flimsy paper so he and Lucas could both read it.

> *My name is Leila Savea and I'm a marine biologist. I was kidnapped while working alone in the Pacific Ocean a mile off the coast of Samoa and I've been held in a cold, gray prison since. They scarred my face, cut it up, said it was so a teleporter who uses faces to go places couldn't find me. I don't know if that's true or if they just wanted to hurt me.*
>
> *I'm often drugged but they're late with the dose today. I can write today.*
>
> *A week, maybe ten days ago, they took me out of this room to test drugs on me and when they weren't looking, I stole a bottle that was on the shelves outside. There were lots of bottles. Like it was someone's collection once, but they're all covered with dust now.*
>
> *I took the paper and pen another time, when one of them forgot his lab coat in my room.*
>
> *I'm going to hide this letter in the bottle and if they ever take me outside this place, I'm going to look for water. Water will carry it somewhere. Carry it to my people.*
>
> *They won't break me.*

There was a subtle change in the ink on the following line, possibly indicating that the next part had been written some time after the first. The words, the tone, it too implied enough of a passage of time that the writer's defiant spirit had begun to crumple under the pressure.

Miane, please help me. I'm so far from home and I hurt. It's cold here. There's snow everywhere but no ocean to feed my soul. I listen so hard for it, but all I hear is the wind and the trees and my captors. The sea doesn't speak here.

Even if I escape this prison, I won't get far before my body gives up. I'm not meant for this kind of cold. They want me to swim to places, do bad things. They think no one will miss me because I prefer to swim alone.

Please miss me. I miss you.

They're trying to break me, turn me into an automaton, a slave.

I don't know where I am. But I saw things when they first brought me here. They miscalculated the drug and I was almost awake. It's a square concrete building in the middle of snow and trees. So much snow that it hurts my eyes when I look out the narrow strip of window at the top of my prison.

The building has this symbol on the side, faded and old.

A painstakingly hand-drawn symbol followed. A triangle with the letters CCE on the inside, the font blocky and squat.

I hear ducks sometimes. As if there's a river or a stream or a lake nearby. I can't see anything but I hear them. And—

The letter just ended, as if the writer had run out of time or been interrupted. What Leila Savea had written was chilling enough.

Lucas's eyes met Clay's before they both looked at the bottle in Lucas's hand. Barnacles crawled up over a quarter of the bottle's surface, betraying a long sojourn in the ocean. The chances of Leila Savea still being alive were low to negligible.

That didn't matter.

His anger a cold, icy thing that burned, Lucas turned to the teenagers who'd had the intelligence and heart to understand what they'd found. "I'm proud of you," he said because cubs needed to hear that from their alpha. "We'll take care of it now." He'd get the bottle and the message to the BlackSea water changelings, to the people Leila Savea had hoped to reach.

"Will we find her?" Jon's fingers were bone white on the edge of his hoverboard.

Lucas gripped the side of the boy's neck, anchoring him in pack skin privileges. Jon might've been born Forgotten, but he was DarkRiver now. And Lucas didn't lie to his packmates. "I don't know, but we're sure as hell going to try."

No one deserved to be tortured and tormented and trapped in the Consortium's clutches.

Chapter 3

MIANE LEVÈQUE, ALPHA of BlackSea, ended her comm conversation with Lucas Hunter with rage in her blood and determination in her bones. Leila, sweet, happily nerdy Leila, who loved the sun and the ocean and who was never more contented than when she was swimming with the tropical fish she studied, was caged in a cold box, drugged and hurting.

Dying.

She jerked as Malachai closed his hand over her shoulder, squeezed. The big male had stayed out of sight of the screen, but he'd been privy to her entire conversation with the leopard alpha. "She gave us clues," he reminded her. "The bottle itself may be a clue."

Miane had asked that DarkRiver give the bottle to a trusted member of BlackSea who'd be able to run tests the cats wouldn't even think to run. They didn't understand water, didn't know all the moods and tastes of it. Not simply salt and fresh. Each ocean had its own complexities. Different *parts* of an ocean had different personalities.

"Leila was always clever." But even the cleverest young woman couldn't share what she didn't know.

The comm beeped again, notifying her of a file transfer from Dark-River.

Downloading it, she saw that Lucas had sent through information on the triangular symbol Leila had drawn. The search had been running as they spoke. "It's the logo for a long-defunct utility company." Canadian Cheap Electric. "Hundreds of possible facilities across Canada."

"Wait." Malachai scrolled down, swore with uncharacteristic harshness.

Miane's right-hand man was usually almost Psy in his ability to control his emotions.

"It says historical records were damaged forty-five years ago," he told her. "The locations of the substations, the part of CCE's infrastructure that best matches Leila's description, were lost."

Some, Miane thought, had undoubtedly been destroyed by time and human interference. Others might be hidden by the kind of tree cover Leila had described, while still others may have been repurposed into legitimate uses. "It's our only real clue. We run it, even if it means tracking down each and every substation one by one."

Malachai didn't tell her that was an impossible task—Leila would be long dead and turned to dust before they found the right location. All he said was, "We have to think smart." His pale gold eyes held hers, the color so clear she sometimes couldn't believe it was real. Malachai's true eyes looked like a beam of sunlight cutting through the clear waters off the most pristine white sand beach.

It befit what he was, a secret unknown to the world.

"We'll have the tests done," he continued, "get an idea of where she might have dropped in the bottle and how long ago."

Because there was a high chance Leila was no longer in that old CCE facility.

Miane refused to believe the bright young woman was already dead, like so many of BlackSea's vulnerable and far-flung members. The ones who swam alone or in small groups. Where the Consortium believed they wouldn't be missed.

I miss you, Leila.

The girl was on their list of vanished members, the disappearance reported by another lone swimmer who'd crossed paths with Leila once a month and who'd searched weeks for her in the warm waters around Samoa. She'd found only Leila's small research vessel; it had been bobbing on waves far from the zone where her friend said Leila would've normally dropped anchor.

"We also have people in Canada," Miane reminded Malachai, ruthlessly silencing the memory of how Leila's friend had sobbed when she'd reported her missing, how she'd begged Miane to find Leila.

She's so gentle, Miane. And she has this childlike wonder in the world, this belief that people are mostly good.

Hand fisting so hard her nails cut into her palm, Miane forced herself to speak. "I'll blast out a notice, put our people in the region on alert." The Canadian landscape was full of lakes and the changelings that called them home also called BlackSea pack.

Malachai's expression darkened. "It could go to one of the traitors."

Bile threatened to burn Miane's throat.

The realization that BlackSea *must* have at least one traitor in their midst was a terrible one. There was no other way to explain how outsiders had so accurately been able to predict the location of BlackSea's most isolated members—those lone water changelings generally had well-hidden places of sleep scattered across oceans and along beaches, riverbeds, and lakefronts.

The ones like Leila, who lived on boats, moved around from day to day, though like any living being, they had favorite spots.

The realization of betrayal would've been devastating for any pack but it was viciously heartbreaking for BlackSea because of the pack's unique genesis. Water-based changelings tended to be made up of pairs or small pods. Some *did* run in large schools, but those changelings thought in "groupmind." It made them smart and strong when functioning as a group, but different enough that they had difficulty dealing with outsiders who demanded to speak to the boss. The schools had no leader, were truly a single multicelled organism.

On the flip side, the water was also home to the dangerous and the powerful, but the lethal predators rarely came into contact with the other species. That had worked fine for centuries, but as the world developed and the oceans and lakes and rivers of the planet became a coveted source of power and trade, fishing going from small boats that changelings could easily avoid to huge trawlers dragging massive nets, their isolation began to kill them.

It had been Miane's ancestors who had reached out to their brethren, after losing half their family to a huge fishing conglomerate that had flat-out ignored the warnings that certain waters had been legally claimed for changeling use. Big business knew that scattered groups of water-based changelings had no way to enforce the rules and as the decades passed, people had become used to ignoring them.

Coming together to form BlackSea had *never* been about power, though power was a much-needed by-product. BlackSea had been born so that their people would be *safe*, so that they could protect and nurture their young in waters unpolluted by outsiders, free of their deadly nets and traps.

Now one of the pack had sold out the members who needed BlackSea most.

"We need eyes out there," she said, her gut churning. "Not just for Leila, for all of the vanished." This was only the second time they'd had any clue where one of their stolen packmates might be. "We'll have to take the risk."

"Let me handle it." Malachai was a wall of strength in front of her, a man she'd never seen lose his temper. "I know several Canadian members personally, people I trust. I'll pass on the information to them, have them feed it out to those they trust. It should lower the chance of treachery."

"Do it." Miane knew her brain was hazy with rage, her decision-making skills compromised. She needed Malachai's calm, his way of being a still pond even in the midst of a crashing sea.

When he pinned her with those clear eyes of pale gold unseen on any human or Psy or terrestrial changeling, she glared back. "What?"

"You need to swim." It was an order. "You've been out of the water far too long."

Unsaid were the words that no water changeling did well after too long a separation. Leila might already be dead because of that need, her captors ignorant that a water changeling needed to swim as much as he or she needed to breathe. A strong adult could survive years deprived of enough water to allow a shift, but they'd probably end up mad. Leila had always been small and a little fragile physically, her mind her most important asset.

In her changeling form, Leila was as delicate and colorful as the fish she studied. A pretty tropical dancer who knew nothing of war or of enemies who would steal BlackSea's members and attempt to turn them into assassins.

Terrestrials often forgot to look at water as a threat, ignoring rivers and streams as roadways when they blocked other routes into an area. It was a detail BlackSea had long used to its advantage. The fact that the Consortium had also figured it out pointed once again to a traitor. Humans, Psy, even land-based changelings, they simply didn't think that way. You had to be a creature of water to understand its full potential.

Leila had loved the sea so much she rarely set foot on land.

Now she was caged in a barren place far from the ocean.

Miane reminded herself of Leila's stubbornness, of how the other woman had become the youngest marine biologist on record through endless dedication and sheer hard work. A woman with a will that strong would fight to survive. "I don't like to be far from Lantia," she finally said to Malachai.

The world didn't know this floating city deep in the Atlantic was their central base, didn't know that the city beneath the waves was far bigger than the city above. This entire region was heavily patrolled by BlackSea and covered by the aquatic equivalent of a no-fly zone. Air traffic was permitted, but only at so high an altitude that it made spying impossible; to make certain of that, the wavelike curves of Lantia were covered with tiny antennas designed to emit a signal that scrambled any radar or sonar equipment pointed at it.

Below the water, the ocean was BlackSea's.

Anyone breaching the city's clearly advertised and legally defined borders did so knowing the penalty was death—and BlackSea *would* enforce it. The world had hurt them too much for BlackSea to believe in mercy. Especially when no one got this far out into the ocean by accident. No, anyone trying to sneak up to or under Lantia did so with full knowledge of what they risked.

"We have so many of our young here," she added.

"Protected by over a thousand of our strongest," Malachai reminded her. "You're making bad decisions because of anger and tiredness. Go."

Miane was the First here—alpha in terrestrial changeling terms—but she knew full well Malachai wouldn't hesitate to throw her bodily into the ocean. Not that he'd succeed. Or survive. Still, the fact that one of her blood-loyal seconds had threatened that, even if by implication, was reason enough to pay attention. "Keep them safe," she ordered, and, swiveling on her heel, headed to the far edge of the city.

She could've gone into the water at various other points on Lantia—the entire city was built to ensure easy access to the ocean—but it was important her people see her, see that she was present and strong and in control.

Especially now.

When she stripped and dived beneath the waves, the salt a familiar taste and the cold slide of the sea over her skin a welcoming kiss, several more bodies slipped in with her. They shifted in the water, sleek and fast and built for the ocean.

This was their home. They would defend it to the death.

And they would find their missing. Every. Single. One.

Chapter 4

"I WANT TO kill the Consortium," Mercy muttered after reading the e-mail Lucas had sent out to all the sentinels about the kidnapped Black-Sea changeling. "Chop them into little bits and throw them into that canyon we visited in Arizona."

"The falcons might object to all that rancid meat in their territory," her mate said mildly from where he stood beside her, reading a message from his own alpha.

"Hmm." Mercy placed her phone on the nearest flat surface, then leaned back against the porch railing of her old cabin.

Given her need to be closer to the DarkRiver healer with the pregnancy this far advanced, she and Riley had made the decision to move down from their usual home a week earlier. They'd requested any open cabin on DarkRiver lands, but the packmate currently living in Mercy's old cabin had cheerfully offered it to them for the duration.

All Rina had asked was that they spill the beans on the number and sex—or sexes—of the pupcubs so she could win the betting pool. When Mercy had threatened to shoot the young soldier instead, Rina had laughed and taken off—but not without hugging Mercy first with the wild affection of a packmate who knew her touch would never be rejected.

The memory had her smiling as she said, "Rancid meat is pretty bad. And the falcons are our allies." Though unlike with the wolves, the DarkRiver-WindHaven alliance was still a work in progress, not in the first stages, but not far past, either.

"I know." She snapped her fingers. "I can dump the pieces on Snow-Dancer land. Wolves have no sense of taste so no one will notice."

Her gorgeous wolf mate growled at her.

Laughing, she ran her fingers through the thick chestnut silk of his hair. He was leaning forward over the railing, eyes on his phone, while she leaned back against it. "Hawke?"

Riley nodded, shifting slightly so that she could pet him more easily, those incongruously pretty lashes of his beautifully visible in this position. "He's called a lieutenant meeting at five today. We'll probably be discussing the BlackSea situation." Sliding away his phone, he rose to his full height, a broad-shouldered man with chocolate-dark eyes that looked at her as if she was his everything.

Woman and leopard, every part of Mercy adored him.

Nuzzling at her, making her smile, Riley placed his hand over her belly. "How are you feeling?"

Heart mush because her mate was petting her, she said, "Like I've been pregnant forever." According to her three hooligan brothers, it was closer to twenty-seven months. According to the SnowDancer and Dark-River healers, it was just past eight months.

Looking down at her belly, Riley's right hand strong and warm on the curve of it, while he used his left hand to massage her nape, she spoke to their pupcubs in her best "behave" tone. A tone she and the hooligans had heard often from their own mother during childhood. "You're meant to come out early," she said to the babies she already loved beyond life. "Multiple births always come early." Likely so the mother wouldn't burst or tumble headfirst right onto her belly.

Riley nibbled at her ear.

Purring, she snuck her hand under his shirt to play her fingers over the ridged lines of his abdomen. God, her mate revved her motor. "Sex could make the babies come out," she said, kissing his throat.

Shuddering, he began to slide his hand up to cup her breast, then suddenly blinked and shook his head. "You just made that up." It was a narrow-eyed accusation.

Baring her teeth at him, she began to undo the buttons of his shirt while he was distracted. "Your children are driving me crazy." Changeling multiple pregnancies never went full-term. Never.

Apparently, the pupcubs hadn't got that memo.

"Is that how it's going to be? They'll be my children each time they're naughty?"

"Of course." Pushing off Riley's shirt, she kneaded at his muscular shoulders in bone-deep pleasure, a purr building inside her. "My children will be angels," she said when they both knew she was the one who'd brought in the hellion genes. Then again, the Kincaid family did boast Drew. "Though, the kidlets *have* given me spectacular breasts."

Riley's gaze fell, his breath catching. "Your breasts were always spectacular."

Sinking her teeth into her lower lip, she crooked a finger. "Come kiss me."

Her mate didn't try to resist. He shifted to cup the side of her face with one big, rough-skinned hand and then his lips were on hers and her entire body was aching for him. When he slid that hand down to touch her heavy breasts, her purr turned into a moan.

Those breasts were a pain in the ass when she wanted to run patrol—not that she'd been able to do that after her balance became that of a drunken goat—but she had to admit they were kind of fun. Especially when Riley did *that*. Shuddering as he just pushed down one shoulder of her loose top and the bra cup on that side to replace his hand with his mouth, she wove her fingers into his hair and held on for the ride.

Thank the heavens the cabin was deep in DarkRiver territory and surrounded by the forest, giving them endless privacy—because Mercy did not want to move right now.

"God," she whispered huskily at some point after Riley had stripped off her top and bra to leave her clad only in a pair of shorts. "Wolves have all the moves."

He chuckled, his pupils surrounded by a ring of wolfish amber when he looked up to meet her gaze before he claimed her lips in a possessive kiss that made her squirm. "I want you inside me," she said, her hands fisted in his hair.

He grazed the side of her breast with his claws. "Be good, kitty cat." A nip of her lip. "You're—"

"Pregnant and in full pounce-on-my-mate mode." Changelings were known to be sexually active all the way through a pregnancy, but her overprotective mate had been obdurate this past week, worried about causing inadvertent harm to her or the pupcubs. "I hurt from missing you."

Yes, she was shameless.

A growl rumbled in his chest. "You can't play me that easily anymore."

Nipples aching from the vibration, she petted his nape exactly how he liked . . . then smiled her most sinful smile. "If I could reach over my belly, I'd take care of it myself."

His eyes heated. "Witch."

"Your witch. Now be with me before I die from want." She petted his amazing shoulders, his incredible chest. His body made her want to bite and claw and climb all over him.

"Mercy, what if—"

Hearing the worry in his tone, she ran her fingers through his hair and stopped playing to hold his gaze. "Nothing will go wrong." They were no longer talking about sex. "I'm as healthy as an ox and so are the pupcubs."

Her mate had lost his parents, all but raised his siblings, then had his sister kidnapped and tortured by a monster. As for Drew, the damn blue-eyed wolf kept getting shot! The fact that Brenna was healed and happy and Drew had promised not to get shot again didn't erase the scars her mate carried on that huge heart of his.

Stroking her hands down to cradle his face, she spoke to wolf and man both. "Any sign of a problem and I'll be at the healer's." She let him see her sincerity, feel it through their mating bond. "I'm awful at being pregnant, but I *want* to be a mom so bad, Riley, and I want to see you being a dad. I'm not going to put that at risk, no matter what."

He took a shaky breath, bending to press his forehead against hers. "I know. I just . . ."

"I know, baby." Kissing and nuzzling at him until he was no longer trembling, she surrendered when he took control of the kiss. That kind of surrender didn't come instinctively to either part of her, but if Snow-Dancer Senior Lieutenant Riley Kincaid could let her see his fear, let her hold him, then DarkRiver Sentinel Mercy Smith had zero problems giving him the control he needed to love her right now.

He was far more gentle than they usually ever were, but that was fine, because gentle or rough, her mate always had her moaning in a matter of minutes. That record wasn't in any danger of being broken today.

They finally made it inside and to the bed, where a certain wolf drove her to distraction, then bit down on her shoulder in a possessive hold as he thrust into her slow and deep and oh-so-hard.

Despite their delicious exertion, the pupcubs stayed smug and stubborn and happy inside her body, exactly like the hellions they were.

Chapter 5

JUDD HAD RETURNED to the SnowDancer den an hour earlier, his excited niece in the passenger seat of the all-wheel drive. She'd found a rapport with her Arrow playmates that Judd hadn't expected, at least not this quickly. Arrow children of Marlee's age were already strictly conditioned, and the changes in the squad hadn't been in effect long enough for them to have broken fully free.

But he'd forgotten to add Marlee into that equation.

His brother's daughter had a way of making friends wherever she went, her personality like a cheerful ray of sunshine. The Arrow children had found themselves caught up in the happy storm that was Marlee Lauren, had come out of it a little dazed but eager to see more of her.

Had he ever doubted his rebel leanings, all Judd would've had to do was think of what would've happened to Marlee in the Net, how her personality would've been crushed into a defined box, her sunshine shut up until her world was gray. It was a hellish image, one that affirmed every decision he'd ever made to help bring down Silence and the rotten structure that supported it.

Now the girl who'd greeted him earlier that day with a huge hug and the words, "I love you, Uncle Judd!" was off learning forest skills with her year group, while Judd stood with several packmates on the lush green grass outside the den and looked at the data sent in by DarkRiver. As he read about Leila Savea's captivity and possible location, he considered whether he had any contacts in Canada.

The answer was no, but he knew a large number of the world's teleport-capable telekinetics, was one himself. They could zero in on this symbol, eliminate locations far quicker than searchers on foot or even in the air.

Then he turned the page on his phone and realized the symbol hadn't only been used on substation walls, but on old-fashioned power poles, on warehouses, on electrical boxes placed in houses and at the ends of streets.

Slipping away his phone, he shook his head at his alpha. The silver-gold of the other man's hair was bright in the mountain sunshine, his eyes the pale, dangerous blue of his wolf. Those eyes could be icy and intimidating, as could Hawke, but today the alpha's expression was hard with anger directed at those who would cage the weak and defenseless.

The alpha of the SnowDancer Wolves had no time for cowards.

Neither did Judd. "Even Vasic couldn't narrow this down," he told Hawke, his own anger a cold kiss in his veins. "Too many options." Even if as much as half had been destroyed over the years, that still left thousands of possible hits. "When I try to focus on the symbol, it scatters into nothing." He tried to find words to explain an ability that was an integral part of him. "My brain can't hold on to a single point, because there are too many identical ones."

Hawke nodded. "I figured, but we had to give it a shot." His black shirt stretching at the shoulders as he put his hands on his hips, the alpha glanced at the others who stood with them in the White Zone just outside the den. "Any other ideas?"

As his packmates frowned in thought, Judd became aware of the silence around them. That would've pleased him once, when he'd first defected from the Net. Now it just felt wrong. There should be pups laughing and chasing one another here at this time of day, while soft hands tugged on his leg and asked him to play ball or to make them "fly."

Instead, only Hawke, Judd, Indigo, Riaz, Drew, and Sienna stood under the mountain sunshine, with lieutenants Cooper, Tomás, Jem, Kenji, Matthias, and Alexei listening in via the mobile comm Riaz was holding.

Also present via the comm was Riley, SnowDancer's most senior lieutenant and Judd's brother-in-law. The other man was currently based in

DarkRiver's lower elevation territory. His mate had wanted to be closer to the DarkRiver healer now that she was so close to giving birth and no one had disagreed with her. This was the first known wolf-leopard changeling pregnancy. Despite Mercy's robust health, both packs were worried about complications.

Riley had it the worst, though he was holding it together in that calm Riley way that made it seem as if he were perfectly fine. The only reason Judd knew any different was because of his mate. Brenna had taken one look at her eldest brother three weeks earlier and given him a hug that Riley accepted with bone-crushing force.

It was in the instant afterward that Judd had caught a glint of sheer panic in Riley's dark brown eyes. Unlike Brenna, Judd couldn't help the other man with affection, but what he could do was take on more of Riley's duties. Every lieutenant in the pack had done the same, and those who weren't lieutenants had picked up the slack in other areas, giving Riley the freedom to focus on his mate and their soon-to-be-born pupcubs.

He had more than earned that right.

However, Riley continued to attend their meetings remotely. He was too much the protective dominant to forget his responsibilities. Hawke had also made it a point to still have Riley take care of certain pack tasks, to keep the other man from obsessing over the upcoming births—especially the possible risk to Mercy.

Voices broke the unwelcome quiet, Tomás and Alexei asking a couple more questions about the entire situation with BlackSea's vanished members. Kenji and Riaz, as the two lieutenants who worked most closely with the water changelings, filled them in. Not at issue was the fact that the Consortium was behind the abductions—the events in Venice earlier that year, on which BlackSea had given SnowDancer a detailed briefing, had proven that beyond any reasonable doubt.

Cooper, however, had a question they'd never previously considered. "How the fuck does the Consortium know where to snatch BlackSea people, or how to handle them afterward?" the lieutenant asked. "I can barely get my head around how BlackSea functions, and they're our allies."

"Well, hell." Jem's voice. "BlackSea must have a traitor, maybe more than one."

Hawke blew out a breath. "No wonder Miane didn't mention it."

Judd didn't need any further explanation—no alpha would ever want to air his or her pack's dirty laundry. That Miane Levèque had trusted SnowDancer and DarkRiver as much as she had was a sign of BlackSea's desperation. They'd tried to find their members on their own and failed. Miane's people might rule water, but they needed help when their people had been abducted onto land.

"There are wolf packs in Canada." Indigo folded her arms across her white T-shirt, her black hair pulled back in a sleek ponytail and her long, lean body standing shoulder to shoulder with the playful blue-eyed wolf who was her mate—and Judd's other brother-in-law. Who also happened to be the pack's tracker, charged with hunting down and executing rogues.

The Kincaid family grew them strong.

Judd's mate was as tough as either one of her brothers.

"We have a good relationship with the majority of them," Indigo added. "Just depends if Miane wants us to reach out."

"I'm guessing not." Drew's handsome face was unusually solemn, his rich brown hair tumbled from whatever he'd been doing prior to this meeting. "BlackSea's made it clear they don't want it known that so many of their people have been taken captive."

Judd could understand the other pack's caution. The water-based changelings held significant power now, but it was a delicate balance. Their dependence on water and their scattered locations made the weakest of them easy prey—and the Consortium had recognized that. BlackSea couldn't afford for anyone else to do so.

"Canada's full of water," Sienna pointed out from her position across the circle from Hawke, her navy blue T-shirt bearing paint streaks and tiny handprints that indicated she'd come from a shift in the nursery—and that the pups had been in a rambunctious mood.

Despite her position as Hawke's mate and her own violent psychic abilities, Judd's cardinal niece had made the choice to go step-by-step through the same training as her peers. As a result, she wasn't technically a senior member of SnowDancer with the right to be at this meeting, but Hawke had asked her to attend such meetings when and if she could, because at a certain point in the future, their packmates would begin to look to her for answers in her capacity as the mate of their alpha.

It was good for Sienna to start bedding into that role now, even as she continued her normal soldier training. Judd had expected his niece to protest, since she'd made it clear she didn't want to leapfrog up the hierarchy—not that anyone would've disputed her right to do so after what she'd done in defense of SnowDancer—but Sienna had agreed to Hawke's request and appeared to be focusing hard on learning all aspects of what it meant to be the mate of a powerful alpha.

Love gives far more than it ever takes. And love makes us want to give.

Words spoken by Father Xavier Perez. Judd's friend and fellow rebel was currently somewhere in South America, searching for the woman he loved. The human male should've already reached her, but he'd suffered significant injuries the day he arrived in Peru, after a driver lost control of his vehicle and plowed onto the sidewalk. It was only a month earlier that he'd finally healed enough to continue his search across rugged terrain.

Judd had offered to teleport Xavier to his destination, as had Kaleb, but Xavier was adamant he had to do this himself.

I have to prove I deserve her.

Understanding the depth of Xavier's need in a way he wouldn't have before he'd fallen for Brenna, Judd turned his attention back to the matter at hand. Riaz was nodding at Sienna's point. "BlackSea must have high-risk people who use Canadian lakes as their primary habitat," the other lieutenant said. "Miane won't want to compromise them. On the flip side, it means the water changelings have plenty of eyes and ears in the country if they need them."

"We take BlackSea's lead," Hawke said. "Riaz, Kenji, stay in touch with them, offer our assistance." He shoved up the sleeves of his shirt. "Lucas also asked that we all keep an ear open for anything related to

Naya. Looks like certain Psy in the Net are looking in her direction, and the interest isn't friendly." The wolf-blue of Hawke's eyes had turned frigid as he spoke, the power that came off him a near-palpable force.

There was a reason even Psy were very careful when dealing with strong changeling alphas. At times, Judd wondered how his niece dealt with her mate. Sienna was a power, one honed in brutal circumstances, but she was young . . . and she had challenged Hawke from the instant she set foot in the den, never backing down, even when it would've been prudent. It was a reminder that his niece had her own wild streak, wild enough to handle the primal wolf who was her mate.

"Is Lucas okay with my passing on the word to my contacts?" Judd asked, not saying Kaleb's name though everyone present here knew he and the most dangerous telekinetic in the world were friends. It was old habit to protect the other man's identity, from the time the two of them—and Xavier—had been rebels working in the shadows.

Hawke gave a short nod. "Use your judgment, speak only to people you trust to look after Naya's interests."

Kaleb wasn't "good" in any ordinary sense of the word, but Judd knew the other man would never harm a DarkRiver child for the simple reason that DarkRiver was important to his mate. And whatever was important to Sahara, Kaleb protected. "I'll do it now." Breaking away from the group, he made the call.

It was early in Moscow, but he had a feeling the other man would be up.

He was right.

"I'll release a tracking program into the Net to listen for mentions of the child," Kaleb replied after Judd explained the situation.

Understanding as he did the complex amounts of data Kaleb could sieve through at any one instant, Judd thanked his friend.

Kaleb's response was simple. "DarkRiver protected and nurtured Sahara when she needed it."

Those words said a great deal about the loyalty of which this deadly man was capable, of the lengths he'd go to, to protect the rare few people who'd earned that loyalty. It also hinted at the other aspect of his personality, of the ruthless vengeance he'd mete out should anyone ever harm Sahara.

Black and white, both existed in Kaleb.

Living in the gray was something he did with ease.

"Have you heard from Xavier?" Judd asked, having long ago accepted the duality of nature that was Kaleb Krychek.

"A week ago," Kaleb responded. "I offered to 'port to him, but he continues to insist that he needs to walk alone during this time."

Kaleb never truly betrayed emotion, not even among friends. Likely Sahara alone saw that side of him. But right then, Judd had the feeling the other man was frustrated by Xavier's intransigence. So was Judd. But some things, no one could force. "He knows he can call on us for help at any point."

That they would respond at once should that call ever come was an unspoken vow.

Kaleb didn't reply to that—nothing needed to be said, not between two men who'd fought side by side for so long. "I have to go," he said instead. "Meeting with Ena Mercant."

Judd raised an eyebrow. He'd been out of the PsyNet for almost four years, but he had deep links with his fellow Arrows. As a result of that connection and the information to which it gave him access, he knew the Mercants continued to be a shadow power. It was said the family had more moles and puppets in the Net than everyone else combined. Silver Mercant had long been Kaleb's aide, but Ena Mercant was the reclusive matriarch of the family, one who hadn't been seen in public for years. "Did you blackmail her?"

"I got an invitation," Kaleb replied. "I'm considering taking Silver along to taste test any offered food or drink for poisons. Ena has a reputation for ruthless efficiency."

There it was, that bone-dry sense of humor the majority of the world simply didn't pick up on, much less understand. Judd knew Kaleb would never be anything *but* gray, but his friend had far more light in him since

Sahara came back into his life. Judd understood what love could do to a man. He, too, had once walked in the darkness, once believed he could be nothing but a murderer, his ability to move the very cells of a body a curse.

It had taken a certain stubborn wolf to teach him different, to remind him that he was a man, that he had a right to a life and to love. Never once had Brenna looked away from the darkness inside him—she'd embraced it as simply another facet of his nature. As Sahara had embraced Kaleb. As they hoped Xavier's Nina would embrace their friend.

"I'll send out a search party if you don't return from your meeting," he said to Kaleb now. "Though even Arrows agree that if a Mercant buries a body, it stays buried." Interestingly, no Mercant had ever been in the squad; that family had a way of holding on to its children.

"You see why I want them on my side," Kaleb said before hanging up.

Judd returned to the meeting to find the others discussing details of something SnowDancer's healer, Lara, had proposed in concert with DarkRiver's healer, Tamsyn, two weeks earlier. The two healers had strongly recommended a SnowDancer-DarkRiver function, to be arranged around the birth of Mercy and Riley's pupcubs. Hawke and Lucas had agreed, so now it was a case of hashing out the details and figuring out who should do what.

"Put Mercy in charge," Indigo said, to Judd's surprise.

It wasn't because Indigo had nominated a leopard—the two women were close friends. No, it was because planning parties wasn't exactly in the dominant-predatory-changeling-female job description. The maternals and submissives were far more experienced at wrangling everyone who needed to be wrangled to pull off an event.

Then Indigo added, "She's going stir-crazy, and this is something she can work on with Riley's input for the wolf side of things. For the physical stuff, she can haul in helpers from either pack."

"Luc suggested the same." Hawke's eyes gleamed with wolfish humor. "I think the cat is afraid Mercy will rip off someone's head if she doesn't have something to do now that she can't run patrol and the healers have asked her not to go in to work at CTX."

Judd knew Mercy worked in communications when she wasn't carrying out her duties as a DarkRiver sentinel. It was a job she could've kept doing, but it would've required daily and likely tiring round-trips to San Francisco, which would also mean she wasn't in close proximity to the DarkRiver healer for much of the day.

No one wanted to take that risk, least of all Mercy or Riley.

"It's a good idea," Judd found himself saying after he'd processed Indigo's points. "Mercy's sociable and she has experience with communications. Plus, with her already off the rotation, it won't mean a change in DarkRiver's duty roster."

"And we don't have to worry that she won't take the wolf perspective into account," Drew said in a voice that held open love for his brother and Riley's leopard mate. "She and Riley want the pupcubs to grow up at home in DarkRiver and SnowDancer both."

Hawke grinned. "My bet is four wolf pups."

Golden eyes going wolf, Riaz snorted. "We're talking about Mercy here. She'll probably smugly produce all cubs. Five of them."

The others booed his prediction, calling out their own bets as they spoke. Judd had placed a two-and-two bet. Word was the pupcubs' changeling animal would be linked to the dominance of each respective parent, and Judd wasn't about to bet against either Mercy or Riley. They were the most evenly matched dominant changeling pairing he'd ever seen. And he didn't think Mercy was big enough to be carrying quintuplets. Triplets or quads were far more likely.

A sudden rise in the noise level broke into the group's friendly argument.

Chapter 6

CHILDREN POURED INTO the White Zone seconds later, having clearly been given permission to escape whatever it was they'd been corralled into the den for. Judd wasn't the least surprised when they made a beeline for the adults—big playmates to climb over were always welcome.

"Hawke! Hawke!" Brown-eyed, silky-haired Ben tugged on his alpha's hand as the lieutenants who'd attended the meeting remotely signed off with good-byes that held smiles. "Are we really gonna have a party with Julian and Roman and Keenan and everyone?"

That explained the excitement in the air, Judd thought as he reached down to pick up a little girl who was too small to push through the pack of pups. Putting her on his shoulders, he held her gently in place with one hand rather than with telekinesis. Children this young sometimes got scared when they couldn't feel his hand.

She laughed and kicked feet clad in sparkling blue sandals. Before living in the pack, Judd would've never understood why changeling parents spent time and money on dressing their children when those children could shift without warning at any minute, destroying the items. Now no one had to explain it to him. Judd had given Ben the superhero T-shirt he currently wore.

The six-going-on-six-and-a-half-year-old was jumping up and down at Hawke's positive reply. "Will we get to play games? And climb trees?"

Ben was one of the few wolves who could really climb, even in his wolf form. All thanks to his leopard playmates—Julian and Roman might be a year younger, but they were as prone to getting into mischief as Ben. The last time the three had been together, when Tamsyn came up to consult with Lara, they'd somehow managed to get into a supplies cupboard and gorge on the fancy chocolate the maternal females had been saving for dessert after a planned working dinner.

The chocolate-smeared miscreants had been found snoring away in the cupboard.

"I don't think it would be a party without play," Hawke answered with a grin before he hitched Ben onto his back, where the little boy clung like a monkey. "I don't know about climbing though. I like the earth under my paws."

"It's fun!" Ben insisted, the chorus repeated by other children nearby.

"Have you been contaminating your packmates with leopard ways?" Indigo asked darkly, though her eyes were dancing.

"No," Ben said, then frowned. "What does contami-ating mean?"

Laughing, Indigo clapped her hands. "Who wants to play tag? Hawke is it."

"Yay!" The sound wave of agreement shook the trees before the kids scattered, Ben scrambling down to run away as fast as his little legs would carry him.

A slightly older group of kids, meanwhile, was huddled in another corner of the White Zone. As a grinning Riaz jogged past them to the den to safely stow the mobile comm, Judd managed to see between the children's bodies, realized they were filling colorful water balloons from large bottles of water they'd smuggled out.

In front of Judd, Hawke narrowed his eyes at Indigo. "Right, I know who's next."

The lieutenant took off without a backward glance, weaving between delighted children while Drew got in Hawke's way. "Can't let you tag my mate," the tracker said, hands open palms-out on either side of his body.

Having lowered the little girl he'd been holding so she could toddle away to hide, Judd used his telekinetic abilities to move Drew out of the way.

"Hey!" His brother-in-law scowled at him as Hawke took off after Indigo, their alpha pretending to growl and go after several small children along the way, who all ran off squealing. Sienna, meanwhile, was laughingly trying to herd Indigo into a trap, with a returned Riaz's help.

"What the hell was that for?" Drew snarled, his shoulders moving fluidly under a dark blue tee with a silver design on one side as he threw up his hands.

"Remember that time we played war games and you almost broke my ribs?" It had been before Judd and Brenna's mating, at a time when Drew was certain Judd was no good for his baby sister. "I decided I'm still holding a grudge."

"You got your own back!" Drew's response was half wolf, his claws sliding out of his skin. "You almost dislocated my shoulder that day!"

Judd pretended to think about it. "I did, didn't I?" Having telekinetically stolen a water balloon from the enterprising group in the corner, he said, "So maybe I just wanted you here so I could do this," and threw the balloon at Drew.

It caught the wolf in the face.

Growling as water dripped from his face onto his chest, Drew body-slammed Judd, and they went down. At which point, the other man clawed up dirt and grass and stuffed the mass down Judd's back. Judd attempted to flip his brother-in-law off him, was foiled when pups drawn by their commotion ran over.

"Here, Drew," one said, holding out a bright pink water balloon.

Drew bared his teeth and smashed the balloon right on Judd's neck, which meant the water went down his back and chest, turning the dirt to mud. "Oops."

Fighting dirty now, Judd got him with a couple more balloons. This time they were supplied eagerly by the children. Then he got lucky and managed to rub dirt onto Drew's face. The pups, young and old, loved this new game. Mud was soon being rubbed onto both Drew and Judd with enthusiastic little hands, while the pups laughed like little demons.

Judd, sitting up now, with Drew behind him, back-to-back, felt something build inside his chest.

"Your fault," Drew growled. "Remind me to wring your neck."

"Noted." That powerful feeling kept building and building.

And then a pup stopped squishing mud into Judd's hair to peer at him with big blue eyes. "Uncle Judd's laughing!"

He was, he realized. Quietly, shoulders shaking, but the laughter, it wouldn't stay inside. Drew elbowed him from the back. "Not funny, man. I had on a new T-shirt."

Judd just laughed harder, until Drew gave in and began to chuckle, too. Judd's stomach was aching when he looked up and saw a beautiful blonde SnowDancer step into the carnage of the White Zone. His mate was dressed in sleek gray pants cropped at midcalf, her formal white shirt tucked into the pants. Colorful orange flats rounded out the professional look.

Her hair, which she'd grown out, was twisted into a complicated knot at the back of her head, her sideswept bangs providing a frame for her fine-boned face.

"I see," she said, coming to stand over him and Drew, fisted hands on her hips. "While I'm off having serious meetings at the university, you all get to play." Her attempt to sound stern was totally defused by the sparkle in brown eyes shattered by spikes of arctic blue that speared out from midnight pupils.

Those extraordinary eyes were all that remained of her trauma at a monster's hands, and she'd made them her own. The vicious Psy serial killer who'd taken and tortured Brenna had wanted to mark her, break her, then end her life. But he was the one who was dead. Brenna had survived, grown strong, reclaimed every part of her self. And the monster? She'd banished him from her mind until he couldn't even stalk her nightmares.

People called Judd tough; he had nothing on Brenna Shane Kincaid.

"Want to join us?" He held up a muddy hand, while Drew said, "Yeah, Bren. Come play." His voice was suspiciously cheerful.

Raising her hands and clearly realizing both her brother and her mate were up to no good, Brenna backed off. "I love you both, but no. Not when I'm wearing these clothes."

She was gorgeous and so incredibly smart, Judd's mate. She was also in the middle of the White Zone with kids who'd figured out the adults were in the mood to play. The first water balloon hit her ten seconds later, catching her on the back. Her yelp of surprise was followed by a second balloon that soaked her front, revealing the lines of the simple white bra Judd had watched her put on this morning.

He loved watching her dress, loved the way she moved about so energetic and chatty in the morning. And he loved that she fed his touch hunger with demands of her own. Judd liked nothing better than to get his hands on her.

"Since you're wet anyway . . ." Rolling to his feet, he started to stalk toward her.

"You keep your distance," Brenna ordered. "Judd Lauren, I mean it! I am not getting mud all over—"

Giving up trying to make him behave when it was clear he wasn't about to listen, she took off into the trees, kicking off her flats along the way.

Judd went to race after her . . . only to be brought down hard by a grip on his ankle. All the air in his lungs exploded from his mouth as he went chest-down right into the spot the pups had made their impromptu mud-creation zone. When he looked back, it was to see a certain blue-eyed wolf smirking at him. "Remember that time you used telekinesis on me?" Drew said. "I decided I'm still holding a grudge."

Judd took a breath then unstuck himself from the mud by pushing up onto his hands.

Drew tightened his grip.

And Judd took a leaf from Ben's book of mischief. The pup was a master at innocent misdirection. Judd's misdirection wasn't so innocent. "Indigo's on the ground," he said after pretending to look to the other end of the White Zone. "I think Hawke's making her eat grass."

Drew's hold grew slack as his head snapped in the direction Judd had been looking. "What?" It was a growl. "Where?"

Breaking free before the tracker could figure out Judd was lying through his teeth, Judd followed his mate's scent into the forest beyond the clearing of the White Zone. She'd made good use of her head start, but while she was a wolf, he was an Arrow. He was also teleport-capable. He didn't cheat though, staying on foot and using only the tracking skills he'd learned since becoming a real part of SnowDancer rather than simply existing within the pack.

When he caught Brenna, it was because she'd paused to take a rest by a large, deep pond. It had a mirrorlike surface kissed by sunlight and surrounded by purple blooms with yellow hearts as well as by tiny white wildflowers that reminded him of daisies, the mountain flora having adapted to survive at this altitude. Careful to stay upwind so she wouldn't catch his scent, he crept up behind her.

"Judd!" she screamed as he wrapped his arms around her and rubbed his muddy face against the side of hers, his equally muddy chest sticking to the back of her wet shirt.

He wasn't expecting her to hook her foot around his legs, unbalance him. They fell into the pond together, came up spluttering.

Splashing water at him, Brenna grinned. "Serves you right."

"I needed to wash off the mud anyway." Going under, he scrubbed his face clean before coming back up and hauling her close with one arm around her waist. Her body was softly curved and lithely muscled both—Brenna was a tech rather than a soldier, but aside from her lupine love of running under the moonlight, she attended certain compulsory training sessions alongside fellow packmates who weren't submissive, but who weren't dominant enough that a protective security role in the pack was a driving force.

They had the combat training so they could provide backup should SnowDancer suffer an assault that broke through the ranks of aggressive dominants. The training was intense and regular, and it satisfied the dominance of the wolf within while permitting Brenna to continue to work in another field.

Because her true asset was her dazzling mind.

"How was the meeting?"

"Good. The university wants me to teach a class."

Judd felt no surprise. Young though she was, Brenna was at the forefront of her field, her ideas cutting-edge. "You want to?"

"I'm considering it." Mind clearly on other matters, she smiled and wrapped her legs around his waist, having already linked her arms loosely around his neck. "Do you think we're far enough away from the White Zone not to be interrupted?"

He knew that tone in her voice, slightly husky and soft at the same time. His body responded as if it had been conditioned. Unlike the brutal suffocation of Silence, however, this conditioning was chosen, was wanted.

Gripping her lush lower curves, he opened to the kiss she claimed, felt his erection harden further as she licked her tongue against his. His hands flexed on her, his body hers to command. His mate had taught him pleasure after a lifetime of cold discipline engendered by torture that had forever ended his childhood, and now he craved that pleasure. Craved *her*. Only with Brenna could he be this man, a man who demanded and gave and who sank into sensation.

Sliding one hand up her back, he was about to deepen the kiss when he heard voices, felt the thunder of pounding feet. He broke the kiss just in time to witness an invasion, as all the adults who'd been in the White Zone jumped into the pond en masse, most with loud whooping and hard splashes. Brenna threw back her head and laughed as she was splashed, broke free to splash back. Judd watched her grin, watched her sparkle . . . and he played.

It was no longer a foreign experience.

As he stole a kiss from his mate a few minutes later, he hoped his friend Xavier would have the same chance at happiness, that he'd find his Nina. Of the three of them who had come together to form their own small rebel cell—Judd, Kaleb, Xavier—the priest was undeniably the only one who was good to the core of his soul. He might've struggled, might've looked into the screaming depths of the abyss, but Xavier Perez had never fallen into that darkness. He deserved joy, deserved to find the love he'd lost under a hail of bloody telepathic strikes over nine years earlier.

Good luck, my friend.

Letters to Nina

From the private diaries of Father Xavier Perez
July 8, 2073

Nina,

I'm sitting surrounded by the phantom image of what was once our village. A bare three months since the Psy attack and there's nothing here anymore. The bodies are all gone, as are the houses. No sign remains of the vibrant place that was our home.

I can hear you laughing at the idea of me writing a letter. I never did write you romantic love notes like Jorge did to Fiorella, even after you hinted so hard you may as well have hit me over the head with a hammer. Why should I write letters, I thought, when my Nina is here beside me, and I can love her with my voice, my hands, my body?

But now I've lost you and all I have left is paper and ink.

I saw you go over the cliff into the river. I made you jump. I thought you'd be safe, that the waters would carry you away from the carnage.

The silence here is ugly, obscene. A heavy shroud.

In the months since the Psy murdered all those we loved, I've returned here many times hoping you'd made your way back, but I've found no trace of you. No one knows of a woman who came out of the river. No one has heard of my Nina. I'm not giving up. I'll never give up. Because from the day I first grew old enough to remember my own thoughts, I knew two *things: That I was a man of God, and that one day, I would marry you.*

I'll find you, Nina. No matter what it takes or how long I have to search. I'll find you.

Your Xavier

Chapter 7

KALEB HADN'T BEEN serious when he told Judd he was thinking of taking Silver along to the meeting with Ena Mercant, but when his most senior aide walked into his office as he was buttoning up the jacket of his navy blue pin-striped suit, he considered it for an instant. Because the Mercants were . . . unusual.

In political terms and in terms of their intelligence network, their importance was far-reaching. Most people saw them as shadow players who wanted to manipulate puppets in positions of power, but Kaleb had always seen something different: a family that had stayed a family regardless of Silence. They were a tightly integrated unit with blood-deep loyalty to one another.

Kaleb had first hired Silver because he wanted an "in" with the Mercants, had kept her on even after he figured out that getting Mercant trust was nothing so simple. It had been an easy decision: Silver was the best aide he'd ever had, one who worked efficiently with and for him—as evidenced by the fact that she was here so early this morning. However, Silver also had the critical capacity to make independent decisions and take the necessary steps to action those decisions.

Kaleb didn't trust her. He trusted very few people, but he had long ago decided that whether she brought the Mercant family with her, or not, Silver had considerable value on her own.

She proved that value with her next question.

"Sir," she said. "Would you like me to accompany you to this meeting?"

"No," he answered, at the same time setting up a psychic filter for any mentions of Lucas Hunter's child. It would run quietly in the background so long as he didn't turn it off. "I think your grandmother and I should speak alone."

Silver's expression didn't change. She was always coolly composed, no matter the pressure, her ice-blonde hair pinned neatly back in a sophisticated roll and her body clad in skirt suits paired with spike heels. Today's suit was gray, the shirt white. The heels were black. Kaleb only noticed things like that because he saw them as tools—Silver was far too intelligent to dress in impractical heels unless they gave her an advantage in some way.

"If I might make a suggestion," she said now.

Kaleb nodded. He was well aware of his own strength and power, but arrogance was a flaw he tried not to cultivate. It led only to bitter outcomes. Look at Ming LeBon, scrambling to make a place for himself in the world after losing his grip on the most lethal squad of assassins ever known. Had Ming still had the loyalty of the Arrows, he'd have held more power than even Kaleb.

But where Kaleb had Sahara to keep him anchored, to keep him as honest as he could ever be, Ming had no one he could truly trust. It was difficult to build that trust when subordinates lived in constant fear of death or torture because Ming didn't tolerate mistakes. Kaleb didn't, either, but he didn't punish mistakes that were genuine—or those that had been made in pursuit of a worthwhile goal. He'd been known to promote not only the winners, but also those who had failed but then dusted themselves off and tried again. To do otherwise was to stifle all innovation and drive.

Most of all, his people knew he never forgot those who'd been loyal.

As he hadn't forgotten Silver when it came time to promote someone to coordinate the worldwide Emergency Response Network. Yes, Sahara had had to nudge him, but only because he didn't want to lose part of Silver's attention to EmNet, not because he didn't have confidence in her competence for the task.

"Grandmother Mercant is predisposed to work with you," Silver said as those thoughts passed rapidly through his head. "Don't insult her intelligence at any point by lying or skirting the truth, and you'll come out of the meeting with everything you want."

Kaleb held Silver's eyes, the color an unusual light shade that was a marker of one branch of the Mercant family tree. Her brother had the same eyes, as did her mother and grandmother. "Understood," he said. "I'm surprised you're offering me advice that might help me best your own grandmother."

"It's not about besting," Silver replied. "It's about ensuring you don't make a mistake that will cost both parties in the long run."

Kaleb understood the subtext: The Mercants had, for whatever reason, decided to welcome him into the fold. All he had to do was accept that welcome and work with them. "Thank you, Silver."

Inclining her head, she passed over a whisper-thin organizer that was a prototype from one of Kaleb's enterprises. "If you could sign this contract before you go."

Kaleb scanned the text to make sure it was exactly as he wanted it, then signed. "No interruptions unless it's an emergency."

"Yes, sir."

Having already gotten a fix on the visual coordinates he'd been given, Kaleb teleported to the location of the meeting—though he could've teleported directly to Ena Mercant. Despite her tendency to stay out of the spotlight, he had a recent visual of her face. Not all teleporters could lock on to people as well as places, but Kaleb had been born with the ability.

Using it in these circumstances, however, would've been a grave insult to his host.

I couldn't resist, whispered a familiar telepathic voice, carried along their bond and augmented by Kaleb's own strength until Sahara could reach him telepathically, no matter the distance that separated them. *What does Ena Mercant's inner sanctum look like?*

The darkness inside Kaleb stretched out under the light that was Sahara. *Are you still in bed?* He'd left her warm and sleepy and flushed from his kiss when he teleported into the office.

Do you know how sexy you are when you dress in those suits? was her response. *Especially when you button up your shirt, then slot in the cuff links. Watching you is like having a waking erotic dream.*

Kaleb smiled inwardly. *Yes, I know.* Sahara had made it clear by the way she watched him, by the number of times she'd hauled him into bed after he'd had his shower and was dressing. *Should I stop?*

Come home and tease me after this meeting. You left too early.

His inward smile deepened even as he kept his face expressionless. *I have an empire to run.*

Pfft. What's another million or five when you have . . . I don't even know how much money you have.

A lot. And it's ours, not mine. He'd built the empire for her, built everything for her. *This location in Ena Mercant's home is identical to the image I showed you.* A cool floor of dark stone, steel gray walls, sofas of a darker gray.

Really? A hint of disappointment. *I expected something unexpected. She's the Mercant after all.*

Kaleb looked around the room, spotted what he'd missed when he first came in. *There's a vase of dark, dark red roses along one wall.* A single, violent splash of color in the gray. *Perhaps a subtle reminder that those who cross the Mercants die bloody deaths?*

Don't joke, Sahara ordered, her tone no longer playful. *These people are dangerous.*

So am I, he reminded the woman who worried about him, who *loved* him, twisted internal scars and all. *But I promise I won't take anything for granted. The Mercants can be lethal foes.*

He walked to the large sloping windows that looked out over a misty gorge. It was heading into night in this part of the world, but Ena's windows didn't look out over a city bright with sparkling lights. No, beyond the gorge was craggy rock and then the crashing sea. *This is interesting.* He sent Sahara an image of what he was seeing.

His senses alerted him to another presence at almost the same instant.

Turning, he saw a woman who was Silver with fifty more years of life.

The same eyes, the same sharply defined face. The difference was that Ena Mercant's hair was silky white and she wore not a skirt suit, but pants that moved fluidly around her legs, the color of the fabric similar to that of the café au lait Sahara had made Kaleb try three days earlier. Ena's top was the same color and of the same fabric and flowed to her hips while covering her arms.

On her feet were black flats. She also wore a long silver necklace that came down to below her breasts and was anchored by an ornate metal pendant with a core of red.

Psy rarely wore jewelry, but Kaleb had a feeling this wasn't just jewelry. "Ena," he said, very deliberately using her first name.

Ena Mercant might be a shadow power but Kaleb was a *power*.

Better she not forget that. His decision wasn't arrogance but the cool tactical thinking that had led to his meteoric rise—and that kept him at the top of the food chain. Even Pax Marshall, who was flexing his muscle against many others, gave Kaleb a wide berth.

"Kaleb." Ena Mercant's voice had a rasp that seemed natural. "What do you think of the view?"

Turning back to it as she came to stand beside him, he said, "It's similar to my own view at home." His deck jutted out over a gorge as steep. "You don't want to be closer to a metropolitan area?" That was the choice made by most Psy.

"Do you?" Ena's eyes remained on the foaming waves in the distance.

"No, but I'm a teleporter."

A graceful incline of Ena's head. "Point well made." She moved her hand. "Come, sit, let's talk."

KALEB left the meeting two hours later with the understanding that the Mercants were in his corner—and that Ena Mercant might be the most dangerous individual he'd ever met. She had ruthless intelligence paired with ruthless ambition. But where others used such ambition for themselves, Ena used it in pursuit of power for her family.

"We've accepted you as one of us," Ena had said to him, point-blank. "Don't betray the family and we will never betray you."

It was a far better outcome than Kaleb could've ever anticipated. "I won't be like the rest of your family, Ena," he'd pointed out. "The only orders I take are my own." And Sahara's. But Ena Mercant didn't need to know that.

The older Psy had given him a look that betrayed nothing . . . but that wasn't as closed as her expression had been at the start of their meeting. "I'm well aware we're welcoming a predator into our midst, Kaleb. But never forget that even predators can be taken down by a single poison dart."

He'd smiled. "So, we understand each other." Two predators who had decided to cooperate and to watch one another's backs.

"Yes." Ena had raised the delicate bone-china teacup in her hand, full of a pale green liquid that wasn't part of the ordinary Psy nutrition list. "Welcome to the family."

Having teleported back to his office rather than to Sahara because she'd had to go into a meeting herself twenty minutes earlier, Kaleb kept the door shut and considered the implications of the day. Mercant help was not to be taken lightly and Kaleb had no intention of abusing their trust. He was a man who knew how to value his assets and the Mercant intelligence network alone held the power to topple countless individuals.

Ping.

The psychic alert was faint and part of the myriad pieces of data flowing into his mind at any one instant, but he took a second to glance at it. Interesting. His search had picked up a mention of the DarkRiver alpha's child.

Stepping out into the PsyNet with his mind cloaked so well that he was a ghost, he shot himself to the exact location of the ping. Around him, the PsyNet was a vast blackness populated with millions of stars that represented the minds of the Psy in the Net. But where there had been only black and white, there was now a delicate golden framework underlying everything.

The Honeycomb, created by the empaths, the fragile golden structure that kept the Net from crumbling. Brilliant in the once pure-black spaces in between the bonds of the Honeycomb were the sparks of color that denoted a psychic network awash in empaths. Research suggested the reason those sparks were so prevalent was because the PsyNet was sick, needed a lot of healing.

Today, however, his attention was not on those sparks or on the fine golden lines that connected people to the Es and the Es to one another. It was on the data that flowed constantly through the empty spaces between minds, endless streams of it.

He was only interested in a particular piece of it.

. . . Psy with shifting powers?

Catching the first hint of the conversation that had prompted the alert, he came to a halt, listened.

Such an individual would have enviable abilities.

Do you truly believe so? Don't forget, the child will be hampered by her animalistic instincts.

The changelings have proven intelligent.

Yes, but Psy are more intelligent. Nadiya Hunter is unlikely to have the same brainpower.

Kaleb didn't need to listen any longer. It took less than a minute to identify the minds as belonging to would-be-intellectuals from a university. Like many academics, their shields were all but useless. Inserting a complex "reporter" bug in each mind, one that would awaken if and only should the mind involved begin thinking about the child in a way that indicated danger to her, he left them to their pontificating.

He returned to his own mind with the awareness that a large cross-section of the Psy race still couldn't see outside their bubble of perceived superiority. Fools. Those who thrived post-Silence would be the ones who knew the truth, knew that their competitors had the same hard-nosed intelligence and capacity to innovate. In the case of humans, they often had more because of the way they had so long been sidelined or abused.

Mention of the child, he messaged Judd. No threat. "Intellectual" curiosity. More like speaking simply to hear their own voices.

The reply was prompt. Let's hope they keep it to that.

Yes, Kaleb thought, highly conscious of what Nadiya "Naya" Hunter represented. Considering the bloodshed that would erupt should she be harmed, he decided to use the NetMind and DarkMind to heighten the watch. The NetMind was the librarian and guardian of the Net, its task to create order out of a chaos of data and minds. The DarkMind was far different, a twisted and homicidal creature.

Kaleb could speak to both. Understand both.

Yin and yang. Dark and light. Innocence and horror.

When the twin sentience came to him, however, they were disturbed. Or, the NetMind was disturbed and the DarkMind was ambivalent. Following them back into the Net, Kaleb found himself being taken to a section that was dark. Dead. No empathic sparks. No minds within the dead section. No Honeycomb strands. That wasn't unusual. Parts of the Net had suffered catastrophic damage before the empaths woke and began to sew it back together.

At the current rate of improvement, it would take years, an entire generation, maybe two, for those sections to recover. No minds could anchor there until then. Nothing would survive—or if it did, it would be a creature of raving insanity.

?!!

Following the NetMind's wordless urgings, he shifted his point of view . . . and saw the problem. The rot, the *disease,* was spreading. Not, however, in a way most people would be able to detect. No, the fine threads of the Net were literally coming apart strand by strand below the surface. Kaleb only saw it because the NetMind had imposed its vision over his. "Did you show the empaths?"

A sense of the negative, of an awareness the Es were already close to exhaustion.

Kaleb couldn't disagree. Sahara worked closely with the Empathic

Collective, and she'd been sharing her worry with him that Designation E was being asked to take on too much too soon. "No one designation can shoulder that much responsibility," she'd said, eyes of darkest blue passionate. "It's getting impossible to juggle the workload. I'm terrified that despite our best efforts not to repeat the mistakes of the past, they'll begin to crumple under the pressure."

The problem was that no one else could do what the Es could.

Now it appeared even their efforts hadn't totally stopped the insidious disintegration of the psychic fabric of the PsyNet. They'd given the PsyNet a fighting chance, but it was struggling not to fray apart. Yet . . . despite his first thoughts, this didn't feel like a resurgence of the disease. Rather, it seemed an indication of a deeper issue, a structural weakness that had permitted the disease to take hold in the first place.

"Is it because there aren't enough Es at this location?" he asked the NetMind, because if that was the case, the Es could rearrange themselves to fix the damage before it became critical.

The NetMind sent him a sense of the negative.

The DarkMind, meanwhile, swam into the dead space, becoming at one with it. The two were created of the same primordial soup—all the rage, anger, jealousy, and other dark emotions the Psy race had refused to feel for so long. Only it hadn't ever disappeared. It had simply collected in dark pockets of the psychic network until it split the NetMind into a stable innocence and a murderous darkness.

Today, neither half could tell him why the PsyNet was breaking apart, filament by filament, even as the Honeycomb fought to hold it together, even as the sparks of color that were the emanations of the Es spread through the black night of the spaces between minds.

The PsyNet should've been healing. Instead, it was simply dying more slowly.

Chapter 8

SASCHA HUNG UP after a troubling conversation with Ivy Jane. Her fellow E and president of the Empathic Collective had called to discuss the information she'd just received from Kaleb Krychek. Coming on top of the possible threat to Naya that Lucas had warned Sascha about earlier that day, it left her worried on multiple levels.

Naya was her first priority and always would be, but there were tens of thousands of children in the PsyNet, too. Even if the Honeycomb meant the PsyNet wouldn't collapse on them as it had done in sections prior to the awakening of the Es, the disintegration and hidden weakness within had to be having an impact on all those developing young minds.

It frustrated her that she hadn't been able to give Ivy any answers. Part of it was because she'd been out of the PsyNet since her defection and was receiving all data secondhand, but mostly it was because they were all stumbling in the dark. No one knew the exact extent of the damage done by a hundred years of forced conditioning, of erasing emotion.

"Coming," she said when Naya made a questioning noise from the living room.

It would've sounded like "da mi" to most people. Sascha knew her daughter was asking after her milk. Setting aside the issues preying on her mind for now—Naya was far too good at picking up emotional nuances—Sascha breathed deep to calm herself. "On its way, sweetheart."

She'd just brought out the milk to warm it on a low setting on the cooker when Ivy called. Naya liked it when Sascha made her milk that way, especially if she dusted it with a little dark chocolate.

"Her mother's daughter," Lucas said with a sinful grin each time he saw Sascha sprinkling chocolate onto Naya's milk. Not a lot, *never* enough to harm their baby's health. Just the *tiniest* taste to make this a sometimes treat now that Naya was almost one and starting to become more adventurous with her food choices. The milk would hold Naya over until Lucas arrived home and they could have dinner together—changelings tried to have meals together with their cubs whenever possible.

Naya's mind touched hers right then, sending her hungry thoughts.

Sascha's lips tugged up at the corners, all stress suddenly melting away. "I know you're not starving, munchkin," she said, layering her response with emotion so Naya would understand her meaning.

Her and Lucas's baby was smart, but she was still a baby.

Guilty giggles sounded from the living area. Even as her smile deepened, Sascha told herself to be firm. It was extremely difficult when Naya was smart enough to know she could get out of trouble by being adorable, and when Sascha was terrified of ever hurting her baby's heart as her own had been hurt when she'd been a vulnerable child. Consciously, she understood that gentle correction was nothing like the harsh lessons she'd been taught as a child, but it took real effort of will for her to put that into practice.

Every time she began to backslide into being too permissive, she reminded herself that Naya was a happy, settled child who knew she was deeply loved. She asked for affection whenever she needed it, with zero expectation that she might be refused or rejected—that idea was simply not part of her worldview, exactly as Sascha wanted for her. She was also secure enough to be naughty.

Lucas had had to chase Naya around the aerie at bedtime last night— her walk might still be a little shaky, but she was a rocket when it came to crawling. Dressed only in a diaper, she'd laughed uproariously and said a loud, firm "No" each time Lucas caught her and put her in her crib.

After which she'd clamber out—she'd figured out how to escape a month earlier—and the game would begin again. Of course, since Lucas was a cat, he'd been having just as much fun as their daughter. Sascha, meanwhile, had sat in the living room with a cup of hot chocolate and just indulged in the sight of her mate playing with their cub.

She'd had to pretend to be stern when Naya ran over and pleaded her case with loud sounds and wild gesticulations of her hands. "No, Naya," she'd said, biting her tongue in an effort not to laugh. "It's time for bed. Go with Papa."

At which point, Naya had growled at her, eyes sparkling with mischief.

And Sascha had cracked, laughing so hard she'd had to put down her hot chocolate before she spilled it. Lucas had shaken his head as Naya plopped down on her diaper-covered butt and joined in, clapping her hands at having made her mommy laugh. "No discipline." Lucas had mock-growled at her before picking up their misbehaving baby. "And you"—a growly nuzzle that made Naya laugh harder and pat his stubbled cheek—"time for bed."

He'd finally got her to sleep—by walking around with her pressed up against his bare chest.

Today, their cub was playing in the living area just outside the kitchen nook. Sascha had locked the aerie door to ensure Naya wouldn't undo the latch and go out onto the balcony, and Lucas had childproofed the entire main area of the aerie, so Naya was free to roam as she liked. A lot of the time she practiced her walking skills. And no matter how often she fell down, she started back up again after a little break.

Stubborn, determined baby.

Peeking out from the kitchen, Sascha found her concentrating on stacking the colored alphabet blocks Faith and Vaughn had given her as a gift. Beside her sat a more than slightly ragged wolf plush toy, aka "The Toy That Shall Not Be Named." Hawke had given that to Naya when she was a newborn, and it remained her favorite snuggle toy, much to her father's despair.

Though Lucas did enjoy it when Naya went leopard on the toy, growling and "fighting" with the wolf. Then he'd smile and say, "That's my girl."

Laughing softly and making a note to steal the toy for a wash after Naya went to sleep one night this week, Sascha returned her attention to stirring the slowly warming milk. As she waited for it to reach optimum temperature, she picked up an organizer with her other hand to finish reading a note from Tamsyn about the joint DarkRiver-SnowDancer event she and Lara had proposed to celebrate the birth of Mercy and Riley's babies.

The pupcubs would, after all, belong to both packs.

It's a good excuse to acknowledge how deeply the two packs are now linked, the pack healer had written. *I think we need to recognize that, start getting everyone used to the fact that with the birth of the pupcubs, we're going to truly become two independent parts of a much stronger whole.*

To her original message, Tamsyn had added an update: *SnowDancer has suggested Mercy take the lead on this. I can see their point.*

Sascha smiled. Lucas had decided on Mercy, too, but had been waiting to hear back from the wolves, see if they'd insist on a more hands-on approach. It would aggravate him that he and the wolves—especially Hawke—were on so much the same wavelength.

Grinning, she tapped back a message to Tamsyn, thanking the healer for the update and saying she'd pass it on to Lucas when he returned to the aerie. She and her mate switched off with child-care duties during the times Naya was home, but they were never out of touch with each other or the pack.

As alpha, Lucas had the heaviest workload, but Sascha had carved out her own place in DarkRiver, was the main point of contact for multiple matters so he could be free to focus on the wider picture. She missed Naya when she was away from her, but changeling cubs thrived on social interaction with other packmates. As a result, Naya was often at nursery school or on playdates with friends.

Conscious of the responsibilities that befell the alpha pair, their packmates were more than willing to take full charge of those playdates, but Sascha and Lucas took their turns as the hosts.

Naya needed to see her parents just as much as any other cub.

Pack was built on the bonds of family.

Putting down the organizer as the milk heated to just a little hotter than the temperature Naya liked, she turned off the cooker and carefully poured the milk into a sippy cup. It would be the right temperature by the time she got it into Naya's impatient hands. She was just sprinkling on the dark chocolate—from her personal stash, courtesy of her mate—when she felt a ripple along the mating bond that connected her to the man who was her heart.

She smiled and looked out at Naya. "Papa's almost home."

Face lighting up, Naya ran to the door on wobbly legs. She banged her small palms against it while saying, "Pa-pa! Pa-pa!" Her speech development and comprehension skills had kicked in closer to the Psy timeline than the changeling one, the likely result of her having constant telepathic contact with her mother.

Sascha screwed on the lid of the sippy cup before she walked out barefoot to pick up her daughter. Only when she had a firm hold did she unlock the door and open it to the early evening darkness. Lucas jumped up onto the balcony less than a minute later.

He'd clearly run full tilt from where he usually parked his car overnight; changelings took care not to ruin the environment in which they thrived, and if that meant a long run home, so be it. Lucas's T-shirt was stuck to his chest, that chest heaving. Given his fitness, he had to have run *really* fast.

"Racing to beat your best time?" Sascha asked as Naya stretched out toward her father, a wriggling, excited armful.

Lucas's grin was pure sin, his green eyes all panther right then. Smacking a kiss on Naya's cheek after taking her into his arms, he hauled Sascha close with a grip on the back of her neck and claimed her mouth in a distinctly adult kiss. Even after more than three years as his mate, Sascha's bones melted.

Pressing her hands against his chest, his heart thumping strong and fast under her palms and the scent of sweat and man around her, she rose up on her tiptoes, only breaking the kiss when her lungs protested. "I'm glad you're home." She hadn't seen him since six that morning, when he'd had to leave for an international conference call held in the comm room of DarkRiver's Chinatown HQ. To do with the fragile new Trinity Accord, it'd had too many participants for him to take the meeting on their home comm screen.

Since Sascha had no external meetings of her own, she'd chosen to stay home with Naya, though they'd barely actually been at home. Aside from the afternoon play session, they'd gone out for an hour in the morning so Naya could play with Anu's toddler—the sweet-natured two-year-old and Naya were fast friends.

Sascha had taken the chance to have a coffee with Anu as the two of them watched their children play. She'd expected stories of juvenile shenanigans from the cheerful maternal female, Anu's task in the pack to monitor the emotional health of the eleven-to-thirteen-year-old group, but Anu had shocked her with the news that the children hadn't gotten up to any tricks over the past week.

"The good behavior won't last," she'd predicted with faux solemnity, her prettily plump face set in suspicious lines. "They're just lulling us into a false sense of security. Then . . . pounce!"

Sascha was thinking she had to share Anu's comment with Lucas when he nipped at her lower lip.

"I'm glad to be home," he said. "It's been a hell of a day." Another kiss, this one hard and fast, before he looked at Naya again. "Why are you pulling Papa's hair?"

Naya's smile was pure gleeful cat. "Ooo!"

Sascha tensed her stomach in an effort to fight her laughter; she knew that only encouraged their daughter. But, God, it was hard—she had no idea how Tamsyn did it with her twins. Who, incidentally, had taught Naya the word "oops" as a way to respond when caught making trouble. She could only enunciate "ooo," but her meaning was clear. She also knew the names of the twins, though she couldn't say Roman and Julian yet, only Ro and Jul.

"Ooo is right." Lucas growled at Naya.

Naya growled back, the sound so adorable and their cub's pride in making it such a huge, happy thing, that, once again, Sascha just *could not* keep a straight face. Turning away to hide her tearing eyes and laughter so Naya wouldn't realize how easily she could cute her way out of trouble, she breathed deep. Only when she had herself under control did she turn and take Naya back into her arms. "Come on, let's go have your milk so your papa can shower."

Following at their backs, Lucas pulled the door closed and locked it again. "It's safe to release the escape artist."

Sascha loved carrying Naya, loved feeling her warm weight, but she'd learned that leopard changeling cubs did best if they were allowed a certain independence from a young age. When Naya wanted a cuddle, she'd find her. So she stole another cheek kiss before putting Naya on the play mat on which her daughter had stacked her blocks. Then she watched her mate walk toward the shower.

Her sigh was deep.

It was unfair, how good he looked in an old pair of jeans and a simple T-shirt.

Glancing over his shoulder as he reached the safely folded and stowed screen they used to separate out the living and sleeping areas when they had guests, Lucas grinned. "Hold that thought until our princess is asleep."

Sascha kept her gaze locked to that of her wild panther, let the cat know she saw it prowling under his skin. "Oh, I intend to."

A chuckle before he went the rest of the way to the shower located off the bedroom area.

Going into the kitchenette, Sascha picked up the sippy cup and brought it out to Naya. "There you go, baby girl."

Naya held the childproof cup with firm hands, little fingers around the handles on either side. Her eyes widened when she took the first sip out of the raised bit designed to ensure the milk wouldn't spill should it fall from her hands. "Cho!"

"Yes, chocolate. You were very good at Anu's—I thought you deserved a treat." Rising to her feet, she went into the kitchenette to finish dinner preparations. Naya's meal was easy—when Sascha dropped off the twins this afternoon, Tamsyn had given her a fresh jar of toddler-appropriate stew that Naya loved.

If only adult food were so straightforward.

"Right," she said, and continued what she'd been doing before stopping to make Naya's milk.

She was still a terrible cook overall, but she'd learned to make a few things that were fail-safe, and since Lucas had made sure they were fed three days running, it was only fair she take a turn.

However, not only were her skills as a cook dismal, she had nothing on how sexy Lucas looked while cooking. Especially since he had a tendency to walk around the aerie wearing only his jeans, those jeans hanging precariously low. Sighing again at the memory—then grinning because he'd probably come out of the shower with nothing but a towel hitched around his hips, she put the potato cheese bake she'd already prepared into the oven.

Her plan was to pair it with the chicken she'd put in to roast prior to the troubling call from Ivy Jane. She crossed her fingers that the chicken wouldn't burn or be undercooked. It remained her nemesis, along with a thousand other things.

Picking up the organizer, she walked into the living room. She'd watch over Naya while Lucas showered, then put away work for the day. But first she had to reply to a—"Eep!"

She jumped at the feel of something biting her ankle, glancing down just in time to see a furry black head disappear back under the small pink play table next to her. Eyes wide, Sascha tiptoed closer, was about to look beneath the table when she felt a deep need to do this with her mate by her side. "Lucas," she whispered, reaching for him through the mating bond.

The shower shut off a heartbeat later, and then a dripping Lucas, white towel wrapped around his hips exactly as she'd imagined, was walking out. "What's the matter?"

Sascha just pointed to the table and waved him down onto his knees.

Awareness dawning in eyes that rapidly went from human to panther, he came down beside her. Then, together, they both pressed their weight onto their palms and looked under the table Naya liked to use to put her toys on when she was "tidying."

Bright green leopard eyes glowed at them before a tiny panther cub bounded out into their arms—or tried to. She wasn't very coordinated, more slid across the floor than ran. Pride burned in her eyes, in her mental presence, in her growling.

Lucas growled back, chuckling and rubbing Naya's little head when she tried to pounce on him. Her concentration that of the very young child she was, she then turned to Sascha and tried to climb into her lap, Sascha having sat up on her knees.

Sascha's heart had burst open at first sight of her child's new form. Jet-black like her father except for those bright green eyes, her leopard rosettes hidden in the black, Naya was astonishingly beautiful.

Fighting happy tears, she said, "Clever, clever girl." She'd been told changeling children shifted around one year of age, and with Naya's birthday a bare week away, Sascha had been watchful—but she'd thought she would feel a mental change when Naya shifted for the first time. "Why didn't I feel you shift?"

"Because it's normal for her." Lucas turned over onto his back on the play mat, uncaring of his wet state.

Taking the silent invitation, Naya immediately ran over to climb laboriously onto his chest. She had to rest afterward, her tiny body heaving up and down under Lucas's hand. Once recovered, she stood on his chest and tried to bat playfully at his face. He deflected her with gentle hands, but in a way that told Naya it was all right to continue this game. "She's always Naya, whatever form she takes."

"But when you shift, you feel wilder." Sascha didn't know how else to explain it.

"She's a baby, closer to her primal state."

Naya looked up and purred when Sascha petted her, then fell flat on her belly, legs splayed out. Sascha helped her get back on her feet, where she once again started to "fight" with her father, safe in the knowledge that Lucas could easily handle her mock-attack.

"No claws." Lucas caught one small paw and tapped on the claws.

When Naya made mewling sounds, claws still out, Lucas released his own claws, then retracted them. One second, two, three, Naya's head tilted to the side . . . and her claws slid back in. "Good girl." Lucas kissed her face.

Happy, Naya turned to Sascha. Unable to resist, Sascha picked up their sweet baby and held her close. Her tiny heart beat so fast, her fur soft. Memories crashed into Sascha of the day she'd first held a cub in animal form. Julian had been bigger than Naya then, but just as gorgeous. Never could she have imagined that one day she'd be holding her own cub. Her eyes stung.

Naya only allowed Sascha's hold for a little while before wriggling to be put down. Circling Lucas and Sascha—falling and getting up and slipping—Naya growled and purred and had a rest every so often against her parents.

Sascha, one hand on Lucas's bare chest, couldn't stop watching her. "Remember that day I held Julian for the first time?"

"You mean the day you gave yourself away?"

Sascha smiled through her incipient tears. "I wish I could've kept that boot he chewed on."

"You kept me. I'm a better souvenir." Lucas raised one leg so it was bent at the knee, the towel immediately falling open on either side of his muscled thigh.

Her mind split in two. "Stop that," she ordered the gorgeous adult panther on the floor while a gorgeous baby panther tried to bite at his arm with tiny panther teeth. "I can't have you being all sexy while Naya's being all adorable."

Her heart might explode permanently.

He chuckled, moved over onto his front—and that towel, it just couldn't keep up. Before she could drag it back into place, the air filled with shattered light and a large black panther now sat beside her.

Delighted, Naya tried to bite at Lucas's tail but she couldn't catch it because he'd swept it over. Moving in that adorable, stumbling way, she tried to chase it—and Lucas swiped it back.

Sascha laughed as Naya tried to catch it again.

The simple game kept her amused and excited until she crawled into Sascha's lap and fell fast asleep with the quickness of the toddler that she was. Stroking her hands through Naya's soft fur, Sascha caught light from the corner of her eye. "Now you're naked." She tried to glare at her mate without looking at his body. "Do you want me dead?"

Chuckling, Lucas moved so that he was leaning on his arm behind her, his lower body mostly out of her range of vision. "I can't wait to take her for runs, to teach her the forest, show her how to climb to the aerie."

Sascha's overworked heart thumped. "Oh God, she's going to be so much more mobile." While still a baby in every other way.

Lucas tapped her on the nose. "She's a cat. We'll also teach her the rules."

"Is she going to start jumping off the balcony?" It was strength in motion when Lucas did it. The idea of Naya's tiny body flying through that much air had Sascha close to hyperventilating.

Rubbing her back, Lucas made a reassuring purring sound in his chest. "Not tomorrow or the day after. She's going to need time to build her strength."

Sascha had the feeling he was easing her into Naya's inevitable jump, and she was okay with that. Any woman would need to be petted and reassured when her baby was about to start flying off a balcony. "She's so beautiful as a cat, too."

"Of course she is." Lucas nuzzled her. "She's your daughter."

"Ours."

"Ours." Fingers weaving into her unbound hair, Lucas kissed her with a smile on his lips while their daughter slept in her lap. Sometime during the kiss, Naya shifted spontaneously back into human form—and the dinner burned. Neither Lucas nor Sascha cared. Not with their child snoring sweetly in her dreams.

Chapter 9

THE ARCHITECT, THE one who'd put together the Consortium, the one who'd had the foresight to see the fall of Silence on the horizon and to understand the power vacuum it would leave in the world, considered the latest data on the Trinity Accord.

If successful, Trinity and the ensuing United Earth Federation would kill the Consortium, though right now, the accord appeared to be barely treading water. Still, the Architect took nothing for granted. The Consortium had made the decision to go under to regroup after a member in the uppermost echelon of its membership was captured by the Arrow Squad, but that didn't mean they couldn't action small-scale disruptions.

The Human Alliance, for example, would have little patience for Trinity business if anti-human insurgents started making trouble in their territory. As it happened, the Architect knew of one such group. All it needed was a nudge to the right location and a catalyst to light its destructive fuse.

It was a small thing, but all chaos had to begin somewhere.

As for the much bigger operation that had been put into motion by another one of the core members of the Consortium . . . The Architect looked down at the brief on Nadiya Hunter. It was pitifully empty, but then the child wasn't even a year old, according to Consortium sources. Her importance as a symbol, however, was starting to grow as the Psy race came out of its post-Silence stupor and began to look around.

The Architect's fellow Consortium member was right: Killing the child in the right way held the potential to incite a bloody war between Psy and changeling, humans caught in the crossfire. It would be a decisive blow that permanently shattered Trinity and any hope of a peace that promised to severely frustrate the Consortium's plans.

However, a *single* mistake and the fury of DarkRiver and its powerful allies would focus solely on the Consortium. The Architect knew predatory changelings well enough to understand they wouldn't stop until each and every member of the Consortium was dead.

The pros and cons of the Nadiya Hunter gambit required further thought—but all the pieces were in place, if and when the Architect decided it was time to press "go."

Chapter 10

LUCAS PUT NAYA into her crib and raised the bars of the safety barrier, which he'd had to extend to their full height after she started escaping. It was to keep her safe. Lucas and Sascha would normally wake at the smallest sound, but just in case.

Covering her with a furry green blanket Tamsyn had knitted for her, he tucked the damn wolf snuggle toy beside her, then touched her soft, dark hair and looked at the woman who stood by his side. "We did good."

Sascha slipped her arm through his, eyes of cardinal starlight touched with sparks of color on Naya. "Yes, and had fun doing it." A sudden frown. "She had chocolate sprinkled milk, and I didn't clean her teeth. She usually doesn't fall asleep so early—she didn't even have her dinner."

"She'll wake if she's hungry, and one night without brushing her teeth won't hurt her," Lucas reassured his mate. "I did that every so often myself as a kid—it's amazing how much candy I got into."

"Thanks for the warning. Now go put on some jeans."

Chuckling, he drew her out of the nursery he and packmates had added on soon after Naya's birth. It was attached to their bedroom, so even if Naya escaped her crib, she'd have to go past their bed to get out.

"Anything salvageable?" he asked after pulling on jeans and following Sascha to the kitchen.

"Hmm. I think the potatoes might still be good."

"Super melted cheese is still melted cheese." Lucas took the pan to the table. "Chicken?"

"Lump of charcoal." Sascha looked morosely at it before shaking off her disappointment. "Want omelets instead?"

"Yep."

The two of them worked side by side to prepare the omelets. "Hear anything about Nikita?" The recent assassination attempt on Sascha's mother had caused significant injuries.

"Sophie says she's pushing herself too hard." Sascha's tone tensed. "She's concerned about a setback."

Running a hand over her hair, Lucas pointed out an irrefutable truth. "Nikita isn't used to giving up control, even for short periods." The former Councilor and current member of the Ruling Coalition of the Psy race was a pitiless operator who was used to power.

Sascha nodded, took a deep breath. "So far, she's fine. Sophie's going to keep me updated on her progress." Unspoken were the words that today, Sascha had to focus on her vulnerable child, not on a mother adept at lethal defense—and offense.

They sat down to eat less than ten minutes later, their chairs beside each other instead of on either side of the table. Lucas liked to be able to affectionately touch his mate, and Sascha had picked up the feline habit, petting him every so often as they ate.

Skin privileges between a mated pair. Simple. Deeply needed.

He felt the worry that rose to the forefront of her mind now that Naya was asleep, but they both spoke only in touches until after they'd polished off the meal and she was cutting up some fruit for them to eat for dessert. That was when Sascha asked him to go over the full details of what Aden's people had heard in the Net.

Her face grew white under the dark honey of her skin as he spoke. "Is it a group like Pure Psy?"

"No current signs that it's anything that focused." Lucas forced himself to be calm; his mate needed that from him right now. "I'd still like to increase security precautions around her regardless. People—and not just Psy—are curious about her."

Dorian had done some research for him today, discovered that the only living child of mixed Psy and changeling blood was of far more interest to various groups across the world than the pack had ever realized. The majority of those groups had little to no information about Naya, knew only that she existed. But Lucas wasn't about to take chances with the life of his cub. "That curiosity is only going to grow and"—his jaw tightened—"some bastards will see her only as a political pawn to exploit."

Sascha nodded jerkily, but her words surprised him. "Nothing that stifles her, Lucas." Her eyes had bled to pure obsidian when he first began to speak, and now they gleamed with midnight-blue lowlights as she fought her emotions. He didn't know if all cardinal eyes did that, or if it was limited to the empaths, but the effect was hauntingly beautiful.

Panther and man, Lucas loved Sascha's eyes in every one of her moods.

"Nothing that cages her," she reiterated.

"I promise." He knew Sascha was thinking of her own childhood, of how her abilities had been crushed and stuffed into a box. "The physical security around her won't change much at all." He'd called a meeting of his sentinels that afternoon, with those not in the city attending via the comm, asked their opinion on the most efficient way to protect the pack's cubs without harming their wild spirits.

"We're going to embed more warning sensors in and around our territory," he told Sascha. "That'll have an impact without affecting Naya's independence or that of any other cub in DarkRiver." In Naya's case, the danger level had risen the instant she began to shift and became more mobile. "I've also asked Dorian and Emmett to liaise with our mechanics and make sure all the pack vehicles are as secure and as tough as they can be, and we're going to quietly up the security presence anywhere our children congregate."

"If they can't get Naya, they might try for another cub," Sascha whispered in realization. "Because of us and what we represent, because of the power DarkRiver has in Trinity." But though white lines bracketed her mouth, she didn't panic. "We need to let all our friends know, not just the Rats and SnowDancer. The more eyes looking out and ears that are listening, the better our chances of catching any attempt before it goes far."

DarkRiver had long thrived in isolation, like the majority of change-ling packs, but that time had passed. First had come the wolves, then friendships that slowly connected them to Psy, humans, more changelings. "The falcons have permission to overfly our territory and might spot sus-picious movements." Lucas frowned in thought, rubbing his thumb over the side of his mate's neck as he cradled her nape. "Who else?"

Together, the two of them made up a list and decided which one of them would talk to which party. He knew it was possible they were both overreacting, but that was significantly better than taking no action when innocent lives were on the line.

Sascha made him coffee afterward, herself a hot chocolate. It was her comfort drink of choice, but what soothed her most was to go into the nursery and look in on Naya. Lucas went with her, his own panther needing to see their cub safe and snug and curled up happily in her crib. "Damn it," he muttered. "She's hugging that stupid wolf to her chest."

Sascha's shoulders shook, the stars returning to her eyes. Baring his teeth at her, he pretended to pounce. She jumped then ran out of the room. His panther immediately sat up in interest and the chase was on. Catching her in the next room, he threw her gently on the bed before coming down over her. "Mine," he said, his lower body pressed to hers.

The smug statement was of the predator he was. But this predator loved the woman he held captive, would never harm her.

Stroking her fingers through his hair, Sascha said, "Something else happened, didn't it?"

He dropped his head for a minute, allowed her to pet him. Then, as they lay tangled, he told her about the letter the boys had found, about the imprisoned, tortured water changeling. His hands fisted against the textured white sheets on their bed. "This is the first new piece of infor-mation we've had on BlackSea's vanished members since the capture of the human CEO, and it's a call for help from a woman who's probably already dead."

Sascha shook her head. "There's always hope. No one thought Brenna would make it and look at her now."

Lucas nodded; it was a good reminder. The SnowDancer had been psychically and mentally broken when rescued. Yet instead of drowning in the darkness that had threatened to suck her under, Brenna had said "fuck you" to the monster who'd hurt her, and she'd chosen to *live*. She'd not only wrenched back control of her own life, she'd taken on an Arrow and claimed him as her mate.

Lucas had a great deal of respect for Riley's younger sister.

"None of us will give up on Leila," he promised. "Unless and until we have a body, we act as if she's alive." A woman who'd fought so hard even when alone, far from the sea that was her home, deserved nothing less. "It would help if Miane would allow wider dissemination of the information, but she's caught between a rock and a hard place."

Sascha's eyebrows drew together, even as she continued to run her fingers through his hair. "There's no way to weed out the Consortium spies in Trinity, is there?"

Nipping at her lower lip just because he could, Lucas said, "Can empaths sense deception?"

"Possibly." Sascha nipped back, making him grin. "But even if the Empathic Collective suddenly abandoned its code of ethics and started scanning everyone, the most dangerous spies will have dense shields. An E might pick up surface emotions, but everything else will be locked down."

Running his hand down her side, Lucas pushed up her lightweight top to touch skin, purring deep in his chest at the contact. At the lush feel of her warmth against his rougher skin. Shivering, Sascha wrapped her legs around him. "Why did you ask anyway?" she murmured, her breath kissing his. "You know no empath would ever be so dishonorable. Scans are only allowed with permission—like in business negotiations where both sides have an E at the table."

Eyes going panther as his feline nature rose to the surface of his mind, Lucas took his time kissing his mate, licking his tongue over hers as he lazily explored her body. "Because," he murmured against her lips several minutes later, "your own research has shown that not all Es are good."

The vast majority, yes, but like any being on the planet, even an E had loyalties. "What if the Consortium has an E in its ranks? What if that E *truly* believes that racial peace and the resulting comingling is bad for the Psy race?"

Sascha blinked, then pushed at his chest until he rolled over onto his back on the bed. Kneeling beside him, her knees brushing his side as he slid his hand under the back of her top to find skin again, she stared down at him. "You're right," she whispered. "'Good' and 'bad' are relative terms. An E, who, for whatever reason, is virulently anti-human or anti-changeling or simply pro the purity of the Psy, could justify all kinds of things."

She rubbed both hands over her face. "I don't know what the impact would be on the E—if the harm they did would rebound back on them, or if they'd be protected by their own belief." Lines formed on her forehead. "We still don't know enough about the E designation, not after the Council spent a hundred years erasing all evidence of our existence."

"Alice's memories still scattershot?" he asked, referring to the brilliant researcher who'd spent a century in forced cryonic suspension, and who now lived among the SnowDancers.

Sascha nodded, her frustration a palpable thing. "She has so much critical knowledge, but it's locked deep inside her." Compassion thickened her voice. "I'm guessing it's a combination of lingering shock and the organic damage done by the amount of time she spent suspended that's behind the gaps in her memory."

"She's tough to have come as far as she has." Lucas couldn't imagine going to sleep one day only to wake in a distant future where Sascha was dead, Naya was dead, his closest friends were all dead. "I think I'd go mad."

"She's stronger than she knows." Sascha's eyes were dark with poignant emotion. "But her heart's broken, shattered into splinters." Shaking her head, she touched her fingers to the hunter marks on his face. "It hurts me to even imagine the depth of her loss."

Taking her hand with his free one, he pressed a kiss to it. He didn't have to say what they both knew: If one of them died while Naya was young, the other one would fight and survive no matter their own shattered heart. "What if an E decided to hide his or her ability?" he asked, taking them back to a less emotive topic.

"That person could be a brilliant spy," Sascha said slowly. "He or she could damage Trinity from the inside by doing things as simple as encouraging dissent or quietly upping people's levels of aggression."

"Your designation is far more dangerous than anyone realizes."

Sascha's expression held a sudden, taut sadness. "Sometimes I wish I hadn't figured out the other side of my ability," she whispered, swallowing hard. "But today, when you told me what some nasty people are saying about Naya, I knew I'd use the dark side without hesitation to protect her. Regardless of any resulting psychic backlash."

Lucas nudged her over to straddle him, then he tugged her down so he could pet her, kiss her. He'd been there the day she'd worked out the brutal flip side to her ability to heal minds, had felt her terrible sorrow. "Nothing is ever black and white, kitten," he reminded her, allowing his claws to slice out to touch her skin. "I can use my claws to protect, but I can use the same claws to rip out an enemy's throat."

A slow nod from his mate, though her expression remained troubled. "Trinity brings with it the potential for a dazzling future . . . but we have to accept that it also provides a forum for those who want to seed chaos and destruction."

"Right now," Lucas admitted, "the Consortium is beating Trinity in the cooperation stakes." Driven by self-interest, the members of the enemy group were willing to work together against everyone else.

Those who'd signed the Trinity Accord, on the other hand, were becoming lost in the rivalries that had divided the world for so long. Psy against changeling. Human against Psy. Big businesses against small, the list was endless.

"The United Earth Federation is a distant dream, isn't it?" Sascha's eyes had once more lost their starlight.

"At least the dream now exists." By the time Naya grew up, maybe the UEF would be a functioning entity.

"Who knows?" Sascha murmured. "It could be our cub who one day leads that federation." Her spine grew stiff under his caressing hand.

Aware exactly where her mind had gone, Lucas gripped her jaw, held her gaze. "We'll keep Naya safe." It was a growling promise.

"Yes." Sascha's tone was resolute. "We will."

Releasing her jaw to run her gorgeously badly behaving hair through his fingers, he tugged lightly on the thick curls, released them, fascinated by the texture and by the way the strands clung to his skin.

"You are such a cat." It was a husky statement.

He leaned up on his elbows to flick his tongue over her lips, teasing her into a kiss that ended up with her pinned under him, tall and curvy in all the right places. Setting aside politics and the outside world, he played with the woman who'd begun the wave of change with her very public defection, this empath with her gentle heart and her wild courage.

The scent of her arousal made his cock throb.

"Lucas." A demanding touch on the back of his neck as Sascha locked her legs around his hips once again, her mouth moving to his throat.

Yes, his mate knew exactly how he liked to be touched.

Just as he knew her every sensual weakness.

Pressing her more heavily into the bed, he slid one hand under her top to cup the lush heaviness of her breast. His panther growled in his chest, full of primal pride that she was his.

A tiny answering growl sounded from the nursery.

Breaking the kiss, they both turned to look that way. The growl came again.

Sascha's body began to shake as her face filled with laughter. "*Someone* is not sleeping."

They waited in hopeful quiet. Five seconds later, just as Lucas was bending his mouth to Sascha's once more, Naya made an adorable sound that might have been her attempt at a grown panther's more guttural vocalization. It held impatience and excitement and zero drowsiness.

Dropping his head forward, Lucas nipped at Sascha's collarbone. "Why did we think having a cub was a good idea?"

Sascha laughed again. "She's probably hungry. Even if she isn't, I don't think we should be strict about bedtime. Not today."

"No," Lucas agreed with a nuzzle of his nose against hers. "Not today." Today, their baby needed a little extra care and attention.

Getting up, the two of them went into the nursery to discover a small black panther trying to shove her head through the bars of her crib. Shaking his head when Naya froze and gave him a look of wide-eyed innocence, Lucas picked up their child and held her black-furred body against his bare chest.

His growl was echoed by an excited one from her.

Lucas nipped her on the nose, the affectionate act of a panther with his misbehaving cub. "Want some food, princess?"

Butting her head against his chin, Naya made sounds of impatience.

"I get it. You want to go for a run in the forest first." He knew Naya couldn't really run. She could barely walk without falling over. But tonight, she wanted to be a panther.

Naya scrabbled at him at the pronouncement, her claws making fine furrows on his skin.

He didn't correct her this time; predatory changeling parents had to tread a careful line between teaching their children not to use claws against their playmates and to use them ferociously if defending against an enemy. In his current protective mood, Lucas decided his cub should learn the ferocious part first.

Her older playmates would teach her the rules of play soon enough.

Putting her on the floor, he pulled off his jeans—to his mate's sigh and his grin—and shifted. Then, before Naya could escape, he used his teeth to grip her by the ruff of her neck. Her tiny body went instinctively limp in his hold as he padded to the front door.

Sascha had already unlocked it, so he went straight out onto the balcony that had a railing only along one side. Glancing back to see his mate had squeezed her eyes tightly shut, he huffed in laughter and jumped off. He landed on the forest floor with the grace of the cat he was, his cub safe. Putting Naya down, he looked up and growled at Sascha to let her know they were unharmed.

She peeked over the edge, one hand on her heart and her hair tumbling around her face. "I'm coming down," she said in a breathless voice. "Don't go too far."

He and Naya had barely gone three feet before Sascha scrambled down the rope ladder to join them. All wobbly limbs and wild curiosity, Naya was distracted by a thousand things at once. He watched her with a father's patience, giving her praise when she did something clever, helping her get upright when she fell.

The night was cool and calm around their small family, the stars overhead a glittering quilt, and when Sascha came to her knees beside him, her hand on his back as they watched Naya try to chase fireflies, his heart felt too huge to stay inside his chest.

For this woman, for this child, for his pack, he'd do anything.

Trinity would not defeat him.

Neither would the Consortium.

Chapter 11

KALEB WAS UNSURPRISED when, late that night, Ivy Jane Zen requested he show her the dangerously subtle new damage in the PsyNet. The president of the Empathic Collective had proven to have a steel will beneath her soft exterior. He *was* surprised that she turned up on the Net without an Arrow escort.

"Where's Vasic?" The teleporter was Ivy's husband and second in command of the squad.

Ivy answered his unspoken question instead of the one he'd asked. "I'm an empath, Kaleb. I know exactly how much you love Sahara."

And Sahara called the Es her friends. Thus, Kaleb would never touch a hair on their heads unless they turned into a threat to the woman who was his heart. Then, of course, he would annihilate them to bloody pieces.

Kaleb didn't enjoy being so transparent. The twisted darkness in him reared up in an aggressive stance, too long used to fighting the enemy to ever trust easily. "Breaching shields, Madam President?"

Laughter in Ivy's reply. "No need. I've seen you two together, remember? You look at her like . . . like she's a rare, beautiful gift." Her mental voice grew softer. "To cherish, to protect. I know, because I see the same in Vasic's eyes when he looks at me."

In the physical world, standing on the deck of his home, Kaleb raised an eyebrow. "Does Vasic know you're here alone?"

"Does Sahara know she's mated to an overprotective Neanderthal?"

Kaleb's lips curved. Ivy's sharp response was so close to what Sahara might've said in similar circumstances. "You're ready? Heavy shields?" He might not appreciate the way certain Es were so good at seeing through a man's skin, but he'd permit no harm to come to them.

Without the Es, the Net was dead and Sahara needed the Net to breathe, to live.

"Yes."

"Meet me at these PsyNet coordinates." He was already in that dark, diseased location devoid of other Psy minds, his shields so effective that he had to alert Ivy to his presence before she could spot him.

Her own psychic presence held sparks of color unseen in any minds except for those of Designation E.

Kaleb had experienced the harsh viciousness of Silence firsthand, but even he had difficulty imagining the brutal extent of the conditioning each E must've undergone to have been so completely smothered.

To Kaleb, the fact that the Es had survived at all proved a mental resilience unseen in any other designation in the Net. "Have you considered working for a corporate?" he asked Ivy as she moved to examine the dead and disintegrating section.

"Why? Looking for a new hire?"

Kaleb already had two Es on his staff. As such, he was far ahead of the curve—the Es were so stretched that even those more suited for corporate work were being asked to take up heavy lifting in the Honeycomb.

Asked, not commanded.

That was the difference between the Empathic Collective and many of the other organizations in the PsyNet. It was as well they had the backing of the Arrow Squad or no one would take their requests to nonempaths seriously. A hundred years of Silence had taught the Psy that only the ruthless and the cold-blooded survived.

Kaleb had believed the same until he found Sahara again. The woman for whom he'd extinguish the world—except that she'd asked him to save it—hadn't lost herself in spite of the horror she'd survived. She'd come out of it with her soul and her spirit intact, was still the same generous

Sahara who'd first extended the hand of friendship toward a boy who knew only pain and isolation.

If there was a ruthless bone in her body, he hadn't found it yet.

Then had come the empaths. Kaleb had seen those empathic sparks of color, begun to comprehend the mental strength it must've taken for an E not to break despite being in a psychic stranglehold for decades. He knew what it was to be leashed, to have that leash pulled until he couldn't breathe.

Those who underestimated the Es would one day get a very nasty surprise.

"I thought you might've become sick of politics by now," he said to Ivy. "I can offer a pay package that'll take you immediately into the top percentile of earners in the world, and you'd be working in a far less stressful environment."

"You're very good," she said with open amusement, "but I've settled into my position in the Collective."

Despite his offer, Kaleb had thought as much; Ivy Jane Zen had started out unsure if she could lead, but these days, she was a force to be reckoned with. "The offer is open to any high-Gradient E who wants a more regular nine-to-five job."

While the Honeycomb needed every E in the Net, it had become clear that not all Es could bear the pressure. Those Es remained useful in other capacities, including in specialized medical professions and to corporates who wanted an edge on their competitors during negotiations. Empathic ethics might not allow for active scans without the permission of the individual being scanned, but as changelings picked up scents without trying, Es picked up the emotional undercurrents in any given situation.

Even in "passive" mode, they tilted the scales to their employer's advantage.

Ivy was quiet for a long time as she focused on the problematic section of the Net, but when she spoke, her answer was unexpected. "I'll keep that in mind. I wouldn't recommend jobs at most of the corporates to my people, but you . . . yes." As if guessing his surprise, she said, "Because of Sahara. She'd never let you mistreat an E."

Again, Kaleb wasn't certain he liked being in any way predictable. *Sahara,* he telepathed to the woman who had held his heart in her hands from the day they met, *please refrain from making me appear "nice" or trustworthy. Especially to those of Designation E.*

Sahara's laughter was light in the darkness, a brightness that encompassed the most twisted corners of his soul. *No chance of that.* Underneath the glittering night sky on the outskirts of Moscow, she came out of the house to wrap her arms around him from behind. *The Es know exactly how dangerous you are—but they also know you and your abilities are on their side.*

I'm only on one side. He closed one of his hands over hers. *Yours.*

Look after my friends, won't you, Kaleb?

Stop making so many.

I love you, too.

His lips curved slightly as he returned his attention to the PsyNet, and Sahara went back into the house—after a kiss to his back that made his battered soul curl up in pleasure. "What do you see?" he asked Ivy.

"The fraying is new, but the disease itself isn't as bad as it was pre-Honeycomb," she murmured. "Back then, the PsyNet was literally rotting away piece by piece, as if with gangrene."

Kaleb waited.

"The Honeycomb isn't visible here," Ivy continued after a small pause, "but it *is* present to my empathic senses. That fine net of emotional strands is all that's keeping this section from collapsing." She indicated the lifeless blackness in front of them.

"But?" Kaleb might not be an E, but he'd spent a lifetime learning to read people. First so he could predict the moves of the psychopath who'd ruled his childhood, later because he'd realized that to know people was to know their secrets. And secrets meant power.

"The disintegration below the surface?" Ivy said. "It's eroding the foundation on which the Honeycomb sits, and with each frayed thread, the weight of the dead section gets heavier. Thin as they are here, the Honeycomb bonds could simply snap, and if they do . . ."

Kaleb scanned the area. The rotten section was unpopulated, but there were minds anchored within touching distance of the black. Should it collapse, it would take hundreds, perhaps thousands of those minds with it, much like a whirlpool sucking in everything around it. "Do you want me to move those minds?" Kaleb couldn't do it himself, but the NetMind could make certain adjustments.

"No." Ivy's voice held an awareness of the risk of her decision, of the lives that hung in the balance. "If they go, they take their part of the Honeycomb with them. There'd effectively no longer be anything holding this section of the Net in place—it might create a tear so massive it could cause a catastrophic chain reaction."

Snuffing out the very minds they wanted to save.

"I'll set part of my consciousness to monitoring this area." It was a task Kaleb would've normally given the NetMind, but he was starting to have the disturbing suspicion that as the Net frayed, so did the neosentience in charge of it.

The signs had been there for a long time, if he thought about it. Lapses in concentration, lost or missing pieces of data, a distinct lack of growth since Kaleb was a child. Yes, the neosentience grew at a glacial pace in comparison to a Psy mind, but it had shown *no* development in over two decades.

In point of fact, it appeared to have gone backward, to an even more childlike state.

The only reason Kaleb hadn't noticed earlier was because he'd been distracted by the violent potential of the DarkMind. Though he'd never differentiated between his acceptance of the twin neosentience, handling the DarkMind had always required more attention.

Inadvertently hiding the subtle degeneration of its twin.

Kaleb considered sharing that suspicion with Ivy, made the decision that the Es were already at overload. One more worry could be the pro-verbial straw that caused a fatal breakdown. "It'll alert you if the risk of total Net failure at this location hits seventy-five percent." At which point, the risk in not moving the minds would outweigh the danger of a possible collapse and chain reaction.

Ivy's attention lingered on him. "Can you maintain such long-term monitoring without risk to yourself?"

Empaths. Dangerous to themselves most of all, with their concern for others.

"Yes," he said at the same instant that thought passed through his head.

As a dual cardinal, the only one in the Net, Kaleb had off-the-scale psychic abilities his mind had learned to utilize without melting down in the process. A single monitoring program wouldn't even register as usage on his internal psychic meter. Not when he could cause a cataclysmic earthquake without coming close to burning out.

Kaleb looked at the dead section again. "That's all you see?"

"Broken threads," she murmured. "Frayed edges. Like a piece of natural fabric coming apart, thread by thread."

"If it was the absence of active empaths that caused the damage, the disintegration makes no sense." Not with so many Es awake now. Kaleb could see sparks of color heading into the rot, to be absorbed by it.

"It's like . . . like something is acting against us and it's stronger." Ivy made a sound of frustration before her mental presence froze in place. "The NetMind, I felt it."

So had Kaleb, and this time, the neosentience had passed on an image that was impossible to misinterpret. "A honeycomb structure, but with approximately every third hexagon missing," he said for Ivy Jane's benefit, not certain the NetMind had spoken to them both.

"We're missing a vital component," Ivy whispered. "Without it, the Net will never be whole." A pause. "Another lost designation?"

Kaleb shook his head on the physical plane. "Impossible. I have access to top-secret data from prior to the dawn of Silence. No other designation was buried like the Es were buried."

"When I ask the NetMind for clarification, all I get is a cascade of emotion—loss, pain, brokenness." Tears filled Ivy's psychic voice. "It's in so much pain, Kaleb. So is the DarkMind."

Kaleb thought of the time right after the awakening of the Es and the creation of the Honeycomb. The NetMind had been a wonder of hope, joyous laughter in his mind. "They've lost hope," he found himself saying, though he was no expert in emotion.

Ivy's response was thick with sorrow. "Yes, you're right. The NetMind held on for so long, hid the Es, protected us, but now it's realized we can't stop the pain. Not totally."

And without the NetMind, the DarkMind couldn't exist.

Opening his senses, Kaleb reached for the twin neosentience, asked what was missing, what they needed. The emotions that came back were of a staggering loss, image after image of a body with organs torn out by uncaring hands, leaving the patient bloody and barely alive.

When? Kaleb asked, using a visual of a calendar and a clock with twenty-four numbers on it.

The pages of the calendar began to flip back at inhuman speed as the hands of the clock spun backward, around and around and around.

It all came to a stop at one minute past midnight in the year 1979.

The dawn of Silence.

Chapter 12

TWO HOURS AFTER Ivy's investigation of the strange and deadly weakness in the Net, Aden Kai, leader of the Arrow Squad, stood in an office awash in the sunshine present on this side of the world, and listened to her report, then offered any assistance he or the squad could provide. Even as he spoke, he knew there was little the Arrows could do except protect the Es and attempt to rapidly patch up any tears in the psychic fabric that kept millions alive.

This was a battlefield for which they simply did not have the right weapons.

As he ended the call with Ivy, he considered the other items on his agenda. The Trinity Accord was at the top, the Ming situation a serious issue that could cause real-world violence if not handled correctly. There was also the case of Leila Savea, one of BlackSea's vanished members.

Miane Levèque had updated Zaira directly on the message from the kidnapped marine biologist; Aden's commander and the BlackSea alpha were fledgling friends, both women as dangerous as one another. The fact that Zaira and Vasic had brought three of Miane's lost people home also had the BlackSea alpha far more apt to trust the squad.

"You understand what it is to treasure a child's life," she'd said to Aden once, her eyes as black as night rather than the clear hazel he was used to seeing. "It gives us common ground on which to stand."

While Aden was already calculating how the squad could help in the retrieval of the BlackSea woman, it wasn't because Leila Savea was an innocent. Aden couldn't think with his heart; he had to think first of the well-being of his Arrows, his strategy a long-term one. The squad needed to continue building relationships with other strong groups. Such relationships would keep their vulnerable alive should the world ever turn against the most dangerous predators in their midst.

That thought in mind, he sent an updated alert on the BlackSea situation to his men and women, then made a comm call to Lucas Hunter. "Lucas," he said when the alpha answered on what appeared to be a small-screen device, the view beyond him of smoothly polished wooden logs.

The sunlight made it difficult to see Lucas's face.

"I received your note." In it, the leopard alpha had suggested they send out a simple vote on the Ming situation to all those who had already signed the accord.

The result could well decide the future of Trinity.

"You agree?" Lucas's shoulders moved under the black of his T-shirt as he shifted to a more shaded spot. The clawlike markings on the right side of his face came into sudden, sharp focus.

"Yes," Aden said in reply to the alpha's question. "We can't move forward while Ming's trying to poison Trinity."

"I'll take care of getting the vote out." The leopard male's eyes glittered a green so feral, Aden knew he was no longer looking at the human part of Lucas, no matter the skin he wore. "Your people pick up anything else about Naya?"

"No, but it's possible some data I just received is related," Aden said. "An unnamed party was searching for a mercenary team five weeks to a month ago. The action was or is supposed to be in San Francisco."

Lucas snarled but managed to keep his voice civil as he said, "Thank you, Aden."

"I'll update you immediately if we discover who took up the offer."

Clearly coldly furious at the implications of the information Aden's people had discovered, the DarkRiver alpha signed off with a nod.

Alone in his office again, Aden considered Trinity. It had been his idea, and while he still believed deeply in the agreement, it was becoming obvious the divisions in the world ran far too deep for this to ever be a smooth journey.

You can lead a horse to water, but you can't make it drink. Even if it's dying of thirst. Not when it would rather fight the zebra on the other side.

Zaira had heard the human saying while she was posted in Venice, muttered it to Aden one night, and added her own pithy coda. Yet, despite her disdain for those who were causing problems, she remained his staunchest supporter. "You'll do it, Aden," she'd told him two nights earlier, the midnight dark of her eyes looking down into his as she rose up beside him on her elbow. "You always do what you put your mind to—even if it takes years."

A sudden, narrow-eyed smile from his most lethal commander, the lamplight throwing a warm glow on smooth skin a shade somewhere between cream and sun-kissed brown, the color beautifully changeable; it all depended on the season and the strength of the sun. "Look at me. Took you decades, but now here I am, naked in your bed. Anyone who bets against Aden Kai is as big an idiot as those horses."

His cheeks creasing at the memory of her acerbic words, Aden left his office and walked out into the sunlit landscape beyond. The Valley, as the squad had taken to calling this isolated piece of land cradled between the craggy peaks of two sets of mountains, was no longer as barren or as spartan as it had once been. Newly built cabins stood in small groupings, while pathways curved gently in and around those homes and across the Valley.

But though the newly planted gardens were blooming and the sun brilliant, he heard no childish voices, saw no young Arrows in the play area. A glance at his watch confirmed they were currently in afternoon classes.

Outsiders would see the Arrow teaching structure and declare it far too restrictive with too little room for innovation, but those outsiders didn't understand that when a child could explode another's mind with a simple passing tantrum, he or she *needed* walls, *wanted* safety and pre-dictability.

Paradoxical as it was, such boundaries made the child feel more free.

The restrictions would be eased as each child became increasingly self-sufficient in terms of controlling his or her abilities. That step had already been authorized and implemented for the teenagers he saw studying in an outside green area when he walked around the corner. Because while structure was important, so was the ability to make independent decisions and the capacity to think creatively.

These children wouldn't be forced into a path as Aden and his brethren had been, but many would end up working in the blood-soaked shadows nonetheless.

It was a dark truth for children born with violent psychic power.

Silence or not, so long as those of the Psy race were defined by their minds, the PsyNet would need the hunters, the ones who kept the innocents safe. Like all power, psychic power had a flip side. Changelings could turn feral. Psy could turn murderously insane.

What was no longer inevitable was being a lone hunter in the darkness. *Every* Arrow had a home here, had family. Even their most broken.

"Aden."

Stopping to speak to the teens when they hesitantly called his name, Aden listened to their feedback on cooperative learning as the sun heated his back through the black of the T-shirt he wore in place of his Arrow uniform. "I'll leave you to your work," he said after ten minutes. "Don't forget that your year group is supervising the under fives this afternoon."

It had been Remi, alpha of the RainFire leopards, who'd suggested Aden utilize the teens to look after the youngest in the squad. It was how changeling packs worked, older children often in charge of younger ones—the arrangement built bonds across age lines, blurring the boundaries that had so often kept Arrows siloed in defined boxes.

The same applied to contact between children and elders.

Aden's parents were technically elders, but he couldn't see either Marjorie Kai or Naoshi Ayze interacting with the young without causing irreparable harm to their soft hearts. Yuri, though he was a number of years younger at forty-seven, was proving a better mentor in that respect.

Aden hadn't expected it of the remote Arrow who'd lived more than four decades in Silence, but Yuri had proven to have endless patience when teaching a child.

And perhaps, just perhaps, those children were teaching Yuri, too.

The truth was that after Edward's suicide, Aden worried about many of the senior Arrows, including the man who was one of Zaira's most trusted people. He knew Yuri had struggled with the fall of Silence, unsure where he fit in this new world. Yesterday, however, Aden had happened upon an unexpected sight: Yuri seated at an outdoor table with Carolina standing on the bench beside him, the six-year-old's hand on his shoulder and her pale blonde hair tied back as she peered intently at the organizer he was repairing.

Her concentration had been fierce, her forehead scrunched up. "I can do it, Yuri," she'd said. "I can. Please, can I try?"

It was impossible for such a scenario to have taken place prior to the fall of Silence, but if it had, Yuri would've acted on his training and shut down the child's request for the logical reason that Carolina didn't yet have the manual dexterity to complete the delicate repair. But yesterday, Yuri had given the six-year-old the tiny laser tool, then held her soft hand steady with his scarred and leathery one as "she" made the repairs.

His expression had never altered, but the fact that he'd stayed there in the sunshine, nurturing a small child's confidence . . . it spoke volumes.

A single act of kindness can change a life.

Zaira had said that to more than one Arrow, and it had slowly become an unofficial motto among the adults. When an Arrow who'd never experienced parental affection—the vast majority of the squad—didn't know what to do or how to react to a child's need, they defaulted to whatever seemed the kindest response, even if that response went against their training. Aden didn't think Zaira realized the staggering impact of her words—adult Arrows liked structure, too, especially in this strange new territory they were attempting to navigate, this family they were building.

Music whispered on the wind, carried to him through the open windows of a classroom, art of any kind a gift that had returned to the Psy after over a hundred years. The century of Silence meant they had no teachers. Humans and changelings did, but the squad would never permit anyone into the Valley they didn't know inside out.

So the children learned from recorded lessons.

From the sounds Aden could hear, at present, they were enthusiastic if not in tune. Smile deepening, he went looking for Vasic and Zaira. The most important people in his life were both in the Valley this morning, and he wasn't surprised to find them together. His mate and his best friend hadn't always been friends themselves, but these days they often ganged up on Aden when they believed he needed a break.

Today, however, they were discussing a troubled telekinetic teenager who needed help of a kind only one adult Tk was qualified to provide. "Stefan," Zaira said to Aden when he came to stand with his body touching hers. "Do you think he has the time to take on a trainee?"

"I haven't spoken to him in over two weeks," Aden said, in agreement with their choice of mentor. Stefan might've been termed "defective" during training and transferred out of the squad, but the Arrows considered him one of their own. "Vasic? Will Stefan's current workload on Alaris allow him time to handle a trainee?" Last he'd heard, the deep-sea station was in the midst of a refit.

Vasic flexed the fingers of his newest prosthetic arm as if testing it, the skin of the unit a gleaming obsidian that meshed flawlessly with his Arrow uniform. "I'm not sure, but I'm seeing him later this week for a telekinetic sparring session. I'll ask."

A born teleporter, Vasic could go to the deep-sea station without problem. To him, it was no different than teleporting to another country. There was no issue with a change in air pressure, either, since the pressure inside Alaris was identical to that on the surface. Not that it would've bothered Vasic regardless.

Unlike everyone on the planet but those capable of teleportation across that vast a distance, he'd suffer no ill effects from a sudden change in air pressure. Researchers had been grappling with that little quirk since the first time a teleporter figured out what he could do, courtesy of a scuba diving emergency.

"See if you can judge his mental state," Aden said. "He might not be alone, but he's still stuck under tons of water on a daily basis." He'd always considered Stefan's choice of work an odd one, given the psychological "flaw" that had gotten the other man kicked out of the squad's training program.

"You know he's as stable as a rock, has been for years." Vasic's smile was more suggestion than form. "At least he can finally openly share the reason why."

Aden couldn't argue with any part of Vasic's statement. "Check anyway, ask if he's happy to remain on Alaris." The fall of Silence had changed everything; there was no reason for Stefan to stay underwater if he didn't want to be there.

"I will."

Nodding at his friend's prosthetic, Aden said, "I could swear I saw you wearing a prosthetic with a metallic finish yesterday."

"I was," Vasic confirmed. "But that's the piece Samuel uses to assess various components. This"—he flexed the obsidian hand again—"is his newest creation."

"Any more effective than his previous one?" The gifted scientist had gone into a deep funk when the last prosthetic had shorted out in sparks, the wrist falling away from the forearm.

"Oh, it's very *effective*," Zaira said, a biting amusement in her tone. "Show him, Vasic."

Vasic glanced around before walking over to pick up a branch.

His hand clamped around it. Dust drifted into the air.

"See, very effective." Zaira's comment was dead serious on the surface. "But not so useful if Vasic wants to stroke Ivy's hair or hold her close—or pick up a glass to take a drink."

Vasic closed his prosthetic hand around a rock. It came to the same dusty end as the branch. "I think I've proven this grasp has only one setting: 'crush everything dead.'"

His friend was amused, too, Aden realized. "Rain will be disappointed," he said as Vasic began to remove the prosthetic.

Floating it neatly to the ground using his Tk, the teleporter pinned up the sleeve of his shirt with his free hand. "Samuel won't give up until he either dies or gets it right. Last time a prototype failed, he pulled at his hair until it stuck out in all directions, then declared he was Ahab and my prosthetic was his whale."

"You've definitely decided on a prosthetic?" Aden hadn't expected that. "Last time we talked, you were leaning against it."

"I don't need one," Vasic admitted. "I've adapted." Sleeve neatly pinned up, he teleported away the malfunctioning unit. "But Samuel saved my life and, oddly enough, this obsession helps keep him anchored. He usually only requires three or four hours of my time a month—it's little enough payment for the life he gave me."

"Does he realize you no longer want a replacement for your biological arm?" Zaira put her hands on her hips, clearly annoyed on behalf of a man she'd ignored for most of her life. "And if he succeeds, what then? You'll be stuck with it."

Unexpected humor in Vasic's response. "I'm certain Samuel doesn't care if I actually *use* the prosthetic. Getting a unit to function with my damaged systems is his whale. Once he does that, I'll fall off his radar and he'll find a new obsession."

Aden was in full agreement: Vasic was a puzzle to be solved for Samuel Rain. That didn't mean Aden wouldn't protect the man for the rest of his life. Mad genius or not, Rain had saved the life of Aden's best friend. That was a debt that could never be repaid. "The BlackSea situation," he said into the undemanding silence among the three of them. "No new data on the kidnapped marine biologist from our sources. Changelings say the same."

Seeing Zaira's body tense to trembling point, he put his hand on her lower back. It was a silent reminder that she was no longer a child in a cage, that she stood with her lover and their friend underneath a sunlit sky. Free.

A dark-eyed glance from his deadly commander before she took a deep breath, and he felt her muscles begin to unlock.

"I'm assuming you've had no success locking on to the Canadian Cheap Electric symbol?" he said to Vasic.

The other man shook his head. "Judd was right. There are too many identical hits on the CCE logo and I can't zero in on Leila's face because of the damage from the scarring." The winter gray of his eyes held an arctic chill.

"Zaira's point on this," Aden told his best friend. "Get all intel to her."

An immediate nod from Vasic. While the teleporter wasn't aware of the details of Zaira's childhood, he'd been with her during the last rescue, understood her hunger to free the trapped.

"Trinity," Vasic said as sounds reached them from another part of the Valley, where it appeared a martial arts class was in session. "Holding?"

"Fragile. There's too much divisive history in the mix."

"A summit would be useful." Vasic hunkered down to pet a small white dog who'd run back from his adventures across the Valley. As he did, the wedding band he wore on his right ring finger caught the light, creating a golden spark. "If not for the obvious risk."

"Yes." Zaira folded her arms, set her feet apart. "It would generate a sitting target for the Consortium or anyone else who might want to take out a large percentage of the major powers in the world."

Aden considered Vasic's words, thought about Zaira's on-point risk assessment, felt the germ of an idea. "We turn the Consortium's tactics back on them," he said. "No big central summit but small ones that introduce the key people in each region to one another."

"Limiting the spread of information about the meetings, while achieving cohesion." Vasic nodded slowly.

"In Venice," Zaira said, her eyes faintly narrowed in thought, "the Human Alliance and I had an understanding. It kept the peace." She bent to pet Rabbit when the dog wandered over, tail wagging triple time. "Simply knowing that your neighbor is open to dialogue could eliminate a large number of localized problems."

"I'll start testing the idea," Aden said, then glanced at Vasic. "How's Tavish?" In keeping with the squad's decision to place Arrow children into families with active-duty Arrows, the young telekinetic boy was now part of Ivy and Vasic's family unit—a unit that included the dog who, at present, was lying on his back, tongue lolling in ecstasy and legs in the air while Zaira rubbed his belly.

"Settling into the orchard." Vasic's voice held a deep, quiet joy when he spoke of his home. "He spends a lot of time with Grandfather."

Then, Aden thought, the child was in good hands. Zie Zen—who, in truth, was actually Vasic's great-grandfather—had more wisdom in his bones than most people would ever gain, not even if they lived two life-times.

"Can you stay?" Zaira asked Aden. "We could spar."

Aden loved pitching his wits and tactical skills against Zaira's, but he had to shake his head today. "I have a meeting with Devraj Santos in five."

The Forgotten had requested the squad's assistance in dealing with the wild new psychic abilities cropping up in their children. Aden was certain the change had begun even earlier, specifically with Santos's gen-eration, but the leader of the Forgotten wasn't giving away anything about his own abilities.

However, after his conversation with Ivy, Aden had another critical issue to discuss with Dev. The Forgotten's psychic network was a vibrant, living thing in comparison to the deadly disintegration pulling the PsyNet apart at the seams. It was possible the other man had useful insights Aden could pass on to the Es. "Can you give me a lift," he said to Vasic, "or shall I ask Nerida?"

"I'll pick you up in three minutes." Vasic 'ported out with Rabbit, leaving Aden and Zaira alone.

At which point the woman who was Aden's hauled him close with a grip on his T-shirt and proceeded to kiss the life out of him. *You've become an expert in that*, he telepathed to her when his brain cells started func-tioning again.

We've been practicing enough. Inside his mind, she was black fire. In front of him, she was kiss-swollen lips and a possessive touch—and icy determination. "I'm seeing Miane later today."

"Be careful." Aden cupped the side of her face. So delicate were her bones, in stark contrast to the intensity of her will. "The Consortium might have gone under but they're only hibernating, waiting for a chance— and they know how important you are to me."

"They also know I fight like a berserker." Zaira's smile was all teeth. "After the last assassin I took down, they're going to have a serious recruiting problem looking for someone to hunt me."

Aden thought of the recording he'd seen of Zaira with the point of a blade touching the assassin's eye. She'd been all cold control on the surface while she fought a primal battle within. She'd won that battle, hadn't given in to the rage that lived within her. And she'd made her point: Do not mess with an Arrow, especially this petite Arrow with her dark hair and midnight eyes and dangerous walk.

"Be careful anyway," he said, his heart right there for her to see. "I need you." Zaira was his, the only person in the entire world who belonged first to him.

"*Aden.*" Zaira touched her fingers to his lips, the ruby in her ring a silent representation of the flame that lived within her. "You stay safe, too. Or I'll kill you."

Aden felt laughter shake his shoulders. "Order heard and understood, Commander."

"Good." Sliding one hand to his nape, Zaira tugged him down. "Now kiss me again before Vasic returns."

Letters to Nina

From the private diaries of Father Xavier Perez
February 14, 2074

Nina,

It's been ten months now since the Psy came. Ten months since I watched you jump into the water. Ten months since I promised I'd be right behind you.

I wasn't. I'm so sorry, Nina. I fought them, fought to keep you safe, to keep them from knowing where you'd gone. I was no coward, I promise you this. I'm not alive and writing this letter because I hid. I fought, Nina. I fought so hard.

They took us down one by one with telepathic blows. The bodies of those we loved fell on me. When I rose to consciousness, they were heavy atop me . . . and I knew they'd saved my life. Because of my younger brother and Jorge, the soldiers missed the fact I was still alive, still had a pulse. I live because of them.

And yet here I sit in a bar drinking away my life because what use is it to be alive when I'm alone, without God, without family, without friends, without you? I would do anything, fight anyone, if only you were here. But you're gone and I've forsaken God for his cruelty.

Xavier

Chapter 13

FORTY-EIGHT HOURS AFTER Aden first told Lucas of the possible threat to Naya, DarkRiver had upgraded all its security precautions regarding their young. The panther inside him in a much calmer mood now that he knew his cub and all the cubs under his watch were well protected, Lucas had far more patience for dealing with the shaky edifice that was Trinity.

"Aden's getting ready to test intimate Trinity 'summits' that would act as introductions between various groups," he told Vaughn.

The DarkRiver sentinel was sprawled in a chair on the other side of Lucas's desk at the pack's Chinatown HQ. With amber hair tied in a neat queue at his nape and eyes more cat than man, Lucas's closest friend wasn't involved in Trinity—politics wasn't really Vaughn's strong suit—but like all of Lucas's sentinels, he was highly intelligent.

Scanning the memo after Lucas turned the whisper-thin computer screen toward him, Vaughn shook his head. "Tell him to nix the idea of planning each of these summits ahead of time. Set up a trustworthy team to throw things together with an hour or two of notice max."

Lucas raised an eyebrow. "Hard to get people together that quickly."

"So it takes longer to make the connections—but if there are no plans, then no one can hunt down the attendees as a group."

It was the answer of a predator.

"You're right." Far better, he realized, to go slow than to rush and give the enemy exactly what it wanted.

"My work here is done." Vaughn rose to his feet with feline grace, a smile in his eyes that had become less and less rare in the years since he'd found his F-Psy mate. Before that, Vaughn had been a loner even in the midst of a pack. A loyal friend, a trusted sentinel, but always holding himself a little separate.

Part of that was his jaguar nature, but part of it had been the echo of a soul-searing grief.

"Hello, Miss Naya," the jaguar said now, reaching down to pick up the tiny cub who'd scampered into the room.

Lucas's panther growled in welcome inside him.

In truth, his cub's scamper was more "attempted scamper," but she was so excited at being able to shift forms that she did it every chance she got. Needless to say, keeping her in clothes had become a losing proposition. Good thing that changelings were used to naked babies scrambling gleefully around.

This baby had been in the nursery next door, must've snuck through the connecting door into the offices. Not that anyone tried too hard to keep the cubs out. The only time that door was locked was when they were in meetings with business associates who weren't trusted enough for DarkRiver to be carefree with its children.

Business trust was a far different beast from the trust that came with being family.

Allowing Vaughn to hold her against his chest with one capable hand, Naya purred. She loved the jaguar.

"Careful." Lucas's heart ached at the sound of his cub's happiness. "She'll be scamming you for chocolate next."

Vaughn chuckled, using one finger to rub the top of Naya's head. "I'm heading home for a run before I meet up with Faith."

Naya roared—or tried to. It came out more a kittenish rumble.

Grinning, Lucas translated. "I think she wants to come. But you won't be doing much running with her."

Vaughn's eyes caught his, the shade near-gold. "You okay if I take her? I've got the jetcycle but I can switch to an SUV."

Fighting his overprotective instincts, Lucas said, "She loves the jet-cycle." Vaughn was a skilled driver, and the jetcycle's maneuverability gave it an advantage should anyone attempt to follow Vaughn and Naya with the aim of doing harm.

Lucas wouldn't steal joy from his child in the name of keeping her safe.

"Yeah," Vaughn agreed. "She's a little speed demon." He put Naya on his shoulder, where she curled up as if she'd been doing it forever, wrapping her tail around his neck to anchor herself. "I'll run in human form, hold her when she's had enough. Message me when and where you want me to drop her off." He tugged playfully on Naya's tail. "Come on, Miss Naya. Let's go run. But first we'll sign you out of the nursery so the teachers don't worry."

Naya growled and made bye-bye noises at Lucas as Vaughn walked out the door. Lucas trusted his friend unconditionally. Yet he still had the urge to lunge up and haul her into his arms.

It took teeth-gritting will to fight the primal desire.

She was safe. Vaughn was a lethal predatory changeling. He'd fight to the death to protect her . . . and it was good for the jaguar to open his heart to such a small, helpless packmate. Lucas hoped Naya's determined love of Vaughn would help the other man heal from the staggering loss that had devastated him as a child.

Lucas's phone buzzed.

Looking away from the door through which Vaughn and Naya had disappeared, he answered to find his mate on the other end. Of course she'd picked up on his silent fight against instincts formed when he'd been a young boy helpless to protect his parents from a deadly attack. He'd been tortured, too, but Lucas could've borne that. It had been watching his parents die in front of him that had marked his psyche in a permanent way.

Sascha understood the brutal competing drives inside him.

"I'm fine," he told her. "Vaughn's bringing Naya home. Where do you want him to drop her off?"

"The aerie. I'll be back by the time he actually turns up." Sascha's smile was in her voice. "You know he kidnaps her for hours and she's a very happy kidnappee."

"He lets her finger-paint the walls of his den, that's why." Their cub always turned up squeaky clean, without a speck of paint on her, but Naya couldn't keep a secret.

"Forget about walls, Faith told me she came home last time to find Naya finger-painting Vaughn."

Chuckling at the idea of the quiet, intense sentinel happily acting as the canvas for an enthusiastic toddler, Lucas asked, "How's the lesson going?" Sascha was up in SnowDancer territory, working with Toby Lauren.

"He's more reticent than usual. Lara warned me, said that he might be in the first stages of teenage-boy-itis."

"I remember that phase. Being surly is a requirement."

"I can't imagine Toby surly." A pause, a rustle. "I'd better go. He's getting restless."

Hanging up, Lucas forwarded Vaughn's suggested changes to the summit idea to Aden, then got up and headed out to a work site. He needed to stretch his muscles, see how the project was going. It would also stop him from worrying constantly about Naya.

Sometimes, an alpha had to let go and trust his pack to watch over that which mattered most.

HAVING driven the jetcycle to DarkRiver's Yosemite territory with a delighted Naya safely tucked up inside his zippered leather-synth jacket, only her head poking out and her eyes squinting against the wind that ruffled her fur, Vaughn parked the vehicle in a designated spot just inside the forest. Unlike when he traveled alone or with Faith, he'd logged this trip with Jamie and Desiree; the two senior soldiers were in charge of keeping track of pack children moving in and out of the city.

No cub was going to disappear and not be immediately missed.

Still straddling the powerful body of the jetcycle, Vaughn used his phone to check in, informing his packmates that Naya was safe inside the heart of DarkRiver territory.

He'd ensured they had no tail, his senses on high alert.

Swinging his leg over the jetcycle after sliding away his phone, he spoke to the cub who was a source of living warmth against his chest. "I hope you appreciate that I drove like an old lady for you." He'd never forgive himself if Naya came to harm while in his care.

A tiny panther head nudged the bottom of his chin.

Scratching her under her own chin, he smiled. Truth was, it still hurt to see Naya, to hold her. She reminded him so much of Skye. His baby sister had been jaguar, not leopard, but she'd had the same mischievous spirit, the same affectionate sweetness. Vaughn might've been tempted to keep his distance from his best friend's cub, protect himself, but it was impossible. From the instant he'd picked her up after her birth, Nadiya Shayla Hunter had owned a piece of his heart.

"Yes, we're home," he said when she made questioning sounds. "Down. Stretch your legs." Placing her on the ground with careful hands, he watched as she got her shaky feet under her.

Then she "ran" beside him while he walked at a pace slower than a sleepy five-year-old's. Tail curled up in pride, Naya growled at all sounds from the forest, the big predator who was going to eat anything that dared encroach on her territory.

Vaughn added his growls to hers, got an approving look in response.

He'd left his jacket with the bike in preparation for his run, but Naya lasted longer than he'd expected. Finally exhausted, she permitted him to pick her up and hold her against his chest as he broke into a full-speed run, the tall firs of Yosemite passing by in a greenish-brown blur while beneath his booted feet, the grass was a lush green that sprang back after the feline lightness of his steps.

Tiny claws dug into him, but he didn't censure her as he would have had she used them in play. She was just holding on. But she wasn't scared. Of course not. She was the daughter of an alpha.

She was exhilarated.

Slowing to a jog when he was almost home, he was down to a walk when he entered the cave system within which lay his lair. The scent he caught in the air made him grin, his jaguar rising to its feet inside him in wild welcome. "Hello, Red."

Faith looked over from the sofa, where, clad in nothing but a short slip of a dress, she was eating a big bowl of cereal. "Naya!"

Her delighted cry had Naya scrambling down to run over.

Climbing up onto the sofa beside Faith through sheer grim effort augmented by a little help from Vaughn, she put her paws on the bare part of Faith's thigh and peered curiously at the bowl of cereal. Clearly deciding that the brightly colored flakes looked delicious, she licked out her tongue.

Faith pulled the bowl out of reach just in time. "No, you don't. I am not getting in trouble with Lucas and Sascha by teaching you bad habits."

Plopping down on her butt, Naya shifted and tugged at Faith's sea-green dress while making sounds that might've been her name. "There you go." Faith fed Naya a spoonful after checking to make sure the cereal was soft enough with milk that it would be easy for her to eat.

Vaughn watched Naya eat it up, then ask for more. "She's hungry after shifting so much today." It took significant energy for the young, likely because their bodies were mid-development *and* because the shift did odd things at this age.

Like giving Naya the cub far more dangerous teeth than Naya the toddler.

"I can't believe she's shifting." Faith fed their little guest more cereal. "Yes, you are clever," she said, leaning down to kiss Naya on the cheek. "And you're really hungry."

Vaughn went into the kitchen area and found the box of cereal, as well as the milk. Putting both down on the small table beside Faith, he grabbed a throw to wrap around Naya so she wouldn't lose body heat. "She's too little to regulate her temperature like we do ours," he told Faith when she looked up with a question in her eyes.

"So I should make sure she keeps the throw around her?"

"For the next few minutes at least." He tugged on Naya's hair. "Don't get cold, Miss Naya."

He got an enthusiastic nod that made the lush black of her tumbled hair gleam under the simulated sunlight of his and Faith's lair. "She'll be fine once she's settled into this form," he told his mate. "Just touch her skin, make sure she's not chilled." Getting a nod of confirmation from Faith, he dropped a kiss on the fiery red of her hair. "I'm going to shower off the sweat."

She tipped up her head so that he could kiss her on the lips. Stroking his hand over the slender arch of her throat, he nipped at her lips, licked over the sensual hurt. Faith's hand was just coming up to cradle his jaw when Naya made a grab for the cereal bowl. "Fae!" she said, as if trying to get her tongue around "Faith."

Faith laughed, managed to steady the bowl. "Yes, I know. Less kissing, more cereal."

Naya clapped her hands. "Kiss!" That was clear enough, especially when she tipped up her head to Vaughn.

Remembering Skye again, emotion a knot in his throat, Vaughn kissed the tip of her nose. Once. Twice. As Naya laughed, Faith lifted his hand, touched her lips to the back of it with a tenderness that said more than any words. He ran his knuckles over his mate's cheek before walking over to the shower—which looked like a waterfall cascading from the stone wall, a feat he'd gone to great lengths to achieve.

Vaughn could hear his mate and his friend's cub talking animatedly as he stripped off and stepped under the water. Naya was so engaged that it sounded like a real—if largely incomprehensible on one side— conversation. The sounds made him chuckle, and this time, his memories of Skye were of when they'd been happy.

She'd been just as chatty, talking his ear off about everything under the sun, including her favorite toys and flowers and how come the sun was yellow and the grass was green? And why did bees buzz? Her little face would screw up as she considered each question while waiting for his response.

He'd often replied with nonsensical answers that made her laugh so hard she'd fall to the ground with her arms wrapped around her stomach.

Grass is green because that's the color of insect poop.

Bees buzz because they're really miniature jet-choppers.

Washing off the suds with a smile born of the memory of his sister's delight, he dried off, then pulled on a clean pair of jeans. He'd just grabbed a leftover slice of pizza for an afternoon snack when Faith got a call. She answered it, Naya busy amusing herself with a cardboard box that had once held a cutting tool Vaughn needed for his sculptures.

Right now, the box was on her head.

His shoulders shook.

Faith's own smile was deep as she spied Naya's antics, but when she spoke after hanging up, it was in a quiet tone. "My father says Tanique is in town."

Vaughn knew it was important to his mate to truly get to know her younger half brother. They'd met, but only in passing. "You want to go?"

Faith nodded. "If we can." She gathered Naya into her lap when the little girl pushed off the box to yawn and rub at her eyes with her fists. "Tanique's on a museum contract, so he's only in town tonight."

"I'll put on a shirt, take Naya so you can dress. We'll head out soon as you're ready."

Faith looked down at the sleepy baby girl she was cuddling. She'd replaced the old throw with a soft pink blanket that Naya was rubbing her cheek against as she kneaded at it with a hand that had sprouted tiny claws. "We don't have to rush that much." A whisper. "I love holding her."

Sitting down beside his mate, Vaughn stretched out an arm behind her. "We could try to make a cub of our own." The idea of being responsible for a fragile new life was no longer scary now that he'd been around Naya for a year, been responsible for her countless times.

He'd kept her safe.

Faith's smile was shy, startled, happy. "I'd like that . . . but not just yet. I'm still adjusting to the dark visions."

Those visions came without warning and could relate to anything from a major disaster to a murder to a small accident. "Today?"

"No." She leaned her head on his shoulder while continuing to pet Naya. "Before we try for a child, I want to be confident that if I have a dark vision while I'm alone with our baby, I'll be able to ride it out." A glance up, her cardinal gaze stripped bare. "I don't *ever* want to scare our child by reacting badly to a nightmare vision."

"No rush, Red." Vaughn nuzzled at her, let her know he was with her. Always. "We've got plenty of time yet." Plenty of years to play and grow together. "We'll know when we're ready."

Faith pressed a kiss over Naya's soft curls as Naya's eyes finally closed, thick, curling lashes throwing shadows over her cheeks. His mate had a gentle smile on her face when she looked up. Her lips parted as if she was about to speak, then snapped shut as her eyes widened.

"Red?" Vaughn sat upright from his lazy sprawl. "You having a vision?"

A shake of her head. "My brother is a Ps-Psy," she blurted out. "A strong one. Nine on the Gradient."

Blowing out a silent breath, he turned boneless again. "Yeah, I know." What Vaughn didn't fully understand was how Tanique's psychometric ability worked. The younger man could sense things when he touched physical objects, that much was clear. But what exactly he saw, if he even had a visual component to his ability or whether he simply heard the echoes of sounds, Vaughn wasn't certain.

"The message in the bottle." Faith's voice was taut, intense. "Can you get it back? It's *really* important."

Realization dawned. Swinging his feet off the highly polished stump that acted as their coffee table, Vaughn got up. "I don't know where BlackSea took it after we handed it over, but I know who to ask."

Chapter 14

VAUGHN LEFT THE room to make the call using the comm in Faith's workspace. As a DarkRiver sentinel, he had a contact number for Black-Sea that was routed to whichever senior pack member was currently on shift as liaison. Today, that happened to be Malachai Rhys. The big male listened to Vaughn's proposal, then connected him to Miane Levèque after a minute-long delay.

Vaughn knew what Malachai had been doing in that minute when Miane appeared on the comm and began to speak without Vaughn having to explain anything. "The bottle's in a lab on one of our floating cities," the alpha said. "I can pledge a BlackSea favor to get it to you via a teleport, but you tell me if I can trust this Ps-Psy."

Vaughn was unsurprised by her wariness; Psy had long been the enemy of changelings and even now, Vaughn himself only trusted a rare few. "I can't give you an absolute guarantee," he responded. "Tanique is Faith's brother, loyal to NightStar. And NightStar is headed by Anthony Kyriakus, who has no love for the Consortium."

Wholesale chaos and violence was bad for the F-Psy who were a vital part of NightStar's power base, especially with so many of them now opening up to visions outside the antiseptic limits of business contracts. If there was one thing Vaughn knew about Anthony, it was that the other man protected his foreseers, including Faith, with a merciless will. "On the flip side," he added, "Tanique didn't grow up in NightStar but with the maternal side of his family, so he may have loyalties we don't know about."

"Faith NightStar was the one who suggested we ask her brother?"

Vaughn saw where Miane was going. "Not a vision," he clarified, "but she had a tone in her voice I've come to know. I'd never bet against her."

"I'd be a fool not to heed the advice of the best foreseer in the world." Miane put her hands on her hips, her cream-colored long-sleeved shirt moving with a fluidity that made Vaughn wonder if it was one of the experimental luxe fabrics BlackSea was famous for creating.

"We'll need the bottle within the next two to three hours," Vaughn reiterated.

Miane's curt nod was a silent promise they'd have it. "This is a massive risk on our part, cat."

"Sometimes even sharks have to take a leap of faith."

Miane's lips curved at the implied question about her changeling nature, but there was no humor in her eyes. "I'll kill Tanique Gray if he betrays us."

Vaughn knew that should Miane attempt to take such an action, he'd have to get in her way. His jaguar, too, would never forgive betrayal, but like him, Faith had already lost one sibling. Vaughn didn't think she could bear the loss of another. But he also had total conviction in his mate's abilities—even when she didn't have a vision, Faith "saw" things.

Like this morning, she'd insisted he wear his leather-synth jacket when he absolutely hadn't intended to go out on the jetcycle today. If he'd refused to listen, he'd have had to return home to get it barely an hour later, after one of his packmates asked him for a favor that necessitated a trip to the city. And three days earlier, she'd called Tamsyn to tell the healer about a deal she'd seen for good quality chocolate chips.

"I bought them," Tamsyn had said to Vaughn when they ran into each other yesterday. "Then today, Roman comes home and reminds me I promised to make chocolate chip cookies for his and Jules's entire class after they finished a big project. I totally forgot, would've had to scramble if Faith hadn't given me that tip."

Small things, miniscule even, but they added up. "I don't think you'll have to kill Tanique," he told Miane, but held her gaze so she'd know he was as big a predator as her, his dominance such that even Lucas couldn't make him do anything. Vaughn's jaguar chose to follow Lucas's panther because that panther had earned its respect and loyalty. "Understand, he's family."

Miane didn't blink. "I suspect you and Malachai would get on well," she said before ending the call.

Vaughn received a message five minutes later asking him to share teleport coordinates. "I'll be back soon," he told Faith and grabbed his dirty T-shirt, which he'd thrown into the laundry basket.

Running out of his lair, he went full tilt for twenty minutes, until he was surrounded by trees that all looked identical. He hung his tee, with its distinctive Celtic design on the front, from a branch. Then he took a photograph to send to Miane. It didn't surprise him in the least when the teleporter who appeared with a small storage box was a tall male dressed in Arrow black.

After his recent lifesaving actions in bombings and disasters, Vasic had become famous worldwide. But Vaughn knew him from well before that. He hadn't been there the day this man with his winter gray eyes brought in the medic who saved Dorian's life, but he'd heard the details from those who'd witnessed the incident. Without the help provided by the teleporter and that medic who the entire world now knew as a *power*, Vaughn's fellow sentinel and friend would be dead.

"Thanks," he said, taking the box Vasic held out. "What did Miane promise you?" Vasic wasn't a commercial teleporter, so it wasn't as if BlackSea could've hired him.

The other man's gaze was pure frost. "What has she promised you?"

Vaughn bared his teeth. "Not a thing."

He didn't think the Arrow would respond, but Vasic said, "Life isn't always a cost-reward ratio. It's something the Psy long forgot. Some things we do in the name of friendship—or because it's the right thing to do."

Vaughn had already liked this Arrow who didn't back down in the face of a predator's challenge, but right then, he had the sense he might one day come to call Vasic a friend.

. . .

NINETY minutes later, Faith and Vaughn dropped a sleeping Naya off at Tamsyn's place, where Sascha was having a meeting with the healer and a number of the pack's submissives. They then drove toward Tahoe in a high-speed vehicle. And now here Faith sat in a small conference room, her mate at her side, waiting for her father and her brother.

She'd become accustomed to keeping her face impassive when walking into meetings with her father. Anthony had made it clear the charade that theirs was, was nothing but a business relationship that had to continue post-Silence. PsyClan NightStar might be powerful, but it had powerful enemies, too. Anthony was a highly visible target. He refused to make Faith one when she'd successfully settled into a non-public life.

"I've lost one child. No more."

Faith remained at some risk because killing or even badly injuring her would significantly affect NightStar's bottom line. However, that risk was nowhere near what it would be should NightStar's enemies realize Anthony would strike terrible bargains to keep her safe. No outsider could ever know that Anthony Kyriakus, head of PsyClan NightStar, former Psy Councilor, and current member of the Ruling Coalition, loved his children.

Her father entered at that instant, a tall man with patrician features and black hair silvered at the temples, his expression the epitome of cool Silence. "Vaughn. Faith."

Safe inside the windowless meeting room devoid of monitoring equipment, Faith hugged a man who had been too long in Silence to easily show emotion. But his arms came around her, his scent familiar, and his voice deep as he said, "You're well?" The simple, toneless question held such a weight of love that it made a knot form in her chest.

Swallowing, she drew back to look up into his face. "Yes, Father. I'm well."

Scanning her face, Anthony said, "I see signs of strain."

"I had a marathon session yesterday," she admitted. "Nothing dangerous. Vaughn was working nearby the whole time and he made me take regular breaks."

"I had to physically disrupt her trance," Vaughn muttered, his scowl in his voice.

"Everything was flowing so beautifully, I wanted to keep going. But"—she held up her hands when her father would've spoken—"I'm having a break today and tomorrow to recharge."

Psychic power burned energy, but in the case of the darker visions of violence and murder and natural disasters, it was also viscerally draining. Such visions haunted her for weeks afterward. Thankfully, she hadn't seen anything too distressing of late, only small warnings she'd been able to pass on so people could avoid bone-breaking accidents or personal catastrophes.

"Faith." Anthony held her eyes with the brown of his, the charisma in his gaze potent. "I know you disliked the Tec 3 uplinked chair you had in your cabin—"

"'Dislike' is too weak a word." The tiny hairs on her arms rising in cold warning, Faith shifted back to stand with Vaughn.

Her mate immediately wrapped one arm across the top of her chest to tug her against the muscled strength of his body. It was a silent promise. A deadly one, too, should it be necessary.

Air rushed back into her body, the painful tightness in her chest melting away. "I hate that chair." A full-length recliner shaped to her personal body contours, it had monitored and transmitted every breath she took while using it during the cold years she'd spent isolated in a one-person cabin.

"You hated the intrusion, the fact that the data was fed to the medics," her father countered. "The chair itself would be invaluable to anyone who needs to monitor your well-being." His eyes went to Vaughn.

The jaguar who belonged to Faith brushed his fingers over her collarbone, a DarkRiver cat calming his mate. "I don't need technology to make sure Faith is safe during her visions."

"He really doesn't," Faith reassured her father.

Despite her strong negative reaction to the idea of a Tec 3 uplinked recliner, she knew Anthony only wanted the best for her, that every action he'd ever taken in relation to his children had been to protect. Losing her half sister Marine to a psychopath had honed that protectiveness to a deadly edge.

"I'm safe," she said. "I promise." She couldn't control the dark or wild visions, but she never went into a controlled one unless Vaughn was nearby.

"I know the bond you two share is powerful," her father replied, "but Vaughn, you can't monitor every aspect of her health."

Faith realized her father had no framework for understanding the beauty and intensity of the mating bond. Deciding not to push the point, she said, "Do you need to get rid of my old chair?"

"No." Anthony's tone was so cool she felt chastened for her flip response. "We have three prototype next-generation recliners with top-of-the-line health-monitoring functions, including a direct emergency link to a medic if your vitals drop below a certain point. I want you to have one."

Faith's skin crawled at the idea of once again using a chair that spied on her. She opened her mouth to speak but Vaughn beat her to it. "Give us a minute, Anthony."

Her father left the room without further words, pulling the door shut behind himself.

"I don't want that chair." Arms folded, Faith glared at her mate.

"Red, you can turn off the monitoring functions, right?"

She stayed stubbornly silent until Vaughn brushed his fingers over her jaw in a caress that she knew came from the heart of his jaguar. "Yes," she admitted. "We can take out the chip, lobotomize it."

"So"—Vaughn cupped her cheek, ran his thumb over her cheekbone—"you accept your dad's gift. He's not the most warm and cuddly guy, but you're his little girl. He's just trying to look after you, same as Lucas does with Naya."

Her lower lip trembled. She'd been so locked up inside the memories of how much she'd hated that chair that she'd forgotten why it had been created in the first place. So she'd be safe. "I love you."

Vaughn's smile was pure feline smugness. "I know."

She mock-punched him before opening the door to let her father back in.

"I'll try the chair on a probationary basis." Too easy a capitulation would make Anthony suspicious. "We'll also be disabling all broadcast functions. Any data it collects"—which would be zero—"will be kept strictly local to our home."

"I don't want to monitor you, Faith. I just want you to have all possible safeguards."

Faith gave in and hugged her remote, dangerous, loving father again. "Thank you."

He touched the back of her head before looking toward the door. A light knock came seconds later. Though the two of them drew apart, Anthony didn't speak or go to the door. When it opened, Faith realized he must've answered telepathically. No one in NightStar would ever barge in on her father.

"Sir." The six-foot-tall young male who spoke was striking, with Anthony's patrician bones under mocha-colored skin, his hair black and tightly curled. He was a Ps-Psy, gifted in psychometry . . . and he was her younger brother.

"Tanique," Anthony said. "You know your half sibling Faith and her mate Vaughn D'Angelo."

Tanique greeted Vaughn with a polite nod, but his attention was on Faith. "I've wanted to speak properly with you for a long time."

"I feel the same." Faith reached out her hands before she remembered Tanique had been raised in Silence and, unlike her, hadn't left the Net to join a changeling pack where touch was an essential and everyday part of life.

Any post-Silence changes in her brother would be slow and hesitant.

Dropping her hands, she said, "You're permanently at NightStar now?" All adult Psy could choose the side of their family line with which they preferred to align themselves. Tanique had done it, not at eighteen but later. Regardless, Anthony would've paid a penalty to the family who had raised and educated him but would no longer have the benefit of his abilities.

Thirty was the point at which such considerations no longer applied. Tanique was barely twenty-four and a half.

"Yes," he said. "NightStar is my home base, though I do travel." Her brother continued to look at her with beautiful eyes of a pale tawny brown that made his face even more striking. They were almost feline, her brother's eyes, with fine striations of darker brown and yellow in the irises.

Faith got the impression that he was as curious about her as she was about him.

"My skill set meshes far better with F-Psy than with the telepathic abilities prevalent in my maternal line," he added in a voice that reminded her of Anthony's, only younger. "They didn't know quite how to make use of me, but Father does. I do a little work for private collectors, but the bulk of what I do involves museums that wish to verify the provenance of exhibits or items the institutions wish to purchase."

Faith shook her head, her pride in her brother a tidal wave of pressure against her heart. "That's not all you do," she corrected. "I know you've helped find more than one lost or kidnapped child."

Tanique didn't blink or shift position, but she caught a subtle change in his expression. "Father's taught me that we aren't only machines bound to our gifts." A glance at their shared father that held unhidden respect. "Yes, we need to support ourselves, but we can also choose to use our abilities in ways that are good for society . . . and for our spirits," he finished hesitantly.

At that instant, Faith saw only a younger brother still struggling to find his footing, not the gifted Ps-Psy who'd once carried a child a mile out of a dense jungle after picking up a lost backpack and catching a glimpse of where the child's abductor had taken him.

"Choosing to do the right thing can be hard at times," she said softly, "but it's worth it." The dark visions used to leave her crumpled in a fetal ball until she accepted them as part of her gift and took ownership. Now, sometimes, she saved a life. Against that, the intense psychic control, the pain of living a murderer's dreams, none of it mattered.

Tanique gave a nod so like Anthony's that Faith bit back a smile. For all his poise and training, her brother suddenly put her in mind of the youths in DarkRiver. Adorable. He'd probably hate that description had he embraced emotion, but she thought an older sister should have leave to think such things. "I was actually hoping to ask your help with something."

"I'd be happy to provide it." His reply came so quickly on the heels of her words that she realized he wanted to build a relationship with her as badly as she wanted to build one with him. "You have an object for me to look at?"

Faith gestured to the box on the table. "It's in there. Can you take a look, see what you sense?" It was a deliberately vague statement on her part; she didn't want to influence him in any way.

"Can you open the box?" Tanique's tone was more sure now that they were in his area of expertise. "It's so I don't get sidetracked by any impressions left on the box by those who've carried it."

"I should've thought of that."

Once she'd opened the box, Tanique simply looked at the barnacle-encrusted bottle for a long minute before he reached in and lifted it out, while being careful not to brush so much as his knuckles against the inside of the box. The letter had been deemed too fragile for handling, but Miane had sent a small piece from it that had broken off during the original transit. A blank corner, the paper was protected inside a small plastic sleeve.

Tanique left it in the box for now.

His first words came bare seconds after he touched the bottle. "Youth, curiosity, a feline energy, cold anger. A surface layer only, likely from the people who handled it over the past few days."

Faith didn't interrupt, though she was impressed by how quickly and accurately he'd picked up all that.

"The sea," he murmured, running his fingers over the barnacles. "I can hear its crashing whisper in my mind . . . but you don't need me to tell you this bottle was in the ocean."

He angled his head to the right, as if struggling to hear a faraway voice.

"Age," he murmured. "There are long-ago echoes here, from decades ago. Of an elderly man cleaning the bottle . . . but there's a new deep imprint, too. A girl . . . no, a woman. A young woman held this not recently but recently enough and for long enough that the imprint hasn't faded."

When he looked at Faith, she had to bite back a gasp.

She'd seen Psy eyes turn black. Her own did that during a surge of emotion or when she was using large amounts of psychic power. She'd also seen the colors in Sascha's eyes when she was using her empathic abilities . . . but this, she'd never seen. Tanique's irises had taken on a shimmer of pale green. As if reflecting the bottle.

"She was afraid, but fierce. Hurt." Squeezing shut his eyes, he lowered his head, only to shake it after thirty seconds. "That's all I get."

It wasn't as much as Faith had hoped, but it was fascinating to see her brother at work. "Thanks for trying."

"I don't think anyone but the old man spent great amounts of time with the bottle." Eyes ordinary now, he looked at the plastic sleeve that held the piece of paper. "May I . . . ?"

Faith nodded. She knew the water changelings wouldn't have offered the piece to a Ps-Psy if they didn't expect it to be touched. While her brother's specialty was esoteric and not well known outside of museums—and some crime departments who'd been able to secure the services of a Ps-Psy—most people could connect the dots.

This time, he didn't have to tell her to open the bag for him. Unsealing it, she shook the piece of paper straight out onto his palm.

Tanique's spine snapped straight, his jaw going rigid. "Pain," he said. "Anger again. More pain. Anguish."

Faith saw her brother's other hand fist at his side and had the startling realization that to be a Ps-Psy was to be bombarded by emotion. How had her brother survived Silence? It was a question she'd ask him one day, when they were alone and he didn't feel so overwhelmed.

"The young woman who touched the bottle, she handled this paper on a boat." His breathing grew ragged as his body swayed from side to side, as if he were on a boat himself. "The boat rocked . . . but not for long. She was frantic to get the paper away before it was too late and they reached land again. Home, she was thinking of home the last time she touched this." Releasing the paper so it floated down to lie inside the box, he opened his eyes.

Faith went to say thank-you, but Tanique wasn't done.

"I have fragments of what she saw," he said. "A glimpse of what might be part of a wall, an image of her toes, what looks like a chain attached to a wrist." Another deep breath, his expression difficult to read but his body vibrating with tension. "An old sign, chipped white paint on graying wood: *Edward's Pier*. Apostrophe before the *s* in *Edward's*. Worn wooden boards under her feet, water below . . . and that's it."

"I've got it," Vaughn murmured, his phone already in hand as he messaged BlackSea the details Tanique had given them.

Faith reached out a hand toward her brother. "Thank you."

Only a small hesitation before Tanique put his hand in hers. "I'm sorry I couldn't be of more assistance. She's in trouble, isn't she?"

"Yes, and you helped." The sign he'd picked up was a highly specific detail. "I didn't really understand until I watched you work, but our abilities are on the same continuum. I don't know why they're not listed together in the Designation charts." She frowned in an effort to find the words to say what she meant. "We both see what isn't there. In my case, I see what will be, while you see what has been."

Tanique blinked . . . and his fingers, they seemed to curl further around hers. "Perhaps we should write a paper arguing the case."

"I think we should." Faith smiled at the excuse to spend more time getting to know her brother. "Do you have to go yet? We could head outside for a while, talk."

But Tanique shook his head. "Since I'm officially part of NightStar, it's not safe for you to be connected to me in a non-business context."

Disappointment was lead in her gut. "Oh, of course."

Vaughn prowled over. "How about you two meet in DarkRiver's home territory? No prying eyes there."

Faith didn't bother to hide her delight when Tanique agreed at once.

"Tanique," Anthony said after Faith and Vaughn finished giving Tanique their direct contact details so he could get in touch when he had a day off. "Your transport is here." A piercing look. "Be very careful. Your ability is rare enough that no one has truly worked out your vulnerabilities, but you're a NightStar. Don't let down your guard."

"Yes, sir." Tawny brown eyes met Faith's. "I hope to see you again soon."

Faith just did it. She hugged him. He froze, didn't respond. But neither did he push her away, and that was enough for today. "I can't wait."

Anthony waited until Tanique was gone to speak. "I'll have the chair delivered to DarkRiver's HQ."

"Thank you, Father." Then, prodded by the silent mischief in the eyes of the jaguar who was her mate, she said, "Is Councilor Duncan well?"

Anthony's response was icy. "You should get going, or you won't arrive home until the early hours of the morning." The faintest touch of his hand to her hair before he was gone.

Vaughn held it together until they were in the car and on their way to a casual restaurant for a late-night snack. "Your father and Nikita. Man likes to live dangerously."

Faith shot virtual daggers at the highly amused cat next to her. "He was so mad."

"No, he was just telling his daughter to mind her own business."

"I would have if you hadn't been egging me on." She fiddled with the edge of the simple white top she wore with jeans and ankle boots. "Do you think they really are? In a relationship?" Faith could imagine her father loving a woman, but *Nikita*? "Sascha's mom is . . ."

"A cold, heartless bitch?" Vaughn supplied before adding, "They do have one thing in common."

"What?"

"Both would kill for their kids."

Faith nodded slowly, though she continued to find it difficult to imagine how a relationship between two such icily controlled people could work. And which one of them would bend in any particular situation when both were used to ruling their domains with iron hands? As for physical intimacy . . .

She shuddered, banishing those thoughts far, *far* from her mind. "Quiet," she ordered when her mate chuckled with a knowing glint in his eye. "Shall we go see Mercy tomorrow afternoon since you'll be off-shift?"

Vaughn's thigh bunched under the hand she'd placed on it. "No. She'll just complain about exploding any day soon." It was a bad-tempered growl. "I've never seen a woman be so bad at pregnancy."

"It's only been the last few weeks, when she can't be as active as usual." Even Mercy's sentinel-fit body had said "Enough" at that point. "You know she'd like the company, and I know you miss her now that you don't run into her on patrol."

Vaughn growled again but muttered that he'd stop by a bakery and pick up Mercy's favorite upside-down pineapple cake.

Faith smiled, wondering if they could steal Naya again and take her along on the visit. But her smile faded as she considered what had happened tonight. "You think Tanique's reading will help?"

"Edward's Pier doesn't sound like an official name," Vaughn said. "If it was put up on private land, it won't be easy to find." He shrugged, the movement quintessentially feline. "But it's a whole lot more than Black-Sea had before." Golden eyes locked with hers for a primal heartbeat. "Now we see how well they hunt."

Letters to Nina

From the private diaries of Father Xavier Perez
March 22, 2074

Nina,

I keep writing these letters knowing they'll die with me, but I can't stop. You're the one to whom I always told my secrets. Now I have another one: I spoke to a man in the bar five minutes ago.

Not a man. A soldier. A Psy.

Like the ones who came to our village, came to annihilate because we refused to allow them to strangle all trade in the region, cutting us off from our livelihoods. The only difference is that this Psy looks even more dangerous. I drank tequila and I told him about the murderous evil of his people.

He thought I was drunk, that I didn't know to whom I spoke.

He was wrong.

I can see him still from my new position in the very back of the bar. He's waiting for whoever it is he's come to see. Dressed in civilian clothing, he's trying to blend in, is fooling most people, but I know the way Psy soldiers walk and I know the way their eyes scan a room.

I'm going to kill him.

I can hear you in my head, telling me not to commit this mortal sin, but the drink and the blood and the grief have washed away my faith. All I want is vengeance. If I can't get the men and women who took you from me, took everyone I ever loved away from me, then I'll take their brethren.

Xavier

Chapter 15

MERCY AND THE always-ravenous pupcubs were having a good couple of days. Not only had Vaughn and Faith brought cake and news and Naya yesterday, today Mercy and the football team inside her were getting all kinds of delicious. As for Naya and her pride in being able to shift, "adorable" didn't begin to describe it.

Far more mobile in her leopard form, Mercy had shifted, too, and played gentle games with her alpha's cub. Because, pregnant or not, she could still shift. Scientists had been trying to figure out the whys of that particular trick for centuries, but so far, all anyone could say was that because a changeling was meant to be both forms, a pregnant changeling who shifted also took control of the cells of her embryo or fetus and shifted that embryo or fetus with her.

Despite that, Mercy had worried about shifting the first time after she found out she was pregnant because it was possible the pupcubs weren't built to shift into the same animal as her. But not only had Lara and Tamsyn both reassured her nothing would go wrong, she'd known that *not* shifting would cause far more harm to her, and thus to her pupcubs.

She'd shifted.

And the pupcubs had continued to grow, happy in either form.

Yesterday, she'd been certain she could feel their delight as Faith and Vaughn played with Naya alongside Mercy. Her jaguar packmate had taken his animal form, while a barefoot Faith had happily tumbled in the grass with Naya. Then Riley had returned from a run to get Mercy something she'd been craving; he joined in and the day had turned from almost perfect to perfect.

Especially given Naya's deliriously excited reaction every time she saw Riley in his wolf form. She seemed to think he was a living version of The Toy That Shall Not Be Named and pounced on him without fail. Once, before Mercy and Riley moved down to this cabin, while they had been babysitting, Mercy had come out of their home to find her mate on the grass in wolf form, snoozing in the sun, while Naya did the same curled up on his back, one little hand fisted possessively in his fur.

The image had slayed her, her knees going so weak she'd had to sit down on the steps leading down from their verandah and just watch the two of them as they dozed. Then yesterday, seeing how patient he was with Naya's antics . . . Mercy blew out a breath.

God, her sexy, quietly stable wolf mate was going to be one hell of a father.

To top it all off, she had a genuine task in putting together the DarkRiver-SnowDancer event. She knew Lucas had assigned her the job to keep her busy and stop her from driving Riley crazy, but though she made growly noises at Lucas and Hawke both when they asked her how it was going, secretly, she was enjoying it.

A sentinel wasn't meant to sit around. She was meant to *do*.

At least neither her alpha nor her fellow sentinels tried to shield her from bad news, such as the developing BlackSea situation and the possible threat to Naya. Mercy had helped Jamie and Dezi rejig the communications aspect of DarkRiver's security protocols when it came to the pack's cubs, was certain that between the three of them, they'd plugged any possible gaps.

She'd also racked her brain thinking of how either pack could assist the captive Leila Savea, but right now, she had nothing. What she *could* do was help nurture the ever-growing bond between DarkRiver and SnowDancer. In their blood alliance was a strength that wouldn't only shield the packs from the bastards who hid in the shadows pulling strings designed to cause as much chaos as possible, it could well lead to the downfall of those same assholes.

Most important to her on a personal level was that the blood bond between the two packs meant her pupcubs would grow up in a cohesive single entity with two independent parts.

"See, babies," she said, patting her hard belly, "you're already a force for peace among mankind—or at least among a bunch of stubborn wolves and leopards."

"You talking to yourself again, Merce?" her brother yelled out from the kitchen where she had him prisoner.

"Shut up and cook, Frenchie!"

Bastien poked his head out the door, the dark, dark red of his hair as pretty as the green eyes that made him such a favorite with the women. Too bad for them that he was head over heels for his sweetheart of a mate. Who was just as loopy over him. Loopy enough to take Mercy on. Since Mercy would've accepted no woman who *didn't* fight for Bas, she loved Kirby.

Bastien's sweetheart came with a spine.

"I thought pregnancy was supposed to make you soft and glowy and smooshie."

"Smooshie?" She threw a wadded-up piece of paper at his handsome head. "Is that even English?"

Throwing up a hand, he caught the paper in midair. "I pick up Kirby after work sometimes, and if she's still got kids in the kindergarten because the parents have been held up, we hang out. Apparently 'ooshie' can be attached to most words." He pointed a large wooden spoon at her belly, his white T-shirt and black cargo pants partially covered by a sleek black apron. "You should know that since you'll be hearing words like it very soon."

Mercy smiled. "Come 'ere."

Her big, burly brother immediately looked suspicious. "Why?" he asked, not moving from the doorway.

"I'm the size of a tank and slow as a drunk bear. I'm not going to bite you." Mercy crooked a finger.

Eyebrows drawn together, Bastien came to where she sat in the large armchair Riley had moved to the end of the dining table; papers and a thin organizer were spread out in front of her. When she waved Bas down, his expression darkened even further, but he bent toward her. She put a hand on his muscled shoulder and kissed him on the cheek, his scent so familiar that she was sure she felt the pupcubs squirm in happiness at having their uncle so close.

Bastien rose to his feet, his suspicious expression having transformed into full-blown accusation. "What do you want me to cook now?"

"Cherry pie with your special crust."

"Cherry *pie*?" Bastien glared at her. "Do you know how much work it is to get that crust exactly right? And I'll have to go get the cherries."

Mercy gave him her best "I'm pregnant with multiples" smile. "I love you."

"*Grr.*" Putting a hand on her hair, Bastien leaned down again and pressed a kiss to her forehead. "I'll make you your pie after I finish the casserole you wanted for lunch."

Smiling as he went back into the kitchen, Mercy patted her belly again. "Yes, Uncle Bastien is the best."

"Stop sucking up," her brother growled from the kitchen. "I'm making the damn pie."

Mercy laughed and picked up the old-fashioned notepad on which she was jotting down ideas for the joint event—officially, it was to welcome the pupcubs, but Mercy knew that was just an excuse.

It was time: DarkRiver and SnowDancer had gone from wary neighbors to wary allies to true allies to blood-bonded friends who'd lay down their lives for one another without hesitation. While they'd never be one pack, their animals too different, they were as close to it as possible. This celebration was about acknowledging that.

Planning a social event wouldn't usually be a task assigned to a sentinel, and it wasn't anything at which Mercy was an expert—but she wasn't doing this alone. Riley was better at this kind of thing. Despite being as aggressive a dominant as Mercy, he'd also long been in charge of Snow-Dancer's overall personnel. His experience at organizing a whole bunch of snarly wolves into some sort of order translated surprisingly well into breaking down the manpower required for a large event.

He'd done just that last night, while she did a few exercises with him playing spotter. And scowling. Her lips quirked. Poor Riley. Ending up with a mate who refused to sit still and let him take care of her. Her gorgeous wolf didn't realize she was taking care of him, too—the last thing Riley needed was peace and quiet. Give him time to think and his worry for her went into hyperdrive.

"I'm amazed at your patience," Indigo had said to her a month ago, the wolf lieutenant's eyes curious. "I'd have expected you to have clawed him bloody by now for his overprotectiveness."

Mercy had promised Indigo a clawing was on the horizon, but the truth was that Riley had earned his right to worry. That massive heart of his? It loved so fiercely that it held nothing back, maintained no protections against hurt. For a man like that, she could give a little, accept what he needed to do to keep himself on an even keel.

Quite aside from her wolf, Mercy had two packs of helpers at her disposal when it came to organizing this event. Plus, thanks to Riley, she knew approximately how many people she needed for each task. "Bas?"

"Yeah?"

"You up for doing some catering for the—"

"N.O. *No.*"

"But you're an amazing cook."

"I'm a genius in charge of DarkRiver's financial assets, not your personal chef slave."

She grinned, because grumpy as he sounded, her brother had taken time out of his genuinely busy day—because he *was* a financial genius—to come hang out with her. The food was just an excuse; this was about family. "Is Kirby okay with you being here today?" Bastien and Kirby hadn't been mated long, were understandably possessive of one another.

"Are you kidding? She loves the pupcubs." He poked his head out of the kitchen again. "I think she still occasionally worries about the fact that she's a lynx and I'm a leopard. The pupcubs reassure her that's not and never will be an issue."

Mercy knew her sister-in-law well enough to guess what lay at the root of her fears. "Just love her." Kirby had been alone for a long time—she was pack now and understood that she belonged, but a little extra affection would help cement that realization.

"I love her until my heart hurts." Bastien's expression softened. "She's smart, sexy, funny, perfect."

"I just threw up a little in my mouth." Mercy pretended to gag, wasn't fast enough to dodge or catch the cushion Bastien grabbed from the closest sofa to throw at her. It hit her in the chest with so little momentum she knew he'd been purposefully gentle. All three of her hooligan brothers had reverted to type now she was pregnant: protective DarkRiver dominants.

You'd think they'd never pushed her into a mud pool or five, or tripped her up, or played hard-out football with her complete with bruising tackles. Of course, she hadn't been innocent of hooliganism herself. In fact, she might've pushed Bas and Sage into a mud pool first.

Grinning at the thought of her own children playing rough and tumble games with each other, she said, "Is your lynx coming over after work?"

"I've messaged to let her know you need another kitchen slave so she'll be roped into cherry pie prep." A deep smile. "She said she'll pick up the supplies on the way."

"Did I tell you I adore your mate?"

"She is highly adorable."

Laughing at the smug cat look on his face, Mercy went back to her plans while Bastien busied himself in the kitchen.

The first problem was location.

Usually when DarkRiver held such gatherings, it was in the Pack Circle. SnowDancer had a comparative space up in their territory. DarkRiver was a much smaller pack and as such had a smaller central gathering space.

However, SnowDancer's celebration area was in the Sierra Nevada and at a higher elevation. If the event was to be held soon after the birth, then Mercy and the pupcubs would have to travel to that elevation.

The babies might feel like linebackers inside her, but they'd be very small at that stage and she didn't want to shock their little bodies. It would've been different were they to be born in the Sierra Nevada, but they'd be born in DarkRiver's Yosemite territory. She wanted them stronger before taking them up.

Any wolves who wanted to visit would be welcome in DarkRiver lands.

"Hmm." Tapping a finger on the dining table, she picked up her phone to contact Riley. Her mate was worried she'd go into labor while he wasn't with her, had only reluctantly left to run an errand for SnowDancer. Mercy couldn't argue with his concern—most changeling multiples were already born by this stage of the pregnancy.

He'd given the pupcubs strict instructions to stay put while their daddy was away. Mercy could almost feel them listening as he spoke, had full faith they'd behave—because she was not having them without Riley next to her. The end.

Location for party? she messaged him. DR circle is too small and I don't want to switch elevations on the pupcubs so soon after birth.

Pupcubs are half wolf, Riley responded. They won't mind.

That was a good point. Regardless of what their babies chose to shift into, they had Riley's genes as well as her own. And Riley was built for the higher elevations, barely felt the cold. He was also tough, gorgeously sexy with those big shoulders and that wall of a body that could take anything she could dish out.

Mercy pressed her thighs together. I wanna pounce on you.

Your pregnancy hormones are going to kill us both . . . and we'll die happy.

She giggled, slapped a hand over her mouth before Bas heard and grew curious.

What about the area around our place? Riley sent.

She knew he wasn't talking about this cabin; he was referring to their permanent home, a home that was part Swiss chalet, part rugged mountain cabin. It'll also mean an elevation change, she replied, but not such a big one. And it's where the older teens and early-twenties group had their new year's party. A successful effort to get that age group talking to one another across pack lines.

Only problem is I'm not sure there's enough open space.

Mercy considered Riley's point. Cutting down trees wasn't an option. No changeling would ever damage the environment for such a fleeting reason. We could use our house and the land around it as the focus and people could spread out into the trees.

Close to the house, those trees weren't packed so tightly together that it would make mingling difficult. We have enough open space for dancing and for the kids to play.

Riley agreed before messaging: I'll be home in a couple of hours. You good?

Getting fatter by the minute but otherwise happy. So are the pupcubs.

He sent her back a whole bunch of hearts. She melted. Senior Snow-Dancer Lieutenant Riley Kincaid *did not* message little pink hearts. Saving the message, she hugged the phone to her chest for a moment before messaging back some hearts of her own. She added puppies. Because she could be goofy and mushy with her mate. He wouldn't see her as any less strong.

Positively buoyant afterward, she sketched out several more ideas. A temporary dance floor—maybe backlit?—was a definite, as were pretty lights in the trees. Beside each point, she jotted down names of packmates and SnowDancers who'd be good at actioning it. Riley could help with the latter when he got back.

Food, of course, lots of it. Everyone could pitch in there—despite her teasing of Bastien, bringing food to share at a pack event was pretty standard in both DarkRiver and SnowDancer. "Bas?"

"Yup?"

"Should we get a special cake?"

"What? Half wolf, half cat, all danger?"

She knew he was messing with her, but she liked the idea. "That'd be fun. The pups and cubs would love it."

Mercy stroked her belly when she paused in her work. Space was at a premium in there. The recent scans Tamsyn had taken showed the pup-cubs wrapped around each other like living pretzels, a foot in someone's face, an arm under a chin, other creative ways of making the most of limited space.

"It's almost time," she whispered to them. "Your daddy and I can't wait to hold you in our arms."

Even as her lips curved in joy and wonder, part of her mind continued to think of the darkness licking at the edges of the world, of the growing threat to a small panther cub, and of a woman trapped far from home. When the Trinity Accord was first proposed, she'd hoped her pupcubs would be born into a world at peace.

Today, she accepted that it was going to be a far more complicated, and far longer, process.

Chapter 16

FORMER PSY COUNCILOR and once leader of the Arrow Squad, Ming LeBon needed to be part of the Trinity Accord, not just for informational purposes but because he might otherwise miss out on lucrative business opportunities. Unlike with Nikita Duncan, business didn't occupy the central role in Ming's personal hierarchy of importance, but he'd long ago learned that money was power.

Since the wolves and the squad would certainly block his application to sign the accord, he'd have to get in via a majority. So he'd play politics. He would far rather use fear to achieve his aims, but that could backfire in this situation. No, it was better if he began making contact with smaller groups and flattering them with his interest.

He'd also sound out a number of large Psy corporations who couldn't be as "happy" about the accord as they appeared to be in public. Together they'd ensure Ming's application to sign Trinity was a success. Of course, he'd then figure out how to take control of the cooperation agreement and use it to his advantage.

The Trinity Accord was too potentially influential to be left in hands that had no experience with wielding that kind of power.

Chapter 17

I THINK LUCAS and Hawke should do the tango to open the party. Yes? p.s. Update on pupcubs: I am still fourteen months pregnant.

Sascha stifled a laugh as she replied to Mercy's message from her curled-up position in an armchair in a corner of Lucas's private office at DarkRiver's Chinatown HQ. He had a much sleeker public office on another floor, but this was the hub of the HQ.

"What's the smile for?" Lucas glanced over from where he stood in front of a comm screen, having just finalized the details of a new business project DarkRiver was entering into with a large Psy family group.

Sascha read out the message. "I'm voting yes to the tango," she added. "I want to see you and Hawke cheek to cheek."

Lucas's scowl was very alpha. "She needs to give birth so she can stop being bored and making trouble."

"I think she'd agree with you." In her last update, Mercy had written: Think belly button has popped off. May have to fashion new one out of a doughnut hole.

Lucas turned back to the comm as it chimed an incoming call. "Black-Sea," he murmured to her before touching the screen to answer.

The woman who'd made the call had sharp cheekbones, her flawless skin a shade that, Sascha suddenly thought, wouldn't have looked out of place in any Psy family. Psy in Silence had a clinical way of mixing and mingling genes to the family's psychic advantage, until skin shades on either end of the spectrum were less common than those in between.

According to Riaz, one of the SnowDancer lieutenants who most often dealt with BlackSea, Miane was the product of a devoted mating between an Egyptian father and an Algerian mother.

The result was a striking, powerful woman.

Her straight black hair was cut in a blunt fringe over slightly uptilted eyes that were currently a translucent hazel. However, Sascha had seen those irises turn obsidian. It shouldn't have disconcerted her, not when Psy eyes could go fully black. But the blackness in Miane's eyes . . . it was as dark as the deepest part of the ocean, a whispering echo of a more primal time.

"Lucas." The BlackSea alpha's tone was cool but Sascha sensed boiling tension beneath the skin. As an empath, she couldn't technically feel a person's emotional resonance from this far a distance, but technicalities weren't everything. It was her belief that empaths learned fine emotional cues without knowing it.

Sascha had discussed that with Ivy Jane and with young Toby. Both agreed, though Toby had put it a different way: "Since we know about emotions all the time, I guess we get used to separating out all the types. Like changelings can with scent."

An astute comment from an astute boy.

"Miane," Lucas responded while Sascha stayed out of the shot. "Tanique's info give you any leads?"

A shake of Miane's head. "We've focused on Canada because we have to start somewhere, but so far, nothing's panned out."

"We're here to assist if you need it."

BlackSea's alpha nodded before moving on to the reason for her call. "I just spoke to Aden Kai. He suggested I attend a Trinity summit in two hours with the head of a Psy family plus a couple of Human Alliance CEOs. All three have interests in coastal areas that touch our waters."

"You wondering why the short notice?"

"Kai says it's to stop the chance of a violent disruption and that I'm getting an hour's extra notice because it'll take me longer to reach the location of the meeting. But while I'm predisposed to like the Arrows,

I'm well aware they have motives and aims of their own, not all of which align with BlackSea's."

DarkRiver, meanwhile, Sascha realized, was an official ally. Changelings didn't make such pronouncements lightly.

"It's legit." Lucas braced his hands on his hips, the fine cotton of his white shirt stretching over his biceps. "I'd take the usual precautions regardless—we don't know the motives of all parties who've signed the accord."

Miane logged off with a curt nod and no good-bye.

Watching her mate use the comm screen to deal with a quick contract update, Sascha wondered if Lucas knew he was becoming a powerful figure worldwide. Likely not. Such thoughts would go against his pack-minded nature. He'd never pursued power for power's sake and never would—but as Miane had just demonstrated, Lucas had come to be considered worthy of trust by an influential network of changelings.

Another call came in just as he finished up what he'd been doing and went to turn toward Sascha. She caught his raised eyebrow. "Jen Liu and I don't have a scheduled call today."

It turned out the matriarch of the Liu family group wanted his feedback on a changeling pack that was pitching for business with Liu. "Our contacts in that area are regrettably thin," said the silver-haired woman with a sharp, pointed face. "I'm not requesting private data; I simply wish to know if they're reputable in a business sense."

"Very," Lucas replied. "They're small but if they take on a project and you don't get in their way once the plans are finalized, they'll finish it on time and within budget."

"Thank you. Should you require similar feedback on a Psy company, feel free to contact me."

That was when Sascha realized Lucas wasn't only trusted by changelings across the world, but that he was gaining a reputation among Psy as well. "Naya," she whispered, understanding settling on her shoulders like a warm blanket.

Her mate sent her a questioning look.

"Changeling and Psy," she said, "they both know that of all involved parties, you alone would *never* jeopardize Trinity. You—we—have a child who needs to grow up in a united world."

Her mate's eyes were suddenly more panther than human. "A fair evaluation, isn't it, kitten?"

"Yes." She uncurled her legs from the armchair and got up to walk to him, wrapping her arms around his waist as they stood face-to-face. "You don't mind that they know?"

Head inclined to meet her gaze, Lucas shook his head. "Not if this is the consequence—if people trust me, they trust in Trinity by default."

An inquisitive mental touch across Sascha's mind. "Naya's having fun with Clay."

The quietest of the sentinels was one of Naya's favorite people. She would snuggle up against his shoulder and watch wide-eyed while he moved around, no matter what he was doing—and unusually for Naya, she didn't demand to be put down so she could explore on her own. Clay said it was because he had experience with little girls, thanks to his adopted daughter Noor.

His mate, Talin, had a different take on it. "He's always had a marshmallow heart," the tawny-haired woman had teased one day while he was cuddling Noor in one arm and holding Naya in the other. "He used to attend tea parties with me when we were kids. He even drank the pretend tea and told me it was delicious."

Clay had glowered at the woman he called Tally. "Wait till I have my hands free."

His glower should've been terrifying—Clay was a seriously dangerous leopard. But Noor had growled and pretended to maul Clay, setting off Naya, who'd burst into hysterical baby laughter that had in turn set off both Sascha and Talin. Clay's grin had creased his cheeks, the once angrily silent sentinel now a man deeply at peace and delighted with his life.

Smiling at the memory, Sascha responded to Naya's telepathic touch with a psychic kiss. *Here I am, sweetheart.*

"I've been thinking that Naya should meet Nikita," Lucas said at almost the same time.

Sascha's mouth fell open. "You don't even like her."

Nikita had been part of a machine that had crushed countless change-lings under its boot, had in fact been a member of the organization that had *consciously* hidden the worst serial killers on the planet. That action had led to the deaths of hundreds, including that of Dorian's younger sister, a loss that had devastated the sentinel and enraged Lucas.

SnowDancer had almost lost Brenna to the same murderous psy-chopath.

"I might not like her," Lucas said, "but she kept you alive in difficult circumstances and she's Naya's grandmother." He ran his thumb over her cheekbone, tactile as always.

Sascha never had to wonder about Lucas's love for her, either on the emotional or on the physical plane. Neither did she have to worry about being touch hungry ever again, as she'd been for so many years of her life. "Still," she said, trying to make sense of his suggestion and failing, "to trust her with access to Naya?"

Her mate's expression grew dark. "I'd rather Naya know her from childhood than that she grow up curious about her—curious cubs have a way of getting into trouble."

Sascha couldn't argue with that. She'd seen exactly how much trouble DarkRiver teens could get into; a teenager curious about her powerful, lethal grandmother had the potential to get into more dangerous trouble than most. "I don't think Nikita would ever hurt her," she said, placing her hand on the taut muscle of Lucas's arm.

"I agree," he said. "Otherwise, feline curiosity or not, I wouldn't let her within a hundred feet of our child." Sliding one of his hands up to curve it around her neck, he locked his gaze with her own. "If we do it, it has to be soon. Nikita's still weak from the assassination attempt, her defenses down. Naya might actually get to meet the woman beneath the mask."

Unlike the panther who was her mate, Sascha's empathic heart wasn't used to thinking with such pitiless pragmatism, but she knew Lucas was right. They had to bring Naya and Nikita into contact while there was a chance Nikita would bond with their baby—because once Sascha's mother bonded with a child, she'd fight to the death to protect that vulnerable life.

Sascha had understood that only after she was out of the PsyNet.

"I'll work out a time with Sophie," she said. "We'll make sure Nikita doesn't know, so she can't prepare." Nikita's most senior and trusted aide, Sophia Russo, was very much her own woman and she would defy Nikita if she thought it good for her boss.

"Sophia still worried about how hard Nikita is driving herself?"

Nodding, Sascha said, "At least Anthony's keeping an eye on her. If anyone can make my mother rest, I'd say it's him." Quite aside from whatever it was that was going on with Nikita and the head of PsyClan NightStar, Sascha knew Nikita respected Anthony.

"Faith's father is a brave, brave man."

Lucas's solemn pronouncement made her lips twitch and her mind stop tugging at the thread of worry that was concern for the mother who'd abandoned her . . . and saved her. "If their shields weren't so airtight," she admitted in a guilty whisper, "I'd probably slip up in the ethics department and take a peek at their emotions."

Panther-green eyes glinted in approval. "You and everyone else who knows about those two, I bet." A nipping, nibbling kiss that was pure teasing cat. "I'll reach out to Vasic," he said afterward, "see if he'll agree to teleport you."

Sascha nodded, aware she and Naya couldn't be seen entering Nikita's domain. "If Vasic can't do it, we'll have to come up with another plan. Mother won't accept any other teleporter in her domain while she's weak."

"Vasic's an Arrow," Lucas pointed out. "Dangerous as they come."

"He's also bonded to an E." Nikita considered empaths weak in their emotionality, but she also accepted that they were good judges of character.

"Plus," Lucas said, eyes narrowed in thought, "Aden's made it clear the Arrows don't want to stage a coup. That has to factor into her decisions."

Sascha had a sudden thought. "What if Anthony's with her when I go in?" she whispered, her mind flicking back to the hospital waiting room and Anthony's silent, intense presence.

Lucas paused in the act of unbuttoning his shirt to change into his preferred T-shirt and jeans now that he was about to head out of the office. Anyone who called him while he was in the field would get the changeling alpha as opposed to the CEO of DarkRiver. It was a fine distinction and it kept people on their toes now that DarkRiver was no longer in danger of being dismissed as a small, unimportant pack.

An arrested expression on his face, he said, "If he is . . ." A very wicked, very feline smile. "I'm all for interrupting them and relieving our curiosity about what exactly they get up to behind closed doors."

Sascha's shoulders shook, her worry about her mother overtaken by delight that Nikita might be doing *something* with Anthony, no matter how unlikely that was, given the individuals involved. Any relationship Anthony and Nikita had would never be predictable or understood by others. "You're such a cat sometimes."

"Meow."

Laughing, she ducked out of his office before she gave in to the urge to pet him—because it wouldn't stop there. Then their packmates would catch them and never let it go. Instead, she went looking for their cub. Naya's animated voice announced her presence well before Sascha saw her. She was still with Clay, who was checking construction specs on a comm screen; far from demanding attention, Naya was happily hanging over his shoulder and talking to Dorian as the other sentinel worked at a drafting board behind Clay.

Another, smaller baby, only a few months old, lay in a plush capsule carrier on the desk next to Dorian. This one was peacefully asleep, all dark lashes and plump cheeks. She was dressed in white socks and a pink one-piece with a daisy print on the front. Tied gently around her head, over a shock of silky dark hair, was a white ribbon.

Sascha just wanted to pick her up and cuddle her close.

"Is that right?" Dorian said to Naya, drawing a line using the old-fashioned set square he preferred over more high-tech tools when it came to his architectural work. His white-blond hair was bright in the sunshine pouring through the casement windows on this level of the midsize building, the open plan area maximizing the space and light.

"You don't say." Glancing at the sleeping baby at the same time that he responded to Naya, Dorian reached out and touched the tip of the baby's nose. She smiled in her sleep and seemed to settle even deeper.

"Yes," Dorian said when Naya talked to him some more.

Included was the word "Dor" several times. Naya definitely knew her packmates.

"This is Mialin Corrina," Dorian said, as if he'd fully understood Naya's question. "She belongs to Ria and Emmett. You can play with her when she gets a little bigger."

Sascha leaned against a wall of the workspace and just watched the four of them. She wasn't the least surprised when Lucas's executive administrative assistant, Ria, came to stand beside her. Shaking her head, the shorter woman said, "I swear, these guys make my ovaries explode."

"It's even worse when it's your own mate, isn't it?"

"Oh God, yes." Ria sighed, her brown eyes warm with love as they lingered on her baby. "Emmett does this thing where he tells her stories while cuddling her to sleep. My heart goes boom every single time. I have zero willpower for hours afterward—the man could ask me to dance naked while playing bongo drums and I'd do it."

Sascha nodded in sympathy. "The first time I walked into the room and saw Naya asleep on Lucas's chest while he slept, too, his hand over her naked baby butt . . ." Sascha sighed, rubbing a fist over her heart. "I don't think I've recovered."

"Even just thinking of Emmett with our baby . . ." Ria sniffed, her lower lip quivering.

Sascha wrapped an arm around the normally tough-as-nails woman. "I know." She dropped a kiss on Ria's mink-brown hair, at home with the affectionate skin privileges permitted to packmates who were close. "Your ovaries will learn to take it."

Ria sniffle-laughed.

Hearing the sound, Dorian glanced over. "Hey, now." The handsome male, who'd been full of pitiless anger and grief when Sascha first met him, walked over to tug Ria from Sascha's embrace and wrap her in his arms. "I thought your eyes only shot fire."

Ria punched him in the arm. It had zero effect, since he was built of pure muscle.

Chuckling, the sentinel kissed her cheek. "You have the specs I asked for?"

"Here." Ria pushed the organizer into his chest, but without any force. "How much did you corrupt my daughter today?"

"She's definitely going to have a thing for blond architects when she grows up," Dorian said with a heartbreaker grin.

Going over to her cub, Ria kissed Mialin's chubby cheeks, brushed back the baby-fine hair that had escaped from under the ribbon, and just beamed. "Look at her, such an angel."

She turned to Naya, took Sascha's baby's face in her hands, and smothered her in kisses. Naya giggled and kissed her back. "Your friend Mialin saves her bad behavior for three in the morning," she said with another smacking kiss before turning to Dorian. "Emmett's bringing my grandmother over in an hour to pick up our cub for a little great-grandma-granddaughter time."

"Oh, man," Dorian complained. "We only got her for a few hours."

"Today." Ria poked him in the gut.

Watching her packmates and the two cubs in the sunshine, Sascha felt no fear, only a fierce determination to keep them safe. Anyone who tried to hurt DarkRiver's young would end up mauled bloody. Even an empath had a breaking point—push her too far and she'd hit back. Hard.

The world thought it knew Es and what they could do. It didn't.

HAVING left his mate and child at the city HQ, Sascha working from his office while Naya played happily with her friends in the nursery downstairs, Lucas spent the second half of the day at a construction site with

Dorian and Clay. He and the two sentinels had just finished their discussions when Clay got a phone call. The other man made a motion with his hand for Lucas to remain as he finished the call.

"Teijan," he said after hanging up. "Rats picked up a whiff of something—signs of mercenaries coming into the general area."

Lucas's eyes narrowed. "What kind of mercenaries?"

"Good enough that the Rats are having trouble getting any kind of a lock on them. All they have are whispers in the African community in the city." Clay folded his arms, his muscles taut under the gleaming mahogany of his skin. "The community's scared of whoever these people are and they're pro-DarkRiver enough to pass on any intel they have, but they don't seem to know much more than that the group's called Death Mask."

Taking off the bright yellow safety helmet he'd been wearing, Dorian thrust a hand through his sweat-damp hair. "Good name if you want to intimidate people."

"It seems like in this case, the name fits." Clay's jaw was a brutal line. "According to Teijan's research, no one's ever caught them, but they're rumored to be responsible for massacres and kidnappings across most of the African continent."

Lucas's mind went immediately to the threatening chatter about Naya, but he knew the mercenaries could be here for a hundred different reasons—including picking off Lucas or Hawke, or even Nikita. "Any point hacking into Enforcement databases?"

It was Dorian who replied. "If the Rats are this much in the dark, Enforcement will have no idea these fuckers are even in the city." The sentinel's vivid blue gaze grew grim. "But whatever's going to happen, it'll be soon. We all know groups like this don't come into an area unless they're setting up to strike."

Letters to Nina

From the personal diaries of Father Xavier Perez
March 23, 2074
Just past midnight

Nina,

I didn't kill the man, the Psy. I had a gun, planned to shoot him without warning because that's the only way you can surprise an elite soldier, but when I would've pulled out the gun in the alley behind the bar, my hand froze in my pocket.

It wasn't fear, wasn't cold feet.

It was telekinesis.

As I watched him walk toward me, I thought he was coming to kill me and I'm ashamed to admit I felt relief. Finally, no more pain, no more hurt, no more seeing you jump into the water over and over again.

But when he reached me, the man didn't kill me. He said, "If you shoot me, you'll be acting against your own interests. I'm here to stop another massacre."

I laughed at him but he challenged me to come with him.

"Or would you rather drown in alcohol?"

His words cut me. To be judged by a Psy assassin? No.

I'm going with this Psy soldier, this man who walks like a killer.

Xavier

Chapter 18

ONE DAY PASSED. Two. Three. On the fourth, when nothing suspicious happened and the Rats reported no new whispers about Death Mask, DarkRiver didn't stand down its alert, but it began to consider whether the mercenaries had simply been passing through on their way elsewhere.

Sascha hadn't stopped living her life in the interim, but she had kept Naya in Yosemite, deep in the heart of the pack's territory. However, that couldn't continue forever. Her cub was missing her friends at the nursery attached to DarkRiver HQ, so Lucas had brought her in this morning. Now, at just after one-thirty, Sascha was picking her up and driving them back home so the two of them could go visit Mercy.

They were in an armored vehicle that didn't even pretend to be anything but a protective tank. None of DarkRiver's children would travel in anything but these for the foreseeable future. The entire fleet had been checked by mechanics when the Arrows first reported the ugly things being said about Naya; the vehicles were then assigned to families who needed to move in and out of the city.

Often they carpooled, but today, Naya and Sascha had the vehicle to themselves.

She pulled away from DarkRiver HQ's parking lot with a wave at Lucas, who stood only a short distance away, having walked her and Naya outside. He blew her a kiss, then bent and blew one to Naya; their baby was safely ensconced in back in her special car seat that protected her while giving her a view out the windows and a clear line of sight to Sascha.

Sascha could hear Naya making kissing sounds as she blew kisses noisily back. "Bye, Papa! Bye, Papa!"

That kept her busy as Sascha merged into traffic. She wasn't alone, of course. Dorian was in a rugged Jeep behind her, his task to escort her and Naya home. DarkRiver had made the decision not to put everyone in the same vehicle when an escort was needed; a second vehicle made it harder for anyone to mount an effective ambush—plus, it put two different sets of eyes on the road at different points.

Flashing her rear lights to acknowledge the sentinel, she smiled when he flashed his headlights in return. Then she focused on the road and on keeping Naya safe as they drove home. She'd made this journey countless times, but she never took anything for granted. Still, she had her favorite sections.

"Look at the trees, Naya," she said as they passed through the Presidio. "Those are eucalyptus trees."

"Eutus?"

"Yes, eucalyptus." It was so easy to praise her child, to make her happy. She'd never understand how mothers under Silence had been able to shut down that violently powerful maternal urge. "Do you know which animals eat eucalyptus leaves?"

"Kila!"

Sascha laughed, well aware there was a good chance Naya didn't fully understand their discussion. But her baby knew the answer after the number of times they'd passed this way—and she got just as excited every single time.

"Good girl," Sascha said. "Koalas eat eucalyptus leaves." As she drove, she told Naya about the marsupials and how they carried their babies in a pouch.

Naya's mental pattern was happy in Sascha's mind, her baby finding pleasure in listening to her mother's voice. When Sascha ran out of koala facts, she told Naya about the upcoming DarkRiver-SnowDancer event. A few more minutes and she knew her cub would nod off. It was good timing; the nap would leave her energetic and active for the visit to Mercy and Riley's.

They'd just passed a private driveway without incident, the curving street ahead empty of traffic, when a large truck fitted with a heavy metal bull bar roared out from that drive at high speed. It was aimed straight at Dorian's Jeep. The sentinel managed to avoid a full-on collision with a lightning-fast turn, but it wasn't enough.

The truck smashed into the back half of the Jeep at full speed, crumpling the powerful frame and causing Dorian's vehicle to flip onto its side. The metal screamed as the truck's momentum shoved it across the tarmac, sparks shooting out from the contact . . . just as a bigger armored truck roared out at Sascha from the other direction.

The gleaming black vehicle screeched to a stop across the road, blocking Sascha's path.

She'd instinctively braked when she saw what had happened to Dorian. Now, she came to a full stop. Anything else and she'd have smashed into the armored truck in her way. An armored truck that held people who wanted to hurt her baby. Who had already hurt Dorian.

A strange calm descended on her.

"No," she said.

"Mama?"

"It's all right, Naya. Mama needs you to be quiet and to hold your shields tight for a second." Even as she spoke, she was watching the doors of the truck in front of her shove open, masked men and women in camouflage gear running out with their weapons trained on Sascha's vehicle. "Okay, sweetheart?" She reiterated her order with a psychic visual. "You understand?"

"'Kay."

Sascha felt Naya concentrating as hard as possible on maintaining her fragile new shields. They wouldn't hold against even a weak adult telepath, but it was another small protection. Sascha had already locked her own defenses around her child while gently blocking Naya's ability to feel what

Sascha was about to do. Naya didn't need to know that thanks to all the developments made by empaths working together as a group, her loving empath mother had figured out how to weaponize her ability.

And she'd learned how to do it against *all* races.

Including the Psy mind that was currently trying to batter down her shields.

It didn't matter that she had no preexisting psychic connection to any of her targets.

Maybe it had been inevitable that Sascha would be the one to figure it out—after all, not only had she been out of the PsyNet the longest, she lived surrounded by non-Psy minds who trusted her enough to act as her guinea pigs. And critically, she was connected to not one, but multiple non-Psy minds. Wary of giving enemies in the Net a tool against humans and changelings, she'd shared her discovery only with four other empaths, all of whom she trusted beyond any question.

None, including a fellow cardinal, had been able to repeat her success outside of the Psy race. The others *could* help humans and changelings in emotional pain by taking away or reducing that pain, but as soon as they tried anything aggressive, nothing happened.

They simply couldn't tune into the right "frequency," which was the best way Sascha had found to describe what she did when she used her ability to affect non-Psy minds. It made no difference whether the mind was human—and thus, usually vulnerable to Psy interference—or changeling, and therefore generally invulnerable to the same types of interference.

"We can't even sense the frequency," Ivy Jane had said to her. "When I try, I get that horrible pain I felt when I was trying to impact people without using the PsyNet."

The others had concurred.

It had been sweet Jaya who'd said, "You figured this out after you had a baby. Maybe it's that bond that gives you the ability." A frown. "It could be *her* brain that's allowing you to find the non-Psy frequency. Once she grows up and the mother-child bond morphs into the mother-adult child one, it may disappear."

It was as good a theory as any, but right now, Sascha cared only that she could hurt the people—Psy, changeling, or human—who wanted to hurt her baby. It had been difficult for her to teach herself to do something that went against her every empathic instinct, but she'd promised herself she'd only ever use that aspect of her ability when there was no other choice and to do nothing would be to let evil win.

"Dor!" Naya's sudden agitation had her twisting in her car seat, as if trying to see Dorian. "Mama, Dor!"

"Don't worry, baby. Dorian is strong. He's going to be fine." The sentinel was alive; she could feel it through the Web of Stars, the same way Naya had realized something was wrong. His star *was* flickering on the psychic network formed by blood bonds with a pack alpha, but not badly—because Lucas was pouring energy into the wounded sentinel.

Changelings didn't know they did that, but Sascha could see it clear as day. Lucas's bond with his sentinel had "woken" in a golden blaze the instant Dorian was hurt. Already Lucas would be tracking Dorian's vehicle, trying to contact him. He'd call it an instinctive awareness; Sascha knew it was an unconscious psychic link. Different from those made by the Psy but a psychic link nonetheless.

Lucas would also already be attempting to contact Sascha, but her phone was buried in the bottom of her handbag, and she'd pushed mute on the car's mobile comm the instant the car came to a halt. She couldn't risk an interruption to her concentration. She also couldn't split her energies enough to reassure Lucas through the mating bond. He'd understand.

After this was over, he'd know why she'd done what she had.

All those thoughts passed through her mind in the split seconds it took her to calibrate it to send out a crippling wave of horror and terror: a concentrated dose of the worst nightmares given potent form. In front of her car, the assault team fell almost as one, their weapons lying unheeded around them as they curled up and screamed and screamed, their hands at their ears in a futile attempt to block the empathic pulse.

Two turned over onto their sides and vomited.

It was just as well that Naya wasn't tall enough to see through the

windscreen. Sascha had already opaqued the window next to Naya; she'd
also blocked a large percentage of her baby's audio channels, leaving only
enough that Naya wouldn't be scared and could still hear her mother.
Now she turned to smile at her child while actually looking out through
the back window to see if Dorian was still trapped inside his vehicle.

The doors of the truck that had hit him were open. One man lay
crumpled by the driver's side door, while others lay on the road between
her car and the truck. They'd planned to box her in on every side. She
didn't really care about their plans; her attention was on Dorian.

Because the sentinel had managed to climb out of his mangled Jeep.

He was limping badly but was mobile.

Stopping partway on his walk to her, he lifted what looked like a phone
to his ear.

When her phone rang heartbeats later, the sound dull, she snatched
up the handbag she'd left on the passenger seat and dug through it with
frantic hands. *There!* "Dorian, are you okay?"

Naya gave a big sigh of relief. "Dori!"

Focused on the sentinel as she was, Sascha felt the deep stab of pain
that pulsed through Dorian as her cub's innocent cry traveled through
the line. "Sascha?" His voice was gritty.

"Yes?"

"Can you shield me?"

Her eyes widened. "How are you still standing?" She immediately
pushed a shield around his mind to block out her own broadcast. "I was
hoping you were too far away." And that he'd forgive her if he caught the
edge of it—she'd had to make certain she caught the assailants in the
truck so they couldn't hurt him while he was pinned down.

"I knew it was you," Dorian said and, voice suddenly far less strained,
gave her a wave. "And it was nothing like what these fuckers are apparently
feeling. I'm guessing the fact you're connected to me through our web has
something to do with it."

"I'll come—"

"No, stay inside the car. Keep the squirt company and tell her Dori says hello." As she watched, he nudged a fallen assailant with the foot of his injured leg. "These bastards are all down and fucked." He sounded pleased by that. "How long can you keep it up? Should I incapacitate?" He had a gun in hand, aimed it at a pair of kneecaps as she watched.

Sweat broke out over Sascha's spine as she thought about what she'd done and what Dorian was asking her. But she had to see this through—the threat to Naya and to Dorian remained. "I can keep it up until help arrives." It was the first burst that took the most energy. Though she couldn't keep up the pulse forever, or even an hour, she knew she wouldn't need to. "Is Lucas on his way?"

"Yes," Dorian replied. "With half the pack—from every direction."

That proved to not be too much of an exaggeration. First, however, came multiple humans who lived in the area and who wanted to render assistance. They'd staggered out despite catching the edge of Sascha's blast. When she quickly pulled back the radius, belatedly realizing the extent of her reach, they ran inside their homes and raced back out with rope to help tie up the assault team.

Afterward, Sascha heard that those humans had begun calling in to DarkRiver the instant they'd seen the deliberate collision. At that point, they hadn't even realized the man inside the crushed vehicle was a leopard—they'd simply seen danger and reached for DarkRiver.

It said a lot about what the pack had become to this city.

The human residents had helped tie up three of the downed attackers when DarkRiver descended on the scene. So did Drew and Indigo. The SnowDancer couple had been in the city when they'd received the emergency alert through DarkRiver's network of local contacts.

Teijan also arrived on a high-speed jetcycle, as did Max Shannon. Sascha hadn't even known the ex-cop—and Sophia Russo's husband—was in the alert network, though she should have. He was Nikita's security chief, and for all Nikita's flaws, she'd already proven she'd protect her child and grandchild.

"We're fine." She scrambled out of the car when Lucas ran to them. She'd stayed locked inside until then, both so Dorian wouldn't worry when he had other matters to handle and so she could keep tailoring her broadcast to keep it clear of any rescuers. "We're fine," she repeated as his arms locked around her.

"Naya?"

"She didn't hear or see anything. Just got a little worried about Dorian." Her heart thumped against her rib cage, her body starting to shake. "He's hurt."

"Jason's doing some first aid." Pulling back so he could scan her for injuries, Lucas said, "After that, he'll take Dorian straight to an ER for deep scans to ensure there are no internal injuries. Tamsyn's been alerted."

"Papa!"

Lucas flexed his fisted hand and took a deep, steadying breath. Then, one hand firm around Sascha's, he leaned down to smile at Naya through the open driver's side door. "Hello, princess. What are you doing? I thought you were heading home?"

Naya's response was earnest and largely incomprehensible.

"Yes," Lucas said, clearly responding more to her tone than her words. "Papa's going to take care of it. Don't worry."

Naya smiled.

Lucas reached in and over to tap her on the nose before rising to his full height beside the car again. "I'll drive you home." It was a growl, his panther prowling behind his eyes. "Don't argue, all right?"

"I won't." Sascha's throat was dry. Her muscles felt like jelly all at once. She needed to have him close as much as he needed to be close. But before she could surrender to the need to bury herself in her mate's arms, there was one other thing she had to do. "I have to see Dorian."

"Go." Lucas stayed by the car, so Naya could see and hear him as he oversaw the retrieval operation.

While Sascha had stopped her broadcast the instant there were enough people on scene to disarm and restrain the attackers, the mercenaries remained disoriented and shaky on their feet as they were thrown into DarkRiver vehicles for transport. Dorian, meanwhile, was seated in the very back of an SUV, the trunk door lifted to block out the sun while Jason patched him up.

Tamsyn had taken the young male on as an assistant after he showed an interest in studying medicine. He didn't have a changeling healing ability but that didn't matter if he proved himself suited to be a medic. Another doctor in the pack would take the weight off Tamsyn when it came to a number of injuries that didn't need her specialist attention.

The interesting thing was that Jason showed no inclination to go roaming anytime soon. It was similar behavior to that of most healers—they loved being near pack too much. If they did travel, it was for short bursts only.

"Even though he doesn't have the healing ability," Tamsyn had told Sascha, "I think he's a healer at heart; he's just going to practice the drive a different way. His grades are more than good enough to get him into medical school."

Calm and collected, the twenty-one-year-old had stopped the blood flowing from Dorian's head wound. He hadn't, however, had the chance to wipe away the rust red that had already run down the side of Dorian's face. He was too busy checking the sentinel for broken bones and internal injuries using a handheld scanner.

Dorian already had visible heavy bruising on one side of his face and no doubt his body. The colors were vivid against the surfer-gold of his skin. And his white-blond hair, it was matted dark red on the side with the wound.

"Dorian." Close to tears, she touched her fingers to the undamaged side of the sentinel's face.

Taking hold of her hand, he pressed a kiss to her palm. "I'm fine, Sascha darling. A little busted up, but that was those bastards and that fucking goddamn truck. You can't scare me."

Sascha thought of the pulse she'd sent out, knew it must've been horrible. And still he'd fought his way out in an effort to protect her and Naya. "Can I make it up to you?"

A curious look that was so feline, she didn't need his eyes to change to know she was talking to the cat now. "Go for it."

He gave a startled laugh as she blanketed him in a wave of innocent happiness that tasted of all the pups and cubs that Sascha knew. "Damn, that's good shit." His grin was beautiful. "You could make a fortune charging for a hit."

Having satisfied himself the sentinel wasn't bleeding inside, Jason glanced up from taping Dorian's ankle. "I want some."

Sascha poured the same sensations over the younger male.

"Whoa!" He grinned, too, held up a hand. She high-fived it before looking guiltily back at Dorian.

The sentinel crooked a finger and, when she leaned in close, he dropped a soft kiss on her lips. The affectionate touch of one of her favorite pack-mates, it told her he really was all right. "I'm tough," he whispered. "Go pet Lucas. He's freaked out."

Still shaky inside, she left Dorian and Jason with another wave of childish joy, so pure and unfettered that it made both men collapse into laughter once more. Then she walked straight back into Lucas's arms. He held her trembling form until she could breathe again. At which point, she stroked her hands down the viciously taut muscles of his back.

"I'm unharmed and so is our daughter," she whispered in a subvocal tone, aware of the sharp little ears in the car. "We're not easy prey."

"Damn straight you're not." A hard kiss, his claws brushing her hair and skin as he cupped her face with one hand. "Come on, mate. Let's get our cub home—we have enough people here we can trust to keep us updated."

Chapter 19

IT WAS CLAY who called them with that update, the leopard having taken charge of the scene after Lucas's departure. They'd reached the aerie in the interim. Leaving Naya busy with her play blocks, the two of them walked out onto the balcony to talk to Clay. Lucas answered the call on visual and put the sentinel on speaker at a volume Sascha could hear but that wouldn't reach Naya.

"It's the same mercenary team the Rats warned us about," Clay said. "We confirmed their identity using various back channels courtesy of Nikita's tentacles."

Sascha had already received a call from Max Shannon. He'd patched her through to Nikita, who'd wanted to see firsthand that Sascha and Naya were all right. Sascha had heard the ruthless tone in her mother's voice, known that had Nikita not been as weak as she was right now, she'd have ripped the truth from the mercenaries' minds. The fact that they'd have been drooling vegetables afterward wouldn't have bothered her in the least.

"How the fuck did they stay under this long?" Lucas asked as Sascha's gut went cold.

Perhaps she and her mother weren't that different after all.

"They're a crack team. They come in and set up, then don't move until the timing is perfect. Makes them almost impossible to catch if you don't get them the instant they enter."

"It sounds like they're talking." Fine tremors started to race once more over Sascha's skin.

The last word of her statement broke.

Lucas squeezed her nape. "Remember," he murmured so low only she could hear, "you did what you did to protect our cub. Those bastards would've taken her, hurt her."

Sascha gave a jagged nod as, on the phone, Clay said, "I got one of them to talk pretty damn fast by threatening him with what happened out on the road." An edge of amusement in the sentinel's voice.

"I would never torture anyone," Sascha blurted out, her stomach churning at the idea of it.

"I know that, Sascha," Clay said with unexpected gentleness. "The assholes don't."

His immediate agreement eased her sudden fear that her packmates would see her as a monster now that they knew what she could do.

"They were aware of DarkRiver's strength before they took the job," Clay continued, "but the money on the table was enough to make up for the risk. They were totally focused on Dorian as the threat, expected Sascha to be a soft target."

Lucas's furious growl reverberated through her bones. "Psy?" he snarled as she petted him to calm as he'd earlier done for her.

"Four Psy and three changelings," Clay replied. "Lion, if you can believe it. Not strong dominants or we'd never have gotten the truth out of them so quickly, but strong enough."

"Lion?" Lucas shook his head.

Seeing Sascha's confusion, he said, "Lions are all about family, all about building a pride and sticking with it, more so than any other feline changelings in the world. Mercenary work is for loners."

"Kicker is that these three *are* family," Clay added. "Brother and two sisters." The sentinel's voice turned harsh on his next words. "They were hired to kidnap Naya. Sascha was disposable, but Naya was to be taken alive or they wouldn't get the second half of their fee."

Fury roared through Sascha, pushing aside any lingering echoes of guilt. She felt the same rage in Lucas. His grip threatened to crack the phone. "Who was the client?"

"All anonymous, with the drop-off to be arranged once they had Naya." Clay's eyes glittered, hard and feral. "But the lioness who's the leader of the mercenaries isn't stupid. She got her electronics person—her younger brother—to run a trace. Brother managed to link the first half of the money transfer back to a small company held by an ocelot pack out of southern Texas: SkyElm."

Sascha frowned, unable to imagine why a pack of the smaller feline changelings, whose markings were also black on gold, would want to attack DarkRiver.

Beside her, Lucas's claws sliced out, but his voice was rational. "We ever have any dealings with them?"

"Mercy was with me the entire time." Clay tapped his ear to indicate how Mercy had attended the interrogation. "She ran the data as I got it and says we've never had any real contact with this pack. From what she was able to dig up, they're well regarded in their region, though they're not the strongest by a long shot. And they're part of Trinity." Clay's voice took on the harsh edge of a growl. "It makes no sense unless it's a setup, or—"

"—or they're in the Consortium, too," Sascha completed softly, because changelings weren't a unanimous group by any measure. Each pack made up its own mind about any political alliances. Given how well the Consortium had almost pulled off its earlier attempts to foment trouble between all three races, as well as their success in snatching BlackSea's most vulnerable swimmers, they undoubtedly had changeling members: advisers who were betraying their own people for power and profit.

"Rip the evidence apart," Lucas growled, then proved his mind remained icily clear despite his fury. "There may be a deeper game in play."

"What?" Clay swore the instant after he spoke. "The Consortium . . . or, hell, Ming LeBon may be trying to enrage us enough to take out SkyElm. Why?"

"To mess up Trinity, to make us the bad guys? Who the fuck knows? Use whoever you need to tear this down to the bones—and tap Nikita's intel system through Max." Lucas fisted his hand in Sascha's hair. "We don't make *any* moves until we know for certain. DarkRiver is not about to be played by a bunch of power-hungry bastards."

PART 2

Chapter 20

SIENNA COULDN'T BELIEVE what Hawke had done. She simply couldn't *believe* it! She'd just returned to the SnowDancer den after lunch with Kit and had intended to update Hawke on what the young soldier had told her about the mood of the city in the aftermath of Naya's attempted kidnapping the previous day.

Kit had also shared some personal news in confidence, but he hadn't asked her to keep it from Hawke. People didn't expect mates to keep secrets from each other. And Sienna knew Hawke wouldn't say a word if she told him it couldn't go any further. In truth, she'd been planning to unload on him, because while she was happy for Kit, the leopard was one of her closest friends and she felt a selfish desire to tell him to delay things a little longer.

Only her mate wasn't here for her to talk to. He'd left her a message on their private comm, inside their quarters. A *message*. "I'm going to kill him," she muttered, stalking down the den corridor near the infirmary. "I'm going to wring His Alphaness's neck, then I'm going to kick his—"

She halted before she slammed into her uncle Walker's chest. "I have to go," she said, trying to swing around him.

He stopped her by the simple expedient of putting a single hand on her upper arm. Sienna froze. She would never disrespect the man who was her father in every way that mattered. "Uncle Walker, I need to leave," she said, her skin vibrating with her urgency. "Hawke's gone out to confront Ming!"

"It's a business meeting," Walker said.

Sienna sucked in a breath. "You *knew*?" Betrayal was a slap across her face. "Why didn't you tell me?" Even though she was furious with Hawke, she could understand his boneheaded behavior. Her alpha mate was so protective of her that, sometimes, he acted before he thought. And when it came to Ming LeBon, he was more feral wolf than civilized man. That didn't excuse what he'd done, but it at least made sense.

But for her uncle to go along with it when he knew exactly how good Sienna was at taking care of herself? She stared uncomprehendingly at the planes of his face, his expression calm in the face of her rage.

"Hawke is incapable of thinking clearly with you anywhere near Ming." Walker held her gaze with the unusual light green of his. "But you would've insisted on going with him."

"Of course I would've insisted!" Sienna fisted her hands. "Ming is a combat telepath!" He could smash Hawke's natural shields open with far less effort than almost any other Tp on the planet, kill him within seconds.

"Judd's with him."

Relief and betrayal punched into her in equal measures. "Him, too?" she demanded. "Was I the only *adult* Lauren who wasn't informed of Hawke's plans?"

Walker closed both hands around her upper shoulders, held her still when she would've broken away. "Hawke did this with a cool head, Sienna." The faintest hint of a smile. "Cool enough to know it'd be better to ask for forgiveness than to convince you of the sense of his plan."

"Don't patronize me, Uncle Walker!" It roared out of her. "I'm not a child anymore! I'm his *mate*."

Walker looked at her for a long moment, long enough that she started to want to fidget. But instead of wearing her down in that way only he could do, he inclined his head. "Yes," he said. "Hawke should've spoken to you. As for Judd and me"—his expression shifted, revealing a tenderness that destroyed her—"we can't help ourselves. You're a piece of our heart."

All her anger crumbled.

Falling into his arms, she let his warmth and love and strength surround her, ground her, her face pressed to the smoky blue of his shirt, her eyes hot. Walker had been the calm anchor in the ugly storm of her childhood after her mother died, the one person she'd known she could count on even when she was caught in a monster's grip. He was the one who'd made the Laurens into a family, refusing to let go no matter what. Never once had he betrayed her.

"I'm sorry for yelling," she said when she could speak past the surge of emotion. "I'm just worried about Hawke."

Cupping the back of her head, Walker said, "Can you sense any trouble through the mating bond?"

She shook her head, the realization calming her enough that she could think past her worry and anger. "Why is he even talking to Ming? Hawke hates him, wants to tear him into tiny pieces with his bare claws."

"Let's walk outside. I'll tell you his reasoning."

"Whatever it is, I'm still going to strangle him when he gets back."

HAWKE knew he'd be heading straight into his mate's fiery temper when he returned to the den, but that didn't matter. Not when what he did here today would spell the start of the end of Ming LeBon.

Being in the same room as the former Councilor and his cold metallic scent and not gutting the other man went against his natural instincts, but the wolf understood what it was to protect pups. And right now, hard as that was to swallow, Ming's stabilizing presence was protecting a heck of a lot of pups in Europe.

That would change.

If Hawke had to nudge Ming slowly out of power to make him viable prey, then so be it; the wolf was willing to listen to the human in this hunt. Because both parts of him knew that sooner or later, Hawke would tear out Ming's throat. For threatening Sienna's life, for hurting her when she'd been a child, for all those Ming had tortured and murdered.

"As I noted in my message, Mr. LeBon, SnowDancer has made a

competing offer." The words were spoken by a slight human male seated behind the desk by the windows. Stenson was doing a good job of keeping his cool, but Hawke could smell the sour tang of nerves on the mustachioed man with pale white skin.

It wasn't every day that a small computronics company fielded two buyout offers: one from an ex-Councilor turned de facto ruler of a large chunk of Europe, the other from the biggest changeling pack in the country.

Hawke, his back to the window, stood to the right of the desk. Sitting next to Ming in the spare guest chair on the other side of the desk wasn't an option. Judd stood outside the office door, but Hawke could sense him, knew the other man was protecting his mind from psychic threats. Whatever tricks Ming had, he'd have to mobilize into full battle mode to use them against an ex-Arrow and an alpha wolf.

"SnowDancer isn't known for its interest in cutting-edge computronics."

Hawke shrugged at Ming's frigid comment. "Those who survive are those who adapt."

"I'll increase my offer by ten percent."

Stenson glanced at Hawke.

"We'll beat that," Hawke responded. "By one percent."

Ming made another counteroffer; Hawke countered it by another one percent. They went on like that until Ming got the point: SnowDancer was determined to buy this company and gain control of its innovative ideas.

That Ming hadn't already stolen the company's secrets was thanks to some very clever structuring. Stenson was in charge of the company's finances and did the deals, but he knew nothing of its technological breakthroughs beyond what he needed to facilitate the financial side of things. The company had also succeeded in keeping secret the identities of its developers.

No Psy could pluck out secrets from a mind if he or she didn't know which mind to target.

"It appears the company is yours." Ming left without further words. Hawke bared his teeth.

When Stenson flinched, he realized the gesture had been more lupine aggressiveness than human smile. Ah well, the man would have to get used to dealing with wolves sooner or later.

Since Yuki and the rest of SnowDancer's legal eagles had already checked the details, Hawke finalized the deal with his signature, then held out his hand to Stenson. "Happy to be working with you."

The bewildered man shook his hand. "You won't be restructuring?"

"Expect a SnowDancer team to drop by, go over things with you. But at this stage, we plan to leave you to go about your business." Hawke had bought the company primarily to frustrate Ming and ensure the ex-Councilor couldn't get a foothold in this part of the world, but it actually *was* a good investment. "Now if you'll excuse me, I have another deal to complete."

Five minutes after that, he'd cut Ming off from acquiring the majority share in a financial entity based out of Liechtenstein, and an hour after that, while Judd drove them back up to the den, he made it clear to a corporation that they would lose their biggest client—SnowDancer—should they agree to work with Ming LeBon.

This was war and people had to choose sides.

When he hung up, Judd raised an eyebrow. "If I didn't know better, I'd think you were a ruthless CEO."

"I *am* a ruthless CEO." It was his official description on all the businesses that ran under the SnowDancer banner. "You're the one who recommended we watch for Ming trying to infiltrate SnowDancer territory through business interests." It was why Hawke had known what Ming was up to—he'd had SnowDancer's Cooper and DarkRiver's Bastien arrange a network of eyes and ears in the region's business circles.

"I never expected you to take to business combat like a fish to water."

"It's not my preferred way to fight"—a slight understatement—"but it's nice to know I just cost Ming millions of dollars." Cutting off a little more of the evil bastard's power base.

"How far will you go?"

"All the way." As long as he played a strategic game, SnowDancer had the strength and the financial reach to not only keep Ming out of this territory, but to break the ex-Councilor's grip on Europe. "I should've figured it out earlier, but I was so set on tearing off his head that I didn't think about other options." Now that he had, Hawke was starting to enjoy the hunt. "I'm going to bring him down so low that he has no allies and is running for his life on the streets. *Then* I'll tear off his head."

Judd's eyes glinted. "Losing power would be worse than death for Ming."

Hawke showed his teeth again. "Then the bastard's going to be in a lot of pain starting today."

His phone buzzed with an incoming message from Cooper confirming that SnowDancer now owned a ten percent share in a company Ming relied on for supplies for one of his other corporations. Give me six more months, Cooper had written, and we'll have a fifty-one percent share. The best part is that SnowDancer will make a profit long term even as we freeze out LeBon.

Hawke's wolf threw back its head inside him and howled in triumph.

Letters to Nina

From the private diaries of Father Xavier Perez
March 28, 2074

Nina,

I haven't written for many days. The Psy assassin and I have been in the mountains, laying a trail to disguise the path that leads to the hiding place of the villagers the other assassins are coming to murder.

I thought we'd fight, spill blood, but this Psy, he tells me to be intelligent, to stop thinking with an alcohol-soaked brain and to remember that we are only two against an entire death squad.

"We can't win one on one," he says. "We can win only by stealth and cunning and being smarter than the enemy."

I've never fought this way, in the shadows. Even when I ran with the human rebels in the first months after our village was sacked, we aimed to do violence against those who'd harm our people. Any rebels who died in the course of our campaign were held up as heroes.

The Psy assassin doesn't know about the rebel cells. I'll never betray those men and women to a man who might turn on me without warning. But he said something to me that was eerily apt: "Don't try to be a hero, Xavier. A dead hero can't help anyone."

Xavier

Chapter 21

NIGHT HAD FALLEN by the time Hawke and Judd drove up the final track to the den.

Impatience clawed at Hawke. Searching for something to take his mind off the hunger to see his mate, he said, "What time are you and Brenna heading to Cooper's territory?" He knew the two had plans to visit friends in the satellite den. "Driving, right?"

Judd shook his head. "We decided to catch a quick flight at eight tomorrow, since our visit's only going to be a couple of days anyway. It'll give us more time on the ground." He brought the vehicle into the underground garage under the den. "Good luck with Sienna." Unsaid were the words that he'd need it.

Leaving the lieutenant to deal with the vehicle, Hawke jogged from the garage to his and Sienna's quarters. He was halfway there when he realized the mating bond was tugging him in the opposite direction. Reversing course, he ran out into the night darkness and through the trees for nearly twenty minutes until he saw her standing on a rise, looking out over the fields below.

The moon was full tonight, her body outlined against a sky dotted with stars.

It hit him again, that she was his. His mate. Extraordinary and strong and . . . furious.

Wincing at the look she shot him out of cardinal eyes gone a dangerous black, he braced himself. "Miss me?"

She growled before hauling him close for a kiss, her hands buried in his hair. It was a kiss of claiming, of branding, of angry welcome. Groaning, he had his hands on her hips, his body having turned rock hard in a single pulse, when she pushed him away. "If you ever do that to me again, I won't forgive you."

He'd expected anger but not this brittle edge to her voice. "Walker was supposed to talk to you, make sure you knew what was going on."

"My mate should've talked to me." The obsidian of her gaze flickered with a translucent flame, her tone flat.

Hawke's gut twisted; this wasn't anger. It was deeper, harder. "You would've wanted to come and there was no way in hell I was taking you." Even the idea of her anywhere near Ming made his wolf threaten to turn into a primal killing machine.

"Look at this!" Sienna held out a hand, on which danced a red and amber flame. "I'm not helpless! I'm the least helpless person in the world!"

Hawke thrust his hands into her hair, gripped. "But you're mine to protect!" His heart pounded like a bass drum. "If anything happened to you—"

He couldn't say it, couldn't even think it. "I've lost too many people, baby. I can't lose you."

When Sienna cupped his face, her hands were fierce and gentle both. "You won't. We're in this together." Her nails dug a little into his skin. "Trust me! Treat me as your mate!"

"I do!" Hawke's voice was turning more and more into a growl. "Why would you think otherwise?"

"Why would you hide things from me?" Sienna yelled, her chest heaving.

They stared at each other for a single, endless heartbeat before their lips were locked in a kiss so passionate that Sienna went up in flames around them. He should've been worried, but he was never worried with the woman who fucking owned him. Her cold fire always knew pack. And it definitely knew her mate.

He took her to the ground, or maybe she took him. He tore off her clothes, she tore off his; their naked bodies slid against one another and when he pulled up her thigh and nudged at her with his cock, he found her wet and ready. Then she bit down on his lower lip while clawing his back and it was all over.

He thrust deep, pinning her to the earth.

One stroke, two, and Sienna was clenching so tightly around him that he couldn't hold back. He gripped her shoulder with his teeth as he came, so hard that he knew he'd leave a mark. Good. He wanted her to wear his mark. Her nails made sure he'd be wearing hers.

The fire flamed hot red, then wild amber around them, a dangerous kiss from his very dangerous mate. A mate who was still pissed off with him when the fire sank into the earth to leave them lying entangled and naked under the stars, neither one able to breathe properly for at least five minutes.

Hawke could've dealt with an angry mate. He couldn't deal with the hurt he saw in her expression.

Hand cradling the side of her face, he said, "I'm sorry." It was difficult for an alpha to say that, but never to his mate, never when he was fucking wrong. "I was trying to protect you, but I did that by hurting you. I'm so goddamn sorry."

Sienna's eyes remained dark, without stars, but she spread her hand over his heart. "I was so terrified for you."

Hawke thought about how insane he'd go if he knew she was alone with Ming, and wanted to kick his own ass. "I took Judd," he said, even knowing that was no defense for what he'd done to her, the pain he'd inflicted. "But I was an asshole. I admit it. I won't do it again."

Sienna's lips kicked up a little at the corners, the first stars appearing in her eyes. "I think this may go down in history," she said as relief punched him in the gut. "An unreserved apology from Your Alphaness."

"Smart-ass." He petted her as he spoke, apologizing with his touch as much as with his words. "Seriously—I was thinking with my heart, not my brain."

"Ugh." Sienna pushed at his chest. "Stop making it hard to be mad at you."

Her expression turned on the next breath. "You won't do it again? Leave me out of a decision that affects both of us?"

Tugging her to his chest as he rolled over onto his back, he brushed her hair off her face. "I promise."

Sienna nodded. "Okay. I know you always keep your promises."

The fist around his heart began to open. "Want to know why I went to the meeting?"

When she nodded, he told her, man and wolf both supremely smug when her expression showed admiration for his tactics. "I wouldn't have expected you to take Judd's idea and run with it like that," she said afterward, kicking up her feet. "You're fiercely intelligent, but you don't usually think sneaky."

His wolf decided to take that as a compliment. "Sneaky is for cats," he growled. "But I have been spending a lot of time with Lucas lately. I guess some of it rubbed off."

Sienna's smile was sharp. "I like the idea of messing with Ming's financial foundation." Her eyes narrowed in thought. "You know Devraj Santos hates him, too?"

Hawke nodded. He didn't have any real details on what Ming had done to Dev's wife, Katya, but he didn't need them—because what he did know was that she'd been kept captive by Ming LeBon. Dev's hatred of Ming was something he'd picked up on the last time the Forgotten leader had visited SnowDancer territory to catch up with the Forgotten children embedded into SnowDancer—protected by being claimed as wolves to the outside world.

Hawke had said something about Ming that involved Ming being dead, and Dev had agreed, his voice holding a near-metallic chill that was almost Psy—except for the fury behind it, the rage Hawke could all but taste.

"Katya shot him in the head. The fucker survived."

Running a hand down the sexy curve of his mate's back as the memory of Dev's angry words echoed through his mind, he said, "Arrows have to hate him, too." That would've been easy enough to guess with the defection of the squad from under Ming's leadership, even without Judd's close connection to current active-duty Arrows.

"Hmm." Sienna tapped her kiss-swollen lower lip with a finger. "Snow-Dancer can blindside Ming a few times, but eventually he's going to figure out all our major business entities and start to avoid anything where we could have an impact."

Hawke bared his teeth. "That's satisfying on its own." It would mean the pack was forcing Ming to make financial decisions that weren't in his best interest.

"Yes, but if we get a few other people involved . . ."

Hawke wasn't used to playing with people outside his pack—and okay, Lucas, since the cat had proven his loyalty to the blood bond between the two packs. But he could see the positives of Sienna's idea. "Enough people in on this and it'll become very difficult for Ming to predict who might have an interest in what—or who might develop an interest."

Sienna nodded. "Dev has financial expertise but I'm not sure about the Arrows—I know Judd didn't get any financial training as an Arrow. He learned what he did on his own. We don't want to put anyone in a bad position."

Hawke nipped at her lips just because, growled when she dug her nails into him in response. It wasn't a complaint. "This is only fun if everyone *but* Ming comes out a winner," he agreed. "I'll ask Judd to check whether the Arrows have someone with financial smarts. We have people we can lend them if they don't." He ran one hand through the dark ruby fire of Sienna's hair. *Yes*, his wolf thought, *this is better. Working with my mate, coming up with ideas together.*

Smiling at him, she ran a finger down his nose. "I feel your wolf prowling in there. You want to run? I have to do a sweep anyway."

"Yes." The wolf wanted her fingers in its fur, wanted to nip at her with its teeth, play with her under the moonlight.

Pushing off him, Sienna held out a hand. He took his time rising, enjoying the sight of her nude body kissed by the moonlight and clothed only in the beautiful hair he loved to play with in either form. Her smile, though, that was the most beautiful part of her. He kept that image in his mind as he shifted, the wrenching pain and stunning ecstasy of the shift rippling through him as his body exploded into millions of particles of light, then reformed in another shape.

It was still him. Always. In either form.

He shook his body to settle his fur into place, discovered his mate was pulling on her jeans. Picking up her T-shirt while her back was turned, he started to pad away.

"Hawke!" Her outraged cry came a second later. "Give that back!"

Huffing in laughter, he upped his pace.

An infuriated scream echoed on the air currents, but Sienna didn't come after him. When he glanced back, he saw her pulling on *his* shirt—which happened to be torn down one side thanks to her angry, impatient hands earlier. Using the torn halves, she tied the shirt off at the side of her abdomen, then smirked at him and picked up his jeans.

"Guess you don't need these?" she said before balling them up and throwing them over the side of the rise.

Dropping her T-shirt, he loped back to her and, without warning, nipped her butt. She yelped, clamped a hand over the part he'd bitten, turned to look at him with temper in her eyes. "You are in trouble."

Fire arced a half centimeter from his nose.

Making a sound more common to a startled pup than a tough-as-nails alpha, he jumped back . . . to hear his mate laughing so hard she could barely take a breath. When he growled again, she just laughed harder. And then she was on her knees and her hands were in his fur and she was pressing her face to his while the jeweled dark red of her hair fell around him and life was perfect.

HAWKE kept Sienna company all night on her security shift. After their run through the area assigned to her, she told him about her lunch with Kit, the baby cat alpha she insisted on having as a friend.

"Stop growling." She glared at him from her standing watch position.

He was sitting in wolf form beside her, his fur rippling in the breeze. He growled again, just to rile her up.

Eyes glinting, she pointed at him. "I think you've been hanging around cats too much. You're getting sly."

This time, his growl was one of insult.

Her lips twitched. "Got you." Coming down on one knee to run her hand through the silver-gold of his fur, while still keeping an eye on her watch area, she said, "City's angry but calm. Word's gotten around about how quickly the attempted kidnapping was defused, and that's helping turn aggression into pride."

Hawke nodded. Strange as it was for a changeling to accept, the humans in the city felt a certain ownership in DarkRiver in the sense that it was *their* pack that held such power. That extended to SnowDancer in the regions where the wolves held sway. The oddest thing was that a number of local Psy seemed to believe the same, feeling more loyalty toward the packs than they did toward the Ruling Coalition. It wasn't something either Hawke or Lucas had expected or were used to, but as alphas they saw the pragmatic benefits.

And as two men born with powerful protective drives, they refused to let down the people who'd given them their trust—even if those people weren't pack. That, too, was a situation Hawke could've never predicted. Changeling alphas didn't run for mayor or for any other political office for good reason; their primary and primal focus was the pack.

The latter would never change, but the line of communication between the packs and the other residents of their territories was stronger and more in use than it had ever before been. A threat to any part of that territory was considered a threat to the packs, and as such, their actions protected all who called it home.

"There's no more news yet on exactly who was behind the mercenaries," Sienna added. "At least not as far as Kit knows." Rising to her feet again, she began to walk the perimeter.

He walked beside her.

"Leila Savea remains missing." Sienna's tone turned somber. "It's going to take a miracle to find her, isn't it?" Her eyes met his, the sorrow in them potent.

She, too, had once been trapped in a nightmare.

Hawke wished he could tell her that they *would* find the vanished BlackSea changeling, but Sienna didn't want empty comfort, had experienced too much harsh reality to accept it.

Instead of giving her words that meant nothing, he held her gaze until she nodded, understanding his promise: *No one would stop looking for Leila Savea until they either found her . . . or her body. If, for some unfathomable reason, others stopped, SnowDancer would pick up the baton.*

Together, they began to walk again.

At times they talked, but mostly, they just enjoyed being together. As night turned to the gray before dawn, Tai came to relieve Sienna. The young soldier with his big shoulders and slightly slanted eyes of blue-green grinned a hello at Hawke, but he had the good sense not to attempt to tease his alpha about being out all night with his mate. Hawke wasn't above teasing, but Tai was too young to have earned the right to that much informality.

Sienna had always been the single exception to that rule. From the day she'd entered the den, she'd seemed to make it her mission to drive Hawke insane. He should've known then and there that she was destined to be his mate.

"Why are you smiling?"

Still in wolf form, he glanced up at her question.

"It doesn't matter what form you wear. I know." An answer to his unspoken question. "I can feel it inside." She touched a fist to her heart. "Something's amusing you."

He bolted into a run without warning, challenging her to keep up with him. Laughing, she pounded toward the den alongside him. They both knew he was throttling his speed for her, but that took none of the pleasure out of it. His wolf loved running with her.

Racing through the dew-laden quiet of the White Zone, they pelted into the den and past startled packmates who jumped out of the way. One yelled out, "Act your age not your shoe size!"

Another growled, "Dignity, Hawke!"

Both of those hecklers were his friends, their words tinged with laughter as well as joy that Hawke had found a mate, found happiness.

Continuing to race through the corridors that were quiet except for the early risers, they tumbled into their quarters together and Sienna locked the door behind them. Hawke shifted in the seconds it took her to do that. Scooping her up in his arms the next instant, he ran into the bedroom to throw her on the bed.

Her hair haloed around her in a ruby-red fan, her face flushed from their run and her breathing rough. "That was *fun!*"

Coming down over her, he took a morning kiss, his wolf rumbling inside his chest. "I was smiling because I was thinking about what a pain in the butt you were as a teenager."

"You liked me even then." She poked at his shoulder. "Admit it."

"Never." He grinned and pushed off the bed before her wandering hands made it impossible for him to do anything but strip her naked, make her sigh his name. "You need to eat and then you need to sleep."

A scowl. "You going to sleep with me?"

Hawke was fully capable of going without sleep, but since SnowDancer wasn't at any kind of emergency alert, he didn't need to. "Yes, Sienna Lauren Snow," he said, drawing out her name because he liked the way it sounded. "I'll be sleeping with you."

She sat up and reached back to quickly braid her hair. "Good. Let's go get breakfast."

Hawke had recovered the jeans Sienna had thrown over the rise, but had left them—and her T-shirt—cached for later retrieval. Grabbing another pair, he hauled them on, then shrugged into an old black tee before taking her hand.

In sync, with no more need for any further discussion, they made their way together to the room where breakfast was laid out for those packmates coming off night shift or going out on an early-morning shift.

"Sin!" Sienna's best friend, Evie, waved them over to a table where she sat alone, nursing a cup of coffee. "Hi, Hawke."

"Good morning." Bending, he pressed a kiss to her temple, her hair cool black silk under his touch and her eyes deepest gray.

It was extraordinary how differently he saw Evie and Sienna, though they were near the same age. Indigo's submissive sister was so young in the life she'd lived, so innocent. The alpha in him felt only protectiveness when he looked at Evie, could never imagine seeing her as a woman.

Sienna . . . wolf and man, he'd always accepted her as a strong opponent, even when she'd been too young for him to see her as anything else.

"What are you doing up?" Sienna asked her friend as Evie rose to pour Sienna and Hawke coffee from the carafe on the counter.

Hawke accepted the small gift with a smile of thanks. Had he insisted on getting his own coffee, she'd have lost that sunny light in her eyes, started to feel redundant. She wasn't. No submissive was. Dominants were the fighters of a pack. Submissives took care of creating the home they protected.

It was a perfect balance in a healthy pack.

"I had breakfast with Tai." Evie's cheeks flushed with happiness. "He told me he was taking over from you, so I thought I'd wait."

Hawke had just accepted a hot bacon roll Evie passed over from the tray that must've been brought in a bare minute earlier, when his attention was caught by another woman who'd walked into the otherwise empty room. Alice Eldridge. A gifted human researcher who'd been forcibly put into cryonic sleep for over a hundred years and had woken to find everyone she'd ever known was dead.

Her hair had grown back in the ensuing time, the spiral curls rich brown and gold against brown skin that had regained its glow. Her body, too, was no longer skin and bones. She'd taken up climbing again, regained the lithe muscle tone she'd had before her long sleep. But Alice's eyes continued to hold a relentless sadness. Unable to see a member of his pack that way, Hawke put down his roll and, leaving Sienna chatting to Evie, walked over to Alice.

She hadn't yet accepted that she was a SnowDancer, wasn't sure what her place was in the world, but she was still his responsibility. Not saying a word, he wrapped his arms gently around her, loosely enough that she could escape should she want. She froze like a startled deer.

One second. Two. Three.

A cautious movement.

Alice placed her head against his chest and slid her arms around him.

He tightened his embrace.

All changelings knew that, sometimes, touch could heal what words never could.

"Thank you," she whispered afterward. "I . . . why does that make me feel safe? You're a stranger, really."

Because even a human recognized the power in an alpha wolf. "You're one of mine," Hawke told her. "Part of this family. Don't forget that."

A shaky smile before Alice nodded and joined the rest of them for breakfast.

Smiling, Evie got her tea and a roll before whispering, "I heard a rumor that a certain dominant is going to ask you out today."

Alice groaned, her lingering sadness fading—at least for now—under a wave of aggravation. Exactly as Evie had likely intended, even if it hadn't been a conscious thought on her part. Submissives were good at that, at giving others what they needed to get back on an even keel.

"What is it with wolves?" Alice said with a feminine snarl of which Hawke's wolf approved. "I've made it crystal clear that I'm not anywhere near ready to date."

Swallowing a bite of her own roll, Sienna shook her head. "You say that and certain wolves hear 'oh, she wants me to try harder.'"

Hawke wisely kept his mouth shut and started on a second roll, having already demolished the first. Evie got up to refresh his coffee, but her attention was on the conversation.

"So I should just go on a date and be awful?" Alice asked. "Bore the man to tears by talking about esoteric research papers on bat guano or the health properties of wheatgrass?" Her eyes gleamed. "It holds a certain appeal."

Shaking her head, Evie said, "No, because then all the others will think they can do a better job and it'll become a contest to see who can make you have a good time on a date."

"Yeah." Sienna nodded. "Also, if the male in question makes a real effort on the date, he might get his feelings hurt and then you'll have to figure out how to deal with a moping wolf."

Alice stared at Hawke's mate. "While the fact I'm turning the men down flat isn't hurting anyone's feelings?"

Both Sienna and Evie shook their heads, with Evie the one who explained. "Wolves love a good chase. I mean, did you hear what Drew did while he was courting my sister?"

The resulting conversation actually had Alice laughing. "No, he didn't!" she said several times, only to be met by confirmations that yes, Drew did go there, and yes, he did do that.

Content to be around his mate and packmates, Hawke just grinned and listened.

AS a result of their lingering over breakfast, he was awake when a call came through that Indigo thought he should answer. He'd just been about to strip for bed, had his T-shirt balled up in one hand.

"Psy called Pax Marshall," his lieutenant said over the comm. "He's got a proposal and I figured you'd want to take his measure."

She was right—Pax Marshall wasn't simply another CEO. He was a ruthless male who'd risen to the top of his family hierarchy at only twenty-four years of age and, according to Judd's intel, was considered one of the new powers in the Net.

Whether he has any loyalty to anyone but himself is up for question. But if he doesn't have blood on his hands, I'd be very surprised.

Judd's words fresh in his mind, Hawke pulled his T-shirt back on and said, "Transfer Marshall through."

Chapter 22

THAT AFTERNOON, SNOWDANCER Lieutenant Cooper was on his way out of the den he commanded on the northern edge of the San Gabriel mountains when he got a call from his alpha. Hawke told him that Pax Marshall, head of the Marshall Group, had proposed a joint business venture in a location in Arizona that was almost right up against the border for which Cooper was responsible.

"I don't trust him," Hawke said flatly. "Word in the PsyNet is that Pax would cut his own mother's throat to get ahead." That insight had no doubt come from Judd.

Cooper shrugged. "Judd's buddy Krychek isn't exactly cuddly." Yet, quite aside from his friendship with a SnowDancer lieutenant or the times Krychek had offered assistance to San Francisco, the male rumored to have murdered his way up the ladder had a mate who worked daily with empaths.

"Exactly." Hawke's eyes gleamed wolf-blue. "Talk to Marshall, see if we can work with him. If this is a real opportunity, dig into the ethics of the entire deal."

"Always." Cooper folded his arms, the deep bronze of his skin soaking in the sunlight that poured through the window of his office, that office hidden high in a natural curve of the mountain that held the den. "Lucas's cub all right?" His wolf growled, still enraged at the idea of anyone harming a child.

Hawke thrust a hand through his hair. "Yeah, bastards didn't touch

Naya. Lucas's people are still turning over rocks, but an ocelot pack named SkyElm has come up in the investigation. Keep an ear to the ground for any intel about them."

"Consider it done." Unfortunately, Cooper had nothing new to report to Hawke on the Consortium situation. His alpha had asked him to investigate the shadowy group using his financial contacts, see if he could pick up any kind of a trail. "These particular cockroaches are very good at hiding," he told Hawke. "Someone thought this through, locked down all the information."

"Keep working on it. I'll update you on anything that comes up on this end."

Meeting ended, Cooper went looking for Judd—the other lieutenant had arrived in Cooper's den midmorning, together with his mate, who happened to be close friends with a technician based in this den. The visit was so the women could catch up, but it also gave Judd and Cooper an opportunity to spend time together. They knew each other as all the lieutenants knew one another, but it was inevitable that they'd be closer to the lieutenants they worked with on a daily basis.

For Cooper, that was Jem, Kenji, and Tomás.

Still, his wolf liked Judd. So did the human side of Cooper. The other lieutenant had proven his loyalty to the pack—and his strong, intelligent mate looked at him with her heart in her eyes. A man who'd earned a SnowDancer woman's admiration and respect? He was all right in Cooper's book.

"Judd," he said, spotting the other man on his way out of the den.

The former Arrow was dressed in what looked like workout gear. Of course, it was all black. Arrows never got over that, apparently.

"Got a minute?" Cooper asked.

"Several if you need them." Brown eyes flecked with gold met Cooper's. "I was just planning to try the new obstacle course your trainers put in. I hear it's good."

"Fiendish is a better description." Cooper scowled. "Diabolical is another."

"Excellent."

Walking outside with his fellow lieutenant, Cooper led him in the direction of the course. "Pax Marshall, can you give me the full lowdown? He wants to talk business with us."

"A previously little-known individual who suddenly rose to prominence in his family group," Judd said. "Instinct tells me he was the power behind the throne before he took it over, at least for the final twelve months of his predecessor's reign."

Judd paused as Cooper caught an errant ball and threw it back to the kids playing nearby. "It's rumored he engineered his father's death in a car crash, but no proof. Could be propaganda he himself started—Psy both fear and admire callous expediency when it's used in a smart fashion."

Cooper rubbed at his jaw, his thumb brushing over the scar that marked his left cheek. "He's young. Twenty-four, right?"

"Yes. Don't make the mistake of underestimating him though." Judd's tone was a cool warning. "Aside from being extremely intelligent, he's a Gradient 9 telepath."

Cooper whistled, aware that the Psy Gradient went up to ten. Cardinals were all off the scale, but he'd heard it said that some of the most dangerous people in the Net were just below cardinal status. Judd was the perfect example.

"Pax hasn't been directly linked to any violence," the other man continued, "but that just means he's very good at hiding his tracks." A pause. "One thing I will say—even the squad can't find any evidence that he's ever been involved in the death of anyone I'd term an innocent."

"A ruthless but fair man," Cooper said. "Or a monster clever enough to conceal crimes that don't add positively to his image."

"Exactly."

He grinned as Judd used his telekinesis to catch a pup in the midst of an uncontrolled fall and floated the wide-eyed youngster to the ground.

"Overall, Pax Marshall is a calculating operator," Judd said, as if he'd done the rescue automatically, his mind on other matters. "My take? This is apt to be a legitimate business opportunity. He's reaching out to

SnowDancer because SnowDancer has a certain level of power in the post-Silence and post-Trinity world."

"Yeah, figures." It wasn't only the pack's own financial might that Pax Marshall would've considered, but also the influence they had on other groups. "You think he's left Silence behind?"

Judd shook his head in a hard negative. "Aden's had contact with him and he's sure Pax is ice-cold beneath the surface. He is linked into the Honeycomb, but that empathic link can be achieved with a very minor shift in thinking—my feeling is that he sees Silence as a weapon in a world where most people are held hostage to their emotions."

Cooper paused at the start of the obstacle course. "That gives me a good bead on the guy. Thanks." He gestured toward the course. "Go on, try the beast. I'll stand over there and laugh at you."

"Challenge accepted."

It wasn't until Judd started that Cooper remembered the other man was a fucking telekinetic. Oh, Judd didn't cheat. No, like all Tks, he simply moved *better*. It was hard to explain to anyone who hadn't seen a Tk in motion, but while they weren't as fluid as changelings, they were damn close. And Judd Lauren was a former Arrow, trained to be a ghost.

He moved like liquid smoke.

He still fell flat on his ass on the same obstacle that had dumped Cooper the first time around. Clapping as Judd got up—with a dark look at the obstacle—Cooper called out, "Don't feel too bad. The pups fail that one, too."

"Funny, Coop." Then the stubborn man went back to the start of the course and began again.

This time, he cleared the obstacle with grace, kept going.

By the end of the day, Judd had started the course seven times and finished it zero times. He had several bumps and bruises as well as a cut on his cheekbone and, after a shower, was sharing a drink with Cooper while they sat at an outdoor table they'd set up. "How many times before you completed it?" he asked Cooper.

"One."

"Do I look drunk?" He held up his orange juice—Psy abilities didn't mix well with alcohol, and the Psy Cooper knew tended to stay away from it.

Cooper's wolf bared its teeth inside him in lupine laughter. "Ten. So you have three more to go before I've officially beaten your Arrow ass."

"I've got tomorrow." Judd put down his drink and got up to examine the grilling machine Cooper had brought out.

Cooper was about to explain the functions when his attention was caught by the sound of female voices.

Three women walked out of the den. One belonged to Judd, one was Brenna's friend, and one was very much Cooper's. Grace came straight into his arms, all shiny and fresh from a shower. "Aw," he murmured for her ears only. "I was hoping to get a chance to clean you up." She'd told him she'd be crawling through internal ducts today as part of a routine inspection of the artificial sunlight system that illuminated the den.

Turning a little pink under the cream of her skin, his mate rose on tiptoe and nuzzled at his throat. "You could make me dirty first."

He almost groaned, his cock reacting to her words like she'd stroked him with her pretty hands—or sucked him with her pretty mouth. "When did you get to be so bad, Grace?" He liked it, liked it a hell of a lot.

"When I had to deal with a certain lieutenant." His sassy mate turned to examine the table. "You guys are all prepared."

Cooper wrapped an arm around her as other packmates came out to join them, all bringing a plate to share. It was a small gathering under a clear night sky, the air redolent with the smell of food and flavored with conversation. People came and went as shifts changed, the atmosphere low-key and relaxed. Cooper ended up sitting on the ground, as did pretty much everyone but for a couple of older packmates who joined them for an hour. He'd tugged Grace down to sit between his thighs and she stayed warm and snug against him.

At one point, he realized her eyes were closing, and as he watched her slip into sleep, he thought back to a time when his deeply submissive mate had worried about having a relationship with a dominant. Back then, she'd have looked at him in total astonishment had he told her that one day, she'd fall asleep in his arms without a care in the world, even though he had his hand gently, possessively, curled around her throat.

His wolf stretched out inside him, pleased and proud. His mate had enough courage for a thousand dominants.

EARLY the next morning, he kissed Grace good-bye, then got into a truck with two other packmates for the drive across the border to meet Pax Marshall. All three of them had rock-solid natural shields, the effectiveness of which had been confirmed by Psy members of the pack. Judd had volunteered to accompany them, but Cooper had shaken his head. "We don't want Psy like Pax thinking we're vulnerable targets without you."

Nodding, Judd had said, "Remember, if it all goes sideways, even a Gradient 9 won't be able to smash through your shields without doing significant damage—and using a ton of power. Claw out his throat at the first sign of a telepathic blow. Don't give him a second chance."

Cooper had considered carrying a weapon, decided against it. Again, it was about projecting a confidence that made it clear no SnowDancer wolf was easy prey. He'd also made a conscious decision to turn up to the meeting in jeans, work boots, and a simple white T-shirt. Pax Marshall was all sharp suits. Cooper had no intention of appearing to cater to him.

As it was, Pax surprised him. The handsome blond male, his features sharply patrician and his eyes blue, turned up in khaki cargo pants and a white T-shirt, his boots very similar to Cooper's. Their meeting place—at Pax's request—was an empty piece of land in Arizona that belonged to SnowDancer, but that they'd left undeveloped because it was too small for anything useful.

The area was open, with no way for anyone to set up an ambush.

"So," Cooper said after they'd introduced themselves. "What's your proposal?" He'd already increased his estimation of the other man's political and manipulative skills—Pax had clearly dressed to put Cooper at ease.

"This piece of land is in a prime location to provide an extension to the computronics factory on the horizon."

Cooper raised an eyebrow. "Except for the fact there's an abandoned warehouse in between on disputed land." That was why SnowDancer hadn't already bought the factory and associated land—the heirs were fighting so bitterly over the disputed parcel that it was too much hassle for too little gain. For any development to be a sound economic investment, the pack needed to own all three parcels.

"It's no longer disputed," Pax said, his expression ice-cold.

So, he wasn't pretending not to be Silent. That, too, Cooper thought, was calculated. Pax had quickly figured out that Cooper had a great bullshit detector, so he'd opted for the straight and narrow. Or was giving the impression of it at least. "Is that so?" Cooper folded his arms across his chest. "Last I heard, they were threatening to murder each other with rusty knives."

Human families could be frankly scary to a wolf.

"I bought it," Pax said. "I paid both parties."

That meant Pax had snuck in under SnowDancer's nose. But in doing so, he'd been forced to invest heavily upfront—and SnowDancer still held the winning hand. "Why would you pay twice for a useful but not prime piece of land?" Cooper asked, keeping the rest of his thoughts to himself for now.

Pax turned that arctic-blue gaze back onto the distant computronics factory. "As of this morning, I also own the factory and the land on which it sits."

"You want to make us an offer for our parcel?"

"No."

"Oh? Why?"

"I don't think you're stupid enough not to realize you own the critical piece on the chessboard."

Cooper grinned. Yes, SnowDancer understood the precise value of its land. This area was known for the kind of quiet needed for the manufacturing of the most delicate computronics. No heavy vehicle traffic, no real population, the sky clear of all air traffic, thanks to an old law no one had bothered to update, *and* no pollution.

Clean air. Quiet environment. A waterway for transport.

The three holy grails when it came to the creation of high-end computronics.

And SnowDancer had the only access to the waterway in question. "We've got you over a barrel, Marshall."

"I could hire telekinetics," Pax pointed out, his tone chilling further.

Interesting. Had the man been a wolf, Cooper would've said he was pissed off. But since he was a Psy widely thought to be deathly Silent, it was doubtless a clever psychological game.

"However," the other man continued, "it would be more efficient to bring you in as a partner."

The resulting discussion was hard-edged and pure business. Cooper made no promises, but he hammered out a deal he could take to Hawke and the other lieutenants, should, of course, Pax pass certain other tests. Ethics and the environment included.

There was also one other thing. "You do a lot of business with Ming LeBon?" he asked off-handedly.

The Psy male paused and Cooper had the feeling it was genuine. Pax hadn't expected that question, wasn't prepared for it.

"A small percentage," he said at last. "Why?"

Cooper shrugged. "Word on the street is that he's going to start to suffer significant losses. You might want to pull out before the shit hits the fan." He wasn't giving anything away, not with Ming fully aware that SnowDancer had declared war on him.

"Thank you for the advice." Pax's tone revealed nothing, but a day later, the financial grapevine was abuzz with the news that the Marshall Group had cut all ties with LeBon Enterprises.

Pax Marshall, it seemed, had chosen a side.

That didn't mean he wasn't a cobra in the grass.

Chapter 23

MING LEBON HAD ended his conversation with Pax Marshall an hour earlier without learning anything about why the Marshall Group had suddenly sold all its stocks in businesses associated with LeBon Enterprises. The arrogant young telepath who'd seized the reins of the Marshall empire had insisted the move was simply "part of the family's long-term business plan."

But Ming had heard whispers from his spies within the Marshall Group that Pax Marshall was pursuing a lucrative contract with the Snow-Dancer Wolves. That could not be a coincidence.

He was sending a message ordering one of those spies to get him more details when he received a letter with the official Trinity seal. It stated that the entire body of signatories had voted on his application to join. Despite the backroom deals he'd made, that vote hadn't come down in his favor.

He crushed the letter in his hand. "SnowDancer."

Ming wasn't used to being so blatantly blocked from anything: the majority of people were too scared of him to attempt it.

He also wasn't about to allow the wolves to push him into a situation where he'd lose face in front of the entire world. The emotions didn't matter to him, but the impact on his power base could be catastrophic. Already, he could visualize the flow-on effect of this single damning rejection, see the missed opportunities, the chipping away at his financial alliances.

Throwing the crumpled-up letter in the trash, he decided that if Snow-Dancer and its allies wanted a war, they'd get one. Ming was a combat telepath but he was also a master at strategy. *No one* could beat him on that field of battle. Certainly not wolves driven by a feral desire for vengeance.

"Send me the draft of my proposal," he said to his aide.

He'd finalize that proposal, then, when the time was right, send it to all parties, including the wolves and the Arrows. He wouldn't do this by stealth. No, he wanted the world watching and witnessing the fall of Trinity.

Chapter 24

LUCAS HAD ASSIGNED multiple people to tracking down data on the ocelot pack linked to the assault on Sascha and Naya, but it was Dorian who ended up doing most of the heavy lifting.

He'd fractured his leg in the crash, but what neither he nor Jason had let on at the scene, deciding Sascha didn't need the additional worry, was that he'd also suffered multiple broken ribs and severe bruising to his upper chest. Broken ribs were a general pain in the ass for everyone—even Tamsyn couldn't totally heal them, so Dorian was off active duty for a couple of weeks.

Tamsyn had also ordered the sentinel to keep the weight off his plascast-covered leg for three of those days. "Or I'll reverse the healing I've already done and you'll be stuck with a cast for months instead of fourteen days."

As a result, Dorian took himself and his computer off to Mercy and Riley's cabin for one of those days. There, according to the message Lucas got from Mercy, the blond sentinel kept her company, made sure Riley didn't stress out too badly, and researched the hell out of the ocelot pack.

I'm pretty sure he's hacking things that could get him locked up, Mercy had noted. Watch out for the men in black suits.

It was on the fourth day of his enforced "vacation," Dorian having spent the rest of the time hunkered down in his own cabin, that he sent Lucas a note: *I have a report on the ocelots.*

Lucas could've requested that report over the comm, but he wanted to check up on the sentinel, see that he was, in fact, following orders and healing properly. Vaughn, Clay, and Emmett—as well as Tammy, of course—had all been in and out of Dorian and Ashaya's home since he was grounded, had kept Lucas updated, but his panther wouldn't be satisfied until he'd seen the other man with his own eyes.

Dorian, more than any other dominant in the pack, could be stubborn about injuries. He'd always pushed himself too hard, too fast, an outcome of the fact that he'd for so long been latent, unable to shift into his leopard form. Where others might've given in to despair, Dorian had channeled his pain into an unremitting drive to excel. It was why he'd trained as an architect, taken up flying, learned hacking, all while being a crack sniper. Not only to sublimate the pain that came from not being able to shift, but to keep his mind busy so he didn't go insane.

Lucas's joy the day he'd discovered Dorian had shifted for the first time had been a raw fury inside him. Today, as the blond sentinel met Lucas in the doorway of his home, Lucas took in his balance on the plascast, then scanned his chest. "How're your ribs?"

Rubbing lightly on the soft dark gray of his T-shirt, Dorian gave a lopsided grin. "Almost fixed and no, I'm not lying. My mate insists on scanning me every night to check the progress of my healing."

Since Ashaya was a scientist—and more important, loved Dorian with a furious passion—Lucas nodded. For once, it appeared the sentinel was following orders when it came to his health. "You want to talk inside or out?" Dorian's architectural skill was reflected in the home he'd built. It was all glass panels covered by greenery and foliage except for cunning clear areas that let in the sunlight, until being inside was like walking in the forest.

Next to Lucas's own aerie, Dorian's home was his favorite design in pack territory. But today, his skin was itchy, wanted to be outside. Still, since Dorian was injured and might want to sit in a comfortable spot within, he'd follow the other man's preference.

But Dorian said, "Definitely out. Look at that sky."

It was a cauldron of color, the sun in the process of setting.

Dorian looked over his shoulder as he stepped out. "Keen! You want to kick your ball around?"

The answer came immediately. "Yes!"

Dorian's adopted son ran out seconds behind him, a soccer ball held in his hands. "Hi, Lucas!"

Lifting the six-and-a-half-year-old in his arms, Lucas said, "What's up, Keenan?"

"I got a gold star at school." Keenan's blue-gray eyes sparkled, the dusky brown of his skin glowing from within. "For helping my friend with his adding."

"Good. You make the pack proud." Ruffling the boy's hair, he put him back down on the ground, man and panther both happy to see such open joy in a child who'd been far too solemn when he'd first come into the pack. "I hear you're having special lessons." It had become obvious that Keenan was highly gifted, but though normal schoolwork was so easy for him that he was bored, he didn't want to separate from his year group.

His parents agreed with his choice, as did Lucas. Even a gifted child should have the chance to be a child, to take music and art lessons with his friends, to play games with them during breaks, to participate in group activities where it was more about communication and working together than specific knowledge.

"Children in Silence weren't allowed friends," Ashaya had said to Lucas when the question of Keenan's education came up, her voice thick with emotion. "I don't want that loneliness for my son, and I'm afraid that's what'll happen if he skips grades and ends up far younger than his classmates."

As a result, DarkRiver had authorized a special education grant that meant Keenan had a teacher's aide whose task it was to work with him on more advanced lessons while he remained among his usual classmates. When the class did math, Keenan did math, too, just at a more difficult level. When it was time for a sports or music lesson, he took it with his classmates.

Ashaya and Dorian could've easily paid for the teacher's aide themselves, but cubs were considered the responsibility of the pack as a whole, for they were the pack's heart.

It was an alpha's honor to ensure they had what they needed to thrive.

"Yes!" Keenan bounced up and down in front of Lucas. "My new teacher's name is Shonda and she makes my brain hurt."

Lucas hunkered down to Keenan's level. "Is that a good thing?"

A determined nod. "I like thinking hard." He glanced up at Dorian. "Will you watch me kick the ball, Dad? I can get the goal sometimes now."

As Lucas rose to his feet, he felt more than saw the emotion that crashed through Dorian at the innocent request. Swallowing, the sentinel said, "Lucas and I will watch you while we talk."

Smile luminous as the sun, Keenan ran off a short distance to the leaf-strewn section in front of the cabin, while Lucas and Dorian leaned up against the trees. "It's a punch to the heart each time he calls me dad," the sentinel admitted in a gruff tone. "Right fucking here." He pressed down on his chest above his heart, as if the organ ached.

"When did he start?"

"After the leg." Dorian tapped the slightly green-tinged transparent plascast. "He said, 'Dad, that's just like the one I had on my arm!'" The sentinel grinned. "He was so excited and it was all so natural. No big deal, you know? Except it is to me."

Lucas understood. To earn the trust of a child, that was a gift nothing could beat. "I heard from BlackSea," he said into the emotional quiet. "They've narrowed Tanique's vision of 'Edward's Pier' down to twenty possible locations and are planning to check them out one by one. Of course, that's if the place is even in Canada."

Dorian folded his arms. "I feel so fucking helpless."

"We're here if BlackSea needs us." Despite his rational words, Lucas felt the same prowling frustration as Dorian. To be a dominant was to protect. "Miane and her lieutenants have to be going crazy by now." Leila Savea was only one of BlackSea's many vanished.

"Yeah." A long pause. "Reminds me of Kylie. How I held my baby sister in my arms and there was nothing I could do to bring her back to life."

Memory smashed into Lucas. Of a laughing young packmate whose life had been stolen in a bloody, brutal way. "We made the fucker who hurt her pay," he said with a growl. "Nothing will ever bring her back, but never forget that we did her memory justice."

Dorian nodded. "I look at Keenan and I feel this pain deep inside because he'll never know the funny, loving aunt he would've had. I can almost see how she would've played with him, how she would've taught him to dribble." Swallowing, he smiled when Keenan kicked a goal. "But I figure she's around, watching over us. Kylie would do that."

Ashaya walked out of the cabin before Lucas could answer, two mugs in hand and her feet bare. Her body was clad in a simple orange shift that set off skin a shade darker than her son's, as well as the arresting blue-gray eyes she shared with Keenan.

"Coffee." Her smile was sunshine, banishing the dark—and her eyes, they were focused on Dorian, as if she'd sensed the pain that had rippled over her mate's soul, come out in response to it.

"Thanks, Shaya," Lucas said, deliberately using Dorian's pet name for her as a silent tug pulling the sentinel back into the beautiful present. If there was one thing Lucas knew, it was that Kylie would've wanted only joy for her adored big brother.

The provocation worked.

Growling low in his throat as he accepted his own mug, Dorian hauled Ashaya to his side, the electric curls of her unbound hair shining with hidden highlights in the sunset light. "Why did you get him coffee?" he grumbled. "Now he'll never leave."

Ashaya laughed and kissed Dorian, her fingers lingering on his jaw for a long moment before she turned to face Lucas. "Did you hear Mercy was trying to do pull-ups?"

Lucas almost spit out his coffee on a bark of laughter. "Did she succeed?"

"She told me she was up to seven when Riley made her stop," Dorian said, his very amused leopard in his eyes. "Can you imagine his face when he walked in?"

It was a priceless visual. "Poor Riley." Lucas had a good idea what Mercy was up to with her antics—because when a dominant predatory changeling female loved, she loved with every ounce of her being.

"While I was there," Dorian added, "I got into the swing of things. Pretended my ribs were killing me and I needed all kinds of assistance. I thought Riley was going to strangle me at one point."

Shaking her head in laughing reproof, Dorian's scientist mate gently patted his chest just as Keenan called out to her. "I'll leave you two to talk. I've been in the lab all day working on the Human Alliance implant." Her smile faded at the edges. "It'll do me good to stretch my legs with our future soccer star."

Dorian closed his hand over hers, his eyebrows drawing together. "Hold up. What aren't you saying?"

Ashaya looked over as if to ensure Keenan was happy in his play before replying. "I don't know for certain yet." Her voice was troubled. "But . . . I have a very bad feeling the implants are going to start failing in months if not sooner. I don't mean simply in effectiveness. I mean a degradation that'll impact the brain."

Lucas sucked in a quiet breath, all amusement instantly erased. "You're talking about the same implant that's in Bo's head?" he asked, referring to the effective leader of the Human Alliance. "The one that shields his mind against psychic manipulation?" Natural human shields were far weaker than the rock-solid ones possessed by changelings.

Nodding, Ashaya said, "I haven't shared my concerns with him yet. Amara and I want to be positive beyond any doubt—because the very first group that received the implants? They're beyond the stage where a surgical removal is safe."

That group included Bo and his top people.

"I won't mention it," Lucas promised as Dorian cuddled Ashaya against him, murmuring things to her that made her nod and whisper back.

"Shit," Dorian said after Ashaya left to play with Keenan. "If those implants fail, we lose Bo."

That would be disastrous. While the other man had made bad mistakes in his original interactions with DarkRiver and SnowDancer, he'd proven to be a cool head with whom they could build a relationship. Even more critically, he had the charisma and the passion to reach millions of humans and convince them to believe in the vital importance of uniting under the Alliance banner. Lose Bowen Knight and the Alliance would disintegrate, of that Lucas was convinced. It wasn't strong enough to survive without him, not yet.

And if they lost the Alliance, Trinity would fall.

The world *could not* afford for Trinity to fall. The instant it did, the Consortium would sweep in and chaos would reign.

Jaw grim, Lucas said, "Let's hope Ashaya and Amara disprove their own theory." It was a very faint hope: together, Ashaya and her twin were the best in the world in their field.

Dorian's eyes reflected the same bleak knowledge, but he just nodded. "So, the ocelots." His expression darkened further. "Our old information was out of date. They did use to be a small but strong and stable pack in their region, but they got caught in the insanity that hit the Psy."

"You're talking literally?" Lucas's gut went tight as he remembered the murderous violence that had nearly overwhelmed the Psy race at the start of this year.

"Yeah. SkyElm was—is—based next to a large Psy hamlet. The ocelots have plenty of room to roam but their main pack settlement has always been near the border—just a historical thing no one bothered to change because the two sides kept to themselves." Glancing over at his mate and son when they laughed, Dorian exhaled.

"But when the Psy started losing their minds because of the shit that was going down in their PsyNet, the pack was caught out." Dorian drank more of his coffee but didn't seem to taste it, his mind on whatever it was he'd discovered. "I can't figure out why the hell the alpha didn't move his people, since the hamlet outbreak happened after the first major outbreaks in New York."

At which point, Lucas thought, the entire world knew ordinary Psy had suddenly become deadly neighbors to have. "How many?" he asked quietly. Dorian wouldn't be this affected if the pack had lost two or three members.

The sentinel's words were brutal. "There are only seven survivors. From a pack that was ninety-three strong."

Lucas's hand clenched so hard around his mug that he almost cracked it. "How is that possible?" The casualty rate was far too high for a predatory changeling pack pitched against the unthinking insane.

"Ocelots were unbalanced." Dorian's eyes turned into chips of ice. "SkyElm had too many elders and children, not enough aggressive dominants physically able to defend the pack."

Claws pushing at his skin, Lucas had to make a conscious effort not to snarl.

He tried not to judge other alphas, but the situation Dorian was describing should've *never* happened. It was an alpha's responsibility to ensure his pack had a balanced complement of dominants in the prime of their life. Sometimes that meant putting out the call to friendly packs for intrepid young men and women who wanted to take up higher-level positions than they could hope for in their own packs at the same age. Other times, it meant making the tough decision to dissolve the pack by requesting integration with a bigger pack.

"Even if the ocelots had no one they could amalgamate with," Lucas said, "they could've asked for recruits from other feline packs." Fellow alphas like Lucas would've even authorized temporary transfers to support SkyElm until the faltering pack had enough permanent packmates. "Why didn't they?"

"They did put out the call," Dorian said, to Lucas's surprise. "Catch was they only wanted ocelots, no other cats. That's why we never got a request for help." A tight shrug. "There aren't many ocelots in the country and while the other packs are healthy, they're also small, can't afford to lose members. But"—Dorian's clipped tone grew harsh—"they all, *each and every one*, offered to accept an amalgamation request if it was made. SkyElm said it wasn't interested."

That was flat-out arrogance, and it had led to the decimation of almost an entire pack. "The survivors, who's left?"

"Two of them are children," Dorian began. "Alive because a submissive grabbed them in the middle of the carnage, threw them in a room, then barricaded himself inside with them, hacking off the hands of anyone who tried to get through."

Lucas growled in approval. That was exactly what a submissive pack-mate was meant to do in such circumstances—take any children in his or her vicinity and *keep them safe*. At least one member of SkyElm knew his duty.

"Only two soldiers," Dorian continued. "Both were badly injured in the fighting but are now up and walking. The pack healer is alive; she was on the front line, but the alpha pulled her back before she was too badly wounded. One of the only good decisions he seems to have made."

"The alpha's alive?"

Expression flat, Dorian nodded. "I spoke to a friend in the area—he says according to a few humans who were trapped in buildings near the Psy enclave/SkyElm border and watched the fighting go down, the pack's dominants protected the alpha above all others."

That wasn't necessarily the wrong move—a dead alpha could collapse a pack's cohesion, especially if it was a weak pack to begin with. However, in a situation where cubs were being killed, protecting those vulnerable lives should've been the dominants'—and the alpha's—*only* focus. In DarkRiver, should it ever come down to such a horrible situation, even the most frail elders would take up arms and form a line of defense.

Then Dorian said the most unbelievable thing. "He lost his own cub and mate."

Blinking, Lucas stared at his sentinel. "How is that possible?" In a battle where Sascha and Naya were under threat, Lucas would fight to the death to protect them. No one would get through him except by tearing him to fucking pieces.

"I don't think it was on purpose," Dorian said, though anger vibrated in his voice. "Far as I can piece together, SkyElm left one side of their settlement unprotected, believing the danger to be only on the border."

A crack of sound, coffee spilling to the forest floor.

"Shit." Putting the cracked mug on the ground, Dorian shook off the coffee that had spilled on his fingers. "You can figure out the rest."

Lucas could and it wasn't pretty. "It doesn't sound like SkyElm would have the capacity to organize a kidnapping of any kind, much less hire a mercenary group. And why the hell would they want to attack DarkRiver when they could've reached out to us for help?"

Lucas would've accepted the refugees without question, DarkRiver more than big and stable enough to integrate the seven survivors and provide them any help they needed. While leopard changelings formed the vast majority of DarkRiver, the pack included Psy, human, one jaguar, and several lynx packmates. It was, in fact, the best pack for SkyElm to have approached in the aftermath of the massacre.

Especially since, unlike the alphas of smaller packs, Lucas wouldn't have worried about a dominance challenge from the SkyElm alpha. He was too strong, had held power too long, and his sentinels were loyal beyond any question.

"Here's the thing." Dorian ran his fingers through his hair. "SkyElm was small but they have a couple of patents, courtesy of two elderly pack-mates who'd invented things and signed over the patents to the pack as a whole. Bastien tracked the money generated by those patents and he says that a month ago, someone transferred two million dollars of it to an offshore bank where the trail goes cold."

From there, Lucas realized, it could've been funneled to the merce-naries. "I need to talk to the SkyElm alpha face-to-face." No matter his disdain for the other man's decisions, Lucas wouldn't judge him guilty of

Naya's attempted kidnapping without firm evidence. The Consortium was too good at setting friend against friend, at creating fractures where none had previously existed.

"You planning to leave DarkRiver territory?" Dorian straightened, his leopard a wild green presence in his eyes. "Luc, you know that's not a good idea."

"I can't ask him to come here, not when he must be all but broken." The other alpha had lost his pack, his mate, and his child in a single horrifying day. Lucas wouldn't wish such hell on anyone. "I have to go to him."

Letters to Nina

From the private diaries of Father Xavier Perez
April 30, 2074

Nina,

The villagers are safe.

The Psy assassins have given up and gone away, and the people we saved know to stay in their hidden new home until things change on a far wider scale.

Today, for the first time since I lost you, since our people were butchered, I felt God in my heart again. And in the ray of dawn sunlight as it touched a child's peacefully sleeping face, I saw hope.

The Psy soldier with whom I work in the darkness to thwart his fellow assassins shows no one his face, but these villagers know mine, trust mine. I am one of them after all, my skin the same dark shade, my features familiar, my language theirs, my race human.

Now, however, it seems I'm also a rebel in a sense I could've never predicted only months earlier. I fight alongside a man I would've once murdered for the simple fact he is Psy and it was Psy who so viciously stole everything from me. That shames me and yet I write it here because I want you to know who I've become since I lost you. The good and the bad.

Nina . . . I miss you.

Xavier

Chapter 25

TWENTY-FOUR HOURS AFTER Dorian told Lucas about SkyElm, Lucas's sentinels and mate worked together to cover his absence while he moved alone out of the territory. It was the fact that he was on his own that had most worried his people, but a single panther moving alone in the night was a shadow. If he could've made the trip overland, there would've been zero risk of detection, even from other predatory change-lings, but that would've taken too long, so Lucas had called on a party he'd never expected to need: Nikita Duncan.

Sascha's mother owned more than one airline as well as a fleet of private craft. She'd got him on an unlogged flight on a small plane piloted by a man she assured Lucas wouldn't betray him, even under threat of torture. Sounded good, but Lucas wasn't about to trust anyone in her employ. Had Dorian not been out of commission, the sentinel would've been his pilot of choice. Still, since Nikita considered Lucas integral to Sascha's continued security, he was probably safe.

Getting into the already-warmed-up and ready-to-go plane on an isolated runway outside the city, he chucked his small pack inside, hauled himself in . . . and recognized the scent of the pilot. "When the fuck did you get a pilot's license?"

Max Shannon put his arm on the back of his chair and grinned over his white-shirted shoulder, his features a handsome mix of Caucasian and Asian and his black hair neatly cut. The dimple in his left cheek had fascinated Naya the last time Max and Sophie visited DarkRiver territory.

Lucas's cub had kept touching it, as if trying to figure out how it was made.

"Seemed a good skill for a security chief to have," Max said in answer to Lucas's question. "Especially when the woman I'm meant to protect is constantly on planes." He lightly tapped the control panel in front of him. "Preflight check's done." The other man began to get up. "I just need to close and lock the door."

"I'll do it." Thanks to Dorian, Lucas was experienced at the process, but he made sure Max had a clear line of sight to his actions. "Pass the pilot test?"

Giving him a thumbs-up, Max angled his head forward. "You want to sit in the copilot chair?"

"Nowhere else," Lucas said before sliding into the seat. He'd forgotten there were two people in Nikita's organization he *did* trust: Max Shannon and his wife Sophia Russo.

Max had helped DarkRiver more than once, plus, since Sascha and Sophia were friends, Max was often in Sascha's orbit. And Lucas's empathic and intuitive mate had never once caught anything bad about the ex-cop. Neither had Lucas. Most importantly, the cubs adored Max.

He was one of the good guys.

"You do realize your current taste in employers is inexplicable, right?" Lucas commented after picking up the headset Max pointed out to him.

The other man shrugged and put on his own headset. "Sophie and I live in hope that we'll drag Nikita over to the side of light." A sudden grin that once again revealed that dimple in his left cheek.

Linked as the sight was to memories of his cub, it had Lucas's panther prowling to the surface of his skin.

"It might even happen this century, now that Anthony's in the picture," Max said.

Snorting, Lucas nodded at the lights of the control panel. "How long you been flying?"

"Don't worry. This is my first real flight, but my instructor said it'll be just like in the simulator."

"Funny, Shannon. You tell Nikita that one, too?"

"I only tell your mother-in-law knock-knock jokes," Max responded with a straight face before he began to taxi down the private runway marked by small glowing beacons. "For some reason, she never says 'who's there,' so the whole process comes to a premature end at 'knock, knock.' I'm constantly dejected."

Chuckling, Lucas didn't speak again until they were in the air after a smooth takeoff, San Francisco a glittering sprawl to their left. "You have the brief?"

Max nodded. "Plan was I stay with the plane, while you prowl off into the dark."

"Plan was?"

"I'm offering to go with you if you need backup."

Lucas considered it. Max was as well trained as his own sentinels, and taking him along would have no impact on the security in pack territory. However, his original reasoning for going alone still applied—if this was about stealth, a panther alone stood the best chance of skating under the radar.

There was also another consideration.

"No," he said to the other man. "I need to know the plane is ready to go the instant I hit the runway. Can't take the risk of someone sabotaging it." Lucas couldn't afford to be away from DarkRiver for long, not given how visible he'd been lately, courtesy of his role with Trinity. Someone would notice his absence. "The man I'm going to see, he's physically far weaker than I am, so the security issue is minimal."

"Could be an ambush," Max said with the grim clarity of a security chief for a woman a lot of people wanted to kill. "You prepared for that? And don't predatory packs have rules about entry into another's territory?"

"I'm going over land unclaimed by changelings until I hit SkyElm's borders." Warning them of his arrival wasn't on the agenda. "As for a possible ambush, I'll see them before they ever spot me." Being jet-black had significant advantages—advantages Lucas intended to teach his daughter as soon as she got a little older.

Of course, it would make it a devil of a thing to find her when she was being cheeky, but Lucas would rather have that than not teach her skills she could use to protect herself should she ever be trapped alone and far from help. She was fierce, his cub, but while she was small, he would teach her to hide and wait. Hide and wait.

A child panther couldn't win against adult combatants.

Lucas knew that firsthand.

"Panther in the dark." Max whistled. "Yeah, okay, good plan. What're you going to do about clothes when you arrive?"

Lips tugging up, Lucas said, "Humans are so hung up on clothing."

"Don't give me that bullshit." The ex-cop pointed a finger at him. "You're not going to confront some other man while he's clothed and you're not."

In truth, Lucas would have no problem doing that, especially since he knew his dominance far exceeded that of the ocelot alpha. But, in this case, he likely wouldn't have to. "Someone always forgets their washing outside. I'll grab what I need." If not, he'd do the confrontation in his skin—which, unbeknownst to Max, would probably unnerve the other alpha even more.

Civilized manners, including wearing clothing, came from the human part of a changeling's nature. Comfort with their bodies, whether furred or the human skin, came from the primal core of their animal. An enemy might be able to negotiate with the civilized half, but the animal reacted on pure, undiluted instinct. And an alpha panther driven by violent protective urges was not a predator anyone wanted to face.

"There's a duffel back there with some weapons." Max jerked his thumb to the back of the plane. "I packed them just in case, but I guess you can't carry anything?"

"No, not without losing my speed and camouflage." He'd run with a small pack as a panther before, but it changed the sleek lines of his body, made him stand out. "I don't think this will be that kind of a confrontation." Because if the ocelots had actually had anything to do with the attack on Naya and weren't just being set up, they could have no reason to believe they'd been discovered.

Dorian had undertaken his data mining with extreme care, while the people he'd spoken to in the region were all allied with DarkRiver. Two had been born as part of Lucas's pack, moved out when they mated, still had plenty of family in DarkRiver. The other was a SnowDancer wolf temporarily based in the region while he completed advanced technical training in an unusual specialty.

No, the ocelots had no reason to watch for a panther coming for them.

IT took Lucas two hours to run to SkyElm's home base after Max landed the plane at a private airstrip that belonged to Nikita. It was hidden in the center of a sprawling spread, the landing strip concealed from casual view by the lay of the land, and even had anyone been curious, the strip was officially used for ranching operations and for the transport needs of the people who ran it.

There were no buildings anywhere within a visual line of sight.

Max had initiated the landing-strip lights by remote control, once he got close enough. The instant he had the plane on the ground and parked, he switched those lights off, plunging the area back into pitch darkness, the moon hidden behind clouds.

The quietness of that strip, however, was nothing compared to the screaming silence that surrounded the ocelot aeries. Though he'd shifted by that point, grabbing a pair of jeans off a line a mile back, Lucas's steps remained panther quiet, causing not so much as a whisper to fracture the disturbing quiet.

Perhaps the crushing power of it was because he knew that a community meant to house near to a hundred people now held only seven. While, like leopards, ocelots were solitary by nature, this pack had a long history of living in close proximity to one another, probably because of the small size of their pack.

The survivors had to be shell-shocked.

Pushing aside the surge of pity that came from both parts of his nature, he reminded himself that SkyElm could have Consortium help. Even if not, wild ocelots were nocturnal for the most part and that tendency showed up in changelings as well, though to a lesser extent. He couldn't count on the pack being asleep, even this deep into the night.

Guard up, he took to the trees and stayed high while he made his way toward the only two aeries where he could detect fresh scents rather than the dusty loneliness of homes left uninhabited for months. The first one he reached proved to house the children. He could just see their small bodies through the locked window: both were in ocelot form and curled up tightly together, while an adult male lay on a bed right in front of the aerie door.

Blocking it. Keeping the children safe.

The submissive.

Lucas would readily accept such courage into his own pack.

Aware he was missing the healer, the alpha, and the two soldiers, he took extreme care as he moved on. He had no doubts that he could take on all three of the dominants, but he didn't want to turn this into a bloodbath when this devastated pack might've had nothing to do with the attack on Naya.

Instead of moving on to the other aerie, within which he could now see a soft glow of light, he went dead still and *listened*. His patience was rewarded ten minutes later. The soldiers were below, running a tight perimeter as they sought to protect the remnants of their broken pack. Those two had to be hurting bad—dominants weren't supposed to outlive their vulnerable. They were built to fight to the death.

If the ocelot alpha wasn't careful, he could lose both to their own demons.

Having gained a fix on them, Lucas padded silently along the tree road until he came to a halt directly outside the large open window of the aerie where two people were talking. The window itself offered a view into an empty kitchen, the speakers most likely in the room beyond.

"You have to sleep, Monroe," a female voice pleaded. "You've been up for five days straight except for a few snatches here and there."

"No, I have to stay awake. Have to protect." The tone of the male voice was wrong, the words a little off.

Jagged. Broken.

"You're our alpha." The woman sounded on the verge of tears. "We need your guidance now more than ever, but the lack of sleep is making you erratic."

Growls sounded from within, along with the slap of feet moving back and forth across the floor, back and forth.

"*Monroe.*" The woman, who must have been the healer, tried again. She'd managed to get her incipient tears under control, sounded gentle and coaxing as she said, "I've made you a cup of tea. It'll relax—"

The sound of china crashing to the earth, liquid splashing on wood. "I don't need any fucking tea!" It was a roar.

Concerned for the healer and aware the two soldiers probably couldn't hear the commotion from their watch positions, Lucas flowed into the aerie through the window. His eyes had already adapted to the light so he padded through the kitchen straight into the living area. The alpha was looming over his healer, his brown hair streaked with gray and sticking up in tufts and the pale skin of his face blotchy red, his fists clenched.

The healer was a fragile-looking woman, maybe eighty years of age. To her credit, she wasn't flinching, was in fact still attempting to reason with her alpha.

"Monroe Halliston." Lucas leaned against a wall, his posture deliberately unthreatening. "We need to talk."

Spinning around with a snarl, the ocelot alpha came at him like a hurricane. Lucas had expected the violent instinctive reaction, had the other alpha on the floor in seconds, the older man's wrists locked behind his back. When the healer went as if to cry out for help, he shook his head. "I've come to talk," he said quietly. "You call the soldiers inside and this could end in blood."

The ebony-skinned woman swallowed, looked at his face, her brown eyes on the lines that had marked him from birth. "Lucas Hunter. Dark-River."

Enraged by the sound of those words, Monroe Halliston attempted to flip Lucas off him. Lucas held him in place with increased pressure. "I came to talk," he reiterated.

"I don't want to talk to the bastard who helped the Psy murder us!"

Lucas's blood ran cold.

Making a snap decision, he returned his attention to the healer. "Call your soldiers," he ordered. "Tell them I'm not here to spill blood, but I will if they don't both come through the door in the next two minutes." Lucas had done a full reconnaissance before he approached the aeries, knew there was no threat out there that could prove a danger while the dominants were away from their watch.

"Don't follow his orders!" the alpha yelled, but the healer seemed to realize Lucas was dead serious.

Running to the door, she called out to the two dominants. They appeared breathless in the doorway within the allotted two minutes, during which time, Monroe raved and ranted. Lucas hauled the other alpha to his feet, but kept his eyes on the soldiers, taking in their ragged condition, the bags under their eyes. "Keep your hands in plain view," he said in a tone that brooked no disobedience. "I've got no fight with you."

"You're holding our alpha hostage." It was a tired statement from the male half of the pair. "We have to act."

"I'll incapacitate you in seconds," Lucas said over Monroe's screaming at them to intervene. "At which point your remaining packmates, including the cubs, will be helpless."

The two soldiers looked at Monroe, who continued to demand they fight. Faces growing tight, they stepped back to take up watchful positions by the door, their hands clasped in front of their bodies as per Lucas's order. Their actions told Lucas this alpha-pack relationship had been all but broken long before Lucas arrived—Monroe's unthinking orders had simply put the final nail in the coffin.

Holding the other alpha's wrists in an unbreakable grip, Lucas grabbed a navy blue scarf from the floor. It must've been the healer's. He dragged the alpha into a chair, then used the scarf to tie the other man's hands to the back of it, so that they could have a face-to-face conversation.

He didn't think Monroe Halliston was thinking clearly enough to attempt to break his bonds by semi-shifting, but if he did, Lucas would do what he had to do to control the other alpha. "You blame DarkRiver for the deaths of your packmates?"

Eyes now a pale greenish brown with an elongated black pupil, the alpha bared his teeth. "It all began with you!" he yelled. "You and your Psy *mate*." He spat on the floor, as if he'd tasted something foul. "Without you, the Psy would've remained in their world and we would've remained in ours. Safe."

This wasn't the time to tell the ocelot male about the rot in the PsyNet and how it had infected Psy minds. The outbreaks of insanity had been inevitable. It was Sascha and other empaths like her who'd stopped the massacres from being even worse. Without the domino effect of Sascha's defection, those Es might've never awoken in time.

"You hired mercenaries to kidnap my child," he said, a heavy feeling in his gut.

A sly look flitted over Monroe Halliston's face as the healer lifted a trembling hand to her mouth, while both soldiers visibly blanched. "Prove it." It was a challenge.

Chapter 26

"DO YOUR PACKMATES know about the two million dollars you transferred into an offshore account in the Caymans?" Lucas asked. "The mercenaries tell us that the full fee was four million." An irresistible amount. "That second payment would've cleaned out your pack's savings."

The ocelot alpha curled his lip, but the healer spoke before he could spit out further insults.

"How *could* you?" It was a shaky whisper. "That money was the only thing we had left to give the cubs. Their parents are gone, their grandparents are gone, their friends are gone! At least with that money, they could have a good life, have choices!"

Baring his teeth at the elderly woman, the alpha said, "Shut up and get out."

He didn't seem to notice the reaction of his soldiers, but Lucas did. The two were staring at their alpha not only in shock . . . but also in disgust. The healer was sacrosanct in a healthy pack. No one, *no one* in Lucas's pack, would ever get away with insulting Tamsyn. He might disagree with her at times, might even get angry with her on very rare occasions, but even he would never talk to her in that ugly tone.

"No!" The healer's entire body trembled as she came to stand next to Lucas. "You don't get to give me orders anymore. I don't know who you are, but you are *not* my alpha!"

Hissing and growling, the ocelot alpha attempted to get up, chair and all. Lucas slammed him back down but didn't speak. Instead, he gave the healer the chance to say whatever else she needed to say.

When Monroe Halliston ignored her to shout, "Get this traitor out of here!" to the two other dominants, they didn't respond.

The once-alpha had lost them.

As if realizing that at the same time, the older man began to yell. "You're fools! Don't you see what he did? He opened the floodgates and *we* were caught in the flood! Your brothers and sisters and parents would still be alive without him! My mate would still be alive. My *son* would still be alive!" Another growling snarl. "Why should he get to keep his mongrel child while my son lies dead?"

Lucas's claws sliced out but he forced his enraged panther into patience. There was more here than met the eye. Monroe was too unstable to have pulled off what he appeared to have pulled off. First of all, according to the conversation Lucas had had with Bastien prior to leaving for Texas, Monroe couldn't have done the financial maneuvering involved.

"He doesn't have the skill," the man in charge of DarkRiver's financial assets had told Lucas. "The steps it took to move that money from the Caymans' account without leaving any kind of a trail? It requires years of experience and an in-depth knowledge of banking systems."

Bastien had thrust a hand through the dark red of his hair, his green eyes sharply intelligent. "To put it another way—you couldn't do it and you've got way more financial expertise than the ocelot alpha. The only person in San Francisco who could is talking to you right now."

And since Bastien's level of expertise was in no way common, it was highly improbable that Monroe Halliston had simply hired someone. *Especially* when Bastien had found zero indications that the ocelot had paid out any money but the two million down payment to the mercenaries. No one that good would work for free.

Unless they had an ulterior motive.

"Mongrel child?" one of the SkyElm soldiers said into the stunned quiet, her voice trembling. "Is that how you think of me, too? My father was human, after all."

Her former alpha stared at her and when he spoke, he betrayed far more than he intended to. "It would've been a lot better for the world if we'd all stayed in our separate corners, human, Psy, and changeling." The ocelot's tone was broken rock, harsh and grinding. "This so-called Trinity Accord, it'll just lead to more death, more destruction." Volume increasing, he said, "The smartest people have already realized it. They're working to get us back to where we should've been from the start!"

That sounded very much like it could be Consortium rhetoric, but Lucas wasn't about to rely on guesswork. Before he could speak, however, the male soldier said, "Those aren't your words." A steady tone but one that demanded attention. "Who did you betray us with?"

Monroe jerked. "I didn't betray this pack!" His voice shook with the force of his passion and resolve. "Everything I've done was for you!"

"Oh?" the soldier asked. "What were you intending to do with the DarkRiver cub? Murder her in vengeance?"

The man who'd once been alpha to these people suddenly paled, as if realizing how far he'd gone. "Of course not," he whispered. "I don't murder children."

"So where was she supposed to go?" the soldier insisted. "Did you expect us to take you at your word and accept her as falling out of the sky, never mind that DarkRiver would've ripped apart the world searching for her?"

The sarcastic question made Monroe Halliston snap. Wrenching at his bonds, he said, "My friends made preparations for the child to be shipped out to Australia!"

"What friends?" the healer asked.

"I never knew their names."

"You trusted anonymous *strangers*?"

"Strangers who saw the truth, who wanted to *help us* get vengeance." A smile meant to intimidate. "The ship was ready and waiting in San Francisco Port. That was the genius of it—our enemies would've been scrabbling to find clues and all the while, the child would've been locked up in a boat in their own territory."

"You're a fool if you think that would've worked," Lucas said quietly, though his blood was raging. He didn't need more from this pathetic excuse for an alpha. Luca's people were more than good enough to find the ship in question, given the relative scarcity of vessels bound for Australia that used San Francisco Port. "Do you really think a single ship, plane, or car would've been allowed to depart San Francisco had Naya been taken?"

"You don't have that much power."

Lucas shrugged. "We have enough." And they had friends, including a woman who had the authority to ground entire fleets of planes, and an ally who controlled vast areas of the sea, but he wasn't about to share those details with this man who was about to die. "Go," he said to the soldiers and the healer. "You know there can be only one outcome here."

Had Monroe Halliston been mentally ill, with no awareness of right or wrong, Lucas would've swallowed his rage and forced himself to show mercy, but grief alone wasn't an acceptable excuse for what this man had almost done. He had taken actions that could've led to the murder of Lucas's mate with her warm, empathic heart and smile that was his world, and the abduction of his barely one-year-old cub. Naya's fear would've been a traumatizing wound carried forever in her heart, as Lucas carried the scars of his parents' deaths.

No, he could not, *would not* forgive such a crime. The world had to understand that DarkRiver protected its own and that to come after *anyone* under Lucas Hunter's protection was to sign your death warrant. Yes, he could act civilized, but he remained a panther under the skin.

At the door, the SkyElm dominants came to attention. "We'll stay, bear witness," the female soldier said in a quiet voice.

Her partner nodded.

Accepting their right to remain, Lucas glanced at the healer. "Go," he repeated in a gentler tone. "You don't need to see this."

The woman was sobbing, but she didn't argue with him.

Waiting only until she'd left, Lucas looked down into the face of the man who'd betrayed his own pack in a selfish desire for vengeance.

"Changeling law is clear. You sent outsiders into my territory. Those outsiders had orders to take my child, even if that meant killing my mate. The penalty is death."

The air around Monroe began to shimmer, as if he'd finally figured out he could shift and escape his bonds.

Lucas didn't hesitate.

His claws sliced through Monroe's carotid and jugular in the split second before the shift took hold.

"**HE** was good once," the healer whispered to Lucas while the two of them stood below the aeries, waiting for the soldiers to return.

They'd gone to bury the man who'd once been their alpha, giving him that much at least, even if they could no longer give him their respect.

"Arrogance became a way of life for him well before the Psy attack." The healer hugged herself. "I could see it settling in, tried to counsel him, but he would never listen. He always knew best." She swallowed. "Even his sentinels couldn't get him to pay attention, see what he was doing to the pack."

"Then they should've walked away." A pitiless answer, but that was how a pack was supposed to function—an alpha had no automatic right to the loyalty of his strongest men and women. He earned it. If he didn't have that loyalty, he didn't have the right to be alpha.

"Yes." The healer sighed. "I think they stayed because we had so many elders and children and . . . because of inertia." Her hand trembled as she wiped away the remnants of her tears. "The money cursed us in a way. It made it easier to stay with the pack than to strike out and find a new life."

Lucas tried to be charitable toward the dead, but the truth was that their choices had helped doom the pack as much as Monroe's mismanagement.

"But don't blame those two," the healer whispered urgently as SkyElm's sole surviving dominants reappeared in the distance. "They wanted to roam and explore, were held back by our lack of dominants. And they're babies for all the responsibility they'd taken up."

Lucas had already figured that out—these two couldn't be older than twenty-two, twenty-three. In DarkRiver, they'd be junior soldiers at most.

Waiting for the two to reach him, he said, "It's done?"

They snapped to attention. "Yes, sir," the female said.

"We didn't place a marker," the male added defiantly. "He doesn't deserve that."

A pause followed . . . before the healer seemed to realize she was now the highest-ranking member of SkyElm. "I don't know what to do," she said bluntly. "I don't know if another ocelot pack will take us—they're all so small, and we'd come with only two soldiers as opposed to four people who need protecting."

"I think you're selling your submissive packmate short." Lucas had silently checked the other aerie after cleaning up the blood on his body, discovered the submissive had armed himself with knives and was waiting behind the door. "Call him down. All the adults need to be here." And the survivors of this pack needed to learn to forget bad habits starting right now.

Submissives in DarkRiver were treated as equal packmates, simply those with a different skill set and strength. Never would they be excluded from such decisions.

Only when all four adults surrounded him did Lucas say, "Did any of you know what Monroe was up to?"

They all shook their heads, the submissive having been briefed on what had happened. Lucas picked up no signs of deception. He'd already been certain about the soldiers and the healer. Now, having just seen an example of how this pack had thought of its nondominant members, he realized the submissive was the last person Monroe would've trusted with any plot.

"I'm extending an invitation for you to join DarkRiver."

Relief crashed over their faces, too powerful to be hidden. Changelings who weren't loners by choice were lost and broken without a pack.

"But," he said before anyone could speak, "we function very differently from SkyElm. You'll have to learn our rules and abide by them." He pointed at the soldiers. "You two will be demoted to what your rank should be, given your age and skills."

Both nodded so quickly that Lucas realized neither wanted to be in a position they couldn't handle. Intelligent then. Good.

"I already have a senior healer," he said to the oldest member of Sky-Elm. "But she'd welcome help." Lucas's pack was growing day by day; there was plenty of room for another pair of healing hands.

"I know Tamsyn," the other woman said with a smile that lit up the weathered lines of her face. "She's brilliant and far more suited to a strong pack like DarkRiver than I'd ever be. And . . . I'm tired." Sad, too, her expression told. "I'll be happy to assist her where I can and to care for our orphaned cubs the rest of the time."

"Those cubs will need parental figures." Lucas included both the healer and the submissive in his next statement. "Do you want that responsibility?"

"Yes." The submissive's voice was firm, though he didn't have the dominance to meet Lucas's eyes. "The less disruption to their lives, the better—they've barely started speaking again after the trauma."

Lucas nodded. "I'm leaving tonight. Pack up what you need and be ready to leave here in forty-eight hours." He'd send a team to secure the aeries, put anything his new packmates didn't need into storage.

By changeling law, the land itself would be forfeit if SkyElm had occupied it through historical rights. By *general* law, humans and Psy were locked out from claiming such vacated land, but it would be available for a changeling pack to claim, so long as they could defend it. If, however, SkyElm had purchased the land, then Lucas would make the decision as to what happened to it. These people were now his responsibility and that included taking care of their financial legacy.

"Can we leave tomorrow?" one of the soldiers blurted out. "It won't take long to pack what we need and the rest we can come back for at a later time."

Looking around, Lucas saw no disagreement on the faces of the other ocelots. There was too much pain here, he realized, too much loss. They needed to escape. "I'll organize it." He slashed a claw down one side of the male dominant's face, did the same to the female dominant.

Neither flinched.

Lucas then touched the submissive's cheek with his palm and pressed a kiss to the healer's forehead. "Welcome to DarkRiver."

The submissive began crying, his shoulders shaking with the force of his sobs.

Lucas embraced him, holding the other man until he no longer needed the touch, until his animal understood and accepted that it no longer had to carry this unbearable weight alone. He had an alpha he could rely on.

"The children," Lucas said in a gentle reminder when the ocelot male could finally breathe again.

Nodding jerkily, his new packmate left, to return with a boy of about seven and a girl who looked at least a year younger.

So young.

And so scared.

Hunkering down in front of them, Lucas simply opened his arms. They came instinctively to him, knowing from the stances of their packmates that he was safe . . . and feeling his strength. From the way they clung to him, they needed that strength as badly as the courageous man who'd watched over them until this instant.

Lucas squeezed both children tight, rising to his feet with them still in his arms. "You'll be coming home with me," he murmured and knew he couldn't leave tonight.

To do so would be to break their fragile hearts.

So be it. He'd figure out a way to adjust his plans.

LESS than twelve hours later, DarkRiver had six new members, no one had noticed Lucas's absence, and Vasic Zen had agreed to teleport Naya to visit her maternal grandmother in the coming week.

"As long as I'm not needed for an emergency," the Arrow said, "you can contact me when you've set up the meet and I'll do the teleport." Icy gray eyes holding Lucas's. "You're sure you want your mate and child within the territory of one of the most dangerous women in the world?"

"Nikita knows not to cross me." Lucas didn't have the emotional connection to Nikita that Sascha did, would eliminate her without hesitation should she prove a threat. "Has the squad heard from BlackSea? Any progress on locating Leila Savea?" It had been well over a week since Tanique Gray's psychometric vision.

Vasic shook his head. "Nothing." A glance at the small jade clock on Lucas's desk. "I'd better head home. Ivy's planning a special dinner for Grandfather for his birthday."

"Ashaya mentioned it was today." The scientist deeply respected Zie Zen, and to Keenan, the elder was his grandfather, too. "She said Keenan made him a gift."

Vasic's smile was slight, but for an Arrow, that equaled a giant grin. "It's a portrait of Grandfather done in rainbow colors that he has solemnly promised to place in his study—I teleported him to visit with Ashaya and her family earlier today."

That promise, Lucas thought, said a great deal about Zie Zen. A powerful man who'd surely made many ruthless decisions in his long lifetime, he'd nonetheless not lost his soul. "Please give him DarkRiver's best wishes. We will always be in his debt." Without Zie Zen, Ashaya would've never escaped the Psy Council's clutches, and without Ashaya, Dorian might still be furiously angry at the world, his leopard trapped in a clawing scream inside his body.

That, however, was simply the most obvious example of how Zie Zen had influenced the pack in a positive way. Lucas knew the Psy elder had his fingers in many other pies and, like Nikita, he protected those who were his own. In this case, that included DarkRiver, since Keenan and Ashaya called the pack home.

"I will," Vasic promised before teleporting out.

Alone, Lucas turned to his desk and slid his computer screen back into the body of his desk. He'd only arrived home at close to one this afternoon, wouldn't have minded a few hours' rest, but he'd come into the office instead so people could see he was in the territory. Once here, he'd spent the time wisely and cleared a backlog of tasks that fell to him as the head of DarkRiver's business enterprises. Not everything, however— that would take another three hours at least.

Walking out to where his admin sat at her own desk, he said, "You going to shoot me if I head out?" He could finish up tomorrow morning, but he needed to know if there was something urgent he'd overlooked.

Ria rolled her eyes. "Like I could stop you."

Grinning, Lucas tapped her on the nose. "We all know you're the boss of this office." Ria might be human but she was one of the strongest members of the pack, her status in the hierarchy that of a senior maternal dominant.

Now, her scowl was thunderous. "Tap me on the nose again like I'm a cub and I'll break your hand."

"Boss of the office," he reiterated before ducking back inside his own space to grab his leather-synth jacket. He'd borrowed Vaughn's jetcycle, and at those speeds, even a panther felt the chill. Shrugging into the jacket, he walked back out to Ria. "I heard Mialin caught a cold."

Her face softened. "Only a sniffle. Emmett's got her with him today." Eyebrows drawing suddenly together over the silky brown of her eyes, she said, "How do you even know that? She just developed it this morning."

"You might be the boss of the office," he said as he zipped up the jacket, "but I'm the alpha of DarkRiver." Every packmate was his responsibility, especially the littlest of them all. "Tamsyn had a look at her?"

Nodding, Ria got up to give him an unexpected hug, the scent of her small, curvy body deeply familiar to his panther. "You're a good alpha, Luc."

The out-of-the-blue words hit him hard after what he'd seen in SkyElm.

He wrapped his arms around her, held her close. "Thanks, Ri-ri."

Elbowing him for using her endearing family nickname, she released him to go over to one corner of the office. "Don't forget your helmet or Sascha will brain you."

Lucas accepted the gleaming black thing. "I'll be at Dorian's, then home if you need me."

His light mood only lasted until he hit the road out of town, his face turning grim inside the helmet. Because he wasn't just swinging by to see how Dorian was healing. The sentinel might be off active duty, but he remained one of Lucas's most trusted people. And as of last night, he had a new task: to find the ship that had been meant to take Lucas and Sascha's cub from San Francisco to Australia.

PART 3

Chapter 27

ZIE ZEN SAT in a chair outside Ivy and Vasic's home, his left hand on his cane, and listened to a young brown-haired boy play under the fiery light of the setting sun. Tavish was laughing more and more as the days passed, and today as he chased a small white dog through the orchard, he hadn't stopped. The sound was joyous music.

Sunny, I wish you were here to see this.

The only woman he had ever loved had wanted hope for their people, wanted joy. Instead, she'd been worn away by their need until her heart no longer beat, until there was no strength in her to breathe. His sweet, gentle Sunny. An empath during the time when the PsyNet turned against empaths, when it wanted only cold Silence. That choice had killed her, and in so doing, killed the best part of him, too.

"Grandfather." Another empathic voice, sweet and hopeful and with a generous warmth that sank into his aching bones. "You're cold. Here."

Only when Ivy put the afghan over his knees did he see that his hand was trembling on the cane despite the sunshine that poured down on him, his wrinkled skin bearing the marks of age. "Thank you, Daughter." He touched his hand to Ivy's soft tumble of curls as she bent over to arrange the afghan, this woman who had brought his son alive.

Vasic might not be that in absolute terms, their relationship two generations removed, but he was Zie Zen's son of the heart. And he'd done what Zie Zen couldn't—Vasic had saved his empathic mate, kept her from being crushed under the endless need of their people. A people who had finally remembered that the Es were treasures to be cherished.

It eased Zie Zen's century-old pain to feel her touch, to know that Sunny's dream was on the road to coming true.

Ivy smiled, the translucent copper of her eyes luminous and her affection and love for Zie Zen an open caress against his senses. Empaths—they had no sense of self-preservation. Never had. Probably never would.

"Would you like a hot drink?" she asked as the sun kissed the gold and cream of her skin.

Sunny's hair had been yellow cornsilk, her eyes blue, but she'd been this way, too, always watching out for others. It was a need in an empath, this nurturing drive. "No," he said. "The throw is enough."

"Ivy!" Tavish rushed pell-mell toward them, the knees of his beige corduroy pants stained with grass and dirt. "Ivy! Ivy!" The seven-year-old all but ran into Ivy's legs, throwing his arms around them in wild affection.

Laughing in a way that told the child he was loved, his affection welcome, she ruffled his hair. "Careful, speedy."

Tavish tipped back his head, looked up. "Did you finish Grandfather's birthday dinner?"

"I did." Ivy met Zie Zen's eyes. "I hope you'll like what I've chosen."

"You could do nothing that would displease me, Daughter."

Ivy's gaze shone wet before she was distracted by two words from the Arrow child who now called the orchard home, and who looked to Ivy and Vasic as family. As parents who wouldn't reject him the way his birth parents had done when he proved to have a dangerous telekinetic gift. "Wanna play?" Wariness was a sudden intruder lurking in eyes of hazel mixed with brown.

Then Ivy leaned down to press a kiss to his forehead. "Why not?"

Wariness wiped away with a smile that was a burst of starlight, Tavish went to run back to the ball the small white dog, Rabbit, was guarding. He paused midstep, came to Zie Zen, his pace far more sedate. "Grandfather," he said respectfully. "Would you like to play, too?"

Zie Zen raised his hand to the boy's cheek, touched the innocent warmth of it, and thought of the children he and his Sunny might've created had they lived in another time. "I will enjoy listening to you play, Grandson."

Tavish made an aborted movement forward, seemed to decide to do it, and threw his arms around Zie Zen. Zie Zen closed his own around the boy, this small, bright spark of life who had learned to laugh under Zie Zen's eyes.

"I'll be over there, Grandfather." Tavish pointed toward the start of the orchard after the embrace came to a natural end. "You can call me if you need me. Okay?"

"You are a good grandson."

Flushing with pride, Tavish took his leave and ran off.

Ivy followed at a slower pace after picking up Zie Zen's fallen cane and placing it against the side of his chair. She was soon caught up in the game, however, one that seemed to involve kicking the ball between two trees, with Rabbit in hot pursuit of the black-and-white object anytime it went past an invisible boundary.

When Vasic 'ported in right beside Ivy, she turned to kiss him in a motion so fluid, it was as if the two were one being. Zie Zen didn't need to be an empath to sense her piercing love for Vasic, or Vasic's passionate devotion to her. Zie Zen's son of the heart loved his empath as Zie Zen had loved his Sunny.

Even as the couple drew apart, Ivy's palm yet on Vasic's chest, Tavish came to tug at Vasic's hand and ask him to join in the game. Vasic touched that hand to the boy's shoulder before turning to meet Zie Zen's gaze. *Grandfather, you are well?* His telepathic voice was as pure as a remote lake of unbroken ice, but there was no cold within Vasic.

Not any longer.

I am very well, Son. And he was. The sunshine was warm on bones that felt far older than his years. It was the weight of sorrow, the weight of memory, the weight of promises he'd made to himself to see through his Sunny's dream.

Here in this sun-drenched orchard while his son played with a child who had chosen Vasic as his father, and an empath laughed in unfettered joy, that dream came true. The Psy race was no longer a place only of chilling Silence, the PsyNet no longer a stark black-and-white landscape devoid of emotional bonds.

The time of endless darkness was over.

There, Sunny. It is done.

VASIC felt his grandfather go. No emotional bonds showed in the PsyNet but for mating bonds, not yet. But Vasic knew they existed, felt them in his soul. And he knew when his bond with his grandfather snapped forever.

Grief speared him as he teleported the short distance to Zie Zen.

His grandfather's cane lay fallen on the ground, but Zie Zen's head didn't loll. It simply leaned gently against the back of his chair. His eyes were closed, the faintest smile on his lips. It was as if he were sleeping, but even as Vasic reached out his fingers to check his grandfather's pulse, he knew Zie Zen was gone.

Ivy's hand locked around his as it fell to his side, the words she spoke breathless from her run to Zie Zen and wet with tears. "He was at such profound peace before he went. It felt like . . . like a beautiful heartsong."

Ivy would know, not only because Vasic's wife was an E, but because Zie Zen had been linked to her in the Honeycomb. Vasic's grandfather had smiled at Ivy's request for a connection, then said, "I have come full circle at last, joined once more to an empath."

"Grandfather?" Tavish's plaintive voice snapped Vasic out of his shock and sorrow.

Reaching down, he picked up the child, his single arm more than strong enough for the task. He needed to hold the boy and Tavish needed to be held. "Grandfather's left us, Tavish," he said, finding it difficult to speak but knowing that at this instant, the pain felt by the small vulnerable heart in his hold was more important than his own grief. "But he was ready to go."

Ever since Zie Zen had told Vasic about his Sunny, Vasic had known that his grandfather was only counting time on this earth. The Psy race might not believe in an afterlife, but Zie Zen had believed his Sunny waited for him. He just had to finish his work here before he could go to her, to the woman he had always loved.

"But he can't go!" It was a child's angry cry. "Tell him to come back!"

Vasic felt Ivy's love, the infinite gentleness of her, surround them both.

Reaching up to cup Tavish's wet face, she shook her head. "We'll all miss him desperately, but you see his smile? It means he was happy to go on his next adventure." She was crying, too, made no effort to hide her tears.

Ivy. Vasic's throat was too thick to speak. *I need you.*

His empath tucked herself against his chest a heartbeat later, wrapping her arms around him and Tavish both. It was enough to keep him going, so he could do what needed to be done.

He couldn't cry, not then. He'd been an Arrow too long.

It wasn't until deep into the night, the world silent and his mate holding his head against her shoulder, that Vasic Zen cried for the man who had made him who he was, a man who had lived a lifetime with his own grief and who had left the world a far better place than it had been before he first turned rebel.

ASHAYA received word of Zie Zen's death directly from Ivy Jane. "He would've wanted you to know," the empath told Ashaya before dawn the morning after Zie Zen's passing, her eyes red and swollen on the comm screen.

"Thank you." Ashaya's own grief was a raw wave inside her. "You'll let me know the funeral arrangements?" Under Silence, Psy had held no funerals, celebrated no lives, but Zie Zen deserved every honor they could do him.

He'd saved Ashaya's son, saved Ashaya herself.

And they were only two of hundreds, perhaps thousands.

"Yes," Ivy said. "You know more of a certain part of his life than we do. If you think there are others who should be told, please do it."

"I will." But first, after Ivy logged off, Ashaya needed to deal with the agony inside her. She slid down to sit on the floor of her home office, her arms curled around her knees. Sobs rocked her, when tears were things she'd never shed in the PsyNet.

It didn't startle her when Dorian entered the room within seconds, though she'd left him fast asleep in their bed. Her mate had felt her sorrow, run to her despite the fact that his leg was still in a plascast. "Zie Zen's dead," she managed to say before she couldn't speak.

Kneeling down beside her, Dorian held her against his chest and he let her cry.

"K-Keen . . ." Her son's heart would be broken; she needed to get herself together so she could deal with his pain.

Dorian pressed a kiss to her temple. "I shut the office door when I walked in. He won't wake."

"I c-can't stop," she said at one point.

"You will when you're ready."

So she cried and she thought emotions were a horrible thing sometimes . . . but she wouldn't trade them for cold peace. Never again. A life of freedom from chains psychic or emotional or physical was Zie Zen's gift to her and she would honor it always.

HIGH in a skyscraper in New York, a woman who'd once been under Ming LeBon's ugly control hung up the phone with a thickness in her throat. Ashaya was devastated by the news of Zie Zen's death but she'd taken the time to call Katya. "I thought you'd want to know," Katya's friend and former boss had said.

Katya couldn't believe Zie Zen was gone. He was like an ancient tree in the forest. Always there, offering shelter under its branches. It was near impossible to comprehend that the tree had fallen, leaving a gaping hole in their midst. She'd never been as close to him as Ashaya, but he'd had a profound impact on her life nonetheless—for it was Zie Zen who'd built the foundation on which every Psy rebel stood, whether they knew it or not.

Conscious her husband would want to be informed as soon as possible, she looked up his private diary and saw he was scheduled for a consult with the Forgotten's head medic.

She knew what "consult" was code for, so instead of heading to the infirmary or Dev's office space, she used her handprint to authorize the elevator to take her to a secret subbasement. Triple-shielded against interference, this was the space where the Forgotten ran experiments testing the limits of the new psychic abilities popping up among their people.

The elevator doors opened to reveal another locked door.

Scanning herself through using retinal fingerprinting as well as a voice code, she entered to find Dev and Glen the only two people in the cavernous gray space that always seemed cold to her.

Rubbing her hands up and down her upper arms, she nodded hello to the doctor, but stayed out of the way. Dev didn't acknowledge her, likely couldn't. Her husband was seated in a chair surrounded by complex monitoring equipment. Hooked up to them by multiple wires, he stared straight ahead at what looked like a computer set to solve logic problems.

As Katya watched, the computer's behavior changed. It began to scroll data across the screen. Katya didn't know what was happening but she knew Dev was behind it. He'd become part of the machine.

Gut clenched, she looked into his eyes. They were the same gorgeous brown with amber, gold, and bronze flecks that she loved . . . only ice-cold, no humanity, no warmth. "Dev," she whispered, unable to hold back the visceral need to claw him back from the metallic ice of the machines.

Though she'd spoken at the lowest possible volume, his response was immediate. Lashes coming down, he said, "Katya, *mere jaan.*" A rusty voice, but his lips curved into a smile as his eyes warmed to shimmering gold on the upward rise of his lashes.

She could barely wait long enough for Glen to unhook him from the monitoring sensors. Wrapping her arms around him the instant he rose to his feet, she shivered and held him even tighter. "You're so cold."

Dev cuddled her to his chest. "I don't feel it, but Glen says there's a definite surface temperature drop when I interface with higher-level machines."

"No need to worry though," was the doctor's cheerful addition. "His vitals carry on as per usual."

Katya drew back, took one of Dev's hands, and blew hot air on it while rubbing gently at his skin. "What about your mental state?" Her skin felt tight over her cheekbones, her heart that trapped bird that returned in times of greatest stress and fear. "What's it do to you each time you become part machine?"

"*Katya.*" Dev tipped up her chin. "You keep me human, no matter how many machines I touch."

Fear still knotted her gut. "You're getting so strong." He did things like turn on household computronics without even thinking about it.

The dark of his hair sliding forward, Dev bent so his forehead touched hers. "And I love you more each day. I'm in no danger of losing myself."

His skin was warm now and whatever he'd done this morning, their psychic connection had never once flickered. She had to remember that, believe in that. Dev might be changing, becoming something new, but he was still the man who loved her.

He was also the leader of the Forgotten, a people who'd had far more dealings with Zie Zen than the rest of the world ever guessed. "I have sad news," she said, her throat thick again. "We've lost Zie Zen."

Dev's grief was a rough, harsh thing, and it was painfully, rawly human.

ADEN didn't want to deal with Trinity or Ming LeBon right now. He wanted to be there for his friend, to take care of details so Vasic didn't have to. But Zie Zen had believed in Trinity, had spoken to Aden at length about it the last time they had a conversation.

It is a construct of raw hope, this Trinity Accord of yours. A bold, audacious, defiant thing that challenges the world to be better and demands that people be the very best they can be. Never let this construct fail, Aden, for so long as it stands, it broadcasts that challenge. Sooner or later, even the consciously deaf will have to listen.

For that reason and that reason alone, Aden forced himself to stare at the proposal that had arrived in the hour directly after Zie Zen's passing, at a time when Vasic and Ivy had told no one but Aden and Zaira, and Ivy's parents. At least Ming LeBon could be acquitted of the crime of trying to use Zie Zen's death to his own advantage. That was the only good thing Aden could say about the letter that had gone out to every signatory of the accord.

Proposal for a European Alliance

The Trinity Accord presents a hopeful view of the future, but in the short time since its inception, it has already proven lacking in the basics and is a group clearly dominated by certain parties to the detriment of others. It is for this reason, and because Europe has needs Trinity simply will not be able to fulfill, that I am proposing a European Alliance.

The proposed alliance would encompass members from across the continent as well as the British Isles, and will provide a vehicle for better growth for all parties.

Membership in the EA will not preclude being a signatory to the Trinity Accord. The two organizations can coexist, though the EA is apt to be the far more useful tool for those who intend to do business in this part of the world.

—Ming LeBon

Aden knew the core of Trinity needed to respond to this, but he also knew that he refused to disrespect Zie Zen by playing politics today. So he'd have faith in his "bold, audacious, defiant" construct and in the people who'd helped him take it from idea to fruition.

He input a call.

Lucas was more than willing to handle the situation. "Anything Trinity or Ming related that manages to make its way to you, forward it to me." The panther held Aden's gaze, his own eyes solemn. "I heard. The world lost a hell of a man yesterday."

That was when Aden realized that, of course, Lucas would know of Zie Zen's passing. A child whose birth certificate listed Zie Zen as his father lived within DarkRiver. "Yes, it did. Thank you for handling the fallout from Ming's EA proposal." He knew the alpha had to still be dealing with tracking down those behind the abduction attempt on his child.

"None necessary."

Signing off, Aden turned to find Zaira waiting for him.

She slipped into his arms, her own locking around him. "I've spoken to Ivy." He couldn't see her eyes, but he knew they remained shell-shocked from a loss no one had seen coming.

Zie Zen had always been there, until it seemed even the most Silent, most pragmatic Arrows had subconsciously believed it would always be thus, that he was a force of nature immune from time and age.

"I know what they need," Zaira finished, her voice husky.

Aden nodded, then together, the two of them started to do what they could to help bear the load.

Chapter 28

HELPED BY FRIENDS who'd been there every step of the way, Vasic and Ivy held Zie Zen's memorial service at the orchard, on a small rise awash in the sunshine his grandfather had loved. Once, when they'd spoken about it, Zie Zen had asked to be cremated and scattered on the winds as he'd done for his Sunny. But first, they would have this ceremony for the living who grieved for him.

Zie Zen had an honor guard of Arrows and empaths—and one gifted scientist.

Ashaya Aleine's grief was as deep as Vasic's, but she walked with pride for the man who had been far more to her than Vasic had ever known.

Another woman, her hair golden brown and her hands covered by black, stood waiting for the procession to reach the rise. Vasic had first met her in a different context, hadn't understood how deeply she'd been entwined in Zie Zen's quiet and far-reaching rebellion until she'd shown him the golden coin carried by only ten people in the entire world: people who'd been Zie Zen's most trusted.

Vasic had one of those coins, too.

Clara Alvarez managed Haven, a place where fragmented F-Psy could live in peace—and where Samuel Rain currently made his home. She was holding herself in fierce check, but her features were strained and she stayed close to her husband, a respected prosecutor.

Next to that prosecutor stood another unexpected holder of a coin: Anthony Kyriakus, former Psy Councilor, current member of the Ruling

Coalition, Vasic's occasional ally, and a man who'd publicly opposed Zie Zen a number of times over the decades. Vasic had known the two were allies beneath it all, but until this instant, he hadn't known how deep ran the trust between them.

Grandfather, I have a feeling I will never know all your secrets.

Ashaya's son, Keenan, stood with Tavish. He cried, old enough to understand that the man he, too, had called grandfather wasn't ever going to wake up. Tavish held the younger boy's hand and told him what Ivy had said to him, while Ashaya's mate, Dorian, stood behind both children, his hands on their shoulders.

Ivy walked with the honor guard, and she was Vasic's strength, the gentle force that held everyone together that day.

And there were a lot of people.

Zie Zen hadn't only been a man who loved a girl called Sunny and a boy called Vasic, he'd been one of the greatest statesmen of their race. Vasic had known his grandfather wouldn't mind being farewelled without fanfare, but he'd also understood that there were others who needed to know of the passing of this great man. He'd asked Aden to release a single bulletin out into the world.

It had gone viral within five minutes.

Had they permitted it, thousands of people would've come here today, thousands of people whose lives Zie Zen had touched, made better. Even his enemies respected him, had sent words to acknowledge the loss of a man unlike any who had come before. The Net had gone silent in respect . . . then filled with stories of Zie Zen's impact on people around the globe.

Vasic had seen nothing like it in his entire lifetime. Neither had the rest of the squad.

In the end, he and Ivy had made the decision to limit the funeral and memorial service to those closest to Zie Zen, the ones with whom Zie Zen had had the most intimate contact. The others had been invited to contribute their memories and thoughts about Zie Zen to an archive being curated by two librarians who were alive because of Vasic's great-grandfather.

A hundred people stood here today.

Though Vasic's heart was heavy, his voice raw, he spoke when it was time. Zie Zen would expect nothing less. "My grandfather lived in Silence when he was a man of passionate conviction not meant for cold emotionlessness, and he worked from within to change that which was broken."

Vasic wouldn't speak of Zie Zen's Sunny, for those memories had been his grandfather's alone to share. But he could acknowledge that Zie Zen had carried on for near to a century, even though his heart had shattered at twenty-three when his Sunny died. Even though he had missed her every moment of every day. "He never gave up and he never believed anything impossible. His courage was endless."

Once, Vasic wouldn't have comprehended the depth of his grandfather's searing grief, or understood his infinite valor. Before Ivy. Before he knew what it was to be entwined heart and soul with another.

He reached for her with his mind, found her waiting even as her hand squeezed his tight, giving him the strength to continue. "But more than a great statesman," he said, "Zie Zen was a great man. I am honored to bear his name. I hope I will do you proud, Grandfather." It was too short an epitaph but it came from his soul.

A powerful silence fell, a hundred heads bowed in respect.

VASIC scattered his grandfather's ashes the next dawn, Ivy by his side. "Good-bye, Grandfather," he whispered. "I hope you find your Sunny."

As Zie Zen's ashes flew on the wind, so did the time of those who had been born in freedom, caged in Silence, only to see it fall. Now . . . now it was the time of those who had been born in Silence, fought for freedom.

It's time for the mantle to pass. Zie Zen's voice from a night when they'd walked the orchard together. *The old must give way to the new.*

Wisdom is never old.

Yes, but the young cherish what they've built. So build, Vasic. This is your time, Son. Gather your trusted allies, your gentle, fierce empath, and build your future.

"We will build," Vasic promised. "Today and tomorrow and every day to come."

Chapter 29

THE ARCHITECT OF the Consortium stared out a window, giving Zie Zen a silent moment of respect. Over the years, the man had been a thorn in the Architect's side in countless ways, but he'd been an intelligent, brilliant thorn.

Had the Architect thought it possible the invitation would be accepted, Zie Zen would've been offered entry into the highest level of the Consortium. As it was, the Architect had sought to learn how to be a leader in the shadows by watching Zie Zen, who'd had decades more experience at being a power very few ever truly saw.

Zie Zen had fought for freedom, while the Architect fought for power, but only those without vision ignored the greatness in their midst.

"Good-bye, old enemy," the Architect said as night fell beyond the window. "Let us see who attempts to fill your shoes." Because the Architect needed to kill that person, as the Architect needed to kill Anthony Kyriakus. The PsyNet could have no more great statesmen respected by enemies and allies alike. Not if it was to fragment and unknowingly hand power over to the Consortium.

Changeling, Psy, and human alike believed Trinity protected them from the Consortium's machinations, but the Consortium's attempts to sow discord between various groups and promote general chaos had been just the first salvo. At their next meeting, the Architect intended to suggest the group move strongly and purposefully into phase two within the next six months, once the world was even more mired in the politics of Trinity.

That phase wouldn't be scattershot. It had already been planned with clinical precision, its intent to purge the world of those who provided a foundation on which others could stand. Anthony Kyriakus was on the list for his charismatic ability to command attention from not just Psy but from humans and changelings as well.

In the Architect's eyes, Anthony was more dangerous to the Consortium's goals than Kaleb Krychek, because while Kaleb engendered fear in people that could be twisted if worked carefully, Anthony Kyriakus engendered heavily more positive emotions and responses.

He had become the trusted face of the Ruling Coalition.

Also on the Architect's phase two list was Silver Mercant. No one much talked about Silver, because she didn't seek the spotlight, but her quietly efficient management of the worldwide Emergency Response Network, or what the media had started referring to as EmNet, had gained her the trust of parties worldwide. There was also the little known fact that Silver Mercant was the scion of the Mercant family, Ena Mercant having skipped a generation when choosing her protégée.

The Architect had only recently realized the latter fact, after a passing comment by a Mercant who thought the Architect was an ally in a certain limited sense. And why not? After all, Ena Mercant herself considered the Architect a valuable connection and had maintained an open line of communication even when the Architect's fortunes fluctuated over their decade-long relationship.

Some would say such a gesture of trust was a thing to be treasured. The Architect had other priorities. Do this right and the Mercants would never know the Consortium had gutted their next generation. Then, once the Consortium gained control and began to flex its shadow power, all it had to do was wait. Sooner or later, it would be offered access to the Mercant intelligence network in exchange for a percentage of that power.

That network would be worth the price.

As long as the Architect gave Ena Mercant no reason to believe her granddaughter's death had been a political assassination, that death would soon be forgotten. A freak vehicular crash perhaps. For while the Mercants' vaunted loyalty to one another was a clever bit of manipulation that made the family appear an impregnable unit, when it came down to it, Ena Mercant had always been a pragmatic woman.

The Architect didn't foresee any problems if the plan was carefully executed.

Silver's death would crash EmNet long enough for the Consortium to create emergencies where confusion reigned and promised help never arrived. The resulting cracks would be difficult to fix when the Consortium would be throwing chaotic event after chaotic event into the mix.

On the changeling side, Lucas Hunter was a problem. His Psy-Changeling child remained a symbolic threat, but the leopard alpha himself was an actual one. It was regrettable that the attempt to abduct the child had failed because had the Consortium had control of Nadiya Hunter, the Architect would've used her to control her father.

Because the most recent reports from the Consortium's spies in Trinity showed that Hunter was steadily gaining the support of not just a dangerous number of changeling groups, but that he had the ear of many powerful Psy families as well.

Bowen Knight and Devraj Santos were also irritants to the Consortium's goals, the reason the same in both cases. Humans had always been easy prey, partly because they weren't united under any one banner. Bowen Knight was changing that far faster than even the Architect had predicted. With his passionate belief that humans deserved to stand alongside Psy and changelings on the world stage, the so-called security chief of the Alliance had a magnetism it had taken the Architect too long to understand.

As for the Forgotten, Devraj Santos was the vital force that kept them united. Without him, and given their geographic spread and disparate bloodlines, the Forgotten would dissipate into small, powerless cells. The Architect knew that because the Architect was no fool. There was a

Forgotten in the Consortium's inner circle, a cold-blooded individual who cared nothing for the Forgotten as a people.

Aden Kai and the Arrows would always be a threat, but the Architect had decided to cut the Consortium's losses there for now. Eventually, when the Consortium held enough power behind the scenes, the Arrow Squad would either be made to see reason, or wiped out in a single, ruthless action.

In the meantime, assassinating Ivy Jane Zen would suffice. Aden Kai's second in command was bonded with her, the bond apparently one of love and devotion. So, he would hurt. In the best-case scenario, he'd fall apart, leaving Aden with no deputy. The attack on Ivy Jane would also strike a secondary blow: The Architect accepted that empaths were necessary, but they needed to be kept in their place. Ivy Jane was too well known and too much a hero after the people she'd saved during the outbreaks.

Those six weren't the only ones on the Architect's list, but they were at the top. The assassinations would have to be spread out, made to look like accidents or illnesses. The Architect didn't want credit. The Architect just wanted these problematic individuals erased from the playing board. As demonstrated by Zie Zen, a single strong-minded individual could change the course of the world itself.

When this was over, the Architect intended to be the only one standing.

All it required was patience and precision.

Chapter 30

HAVING POSTPONED NAYA'S visit to Nikita in the face of Vasic's loss, Lucas used the time to hold a much-needed meeting with his sentinels. Naya was on a playdate deep in DarkRiver territory, while Sascha was working at the aerie with a comm conference scheduled for later in the day.

The two pieces of his heart were safe, and all intelligence from the Rats, as well as other sources, pointed to business as usual in the region. No whispers of mercenaries or other enemy incursions. So his pack was safe. The hunt for the ship meant to have carried Naya away from her home continued, but despite his primal need to destroy anyone who'd tried to harm his child, Lucas had never expected that hunt to be an overnight operation. The searches were running, the information filters all in place.

He lost nothing by pulling Dorian from his duties so this meeting could happen.

The alpha and sentinel relationship was critical to the health of a pack and, snarling need for vengeance or not, Lucas had no intention of allowing his to be damaged by a lack of care. For obvious reasons, he'd decided to hold the meeting at Mercy and Riley's cabin. Mercy was not up to making the climb to his aerie, though he knew damn well she'd have given it a try had he been fool enough to schedule a meet there.

As for Riley, the lieutenant was nearby, having a sparring session with Indigo.

Now, Lucas called the meeting to order.

Mostly that involved telling everyone to stop trying to get Mercy to spill the beans on the number and sex of the pupcubs so DarkRiver people could win the betting pool.

Mercy, of course, wasn't budging.

Seated on a comfortable sofa with her legs up on an ottoman Lucas had nudged over and her body leaning against Dorian's—who had his arm affectionately around her shoulders and his plascast-covered leg on a matching ottoman—the redheaded sentinel just gave her fellow sentinels a feline smile and said, "Curiosity killed the cat, didn't you hear?"

The others responded with creative threats that made her laugh. Then the entire group naturally fell quiet, their attention on Lucas.

He knew exactly what he wanted to discuss. "I'm fucking sick of people trying to hurt this pack."

Growls filled the room, every single one of his sentinels in agreement.

"Zero tolerance," Lucas said, making that call as alpha. "As of now, *any* individual caught planning or in the midst of trying to harm a Dark-River child or adult will be executed. We might lose some intel in the process, but fuck that—I want these assholes to think a thousand times before they set foot on our land." Some predators understood only violence.

"The mercenaries we're holding, the ones who tried to snatch Naya," Clay said from his position in an armchair opposite Mercy and Dorian. "What're we going to do with them?"

"I'm not rational there," Lucas answered with blunt honesty. "I want to tear them to shreds."

Clay leaned forward with his hands between his knees, forearms braced on his thighs. "Sascha scrambled two of them. Permanently," he said quietly. "Tamsyn confirmed it just this morning. We can ship them straight to a secure psychiatric unit."

"Shit," Dorian muttered. "Don't tell Sascha. She'll feel guilty when she has no reason to."

Lucas was tempted to follow the sentinel's advice, but keeping secrets from his mate wasn't ever going to be on the agenda. "She'll handle it." It would stun and disturb her, but Lucas's mate was strong and she understood what had been at risk. She'd used her claws in defense of her child and no one, not even Sascha herself, could see a crime in that.

Returning his attention to Clay, he said, "The others from the mercenary team?"

Clay shrugged. "I'm okay with an execution order." His tone was cold, that of a man responsible for the safety of a little girl not so much older than Naya. "They did this for money, took the risk with open eyes."

"Fuck, I want to do that, too," Vaughn said quietly from his chair opposite Lucas, Mercy and Dorian on one side, Clay and Nathan on the other. "But news of the kidnapping attempt went international. Everyone's waiting for the other shoe to fall."

The jaguar pushed back the unbound amber of his hair. "We have to decide what impression we want to make on the world. There's a fine line between fear that keeps our children safe and fear that turns DarkRiver from harsh but fair, to monstrous. You know most Psy and humans have difficulty understanding our laws."

Lucas growled at his best friend, who, right now, was showing an acute grasp of politics. "We'd be handing our enemies a victory by alienating a massive swath of the world."

Vaughn nodded. "The same doesn't apply *post*-warning. At that point, people will blame the assailants for digging their own graves. Pre-warning . . . well, the mercenaries came knowingly into leopard territory. I say we claw them up enough that they'll always bear the marks"—his own claws sliced out—"then we turn them over to Enforcement. Playing nice with local authorities while making it clear this is the last straw."

"I like it." Mercy nodded. "It'll also calm anyone who might be worrying about our growing power in San Francisco."

The reality, as demonstrated by the citizens who'd called DarkRiver rather than Enforcement when they saw the truck smash into Dorian's vehicle, was that DarkRiver could rule San Francisco if it so wished. Lucas wasn't interested in setting up a fiefdom, but he did want this city to be known as a leopard city, a place only the stupid would attempt to hurt.

Vaughn's suggestion would achieve both those aims.

"Done," he said. "I'll mete out the punishment."

Any one of his sentinels would've done it in a heartbeat, but these men and women had threatened Lucas's cub. "Mercy, you set up the press conference. We're going to make a statement tomorrow morning."

No one would see an out-of-control leopard there. No, what they'd see would be a deadly predator in a suit. Smart and ruthless and no one you wanted to piss off—rather, a man you wanted to keep as a friend. Because he looked after his own.

Mercy made a note, her expression approving and her hand on the curve of her belly. There was no one on the planet as dangerous as a dominant predatory changeling woman whose cubs had been threatened.

Calmer now, he was about to move on to another matter when Nathan brought up Trinity. "Luc, what's the response been to Ming LeBon's proposal?"

Lucas smiled and, leaning back in his armchair, put his feet up onto the same ottoman as Mercy. "You should ask our communications expert. She helped me draft the official Trinity reply."

Mercy bent her head and moved her hand in a flowery gesture, as if taking a dramatic bow. *"While we laud former Councilor Ming LeBon's initiative,"* she recited in a deep voice, *"Trinity is unique in its tri-racial structure and world-spanning network. Of course, those European signatories of Trinity who prefer to do business only with other local Psy groups are welcome to join what may well be a very useful entity in its own way."*

Dorian whooped and began to clap. "Tell me if I got the translation right: Hey, if you want to turn your back on changeling and human contacts, as well as on all contacts outside Europe, feel free to join this amusing little group formerly important Ming LeBon is trying to cobble together. The rest of us aren't interested in those who aren't fully supportive of Trinity."

"Perfect." Mercy winked.

Nathan was the only one who didn't smile. "It's a lot of power to have, Lucas," his most senior sentinel said in a quiet tone that held a potent clarity. "Yes, Ming's a monster, but it's a slippery slope if the core members of Trinity start picking and choosing who gets to sign the accord and who doesn't. That'll lead eventually to a world divided in two."

Lucas wished the sentinel wasn't right, but even as he celebrated Ming's slow downfall, he'd been struggling with the long-term ethics of the situation himself. "I don't think we'll ever get agreement on Ming." The telepath had murdered too many, hurt too many, made too many enemies. Having him in Trinity would poison it.

Nathan nodded, his black hair threaded with a few rare threads of silver. "I know and I know Trinity is in the process of being built. But think about the foundation you lay."

This was why Lucas was so damn glad Nathan had chosen to give Lucas his loyalty when Lucas became alpha. He'd lived longer, seen more, had a bone-deep maturity. He made Lucas think about his actions. "I've been considering proposing an adjunct status for cases like Ming's." Not for the ex-Councilor's benefit, but for the reason Nathan had pointed out.

"It'd give the individual or group access to business contacts," Lucas continued, "but they wouldn't be considered a full signatory, would have no voting rights. Their adjunct status would be based on the fact that multiple other signatories have grave concerns about the sincerity of their application." He breathed out, forced himself to continue, though his panther was growling and clawing at him.

This time, the human side had to take precedence. "If, after five years, they've upheld the values of Trinity and not caused any other signatory criminal harm, they would become a full member."

Mercy was the one who broke the silence. "Will the others accept something like that?"

"I don't know." It'd be a hard battle, but Lucas would fight it. He had to or, as Nathan had pointed out, Trinity would be built on a foundation of exclusion rather than inclusion, negating the very reason it had been created. "I think the fact that Ming is too arrogant to ask again should make it easier." No one else in the world was apt to incite this depth of negative reaction.

"We can fix any damage already done by making it clear that even when multiple current signatories have problems with an individual or a group, that individual or group will still be given a chance to prove their authenticity."

Dorian was staring at Lucas. "I always knew you were tough, but you're about to try to take on the wolves, the Arrows, the Forgotten, and God knows who else, all at once." A sudden grin. "Forget brass balls. Those things are goddamn titanium!"

Laughter tore through the tension, and when Clay got up to make some coffee, Lucas asked for a double shot.

"Can you get me a glass of warm milk?" Mercy asked, then pointed a finger at a spluttering Dorian. "Not a word. I happen to have developed a taste for it." A pause. "It's weird."

Nuzzling at her with the affection of a man who'd known her since they were children, Dorian said, "Dude, you're growing tiny people inside you. You can be as weird as you like." He rose to his feet as Mercy smiled. "I'll get your milk."

Only after everyone else was caffeinated did they return to pack business. Which happened to once again be connected to Trinity—but this time in a far less fraught way. One of the most basic tenets of the accord was that all parties could contact one another and open lines of communication existed for people across racial, pack, and family lines.

An unfortunate side effect had been a barrage of calls offering DarkRiver various "amazing" business "opportunities," the offers made by Psy, humans, and changelings alike. Lucas had put Nate in charge of the flood because he not only had the most even temper of them all, he also had the experience to glean real opportunities from the dross.

"It's died down a little," Nate reported after retaking his seat, coffee in hand and the sleeves of his blue-and-red-checked shirt folded up. That shirt was clean except for a smear of purple near the collar where one of the twins had gotten jam on it while hugging him good-bye that morning.

"I've actually got two good ones to share."

The first was from a tiny human company founded and run by a couple out of their own home. "Scratch-proof coating for wooden floors,"

Nathan told them after introducing the founders. "They swore it'd work against changeling claws, so I had them send me a sample, put it on over a miraculously unscratched part of an upstairs room, then had the boys go to town on it."

"I don't have a cub," Vaughn drawled, "but even I can tell that might not have been the best idea."

Nathan grinned. "No, the twins understood this was a special treat. Any rampaging through the house and they'll be facing their mother's wrath."

Saluting Nate with his coffee cup, Vaughn took the organizer the other man passed over, then moved to sit on Mercy's other side. "Wouldn't have expected a human company to come up with this," he commented as he, Mercy, and Dorian studied the images on the organizer.

"Me either," Nathan said, "but you can see it works. I tested it myself, too, to see how it held up against adult claws. Not a scratch." He took a drink of his coffee before continuing. "I think we should set up a more in-depth talk with them, with an eye toward investing in the company."

"Do it." Lucas trusted Nathan's judgment and if DarkRiver was going to continue to thrive, they had to be open to new partnerships and concepts. Because if Psy could be arrogant to the point of hobbling themselves, Sascha had made him realize that changelings had a parallel failing—a tendency to look inward.

Next, Nathan briefed them on the second possible investment opportunity, before Clay took over to talk about operational security matters. Then it was Dorian's turn to update them on his hunt for the ship that had been meant to be Naya's prison. That, of course, turned the mood angry again, as they all thought of what had almost happened.

"Look," Mercy said afterward, her own anger a hot burn across her skin, "I know we have a ton on our minds and there's all kinds of shit going down in the world, but we need to talk about this joint party." She stroked her bump in a self-calming gesture. "It's important."

Lucas nodded. A changeling's strength came from his family, and this celebration, it was all about family. Lose sight of that and they lost what made them changeling, leopard, DarkRiver. "The cubs and pups are excited for it." The thought brought a smile back to his face.

"Riley's got intel that says Ben, Jules, and Rome are already plotting a cake-eating contest." As Mercy spoke, she stretched her ankles by flexing them back and forth.

"Wait." Dorian peered at her toenails, currently painted a hot pink. "Did *Riley* do that? I mean since you can't reach your toes?"

Every cat in the room stared, agog at the idea.

Mercy growled low in her throat. "If he did?"

"Huh?" Dorian scratched his jaw, then smiled that heartbreaker surfer boy smile that had charmed many a woman before he fell madly for his scientist mate. "I'd do it for Shaya if she was a crazy pregnant chick like you."

"Watch who you call crazy, Blondie." Mercy gave her best friend a death stare while the others grinned. "As it happens, it wasn't my wolf. Anu came over with her kit." She held out her hands. "I went for a metallic-blue accent nail on this end. See?"

Taking one hand, Dorian studied her fingertips. "Does this stuff last when you shift?"

Lucas coughed. "Back to the meeting. You two can have your beauty-therapy discussion later." Catching the cushion Mercy lobbed at his head, he put it behind his back, then caught a cookie Vaughn threw over, the jaguar having sniffed out the stash Bastien had left Mercy. "Party. Go."

"Right." Mercy laid out her choice of location plus the general details of how she thought the event should be run. Then she brought up the guest list. "SnowDancer and DarkRiver yes, but do we want to invite our other allies, or those who've helped the pack or are connected to us in nonlinear ways?"

The question felt all the more significant after their discussion about Trinity.

Vaughn was the one who spoke, his voice holding a quiet intensity. "When Faith left the PsyNet, she did it believing she'd never again have any real contact with her father." Eyes of near-gold met Lucas's. "It turned out Anthony isn't an asshole and he loves his children. I think it'd mean a lot to her to be able to invite her father to a pack function."

Lucas knew Sascha wouldn't be inviting Nikita, even had DarkRiver trusted the ex-Councilor not to turn around and stab them in the back. Their relationship was very different from the one Faith had with Anthony, but he could see Vaughn's point.

"There's also Kaleb Krychek," he said. "Man can go wherever he wants, find whoever he wants, so there's no security issue with him." Not all teleporters could lock on to people as well as places, but Krychek definitely could. "He's also been a source of assistance and information multiple times. And his mate is family through Faith."

Vaughn nodded. "Sahara's tightly linked to the Empathic Collective because of the work she does monitoring their work levels and collating reports on the health of the Honeycomb itself, but Faith still worries about her being isolated."

Lucas had felt the same concern when Faith's cousin went back to Krychek after a sojourn in DarkRiver. However, though the dangerous cardinal telekinetic wasn't sociable by any measure, he appeared not to begrudge his mate the social or familial contact she needed to thrive—he'd teleported Sahara into DarkRiver territory multiple times so she could visit with Faith, Sascha, and her other friends.

"I don't see a problem with inviting Sahara and Kaleb," Dorian said. "And Faith's father seems like one of the good ones. Shaya likes him."

Clay simply nodded in agreement.

It was Nathan who spoke next. "I'm fine with inviting them, too, but we'll have to change the location. Currently, while neither pack circle will be compromised, Mercy and Riley's home *will* be—and they'll have pup-cubs there very soon."

"That's a big minus." Mercy worried her lower lip. "The only other possible location is the empathic training compound, but they're running full classes back-to-back."

Lucas frowned. "I'm not sure that's right. Give me a second." Taking out his phone, he sent a message to Sascha, got a response back nearly immediately. "The current class closes in just over two weeks and the next one won't start until two weeks after that. We can hold the event during the time the area is vacant."

"Perfect." Mercy patted her belly. "If these little guys are still snuggling inside, we'll celebrate their impending birth rather than their actual birth."

"And," Clay said, "there's no security issue with the people we want to invite. They all have to know the location by now."

"Anyone else outside the pack we want to invite?" Lucas asked.

"Max and Sophia." Clay placed his empty coffee mug on a nearby table. "They're friends, but they've also earned an invite after the number of times they've quietly assisted the pack."

"I think leave off the falcons and BlackSea this time around," Nathan said. "They're allies, but the relationship is still in progress in both cases. We're better off sticking to one-on-one meetings for now."

Mercy nodded. "I don't think they'd expect an invite at this point."

No one disagreed.

It was Clay who spoke next. "There's another group that also won't expect an invite but that I think has more than earned one—trouble will be convincing the wolves of that."

In the end, they found themselves with a fairly limited list of outside-pack guests that Lucas would discuss with Hawke. This was a joint event all the way, so neither side would be making unilateral decisions. "If SnowDancer agrees," he said, "we'll probably end up hosting a few Arrows, too, courtesy of Judd's connections."

His phone beeped before any of the others could answer. It was an alert from BlackSea requesting that, as an ally, DarkRiver stand by for the next forty-eight hours ready to render assistance should it be required: I hope we need it, Miane had written. Because that would mean we've found Leila and are in the process of ripping another head off the hydra that is the Consortium.

Chapter 31

IVY GRIEVED WITH Vasic in the days following Zie Zen's passing, but like him, she couldn't switch off. They both had responsibilities, not just to Tavish and the squad, but to many others. In her case, that meant the health of her empaths and, of course, the tense issue of the hidden disintegration of the psychic fabric of the PsyNet, a disintegration that was weakening a psychic structure that supported millions of minds.

In Vasic's case, it meant his duties as Aden's deputy, as well as the commitments he'd made to friends and allies. It was on the day after they'd scattered Zie Zen's ashes that Ivy, Vasic, Tavish, and Rabbit returned home from a morning walk through the fruit trees to find Miane Levèque had left a message on their comm and on the phone Vasic had forgotten in the cabin.

"Vasic, I know you lost your grandfather only days ago," she'd said, her voice somber, "but we have what might be a real, viable lead on Leila. We need to move on it as soon as possible. If you can't do it, I understand." Compassion in the alpha's tone, no judgment. "But please let me know within the hour so I can rework our plans."

Ivy's husband would've been justified in saying no, but he didn't. He put on his Arrow uniform and slid a single gold coin into an inner pocket in memory of his grandfather. "If we save this BlackSea changeling," he said, his voice potent with memory and with resolve, "we strike a blow to the Consortium. Zie Zen would've appreciated that."

Because, Ivy thought, all of Zie Zen's plans and intrigues had flowed from a single overriding goal: to return freedom to his people. "Yes," she whispered. "He wouldn't thank us for leaving a woman caged when we might be able to free her."

Smoothing her hands over the front of his uniform, she carefully folded up and pinned the sleeve of his missing arm. Vasic could've had his uniforms altered so this wasn't necessary, but with Samuel Rain continuing to experiment with prosthetics, he'd left it.

That choice said something powerful about the man she loved. Though he'd adapted to the loss of his arm to the point that the prosthetics often annoyed him, he kept giving Samuel a chance. All for a simple reason: the other man's mind was such that it needed a challenge and this challenge kept him focused and mentally healthy.

"There," she said after completing her self-appointed task. "You'll be careful?"

Vasic cupped her cheek with his hand, his eyes a stormy gray today. Filled with echoes of grief. "Yes," he promised. "I need to come back home to you."

Ivy's heart ached at the raw power of his words, at the love that lived in his touch. Turning her head, she pressed a kiss to his palm. "Your grandfather was so proud of you, Vasic," she said to him afterward, her eyes locked with his. "Don't ever forget that."

Drawing her close, Vasic held her for long moments. "You'll take care on the PsyNet? This strange disintegration you showed me, it may be as insidious as the original rot."

"I will, I promise." Ivy had no intention of bringing their journey together to a premature end. Yes, there was grief here, but there was also love, laughter, hope. "I'm having a comm conference with Sascha and several of the other Es to brainstorm solutions and explanations." She forced herself to step back. "I love you."

You're my heart, Ivy.

Holding the words close after he teleported out, Ivy sniffed back her tears, put a smile firmly on her face, and went to find Tavish. She and Vasic had permitted him to stay home from the Valley school to this point, but she decided that would change come tomorrow morning. Like any Arrow child, he needed the certainty of routine—and being with his friends would hopefully help take his mind off the loss their family had so recently suffered.

"Tavish? Rabbit?"

Scrabbling claws on the floor as a small white bullet shot out of Tavish's room to come over to her, tail wagging. She knelt down and petted the dog who'd been with her since before she'd found her strength, who had, in fact, *helped* her find her strength with his own brave fight to survive. The act of stroking his fur comforted her as it had always done.

"What have you two been up to?" she asked Tavish when the seven-year-old came to the doorway.

"The schoolwork the teacher sent," he answered, a faltering smile on his face. "Is Vasic gone?"

"Yes, we're all getting back to work." Giving Rabbit one final pat, she moved over to hug Tavish.

Rabbit had padded alongside her and now leaned his body against Tavish's.

"I have to go to school tomorrow?" A quiet question with a tremor behind it.

Tavish had been abandoned by his family when he was signed over to the squad, at which point, he hadn't been encouraged to form any bonds at all. Then had come this new family and a wary dawning of hope.

Zie Zen's death had struck a harsh blow to that hope, but Vasic and Ivy were helping the boy work through it by always reiterating that unlike the members of his biological family, Zie Zen hadn't chosen to leave him behind, that it had simply been time for the older man to travel on to the next stage of existence, whatever that might be.

Going down on her knees in front of the boy, Ivy took his hands in her own. "What did Grandfather always say?"

"That education is important, and that the man who has the most information is the man who can change the tides of the world itself," Tavish repeated almost word for word.

It was clear he didn't understand it all, but he understood enough. "So," Ivy said, "school tomorrow." She smiled. "Your friends are missing you, you know. The teacher told me."

A whisper of a smile warmed Tavish's eyes. "School tomorrow," he agreed, then bent down to pet Rabbit. "Can you play with Rabbit and me today?"

"Not just yet." Ivy kissed him on the cheek before rising back up. "I have a comm conference, then some other work to complete. But my mother would like your help in her garden. You can finish your schoolwork later."

Tavish's face lit up. Ducking inside his room, he came back out having changed into his designated gardening clothes and with a hat on his head. They picked up his child-sized gloves and tools from the outdoor shed before Ivy walked him over to her parents' home. Her mother was already outside in the vegetable garden.

Thank you, she telepathed to the woman with the strong, rangy body who'd given birth to her.

Gwen Jane would never be the warm and cuddly epitome of the maternal instinct, but she'd *fought* for her child's right to live and to be happy. As had Ivy's father. She loved them with every beat of her heart.

It's not an issue, her mother telepathed back. *The child has a green thumb and a willingness to learn. And it's useful to have a telekinetic around when I need a spade or forget my gloves in the house.*

Ivy's lips twitched. She was certain her mother was developing a sense of humor, but she was never quite sure. "Have fun," she said to Tavish, who was already pulling on his gloves and getting ready to weed.

She'd asked her mother to watch him until noon because the comm conference she was about to have was nothing a child should accidentally overhear. Especially not a child whose mind was anchored in the PsyNet.

She initiated the conference as soon as she arrived back home.

After clearing some minor operational details, she and her team moved on to the real reason for this meeting. The weakness, the fracture lines, the disintegration that threatened to collapse the Net. A number of the team had received reports of unstable areas from empaths in the zone for which they were responsible. When they put all the pieces together, it made for an upsetting picture.

"It's worse than I thought," Ivy said, dismayed. "Sahara, has Kaleb been able to dig up any further data on this?" The powerful Tk knew the DarkMind best of all and the neosentience had an affinity for the rot that overlay this disintegration. And though its twin, the NetMind, loved empaths, it had known Kaleb longer; he seemed to be able to talk to it in a way even Es couldn't.

"No, I'm sorry, Ivy." Sahara's dark blue eyes were solemn. "I asked him to make contact before this meeting and he says he's getting the same images he did before—of bodies having their organs forcibly torn out, a calendar that stops at the dawn of Silence."

The hairs rose on Ivy's arms as they'd done the first time Kaleb shared the information with her. "What the hell are we missing?"

No one had any answers, not even Alice Eldridge, who'd completed a groundbreaking and in-depth study of empaths. "Regardless of my spotty memory," the other woman said, rubbing at her forehead, "I'm not sure I could help here. I don't have any proof but I don't think this is an empathic issue. There's another problem, one we're blind to for some reason."

Slowly, faces drawn and worry a heavy weight on their shoulders, the team began to sign off, until only Sascha and Sahara were left. Ivy had been disappointed by Sascha's lack of participation in the meeting—the cardinal was the most senior E in the world. She'd been "awake" the longest, had run countless tests on her abilities while the rest of them were still mired in Silence.

Yes, Ivy and the others had made certain breakthroughs, but Sascha's years of intensive study and experimentation gave her a depth of knowledge nothing could beat. Especially with the Es in the Net strained to their limit handling not just the Honeycomb but the confusion and need of a population staggering awake from a long, Silent sleep.

No one had time to do anything but react.

A dedicated E designation research team was a pipe dream.

As a result, Sascha had unofficially taken up the research baton, and Ivy had been hopeful of her contribution. Assuming the cardinal empath's reticence had to do with the fact that, having defected from the PsyNet, Sascha no longer had real-time data, Ivy went to reiterate the Collective's need for Sascha's advice.

But the other woman spoke before she could and it immediately became crystal clear that Sascha *had* been engaged in the meeting. She'd simply been absorbing all available data and putting the pieces together. "Sophie," the cardinal said with a frown. "Have you checked her section of the Net?"

Ivy nodded. She didn't know Sophia Russo well, but every E in Sophia's part of the world was aware that the section of the PsyNet immediately around Sophia's mind was different. Stable. Deeply peaceful.

So much so that tired Es strained to the limit had been known to deliberately linger in that section to catch their breath.

What nobody but a rare few knew, however, was that the difference had to do with how Sophia Russo was anchored into the Net—the mind of Nikita Duncan's senior aide was woven into the PsyNet by millions of fine connections, rather than being linked to it by a single biofeedback link.

In essence, Sophia Russo wasn't jacked into the Net, she was *part of the fabric of the Net itself.* And in her mind, the mind of a J-Psy who had always accepted darkness as well as light, the NetMind and DarkMind were one. No division, no fractures, no damage, that joyous wholeness reflected in the cool clear pond that was Sophia's anchor point.

"Sophia's area is as stable and peaceful as always," she told Sascha, the fact one that gave her hope.

"Totally stable?" Sascha pressed. "No shrinkage of her zone of influence?"

Ivy frowned. "I checked after Kaleb first showed me the disintegration, but I wasn't looking for that in particular." Dread coalescing in her veins, she said, "Give me three minutes. I'm going to make a more detailed assessment."

What she found was extraordinary.

Dropping out of the Net, Ivy stared at Sascha. "How did you know?" It came out a husky whisper.

"What did you see?" the cardinal Psy asked.

"Sophia's zone of influence has *grown*, Sascha. Not enough to be noticed on a casual pass, but look again and it's obvious." Where once, two or three empaths could've lingered in that area at any one time, it could now accommodate four, maybe even five.

Sascha blew out a breath. "I didn't know," she said. "I was hoping, because so long as Sophia is holding steady, there's a chance to save the Net before it collapses. We just have to figure out what makes her unique."

Frowning, Sahara said, "It can't just be that she accepts both sides of her nature, allowing the NetMind and DarkMind to be one at that point, because if that was true—"

"—then the Net should be healing, even if at a glacial pace," Ivy completed, because with the fall of Silence had come a tumultuous surge of emotion into the Net. "Is it because of how Sophia's mind is woven into the Net?"

Tucking back a strand of hair that had escaped her braid, Sascha said, "It's possible. Sophie is more deeply integrated into the PsyNet than anyone else on the planet."

"How could we ever duplicate that?" Sahara's question was stark. "It might help if we knew how and why Sophia Russo's mind anchored that way."

Sascha gave a gentle shake of her head. "Sophie's story is hers to tell, but I asked her once what I could share should the question of the genesis of her anchor point ever come up, and she gave me leave to tell you that it was an instinctive survival act. I don't think even she could provide us with instructions."

Head beginning to pound as if it were being struck repeatedly by a hammer, Ivy looked down at a small bark to see that Rabbit had run back from her mother's home to pay her a visit. He always did that, happily running back and forth when his people were in two separate locations in a single area. "Let me get Rabbit some water," she said to the other women and went to refill his bowl.

As he began to lap it up, his tail wagging, she found herself thinking of the community her parents had helped build in this corner of North Dakota, how it was a living organism of a kind. Each individual unique and separate, but together forming a cohesive—

Her eyes widened.

All but running back to the comm, she interrupted Sahara midword. "Can you ask Kaleb to help rope in the NetMind to search for any other healthy sections? Areas like Sophia Russo's?"

"That's brilliant, Ivy." Sascha's eyes bled to pure black. "With Sophia alone, we have only guesswork, but if we can find a second mind that's helping the Net to heal, we can compare similarities and differences."

"But wouldn't your Es have already spotted such sections?" Sahara pressed her fingers against her temples, as if she'd caught Ivy's headache. "I first heard about Sophia from one of them."

"I'm going to alert the entire Collective to be on the lookout," Ivy said, already drafting that message in her head. "That might be enough to jar loose important memories—because if the area is small, an E might not have noticed except to think he or she felt good when passing by."

Ivy hoped that was the case, because the other scenario was bleak: that Sophia's was the solitary healthy area.

Chapter 32

VASIC ARRIVED AT the coordinates he'd been given by Miane Levèque to find himself on one of their floating cities. The BlackSea alpha was dressed in camouflage gear, her face painted with stripes of black and her above-shoulder-length hair scraped back into a small tail. There were five others with her, including a large male Vasic recognized as Malachai Rhys.

"Vasic." Eyes softening, Miane touched her fingers lightly to his forearm. "Thank you for coming."

He accepted the tactile gesture of sympathy with a quiet nod. "Where do you need to go?"

Miane held out her hand. On it was a small disk that she pressed down on to bring up a detailed hologram of an old pier. The battered sign at the end identified it as Edward's Pier.

Vasic looked at the image, tried for a teleport lock, achieved it. "This is perfect. How did you get the original image?"

Miane and Malachai exchanged a look before seeming to decide to trust him. "We sent in a packmate who can shift into a snake—freshwater," Miane said. "He's unusual in that his snake form is relatively small. We took the risk that it wouldn't set off any sensors calibrated for changeling water creatures."

Vasic nodded, realizing they'd asked for a 'port because a bigger team couldn't replicate that stealth sweep. "Let's go."

"It's not dark there," Miane said. "Your uniform—"

Vasic had touched a control on his shoulder as she spoke. It was usually located on the left wrist, but had been moved to the left shoulder for him. One touch and his uniform morphed into a camouflage pattern.

"Handy." Malachai took in the change with interested eyes. "Want to share that tech?"

Vasic took the grease pot Miane held out, striped his face. "Talk to Aden." He knew it was unlikely his friend and the leader of the squad would agree to it. Arrows still needed certain advantages and this technology was cutting edge, created by scientists the squad had saved from death and who now worked for the squad—not under duress, but because the squad gave them the funds and the freedom to explore their ideas.

Throwing the grease pot to one of Miane's people who was dressed in civilian clothing and who had just finished checking the earpieces to be used by the incursion team, he said, "Move into a tight formation around me." He could teleport the six-strong BlackSea team at one time, but only if they minimized the distances between their bodies. "I'm going to 'port us into the area between the trees to the left of the shot."

It took three seconds for them to organize as he'd requested and then he was making the 'port. The team melted against the trees and into the long grasses the instant after arrival, and so did Vasic. They were good, Miane's people. If he hadn't known they were there, he might not have seen them immediately.

On his first visual scan, he saw nothing except the pier, along with scattered trees. The knee-high grasses waved in the breeze. There were no indications that their slender forms had been pressed down by the passage of even a single pair of feet. That didn't rule out teleporters, but given that there were a limited number of teleport-capable Tks in the world, the possibility was low. Not negligible, however.

It was on his second visual sweep that he spotted something on the other side of the most open patch of grass directly beyond the pier. Making a sign for Miane to wait, he teleported to the site. It was what he'd suspected—a surveillance unit. A closer look showed it to be dead.

Taking it back to BlackSea, he pointed out the water damage and ingrained dirt. "Doesn't look like anyone's bothered to maintain it." As if this location had been abandoned.

Miane's jaw tensed. "We still stay low, stay quiet, on alert."

"Agreed." He let the BlackSea team take the lead because he needed to be able to see everyone so he could pull them out if there was a problem. With them now spread out, he'd have to do it in bursts.

Two seconds after they began, the entire team froze at a gust of sound, but it was only waterfowl taking flight from the waterway beyond the old wooden pier.

It took an hour for them to move from their start position not far from the water's edge and up along a line following the open strip on which there were no trees, only what appeared to be the kind of grasses and weeds that grew quickly on land that had been cleared by outside forces.

Miane clearly believed this had once been a dirt track. She was proven right when a couple of minutes after the hour mark, they turned a slight corner and came within visual sight of a squat man-made structure.

Vasic hadn't asked for an earpiece to match those worn by the Black-Sea team, now realized that had been a mistake. If he had one, he could've spoken to Miane, who was in the lead, told her it made the most sense for him to teleport there. Even as the thought passed through his head, the BlackSea alpha turned to look at him. She made a motion toward the structure.

He teleported, taking care to ensure he didn't end up right next to the building but nearby. Then he made his way closer with painstaking focus, crawling there on his front. Having only one upper limb made the task a little more difficult, even given his Tk—this was a situation where one of Samuel's prosthetics might've come in useful.

He knew they were too late the instant he saw the slightly open door, spotted the browned leaves piled in that narrow gap. Still, he took no risks. Retrieving a low-tech tool from a thigh pocket, a tool that was basically a slender piece of metal with a small angled mirror at the end, he used it to look inside the building.

All he saw were signs of neglect.

Including thick cobwebs that crisscrossed the space and couldn't have been spun had anyone been moving in the area even a week earlier. He was too much an Arrow, however, to take it as a given that one empty room meant the entire structure was empty. Sliding away the mirror, he made his way around the side of the building and to the back. There was a small hole at the bottom that looked like damage caused by wear and tear.

Again, he used his tool to look inside.

More cobwebs.

The structure had no other rooms from what he could tell.

Lifting his hand, he waved Miane's people over. They came in quiet as ghosts, but one look inside the structure and it was confirmed they were weeks, more likely months, too late.

"She *was* here," Miane said, striding to a dusty corner and pointing to a green bracelet that appeared to have been forgotten there. "I saw her wearing this at our last Conclave."

Vasic glanced at her. "Why aren't you picking it up?" It should've been an instinctive act for a woman born in a tactile, emotional race.

"Because I'm hoping we can get a psychometric in here." She looked at her people. "Everyone out. Let's leave this place as clean as possible for the Ps-Psy, if we can get him." Miane turned to Vasic. "Can you 'port me back to Lantia? I need to make some calls. The others will stay here and we can move them out on water transport now that we know this location is abandoned."

Vasic got her to the floating city, said, "If you need someone to take the psychometric to the site, I'll do it."

"We're starting to owe the Arrows far too many favors," Miane said without heat. "Thank you. Now let me see if he's willing to do this."

VASIC was both surprised and not when the Ps-Psy proved to be Tanique Gray. Anthony Kyriakus's children had never been ordinary and, given their father, their rebel leanings were almost to be expected. Because he'd seen psychometrics at work before, Vasic kept Tanique within sight once he'd 'ported Miane and the young male to the location of Leila Savea's captivity, ready to get him to a medical unit should it be necessary.

He didn't think Miane and the other changelings realized the cost of a Ps-Psy's abilities. Likely because psychometrics were rare and tended to work mostly with museums and the like. That didn't negate the danger; it simply kept it out of public view. The last emergency Vasic had heard of, had involved a Ps-Psy who'd been asked to verify the provenance of an old sword.

He'd been paid a considerable sum to handle the weapon because most psychometrics wouldn't touch anything with a known history of violence. As it happened, the compensation could never have been enough. The Ps-Psy had managed to scream that the weapon had been used in a *recent* massacre before he stopped talking and started convulsing.

He was still in a high-dependency unit in a private medical facility. The chances of his waking up were slim, but he was kept alive because there *was* a chance, and Ps-Psy were valuable enough that no one wanted to squander the opportunity, should it exist.

Today he saw Tanique freeze to a stop on the floor of the main room, well before he reached the entrance to what must've been Leila Savea's cell. The younger male's muscles contracted, his hands fisting as his breathing turned ragged.

Vasic didn't hesitate. He teleported the other man out of the building and into the trees just outside.

Miane spun around to face Vasic. "What the hell? He was getting something."

"He was about to go into a seizure." Shifting on his heel, Vasic walked to where he'd teleported Tanique.

Faith NightStar's brother was bent over with his hands on his knees, his chest heaving as he sucked in gulps of air.

"What's wrong with him?" Miane asked, but didn't wait for an answer before pulling out a bottle of water from the pack of a nearby BlackSea soldier and walking over to put it by Tanique's feet.

Vasic liked her better for the action, for her awareness that her packmate's life wasn't the only one that held importance. Waiting until she'd returned to his side, he said, "A psychometric picks up echoes. The older the object, the duller the echo. The newer the object, the harsher and louder."

Frowning, the BlackSea alpha said, "He wasn't handling anything at the time."

"Why do you think he took off his shoes before he went inside?" The building itself was an object and Tanique's bare feet had been on a critical part of it.

Realization chilled Miane's features. "Leila was tortured on that spot," she said in a cold, hard voice. "And that kid relived it?"

That "kid" was a highly gifted psychometric who cost hundreds of thousands to the institutions that hired him. But yes, he "felt" young. Innocent. Enough that Vasic was compelled by the urge to protect him as he would young Arrows who were out of their depth. "We'll find out soon." Because Tanique was picking up the bottle of water and drinking.

"Is he sensing things from the bottle?" Miane frowned. "Shit, I didn't even think about it hurting him."

Vasic shook his head. "He can shield against his sensitivity to physical echoes the same way powerful telepaths can shield against the noise of the world." Tanique had to deliberately lower his shields to sense anything from the objects around him.

"I'm glad for him." Miane folded her arms. "It'd be hell to walk through life never knowing what object or place might send you right into a nightmare."

The psychometric finished half the bottle, capped it, then came to stand opposite them, more on Vasic's side than Miane's. "Thank you," he said to Vasic, his pupils still hugely dilated. "I've never been near such a recent violent event."

Some might have been surprised by that, since Tanique was Anthony's son and Anthony was known to be a ruthless operator. But Anthony didn't think in terms of exploiting his family. He had to understand what Tanique's ability demanded from him, must've ensured his son was never asked to take on tasks that could permanently compromise him.

Vasic inclined his head. "Did you pick up anything useful that might help us track the BlackSea changeling?" He'd phrased the question very deliberately so Tanique wouldn't feel forced to detail Leila Savea's torture.

That would help no one, and while Miane Levèque could put on the appearance of calm, Vasic knew she was changeling under the skin, had the same primal drives. There was no point in enraging her any further.

"Nothing," Tanique said after shooting Vasic a grateful look. "I think I should focus on the doorway. Since it's the only route by which they could've left, I stand a higher chance of picking up facts about their departure."

"Wait." Miane went as if to touch Tanique's upper arm, dropped her hand partway. "Do you sense things from people, too?" she asked, though Vasic didn't think that had been her original intention.

Tanique shook his head. "Only inanimate objects, though the size of the object doesn't have a bearing on my ability. I have picked up echoes from trees in rare circumstances, but that's about as close as I get to reading a living creature."

"Good to know." Miane accompanied them back to the doorway. "Did you pick up anything about the people who are keeping Leila captive? Are they Psy?"

Tanique took several seconds to reply. "You must understand," he said at last. "What I see, I have to interpret. It comes in kaleidoscopic pieces in a massive rush . . . like I'm standing in a wind tunnel with images blowing past me at rapid speed, and those images are in splinters."

The young male had left out a critical word: "emotion."

That was the secret psychometrics had somehow managed to keep through Silence—that when they read an object, they felt the emotional resonance attached to it. It was why so many of them had switched to dating *only* paintings or other objets d' art. Things that were highly unlikely to have an intimate history of violence. Weapons had been off the agenda for most Ps-Psy for far longer than the span of Silence.

"You're telling me you can't say anything with certainty?" Miane asked, and though she had to be fighting a brutal tumult of emotions, her tone was even. "Without that clue about Edward's Pier, we'd never have got this far."

"It's different with people," Tanique said. "Especially when it comes to race. Unless a changeling shifted right at the moment I pick up, or a Psy used his or her ability in an obvious way, all I can give you are my impressions."

Again, he was leaving out the impact of emotion. A holdover from when he'd had to hide that aspect of his abilities under Silence?

"Understood," Miane said. "What did you get?"

"Two people. One female, one male. No real impression of their faces." *Leila was bleeding, had been recently beaten, her face cut. Should I tell the alpha?*

That last statement was sent telepathically to Vasic. *No,* he answered. *Focus only on the practical facts.*

Aloud, Tanique said, "My impression is of weapons around the male, not so much around the female, but that's it. Nothing you can use for identification purposes."

Miane's mouth tightened but she didn't push any further as Tanique went to the doorway. Keeping her voice low, she spoke to Vasic. "He's more green than I realized. Pull him out if you think he's in trouble—he helped us get this far and I'm not repaying that by screwing up his head."

Vasic didn't take his eyes off Tanique. "Even at the cost of your pack-mate's life?"

Voice grim, Miane said, "He's someone's kid, too." That statement was followed by one that was far more pragmatic. "And he can't help us if he's dead or if his brain is damaged by convulsions."

In front of them, Tanique was running his hands all around the door-way. Satisfied with whatever he sensed, he put one foot inside, then two. He stayed there for about a minute before he walked back to join them. "Water," he said. "The overwhelming impression is of water. Saltwater," he specified. "They're heading in the direction of saltwater."

Vasic could sense Miane's frustration. There were oceans filled with saltwater.

Then Tanique said, "Contained. The saltwater is contained." He frowned. "Old concrete and saltwater."

That immediately narrowed the focus but it still cast a wide net. Somewhere out there, there was a saltwater pool or reservoir where Leila had been taken either so she could swim and regain her muscle tone, or where she was being trained for an operation.

"Anything else?" Miane asked. "Even the smallest crumb could help us narrow down the search area."

Tanique rubbed his temple. "It doesn't make sense, but I did catch an image of a feline of some kind." He lifted his hands instinctively above his head, cupping them in the shape of ears before he seemed to realize what he was doing and dropped them. "Its ears stood straight up and they had black tufts on the tops."

"Could one of them be a changeling?"

Vasic had pulled out his palm-sized organizer and was scrolling through images of felines as Miane asked that question.

"I don't know," Tanique said. "It was a very faint impression, could even have been from a feline incursion into the building prior to your packmate's captivity here."

Vasic turned the screen of the organizer toward Tanique. "Did the feline look like this?"

"Yes. What is it?"

"A Canadian lynx."

Miane blew out a breath. "There are multiple lynx packs across Canada, never mind the world, but at least we have a place to start." She held out a hand toward Tanique. "Thank you. We owe you one."

Vasic wondered if the alpha realized she'd just pledged a favor to PsyClan NightStar.

As he watched, Miane walked to the building, pressed her hand against it, and said, "We'll find you, Leila. Don't give up. Your pack is coming."

PART 4

Chapter 33

MIDMORNING THE DAY after the unsuccessful attempt to rescue Leila Savea, and Dorian had tracked down the ship involved in the abduction attempt against Naya. Lucas had just authorized the plan the sentinel had put together for the capture of the ship's captain when Devraj Santos arrived in DarkRiver territory with his wife, Katya, and a boy named Cruz.

The leader of the Forgotten had become a stronger and stronger ally over time, the relationship between DarkRiver and SnowDancer and the Forgotten such that he'd asked the packs to offer sanctuary to gifted Forgotten children and their families. That sanctuary was needed because the world had more than one mercenary individual who wanted to control the children's unique new abilities.

Lucas had known Dev was coming, and now the two of them stood to one side of a small open area in the forest, where Naya, Keenan, and Noor were playing with Cruz. The older boy was good-natured about the younger children's enthusiasm; nothing about him betrayed that he was a telepath of cardinal-level power, his eyes near-black with unexpected flickers of dark gold rather than night sky. Because Cruz was one of the Forgotten, not Psy.

As Lucas watched, Cruz went to say something to Sascha before he smiled and returned to the field of play. Lucas's mate was standing with Katya and Ashaya, the three women having a quiet discussion. Dev's wife and Ashaya had once been scientists in a lab controlled by Ming LeBon.

Both had helped children even when they couldn't fashion an escape for those children, and both had paid a price for that help. While Lucas didn't know Katya as well as he did Ashaya, he had a soft spot for her.

Katya, in turn, had a giant one for Noor and Keenan, the bond between them formed out of bleak despair that had been transformed into incandescent joy.

His and Dev's current conversation, however, had nothing to do with either the children, the Forgotten hidden in DarkRiver and SnowDancer, or Cruz. It involved a Forgotten teenager who Lucas had claimed as part of his pack.

"I've confirmed the rumors your Rats first picked up," Dev said to him, the golden brown skin of his face all harsh lines. "There's a bounty out on Jon. Five million to anyone who can capture him alive."

Lucas's claws pricked at his skin. When the Rats reported the rumor over a month earlier, he'd immediately gotten in touch with Dev. Both because the Forgotten had made it a point to infiltrate networks that might pose a threat to their people and because if someone was after Jon, it was possible he or she—or they—would also attempt to snatch other Forgotten children.

Such abduction attempts had already occurred more than once.

"Our message wasn't an empty threat," he said in a tone that held the panther's harsh rage. "Anyone hurts or tries to hurt or take one of Dark-River's young, and they'll die by claws and teeth."

"You haven't heard the best part." Dev's voice was both approving and amused.

Lucas went to answer, was distracted when Cruz came running over.

"I forgot my juice," the boy said, his face hot from exertion.

Dev picked it up off the picnic blanket Sascha had brought, on which she'd placed snacks and drinks for the children. "Here you go," he said, bumping fists with the eleven-and-a-half-year-old. "Don't let those three"—a nod at where a ferocious and tiny black panther was pretending to bite Keenan while Noor tried to tackle him—"give you too much trouble."

Cruz rolled his eyes after taking a drink. "They're *babies*." A put-upon sigh. "But I better play with them so they don't get bored."

Lucas's lips curved as Cruz ran back to enthusiastically join in whatever game it was the three DarkRiver cubs and one Forgotten boy had thought up. "Kid's looking much better," he said to Dev. "Sascha says his shields are phenomenal." Lucas's mate was the one who'd helped create those shields, Dev having asked for her help after discovering that Cruz had no shields of his own, his mind naked to the world.

"She gave him the base." Dev slid his hands into the pockets of his black pants. "And fuck she's good, Lucas. The more we study Cruz's shields, the more we realize what she built, and it's extraordinary."

Lucas's panther stretched out in pride inside him. "Yes," he agreed. "But I can tell she's pleased with the progress he's made on his own." That checkup was part of the reason Dev and Katya had made this trip.

"He's a tough kid." The pride was Dev's this time. "Resilient doesn't come close to describing it." The other man was quiet for a moment before adding, "He's still mourning his mom and dad, but he's not dwelling on the horrific way he was diagnosed as schizophrenic and drugged. The nightmares are all but gone."

Lucas knew it wasn't only Cruz's resilience that had permitted the boy to heal; it was the fact that he was surrounded by a shield of love and fierce protectiveness. Cruz had the air of a child who knew nothing could get to him. A lot of that fell at the feet of Katya Haas and Devraj Santos. Which brought Lucas back around to the protection of the children in his care.

"The bounty," he said. "Details?"

"I'll send you what we have. The offer was sent *directly* to a number of for-hire black ops and mercenary units. The best of the best across racial lines. Whoever it is means serious business."

Folding his arms, Lucas said, "It also means we can't play the client by creating a fake team to take up the offer."

Dev nodded. "We tried talking around our contact into playing the client, asked him to send in fake images of Jon bound and gagged." A shake of his head. "He's too terrified of the retaliation from his own team if they find out he's been feeding us intel. They don't know he's Forgotten."

"Shit." Lucas unfolded his arms before he clawed himself. "Contact details on the offer?"

"Throwaway e-mail address. No way to trace it—and we've tried."

"So what's the good news?" This time, he had enough of a snarl in his tone that Naya's ears pricked up, but she was soon distracted by Noor calling for her.

"No one is eager to take up the offer."

Lucas glanced at the leader of the Forgotten, his panther looking out of his eyes in disbelief. "Five million and no one's eager?"

"Our contact says his own group was considering it, and we have indications that two others were as well, but all of them pulled out last night." Dev's eyes glinted. "It was a stroke of genius to follow up your statement by leaking images of that bloody room where you executed the alpha who came after your cub."

It wasn't Lucas who'd leaked those photos. He hadn't even been aware they'd been taken. It had been one of the ocelot soldiers—the female. She hadn't done it in defiance or rebellion. No, she'd done it to make it clear to other changelings that the surviving ocelot dominants had witnessed the execution and that it had been a righteous one. Her act had been one of solidarity with her new alpha.

Despite her unauthorized actions, Lucas had to admit he liked the young ocelot. Especially when she accepted her punishment for those actions without complaining. He hadn't hurt her, but he had put her on the worst duty shifts for six months.

"Worth it, sir," she'd said when he'd shaken his head at her afterward. "I didn't want any rumors out there, just the cold, hard facts. You don't deserve to have anyone questioning your actions."

Hugging her against his chest, one hand cradling her head, Lucas had pressed a kiss to her hair. "You're going to be trouble, but it turns out this pack likes trouble."

She'd left with a dimpled smile, Rina by her side. The twenty-four-year-old DarkRiver soldier was helping the younger girl settle into the pack, and it wasn't a chance partnership. Rina had made more trouble than most of her yearmates combined before Lucas put Dorian in charge of her training and development. Faced with a trainer who accepted zero bullshit, she'd exceeded all expectations without losing the edginess that made her Rina.

Lucas knew she'd be good for the high-spirited ocelot soldier.

"A bloody room," he said to Dev now, "wouldn't normally put off the kind of mercenaries who kidnap children."

"Maybe not, but the idea of having their entrails clawed out and tied into knots in front of them, or having their dicks cut off while they scream, or their eyes plucked out before they're released, just so you can hunt them and tear them apart with your teeth, isn't sitting well with most. Especially when the failed attempt to snatch Naya has skewed the risk of capture into the 'ninety-nine-percent certainty' category."

Lucas stared at the other man. "Knotted entrails and dicks being cut off? Blinding people so I can hunt them?"

Cheeks creasing, Dev angled his head. "Yeah, I didn't think that was your style. Looks like someone's been embellishing on your behalf and doing a damn good job of it. You've now got a reputation as a scary motherfucker with no limits when it comes to your kid and your pack."

The Forgotten leader leaned back against a tree. "Oh, and the rumors make it clear you're also brutally intelligent and your pack has the smarts to dig out financial connections, no matter how deep a mercenary team might bury those connections in an effort to avoid retaliation."

Dev smiled at Naya when she padded over to growl playfully at them before making her way back to her playmates. "It's also gotten out that you confiscated the captured assault team's money—mercenaries hate working for free even more than they do being subjected to torture."

Lucas had put that money into a trust for the ocelot children, with the unanimous agreement of the adult ocelot survivors. He'd have put all four million of SkyElm's money into that trust, but the survivors had been adamant that they wanted to contribute to their new pack, so one million had gone into the DarkRiver fund used for the education of cubs.

None of the adults had wanted to take any of the remaining million, but he'd made each one accept an amount that would give them room to breathe while they settled into their new lives. The rest, at their request, would act as the capital for a scholarship for young inventors. Named the SkyElm Grant, it would ensure the pack's name lived on as part of something good, not simply in memories of horror.

"Huh," he said in response to Dev's revelations about his own apparent reputation for meting out horrific torture.

Lucas would savage the world for those who were his own—but he wasn't into torture. Never had been. Still, it was a useful reputation to have if it helped protect the most vulnerable members of DarkRiver. "That explains the sudden wary respect I'm seeing in the eyes of Psy corporations we're working with on business deals."

"Business gone down recently?"

"Up. Appears the Psy respect that kind of merciless retribution." Lucas smiled, his panther amused as it realized the identity of the person most likely behind his new reputation.

Nikita Duncan was more than deviously intelligent enough to figure out how to protect her daughter and grandchild long-term *and* what would scare even the most hardened men and women. The fact that his reputation would also protect other children was a side effect that wouldn't matter to her, but it mattered a heck of a lot to Lucas.

"So it's done?" Dev asked. "The trail ended with the ocelots?"

Lucas shook his head. "No, the alpha was just a useful weapon to point in our direction. Someone else was driving the operation." Hopefully, the captain of the ship Dorian had pinpointed would provide further intelligence.

Jamie was leading the op to intercept the ship in question, which involved taking a flight to one of BlackSea's floating cities in a craft capable of water landings. Miane had made one available for their use after Dark-River and SnowDancer allied with her pack. From that point, Jamie would get on a BlackSea underwater craft and sneak up on the ship, then climb up and into it with a small team of water changelings.

It seemed an appropriate operation for a cat who'd taken up deep-sea diving.

"We'll get them," he said to Dev. "Sooner or later, we'll find the people pulling the strings." It was the unyielding promise of an alpha—and of a father.

Letters to Nina

From the private diaries of Father Xavier Perez
May 7, 2075

Nina,

He's trusted me with his name, the Psy soldier. I won't write it here—if my letters are ever found, I don't want to betray my friend.

I know you must be thinking that this is surely a double cross, that he'll betray me. I thought the same until I realized he had no reason to approach me, or to want me with him. I'm no one, a broken fragment of a lost village. At the time he and I first met, I was a drunk, a fool who was more hindrance than help.

No, my new friend had no reason to take me into his confidence except that he saw I needed a mission, a reason for being. In giving it to me, he has given me more than he'll ever know. For the first time in an eternity, I feel like Xavier again. I feel like the man I was before the day murder stained our village and I saw you jump into the water.

At times, I even glimpse the rare flame of hope.

Your Xavier

Chapter 34

IT WAS VASIC who Miane Levèque most often contacted now with updates on the Leila Savea situation and Zaira with whom the BlackSea alpha met with simply to talk—one dangerous woman to another, their friendship a growing thing. As leader of the Arrow Squad, Aden might've been expected to be dissatisfied with that state of affairs, but he felt the opposite: his mate and his best friend were building powerful bonds of their own.

Should the worst ever happen, should Aden be assassinated, Vasic would have the skills and contacts to step in and Zaira . . . No, Aden couldn't predict what Zaira would do except seek vengeance. And after that was done, he had the haunting conviction that she'd choose to join him. So he'd have to stay alive. That was all there was to it.

The thought echoed in his mind as he grabbed a handhold on a rock face not far from the RainFire aeries and swung over and up. A couple of meters from him, Remi, the alpha of the small leopard pack, was doing much the same. They were dressed similarly, too, in dark outdoor pants and T-shirts, boots on their feet and gloves on their hands; the only real difference was that Remi's T-shirt was white, Aden's olive green.

"So," Remi said, his biceps bulging as he attempted a particularly difficult crossing over a jagged gap in the rock face, "since the wolves are keeping Ming busy for now and Trinity hasn't collapsed, what's on your mind?"

Aden held his position until he saw that Remi had made it safely. They were climbing separately but acting as each other's spotters, ready to send out an alert in case of an accident. Such an accident was highly unlikely, not with Remi having claws with which he could hook into every tiny crevice and Aden a far more careful climber than his more instinctive friend. However, taking things for granted got people—and Arrows—killed.

"Did you know BlackSea holds regular gatherings of its people?" he asked after they'd both begun climbing again. "They come from every corner of the globe." He pushed off with his feet, caught an overhang, kicked up so that he was in a crouched position vertically for a second before he managed to get himself on the overhang and ready for the next part of the climb.

Remi whistled. "Nice move."

"Zaira taught me that one." His lover was currently "cat climbing" the internal RainFire rock wall. She'd been press-ganged into it by the smaller, less powerful cats who wanted to know how she did it without claws.

Them, Zaira could've resisted. But when little Jojo had jumped up and down at the idea of watching Zaira do another climb, well, his tough commander had a mile-wide vulnerable streak there. *How's the climb going?* he telepathed to her, the connection flawless at this range.

Fairly uneventful. I threw in a semi-slip to make it more exciting, but now that I've done it once, it's not a true challenge.

Because Zaira climbed as much with her mind as with her body, would've remembered every grip, every successful move. *Don't show up the cats too badly.*

Soft laughter along the black-on-black bond that connected them, his lover's firelight hidden within the black. The entire squad needed her fire, thrived on it, whether she accepted her importance or not.

Their honor is safe with me. Zaira rarely laughed aloud, but mind to mind, he was becoming addicted to the sound of her happiness. *Are you done?*

Halfway.

They disconnected without need for good-byes. He and Zaira lived in each other's minds, never intrusive, just . . . present. He loved being able to feel her blade of a mind at the edge of his consciousness, liked knowing that should she need him, he could respond within split seconds.

"Sounds like our pack circle events." Remi's voice brought him fully back to the here and now. "All packs have gatherings, and as different as BlackSea is, they're still changeling, still a pack."

"The goal is to reinforce pack bonds?" Aden was still rebuilding his own "pack," trying to heal his broken family, and he wasn't so proud as to ignore advice from a race that was all about family. Especially when the man giving that advice was a self-confessed "remedial" alpha who was learning right alongside Aden.

"Sure," Remi said, as above them, an eagle flew with stately grace, circling the rock face, as if taking in their activity. "But it's also about celebrating important events like matings, births, the achievements of our cubs." He hauled himself over a near-smooth section of rock. "Why? You thinking of a gathering?"

Aden nodded when the other man glanced over, Remi's shaggy brown hair damp with sweat and pushed off his face. "If a pack whose members often swim alone can do it, why not the squad?" Ivy Jane had already begun the process by inviting Arrows to her home for dinners. She'd even held an informal party of sorts—though with a guest list made up mostly of Arrows that party was never going to be raucous. However, it would take a coordinated effort to get the majority of his people home for an event.

"Hell, Aden," Remi said, "from what you've told me, your people deserve a seriously epic shindig."

Aden and the leopard alpha were now side by side, having come closer as the rock face narrowed. Meeting Remi's eyes, the color a clear topaz striated with light, he said, "I don't think my Arrows, child or adult, are ready for such an unstructured event."

The reason Ivy's party had worked was because it had been small enough that she'd been able to have one-on-one contact with her guests, easing their way into the gathering. Any bigger and Arrows would start to withdraw behind an instinctive protective shielding. They'd bury their newfound emotions, fall back on decades-long training designed to turn them into remote, inhuman machines.

For to be an Arrow was to live within a strict set of rules.

Aden could soften that but he couldn't erase it. Not when the people in his family were some of the deadliest on the planet—the rules and structure gave them a chance to have lives, and now, to have families. A telepath who wasn't terrified of destroying a child's mind with a simple slip made for a far more stable and happy parent, as did a telekinetic who didn't have to worry he'd crush a child's windpipe by being unaware of his strength.

Those mistakes simply did not happen inside the squad.

Silence had been an ugly construct, but it had taught the squad some good along with all the bad.

"Hmm." Remi took a grip, then grinned. "Let's talk about it at the top. See you there, Arrow."

They began to climb with single-minded focus. As a changeling, Remi's greater strength and flexibility gave him a natural advantage, but Aden had mapped out the entire climb in his head before he ever started. He didn't need to pause or to rethink. As a result, they were evenly matched—and pulled themselves over the edge at the same time.

Laughing, Remi slipped out the bottle of water he'd carried strapped to his thigh. "Fuck, that was impressive for a man with no claws."

Aden took a drink from his own bottle. "You didn't use your claws." Remi's gloves were undamaged.

The other man put aside his water to tug them off. "Yeah, well, it's only fun if it's a fair fight. Now if you'd been like your friend, the Tk, it would've been no holds barred."

"Vasic has only one arm." Samuel Rain's attempts at making Vasic a working prosthetic continued to fail—the last one in spectacular fashion. "The newest iteration of the prosthetic currently in play shorted out in a shower of sparks that set fire to Ivy's new tablecloth."

Aden had been at the orchard during the incident, so he knew first-hand that the empath had *not* been happy when she saw the damage. "She took a hammer to that particular prosthetic." And if there had been a little too much force in her blows, well, even empaths needed outlets for grief.

Not cognizant of the sadness that had driven Ivy's incensed reaction, Remi's shoulders shook. "Vasic might have only one arm, but he's a tele-kinetic. They move in a way that's almost like a changeling but different. Can't explain it."

Aden didn't need more of an explanation; he'd seen Vasic climb, knew exactly what Remi was trying to describe. "Yes, he'd beat both of us, even with only one arm."

"Talk for yourself." Remi's tone was mock-insulted. "But the party thing—you need an excuse to give it structure. Anything good happen that you want to celebrate?" A pause. "I know your squad lost an elder recently. It's even more important that you celebrate joy in the aftermath, that you show your Arrows that life, it's got a lot of different faces."

Aden thought of the children's achievements, decided their confidence was too new and fragile yet to put even under a celebratory spotlight. Then he sensed Zaira at the back of his mind, happy in whatever she was doing, and knew. "We've had a number of bondings. Matings." The squad had picked up and begun to use the changeling term, and they weren't the only ones in the PsyNet.

"Ivy and Vasic had a wedding," he continued, thinking back to an orchard dressed in sunshine and scented with spring blossoms. "As did Abbot and Jaya." Held in the Maldives, the traditional Indian wedding had been a feast of color and sensation that made Aden doubt very much that the vast majority of Jaya's family had ever truly been Silent. "The rest of us had no familial or cultural need to celebrate that way."

"A mating or a long-term bonding is a big thing," Remi countered. "It *should* be marked and celebrated." The alpha's eyes were leopard when they met Aden's. "Your cubs have to follow rules, as do mine, but we have to balance that by giving them a chance to run wild." A slight grin. "Your

kids are probably far better behaved than ours, but give them an opportunity to realize the rules have been relaxed and I predict sweet mayhem."

Aden couldn't imagine the children under his care ever causing
mayhem . . . but then he thought of how little Jojo had "attacked" him on
his last visit, growling and snarling playfully without so much as scratching him, and knew he wanted his tiny Arrows to feel the same freedom
even as they continued to learn how to control their violent abilities.

"An event to celebrate the bondings in the squad." He nodded, his
eyes on the sprawling vista of trees and mountains visible from this van-
tage point. "I'm going to speak to my senior people, see what we need to
do to pull it off. Thank you for the advice."

Touching his water bottle to Aden's, Remi said, "I knew I was the
brains of this outfit."

Aden felt his lips curve at the leopard alpha's statement, right as
another mind touched his. "Vasic just asked if I have time to meet him
for a sparring session." The request had been between friends, rather than
Arrow to Arrow. "I've invited him to join us instead."

"Hell, yeah," Remi said. "I want to see him climb."

Vasic 'ported in at the bottom of the rock face ten minutes later, having returned home first to change into clothing and boots suitable for
climbing.

Instead of telepathing—that would shut Remi out of the conversation—
Aden yelled down his and Remi's climbing time. "See if you can beat
that!"

Vasic's wintery eyes were brilliant in the early evening sunlight when
he looked up and pointedly raised his single arm. Aden shrugged, as
beside him, Remi said, "Minimal use of your telekinesis permitted—just
enough to compensate for your other arm!"

Vasic's eyes narrowed. Stepping back from the rock face, he looked at
it carefully for several minutes before returning to take his first grip. Aden
could tell within minutes that Vasic was actually using far *less* Tk than
would've been permitted under Remi's rule. "He's utilizing pure muscle
and intelligence."

Remi whistled. "I told you. Man moves like a cat."

Watching his friend, Aden thought of the endless training sessions they'd done together at the orchard, of how hard Vasic had worked to regain his balance and fluidity in movement. Losing an arm changed everything about how a person moved, but Vasic had never complained. He'd simply learned to adapt.

Because the man who had once wanted only to die now had multiple reasons to live.

"You're getting slow in your old age, Zen!"

Vasic glanced up at Remi's heckling and Aden saw the shadow that passed across his face at the reminder of the man whose name he bore—a name he'd chosen to bear. On its heels came determination. "Want to put a wager on it?"

Remi snorted. "Do I look mentally challenged? Only an idiot would bet against a Tk, one-armed or not."

Laughter dawned in Vasic's eyes before he returned to his careful yet strangely fluid climb. As Aden sat there under the light of the evening sun and watched his best friend take on what should've been an impossible challenge, while a new friend sat beside him, and Aden's mate spoke with friends of her own, he felt a dizzying sense of possibility and hope.

Ming LeBon might be stirring trouble, the Consortium was waiting in the shadows, and BlackSea's vanished remained lost and alone, but today, this night, it was a dream an Arrow would've thought impossible even six months earlier.

Chapter 35

CHANCE PUT LUCAS with Devraj Santos again when Jamie sent in a note the next day confirming mission success, with details to follow. Lucas glanced at the message with grim satisfaction, then slid away his phone so he could start the car. He'd offered to drive Dev up to SnowDancer territory, where the leader of the Forgotten planned to check in with the children and families SnowDancer had given shelter.

Since Lucas had business with Hawke, it was convenient for them both.

It turned out Dev was thinking of pulling his people out of pack lands. "Not that you haven't kept them safe and treated them well," he said to Lucas, "but the kids are starting to need more and more specialized help as their abilities develop. And while Sascha and the others here have been incredible, I think they'd do better under the training programs we've been figuring out with the Arrows."

Lucas nodded. "Judd's really the only one with the kind of skills to teach those of your young with dangerous new abilities, and he can't handle them all." Sienna was assisting, but her training differed from Judd's and a lot of it wasn't transferable.

"There's no question of moving William," Dev clarified, referring to a boy born with the unusual telekinetic gift that made Judd so deadly and so extraordinary at the same time. "Judd can help him in ways no one else can, but the others? I'm going to talk them through the programs we're developing, give them the choice."

"What about the reason you moved them here in the first place?"

"We've been quietly buying up land in a remote part of New York State," Dev replied. "It's secure but large enough that no one will feel penned in. I got the idea from DarkRiver's Yosemite territory, to be honest—though our area isn't as large, it's plenty big enough for humans and Forgotten." The other man ran a hand through his hair. "I actually wanted to run something by you in terms of our security protocols."

Lucas listened, gave his opinion, then asked Dev if he'd had a chance to think about the dangerous disintegration of the PsyNet, an issue Sascha had brought up at dinner the previous night. While the Forgotten had no reason to love those in the PsyNet who had once hunted them, Dev and his people understood that the majority of Psy were ordinary people fighting to survive.

The other man had offered to assist Sascha in any way he could.

"I can't figure it out." Dev braced his arm on the door, his window down as they reached the foothills of the Sierras. "If the Es are awake and emotion is back in the Net, then it should be healing. The Forgotten didn't do anything extraordinary when we defected." His frown was in his voice. "We just stayed what the PsyNet was pre-Silence."

The two of them talked it through but hadn't come up with anything new by the time Lucas brought the vehicle to a stop near the den.

TWENTY minutes later, as he stood waiting for Hawke just outside the White Zone, Dev having already met up with his liaison, Lucas made a note to ask Jon if the teen wanted to join the Forgotten's new training program. If he did, DarkRiver wouldn't send him alone; he'd have a pack escort, someone who was his friend as well as being tough enough to protect him.

Not because Lucas didn't trust Dev, but because Jon was a child of the pack.

His phone beeped right then, with the promised report from Jamie. The senior soldier had written up his conclusions and sent the result over a secure line. Everything had gone according to plan—they'd invaded the target ship without setting off any alarms, then interrogated the captain.

Jamie was certain the man had simply been another cog in the machine.

All he knew was that he had to pick up live cargo at a certain time and place. That time and place would've lined up perfectly had the snatch on Naya been successful so I don't think there's any question Dorian zeroed in on the right ship. The captain was told he'd receive further instructions for care of the cargo once it was on its way but that he was to set aside a cabin for the time being, a cabin that had been stripped of all small items and was capable of being locked.

He figured it was going to be an animal of some kind, an exotic pet "for some rich asshole." He swears up and down that he had no idea he'd been hired to transport a kidnapped child. His exact words were: "I don't do people. People have other people who look for them and some of those other people are fucking scary like you and your friends."

I tend to believe him.

His record isn't exactly squeaky clean but he's never tried anything this ambitious or dangerous. He's a smuggler, back and forth with low-risk goods most of the time, spiced with the occasional legal job.

He was paid twenty-five grand upfront for the transport. That wasn't enough to buy his loyalty when his life and livelihood were on the line. BlackSea did us a solid there, threatened to ban him from all the commercial waterways they control and they control a shitload. I didn't have to show him my claws before he started spilling his guts.

Lucas made a mental note to thank Miane, knew the alpha would say she was simply repaying DarkRiver for the introduction to Tanique Gray. Faith's brother had brought BlackSea far closer to their vanished packmate than they would've been otherwise.

Jamie's report continued:

My gut says we got everything out of the captain. He even gave up all his commercial and personal codes. I sent them through to Dorian and Bastien so they could dig through his transactions and transmissions and they haven't found any evidence of greater involvement on his part. He was the unwitting mule hired to be the fall guy should Naya be found while he was crossing the ocean.

Bastien's tracking the source of the twenty-five-thousand-dollar payment. It was all anonymous of course. Pretty standard in a smuggler's line of work so the captain had no reason to dig any deeper.

I made the call to let him go, but we've bugged the hell out of all his systems. He doesn't know, thinks he was released with a warning. He's promised to share any new approaches from the individual who hired him, but for some strange reason, I don't believe him.

I've asked Bas to tag all his financials and Dorian is monitoring all his personal correspondence using various data backdoors. We'll know if he's approached again—I figured it was better to let this piece of bait sail away, see what he might attract, but if you think I should take him in, we can easily catch his ship.

One more step in hunting down their prey, Lucas thought, one more step in the right direction. It was slow progress, but it was progress. Sending a message to Jamie confirming receipt of the information and backing the senior soldier's decision to release the captain, Lucas told him to return to DarkRiver territory.

The work on the water was done. Now it was up to Bastien to hack through the financial jungle that no doubt awaited.

"Luc." Hawke's voice came just as he was sliding away his phone. "Sorry for the delay—was up in the higher elevations, hit a rockfall on the way out and had to navigate around."

Lucas shook the other alpha's hand. "No problem." Where before they'd both circled around each other, their animals ready to attack at any behavior that even hinted of a dominance challenge, their relationship had changed into something far different over time.

Lucas had allowed Hawke to hold Naya.

That said everything.

"You want to walk to the waterfall while we talk?" Hawke asked, thrusting a hand through the hair of silver-gold that echoed his wolf's pelt.

At Lucas's nod, the alpha fell in beside him, and they moved at a steady pace as they spoke about a number of matters related to the increasing interaction between the packs, as well as a construction project DarkRiver was heading, with SnowDancer a thirty-percent silent partner. They'd worked on several such projects by now, the wolves content to remain in the background, given DarkRiver's expertise in the area.

The two of them had just completed their discussion and returned to nearer the den when Dev joined them. After explaining to Hawke what he'd already told Lucas about the better training opportunities for Forgotten children back in New York, he said, "Excluding Will's family, it looks like my people will be out of your hair within the next month."

Hawke nodded. "Everyone fit well into the pack, and adults and children both made friends. If they want to visit afterward, they'll be welcome."

"I can tell you right now that they'll be taking you up on the offer— leaving their new friends was the children's biggest concern." Dev's eyes met Lucas's and, all at once, those eyes didn't quite look human.

The irises remained brown but the flecks of color inside were suddenly glittering so bright they appeared like pieces of precious metals.

"Dev, what the fuck is happening to your eyes?" Lucas asked before the other man could say whatever it was he'd been about to say.

"Shit." The leader of the Forgotten squeezed his eyes shut as he lifted one hand to grip his temples in a vice. "It comes and goes, and it doesn't look like I can control it, though I'm trying the fuck hard."

Hawke folded his arms. "You developing cardinal eyes?"

"Or something." Scowling, Dev dropped his hand and opened his eyes.

The flecks continued to glitter. Eerie, but oddly compelling at the same time.

"I'm not the only one." The other man blew out a breath. "Cruz's eyes are changing the more he uses his ability, and so are those of a number of others. This"—he pointed to his own eyes—"it's not what Cruz's eyes are doing. None of the changes are the same and none of the changes are stable, but there *is* a definite change in the eyes of the majority of Forgotten with high-level abilities."

Lucas whistled, suddenly understanding why Dev was so pissed off. "It'll put a marker on the backs of all your most gifted members."

A hard nod. "It's like we've hit a default setting," Dev said. "As if once an individual reaches a certain level of active psychic power, previously dormant genes turn on and start to fuck with their eyes."

"Maybe Dev's people can modify the contacts we developed for Sienna and the others," Hawke said to Lucas. "Has to be easier to hide these fluctuations than it was to hide cardinal eyes."

Dev looked immediately interested. "Seriously, any help you can offer, we'll take," he said before locking gazes with Lucas again. "I think Jon was the first to exhibit the change. When we spoke, he told me he doesn't remember people commenting about his eyes until he turned eleven or so."

Since the remarkable violet shade of Jon's eyes definitely invited comment, Lucas could find no fault with Dev's theory. "Jon was on his own, forced to use whatever he had to survive." Ethics made for cold comfort when you were a starving child.

"No surprise his abilities woke faster as a result," Dev agreed without hesitation.

The response further strengthened Lucas's liking for the Forgotten director. "We'll forward you the information on how to produce the contacts." They were highly specialized and had to be custom-made for the individual, but the Forgotten had the resources to do that. "You ready to head down?"

Dev nodded and, saying good-bye to Hawke, the two of them were soon back in the car. They were a half hour out from the aerie where Dev, Katya, and Cruz were staying when Dev received a message on his phone that made him frown. "You know a lynx pack in Calgary?"

Lucas thought immediately of Bastien's mate, Kirby. Her grandparents' pack, IceRock, was the only one in that immediate region. "Yeah. What's the issue?"

"There's a small Forgotten population just off the pack's eastern border. They've had a good if not close relationship with the pack to this point, but they're getting nervous about vehicle movements late at night that seem to be going in and out of pack territory—black SUVs that look military grade to them, but they're not trained."

The information didn't fit with Lucas's impression of IceRock. "I'll ask, but as far as I know, the pack's a peaceful one." A family-centered group that was happy to be left alone, though it was cautiously following DarkRiver's lead in making friendships with its neighbors.

"Appreciate it." Dev slipped away his phone. "My people tend to be jumpy, especially with children in the mix."

"Don't blame them." The Forgotten had lost a number of their young in horrific circumstances. "I'll touch base with the lynx alpha soon as we get back."

"We're leaving in two hours, so if you get any information after that, give me a call."

Letters to Nina

From the private diaries of Father Xavier Perez
October 19, 2075

Nina,

I've been working with my Psy friend whenever possible. He appears only rarely but we've found ways to stay in touch while he maintains his cover. In his absence, I use the welcome provided to me as a man of God to uncover information that helps us fight the evil that rules the Psy race.

I've been surprised at how many of the Psy treat me with respect, despite their official disbelief in any plane of existence beyond this one. Again, it's shown me that not all Psy are the same. They have their good and their bad, their lazy and their strong.

I'm still angry at God, still full of rage, but there are glimmers of hope in the darkness. I don't know if I'll ever again be a man of absolute faith as I once was, but it seems my faith is too powerful to be killed even by horror.

But one thing I know: I'll never be fully at peace with God until the day I see you again . . . whether in this lifetime or the next.

Xavier

Chapter 36

LUCAS WAS MEETING Sascha and Naya at Tamsyn and Nate's, the other couple having invited them for dinner, but he stopped by his own aerie to make the call to the lynx alpha. Kiya Teague was around Lucas's age but had become alpha far more recently; the pack's previous alpha remained strong and healthy and respected though he was in his seventh decade of life.

He'd had the support to keep on being alpha, but had decided to pass the baton to Kiya rather than see her move away from IceRock to establish her own pack. He remained available to her should she need his advice, the transition apparently seamless from what Lucas had heard. It was exactly how a healthy pack was supposed to function, how the switch had happened in DarkRiver until Lachlan died unexpectedly two years after stepping down; the loss had left Lucas without guidance when he'd been a bare twenty-five years old.

He'd never have been able to do it without his sentinels, particularly Nathan. The current most senior sentinel had been Lachlan's youngest sentinel at the time; he'd provided a crucial link between Lucas and Lachlan's older sentinels, men and women who were now all retired but who'd always been there for the young panther who'd had to rebuild a heartbroken pack.

"Lucas," Kiya said with a smile that lit up her pixyish face, her skin a tawny shade of brown and her eyes shaded by lashes that reminded Lucas of a doll's.

Petite Kiya Teague was the most cheerful alpha Lucas knew. It was mildly disconcerting. Lucas's panther kept wanting to pat her on the head, but the human side of him knew never to try the condescending gesture. She'd probably rip off his arm because, bouncy personality aside, Kiya was a true alpha. Nowhere near as powerful as Lucas, but powerful enough to nurture a healthy pack and to hold his gaze.

"What can I do yer for?" she asked, her hazel-brown eyes sparkling. "This about our Kirby?"

Lips curving at the possessive emphasis on Kirby, Lucas shook his head. "Got a question for you from the neighbors on your eastern edge."

"The human settlement?" Kiya's smile faded into a frown. "Why're they going to you instead of coming to me?"

Interesting that she didn't seem to know her neighbors were Forgotten . . . but then the Forgotten didn't exactly advertise their presence. Lucas sometimes forgot that he had far more information about them than the average alpha. "We have a mutual acquaintance," he said, then grinned. "And they're scared of you."

She drew up the entire five feet and one inch of her body. "You making fun of me, Lucas Hunter?"

He held up his hands. "Wouldn't dare. They really are worried—it's to do with the late-night SUV movements in and out of your territory."

Kiya's scowl faded at once. "Well, damn, I could've put their minds to rest in a heartbeat. I'll do that today unless you have objections?"

"No, I think they'd probably appreciate a personal response." Lucas was guessing at the Forgotten's reaction, but in the back of his mind he was also always thinking about Trinity; the accord would only work if friendships and relationships developed across racial lines. "So, what're you doing so late at night?"

"It's not us," the IceRock alpha replied. "*We* were worried about those SUVs, too. They didn't quite come onto our territory, but they were passing right by and, well, we're not a big pack like DarkRiver, don't have a sprawl of land. We wanted to make sure no one was setting up to steal some from us."

Lucas knew cats, knew exactly what the lynx pack would've done. "What did you see when you followed their trail?" He couldn't have asked the question so directly had he and Kiya not already developed a good working relationship built on the fact that they were now family.

Eyes gleaming, the lynx alpha said, "The SUVs are going into the massive old estate on the other side of our territory. It used to be owned by a human CEO who went bankrupt back when I was a cub. Been left to crumble into a ruin ever since—our cubs used to sneak over to play on the property until we built a fence they couldn't climb."

"Why?" If the place had been deserted, most alphas wouldn't have minded cubs playing there so long as they didn't cause any damage.

Kiya's expression turned dark. "The CEO built a big-ass pool and even though it was emptied out, it was still a large concrete hole in the ground—and when it rained, the water gathered. Wasn't safe and we couldn't get the owners on record to fence it up, so we just built our own fence."

Lucas's pulse had kicked up at the word "pool," stayed that way. He thought of what Miane had told him about Tanique's psychometric readings. Saltwater and lynxes. "That pool full now?" He knew she'd know—cats couldn't help being curious, especially about a neighbor so close to their border.

A nod that caused her ponytail to bounce, her hair dark, dark brown with glints of red highlights. "Construction folks started coming in about a year ago, when the new owners must've bought it. They put a glass building over the pool and cleaned up the house, which was in pretty good condition surprisingly.

"Can't see through to the pool anymore—smoked glass. They've also added to our fences, put up opaque ones on their side." Disappointment and approval vied for lead position in her tone. As alpha, she obviously appreciated the better safety measures, but feline curiosity had her itching to know what the heck was going on with IceRock's new neighbors.

"It's clear it's someone with money," she added, folding her arms. "We figure maybe a celebrity, what with the cloak-and-dagger blacked-out SUVs in the night and the bodyguards."

"Weapons?"

Her eyes cooled. "I paid the bodyguards a visit when my dominants told me they were patrolling our border with guns, pointed out that if they so much as touched a hair on my people's heads, I'd rip off their own heads and use them for football practice." She smiled that bouncy smile. "They electrified their fences after that and stopped the patrols. Fair enough. All our people know not to go beyond our own fence in that area."

Lucas chuckled but his mind was racing. "Look, Kiya," he said. "There might be more going on than a publicity-shy celebrity. Can you get me images a teleporter can use to 'port inside the compound?"

"No problem." She braced her hands on her hips on the heels of the confident statement, her shoulders squared. "You going to get my pack in the middle of something, Lucas?"

"It's possible." He held her gaze, a gaze gone the yellowish-hazel of her lynx. "But it's also possible there's a changeling or changelings being held captive in that compound."

Kiya's hiss was violent. "I'll get the images to you later tonight," she said, her lynx still in her tone. "If your teleporter friend needs assistance, you give him my number and tell him to call."

SASCHA was seated at Tamsyn's kitchen table chatting with the healer when a vehicle entered the drive. She expected Lucas to walk through the door, but it proved to be Clay and Talin with the kids. All four, Jon included, had gone to a tea shop for Noor's requested birthday tea party, had decided to say hello to Tamsyn and family before they went home.

"We had this many cakes!" Noor held her hands as far apart as they'd go, her dark eyes shining.

Scooping up the little girl, who had on a pretty blue dress with white lace and ribbons, her glossy black hair tied back with more ribbons, Sascha cuddled her in her lap. "Let me see how full your tummy is," she said, gently patting Noor's abdomen. "Uh-oh, I think it's about to explode."

Noor giggled. "Kee got cream all over his face!"

Sascha wasn't surprised at the news that Keenan had been present at the tea party. The two children were best friends—the fact that their psychic gifts worked in concert was a peripheral matter. It was their friendship that was most important. "Who else did you invite?"

"Ben!" Noor beamed at the mention of the mischievous little wolf. "He came with his mom. Issy and Behali came, too, but Jules and Rome couldn't come because they went on a special date with their grandma. We brought them a big box of cake." She went quiet all at once, her next words a worried whisper. "Will Naya be sad she didn't come?"

Such a generous heart, Sascha thought, her own aching with love for this child of the pack. "No, baby," she said, "Naya's too little." Talin had offered to take her along after Noor invited both Naya and Anu's toddler, but Sascha knew her rambunctious cub wasn't yet at an age where she could sit in a tea shop and behave. Anu had made the same call. "She had a party at the nursery with the other little cubs to celebrate her own birthday."

It was DarkRiver tradition for first birthdays, with parents invited along to join in, and Naya had loved it. "We got her a cake shaped like a leopard paw, and she and her friends got to make mud pies and dance while wearing dress-up clothes."

"That's fun!"

Utterly delighted with this sweet girl who'd survived so much, Sascha kissed her on the cheek just as the twins, who'd returned from visiting Tamsyn's mother an hour earlier, stuck their heads inside the open back door and yelled for Noor to come play. Wriggling off Sascha's lap, Noor ran to join her playmates, calling out for Jon—who was standing next to Clay—to come with her. The sixteen-year-old ambled out, his phone in hand and his ball cap worn backward.

Naya was already in the backyard with the twins.

Sascha had no idea what Tamsyn's cubs were teaching hers, but she had a feeling it involved getting into as much mischief as possible in as short a time as possible. The one thing the boys would never do was allow

Naya to come to harm, and even if the kids wandered off, this was central DarkRiver territory.

Zach and Annie were the closest neighbors but other packmates roamed nearby. The children could explore in safety and freedom. She had to keep telling herself that, keep reminding herself that no one could snatch Naya while her cub was out of her sight.

Talin's cloud-gray eyes met hers at that moment, and the tawny-haired woman walked over to touch Sascha's hand in silent comfort. Talin knew what it was to lose children she'd sworn to protect, and that sorrow would never leave her.

"Noor and Jon," Sascha reminded her softly while everyone else was distracted, Tamsyn having risen to make sure the children drank some water before continuing to play. "They survived and thanks to you and Clay, they're thriving."

Talin swallowed. "It's tough though, isn't it, Sascha? My heart pounds so hard whenever either one of them goes missing for even a short time. I have to physically stop myself from messaging Jon every hour when he's out with his friends." A shaky smile. "You think it ever goes away? This worry?"

Sascha shook her head. "Dezi's mom used to make her check in after a night shift for years." The only reason she didn't anymore was that Dezi was no longer living alone; her mate would raise the alarm if she didn't make it home.

"But she's a senior soldier!" A startled response.

"You see my point." Sascha's dry response made the other woman laugh. "It sounds like the tea party was a success," she said at a normal volume, which she knew would be audible to all the changelings in the room.

"Noor loved it." An affectionate glance over at where Clay was helping himself to a cup of coffee from the carafe. "Jon and Clay liked the scones."

Clay, the sentinel who'd been the most remote and dangerous when Sascha joined DarkRiver, offered a thumbs-up. His dark green eyes were feline, his body relaxed. "Good stuff, scones." He glanced at Tamsyn, who'd returned to take her seat at the kitchen table. "You should make those."

The healer grinned. "I do. You've just never been fast enough to get any."

Moving over to perch on one of the breakfast stools at the counter, Talin stole Clay's coffee cup when he came around. She took a couple of sips before handing it back, pressing a kiss to Clay's jaw at the same time. Smile quiet, Clay took the mug in one hand, then braced his other one on the counter behind Talin. "I'll work on my scone-racing skills."

The solemn comment had them laughing.

Nathan walked in at that instant, his black hair tumbled as if he'd been running his hands through it. "Stealing all the women, Clay?"

"I can barely handle the two women I have now," the sentinel replied. "And one of them is less than three feet tall."

"You're late, Nathan Ryder." Having risen even before he appeared in the kitchen, Tamsyn embraced her mate.

Nathan kissed her temple as he held her close. "Got held up helping Emmett deal with a couple of cubs who need a little extra supervision."

The healer and senior sentinel were the longest mated couple Sascha knew this well, and their love, it was a deep, warm pulse that existed in their every breath. There was passion, too, but that was a private thing and Sascha would *never* intrude. What she picked up was what any cardinal empath would pick up simply by being in the same room with the mated pair.

Watching them, she saw what she and Lucas would one day become. So very rooted in one another that they were woven into the very fabric of each other's being. When Nathan held Tamsyn, when she placed her hand over his heart, they needed to say no words, ask no questions.

Today, as Tamsyn shifted to stand by his side, Nathan tangled his hand gently in her deep brown hair. He was a handsome man, with a face that held enough lines to be interesting, including the grooves around his mouth that said he laughed often.

"You hear the latest odds on Mercy?" he asked the room at large. "Rumors are four girls."

"I don't believe it." Clay's eyelids lowered to hood his eyes. "I'm sure those two are playing everyone."

Talin grinned. "Mercy's probably having a great time dropping 'inadvertent' hints to start these rumors—and I bet you she's talked Riley into helping." She waggled her eyebrows at Tamsyn. "I don't suppose you want to end the speculation?"

"When it's so much fun watching you all try to figure it out?" The healer shook her head. "Plus, it's not going to be long now."

"I wouldn't bet on that," Talin said. "Last time I spoke to Mercy, she said the pupcubs are having too good a time inside her. She's convinced she's going to be the first ten-month multiple pregnancy on record."

As everyone chuckled, the children padded inside, Jon included. He was carrying a cheerfully naked Naya in one arm. Sascha's daughter was currently smacking kisses on his cheek and saying, "Pe! Pe!"

"She's calling you pretty," Sascha translated for the bemused teenager.

Jon sighed. "I don't want to be pretty. I want to be dangerous and kick-ass."

"Pe! Jon!"

Jon blinked, grinned at Naya. "Hey, you know my name. You can call me pretty."

Naya kissed him on the cheek again before stretching out her arms toward Sascha. "Mama."

"Come on, baby." Settling her little girl into her lap, Sascha went to ask if Jon could grab the baby bag turned toddler bag, only to discover the boy had already put it within reach.

"We get any news from the water changelings about the woman who wrote the message in a bottle?" he asked when she smiled at him in thanks.

"No, not yet, but they're working hard to find her."

Worry radiated off him. "I heard Faith's brother helped." The rough edge of frustration in the set of his shoulders, in the way he pulled off his cap and began to twist it in his hands. "I wish I could do something."

"You plucked out that bottle," Sascha reminded him. "We wouldn't even know Leila was alive without that." This tall, beautiful boy, he still carried a lot of hurt in his heart that made him act out on occasion, but when it came down to the bone, he was one of the good ones, with more compassion in him than the world had any right to expect.

His own scars were healing day by day, surrounded as he was by love and by pack. And by a little girl who adored him.

"Jon, look." Leaning against his leg, her blue dress now bearing streaks of dirt and her hair ribbons threatening to slide off, Noor showed him something on her palm. "It's a ladybug," she whispered.

Jon hunkered down. "Wow, it's blue."

"Jules showed me, but we have to put it back. He says we always have to put them back."

Tugging on a lock of her hair, Jon said, "Yeah, Clay made me put back the wolves I caught, too." His eyebrows lowered, his tone dark. "And I had them all neatly wrapped, ready to ship to Timbuktu. I'd even stuck on the postal stickers."

Sascha bit back a laugh, well aware she shouldn't encourage the pranks Jon pulled against wolves his own age, even when those pranks were inspired. Not that the SnowDancer juveniles were taking it lying down. The last retaliation had involved a slime pit and a sulfurous stink so noxious he'd had to bathe in antiseptic wash to get it off.

"You shouldn't catch wolves," Noor scolded her adoptive big brother. "The wolves are our friends."

Jon clutched at his chest with melodramatic flair. "But yeah," he added after Noor laughed, "you should put the ladybug back. It's meant to live outside and you can see it when you come again."

He walked out with Noor as she held her hand carefully half-cupped to protect the ladybug.

Julian and Roman meanwhile had stayed in cub form and were currently being petted by their father, who'd crouched down to rub their heads. When they shifted without warning, Nate didn't miss a beat, just wrapped them in his arms and rose to his feet as they began to talk his ear off about their adventures.

Tamsyn brushed her fingers through the twins' hair before she went to the other side of the counter; her intense joy at having a busy home filled with packmates was a warm taste in the air to Sascha's empathic senses.

"You're all staying for dinner." It was less a question and more a command.

Talin groaned. "I'm so full of cake. Don't make anything delicious."

"I was thinking Vietnamese chicken with glass noodles."

"I'm going to go run laps with Noor so I can make room in my stomach."

Smile deep at that solemn response, Tamsyn said, "Nate, honey, do you want to give Zach and Annie a call, see if they want to come over, too? It'll probably depend on how exhausted they are. Annie said their cub's fond of four a.m. wakeup calls."

Having finished dressing Naya in a soft blue jumpsuit, Sascha put her down so she could toddle around. Her balance had improved in leaps and bounds since she started shifting—as if her brain was using what she was experiencing in cub form to assist her in human form. "I'll call Lucas," she said as Naya wobbled off after Jon and Noor. "He might've been held up."

The mate of an alpha knew too well that his time wasn't always his own.

Chapter 37

ZACH AND ANNIE arrived before Lucas. The DarkRiver senior soldier and his elementary school teacher mate had walked over with their one-month-old baby, even though Annie was currently using a cane to support the leg that had been injured in a train derailment when she was a child.

"I need the exercise," the brown-eyed woman said, a little breathless upon arrival but flushed with health under the delicate cream of her skin. "All this baby weight isn't going to shift itself."

Behind her, her taller mate—their baby boy cradled in one arm—bent down to nip at her ear.

Annie yelped. "What was that for?" she asked, rubbing at the abused ear.

"I seem to remember you throwing up for most of the first half of the pregnancy," Zach replied. "I don't see any extra weight." Bad-tempered words from the copper-skinned male with aqua eyes but the raw tenderness he felt toward his mate made Sascha's heart hurt in the best way.

Annie tilted back her head to scowl at him, the deep black of her unbound hair brushing over his chest. "You need your eyes examined."

Growling, Zach maneuvered her into a chair. "Let me massage that leg."

Annie, who'd always been shy, blushed a little but didn't push away her mate's gentle hands when he hunkered down beside her after handing her their cub.

"Hey, sleepy." She nuzzled their child. "Your daddy's being a grumpus."

Growling deep in his chest, Zach continued to massage Annie's leg.

Sascha smiled. The couple was adorable.

"Did you two settle on a middle name yet?" she asked, leaning over to look into the baby's sweet face. Annie and Zach's first child had his daddy's skin and straight black hair and his eyes looked like they might end up the same stunning aqua as Zach's. But there was a sweetness to his drowsy baby smile that spoke of Annie.

"We're going to leave it as Rowan Quinn for now," Annie said, a stark poignancy to her. "If I ever find the boy who saved my life, I want to use his name as Rowan's middle name."

Sascha could understand Annie's desire to honor that unknown telekinetic boy—if he hadn't lifted the train off Annie, she wouldn't be here today, wouldn't have a mate or a child. And the world would've missed out on the beauty and gentleness of Annie's spirit.

"Zach understands." Allowing Tally to take Rowan for a cuddle, Annie ran her fingers through the hair of her still-scowling mate, who growled at her even as he continued to massage her thigh.

"What I don't understand is why you keep overdoing it," Zach said, then looked at Sascha. "This morning, I stumble bleary-eyed into the kitchen, thanks to the alarm clock called Rowan, and what do I see but my mate on a *stepladder* trying to fix a malfunctioning kitchen light."

Screwing up her nose, Annie pulled at the hair she'd been petting. "I was being nice, letting you sleep in."

"You were giving me a heart attack, that's what you were doing. It's like you're taking lessons from Mercy."

Tamsyn frowned from where she stood on the cooking side of the counter. "How bad is your leg, Annie?"

"Not too bad really."

Zach spoke without stopping the massage. "In Annie terms, 'not too bad' equals 'yeah, it hurts like a bitch.'"

"Zach's exaggerating." Even as Annie glared at her mate, she was petting his shoulders with the caressing touch of a woman who sensed her mate's very real worry and was trying to alleviate it. "It hurts but nothing major."

Tamsyn's response was a "hmm" of sound.

Leaving Clay to look after the vegetables she'd put on to stir-fry, the healer retrieved a scanner from her kit and, coming down beside Zach, ran it over Annie's thigh and lower leg. "No signs of strain or degradation in the plassteel itself," she said, referring to the way Annie's leg had been rebuilt after the train accident, "but I see a little inflammation in the tissue around it."

Her eyes met Annie's. "I can give you a localized and gentle anti-inflammatory that'll alleviate that and make you more comfortable."

Annie bit down on her lower lip. "Will it—"

"It won't have any impact on Rowan," Tamsyn promised. "You can continue to nurse him."

Nodding, Annie allowed the healer to administer the anti-inflammatory. Afterward, Tamsyn gave a preloaded injector to Zach before talking to both Zach and Annie. "There are ten doses in there. You can use it a couple of times a week without issue—and less discomfort means less stress on you, which is good for your cub, so *do* use it." The last words were an order.

Annie smiled. "Yes, Tamsyn."

"You're getting as cheeky as your students," Tamsyn said, rising to her feet to press a kiss to Annie's cheek just as Lucas arrived.

So did Dorian, Ashaya, and Keenan. The three had detoured to run an errand after the couple picked up Keenan from the tea party, then decided to swing by. Tamsyn was delighted to have so many packmates in her space, put a couple of them to work helping her prep for dinner.

"Dev might've inadvertently pointed me to a possible lead on Leila Savea," Lucas told them after claiming a hot, wet kiss from Sascha that left her flushed and breathless and happy he was here, safe and strong and with his heart beating under her palm.

She felt his own protective need to be certain of her welfare in the way he held her snug against his side. The only reason he hadn't hunted down Naya was because they could hear their cub giggling wildly as she played a game with the other young children that had them all in hysterics.

But where her and Lucas's impact on one another was an exchange between mates, he also had a subtle effect on the others in the room. Each and every one of their packmates had become more calm and steady in his presence. For an empath, it was fascinating to witness the primal impact of an alpha—but for Sascha, a member of DarkRiver, it was simply right.

Lucas was the pack's alpha. This was what he did.

Today, as they listened, he laid out the trail of bread crumbs and connections that had put a bull's-eye on the estate next to the IceRock pack's territory. "I spoke to Miane, let her know. We're just waiting on the images from IceRock."

That wasn't the only news he had.

Sascha listened intently as he shared the report from Jamie. "I had a quick chat with Bastien on the way over," he added afterward. "He says the transfer of the twenty-five thousand to the captain was as highly sophisticated as the financial transactions purportedly completed by the SkyElm alpha. He's started pulling things apart, is hoping to get a bead on the person at the end of the money trail."

Sascha couldn't wait for that to happen; she'd accepted that Naya would always attract attention, some of it dangerous, but she wanted at least one threat off the table.

"Couple of Trinity things came in while you were meeting with Hawke," Nathan said after they'd discussed Jamie's information. "I handled it. Basically, Ming's continuing to stir up trouble but Hawke's keeping him too busy shoring up his business interests for it to do much damage."

Sascha had been impressed by Hawke's plan when Lucas first shared it. She was even more impressed by how well all the people who hated the venomous ex-Councilor had worked together to thwart him. As the daughter of a former Councilor herself, Sascha knew enough about Ming to know the combat telepath treasured only one thing more than his psychic skill—his tactical intelligence. To have that so publicly beaten would burn.

"I also wanted to discuss Jon," Lucas said after glancing outside to ensure the kids were all still out there. "I think we should offer him the chance to attend a training camp with the Forgotten. Dev's people have come up with techniques that might help him get a better handle on his abilities."

Talin's expression was tight, but she nodded. "I'll talk to him," she said, and Sascha knew she was having to fight her protective instincts to even consider the idea of allowing Jon to go that far away.

Pulling her back against his chest with his arm around her front, Clay nuzzled gently at her. "We can discuss it with him tomorrow. No need to mess with his mood today."

No one argued, well aware that while the idea was a good one, Jon might well prefer not to go. He'd been lost and alone too long, tended to stick tight to his family and packmates. Today the teen ended up the de facto babysitter when the children eventually decamped to the large living area to play with toys.

He wandered into the kitchen twenty minutes after that, while dinner was still cooking.

Tamsyn pointed to the fridge without looking up. "Leftover lasagna from last night. All yours."

A grin split Jon's face. Taking the lasagna and a fork that Nathan passed over, he would've left to return to the living area if Nathan hadn't made him heat up the lasagna. The teenager had already taken the first bite before he left the room.

"Do all teenage boys eat like that?" Sascha asked, wondering where it all went. Jon was thinner than he'd ever been.

Tamsyn nodded. So did Clay and Nathan, Lucas and Dorian.

"My foster brothers used to get hungry every two hours," Talin shared. "Ma Larkspur bought sandwich fixings by the bucketload."

"I once ate an entire roast chicken my mom had cooked specifically so she could make sandwiches the next day." Dorian winced. "Boy, was she mad when she woke up to a pile of bones."

"But he's so thin." Sascha couldn't help but worry, saw the same concern in the blue-gray of Ashaya's gaze. "Are you sure he's not sick?"

Nathan disappeared for a minute, to return with a photograph. It was of a skinny teen with black hair and midnight blue eyes. "Is this you?" Sascha couldn't believe it, Nathan was so strongly muscular now.

"Skinny as a beanpole until I was about sixteen, seventeen." The senior sentinel touched her cheek with the easy skin privileges of a packmate, including Ashaya in his reassuring look. "Don't worry about the boy. Tamsyn's keeping an eye on him—he's just going through a growth spurt."

"I guess," Ashaya murmured, "we never noticed in the PsyNet because our diet was based on nutrition bars and drinks."

Sascha saw what the scientist was saying. "The menu plans must've compensated for that teenage growth spurt, allowed for extra calories when teens needed it."

"You caught the tail end of it with Kit," Tamsyn pointed out. "He had his main growth spurt earlier, but he was still eating the pack out of house and home until he turned twenty-one." The last was said with so much love that Sascha knew Tamsyn would've fed the young male had he turned up every single day.

That was when Lucas's phone rang. "IceRock just sent through the images," he said after he'd hung up following a short conversation.

He checked the download, then forwarded it to Miane, giving her a call to alert her it was coming through. Simply taking over the operation wasn't on the agenda, not when it was one of Miane's people who was being held hostage. If BlackSea asked, Sascha knew DarkRiver would respond.

Until then, they'd wait and hope that Leila Savea's captivity was about to end.

Chapter 38

HAWKE WAS ABOUT to hold a working dinner with his lieutenants when he received a message from Lucas updating him on the hunt for Leila Savea and on the BlackSea op currently being planned. Sliding away his phone, he decided to give his people a little more time to talk before they began to discuss that situation among others—including the unexpected wrench Lucas had thrown into Trinity by proposing an "adjunct" or provisional signatory status.

The DarkRiver alpha had sent the idea only to SnowDancer and the Arrows at this stage, for their input. Hawke's initial reaction had been a firm "hell, no." He couldn't understand why the fuck Lucas would propose something that could give Ming a way in should he want to take it; it was Riley who'd made him see the reason behind Lucas's idea.

"Trinity is about creating a world without divisions," his best friend and lieutenant had said. "There has to be a way for former enemies to prove themselves, or Trinity fails before it ever really begins."

Hawke wasn't sure he was civilized enough to accept such rational necessities, but since they had Ming on the ropes, he was at least willing to listen to feedback from the rest of his lieutenants. Having Riley's calm presence anchor the discussion was partially why this SnowDancer meeting was about to take place in DarkRiver territory.

He and the lieutenants who were based in the Sierra Nevada den had arrived a couple of minutes ago with insulated carriers holding dinner, to find both Mercy and Riley strolling outside their cabin, soaking up the red-orange rays of the setting sun. Alone with Mercy when Riley was pulled into a back-slapping hug by Riaz, Hawke leaned down as if to kiss her on the cheek.

She growled low in her throat. "Try it, wolf, and lose your face."

Grinning, he instead gave her what he'd been holding behind his back. "A little present."

Another growl as she narrowed her eyes. "Why are you giving me gifts?"

"Your pupcubs are half SnowDancer."

Mercy's eyes went to where Riley was laughing with Riaz, Indigo, and Judd, the four lieutenants apparently deeply amused by something. Expression softening, she turned her cheek slightly. "You may kiss me," she said, like a queen bestowing a favor. "But only because you moved your lieutenant meeting all the way down here mostly so Riley could see everyone."

Hawke didn't dispute her interpretation of his actions because she was dead right. The agenda for the meeting offered a good excuse, but this was really about looking after a packmate who'd given so much to Snow-Dancer. Accepting the invitation to kiss Mercy, an invitation she'd never before extended, he drew in her scent. His wolf considered her part of his pack, especially now, when she carried the twinned scents of leopard and wolf far more strongly than usual. "Open your present."

Gaze suspicious again, she took a seat in an outdoor chair, then tore away the wrapping paper to pick up the baby-sized item on top. It was a legless one-piece bodysuit in SnowDancer blue, with "SnowDancers Rule" written on the front in white and a wolf silhouette on the back in the same shade.

The next item was a tiny white T-shirt with wolves gamboling all over it.

Mercy looked up, her lips trying not to curve. "You're doing this to mess with Lucas."

"I'm astonished you'd say that." Hawke pressed a hand to his heart. "I'm just proud of my soon-to-be-new packmates."

Shaking her head, Mercy gave in to her smile as she continued to go through the miniature pieces of clothing, all of them SnowDancer branded . . . except for the last set, every one of which had "Pupcub" written across the front, above a cartoon of an adorable half wolf–half leopard pupcub drawn by Toby.

The thirteen-year-old had shown it to Sienna, who'd shown it to Hawke.

The rest was history.

Mercy's face lit up. "Riley! Come look!" She held up a little yellow jumpsuit that came complete with a hood that sported two pointed ears.

Cheeks creasing in a deep grin, Riley said, "Perfect."

The other lieutenants hadn't seen the gift pack, came over to go through it together with Riley and Mercy, all of them laughing as they debated their favorites. Including Riaz. The dark-haired lieutenant with eyes of beaten gold had been in one hell of a good mood for the past month, stayed that way throughout the working dinner—where Mercy told them what Nathan had said about the terrible error in building Trinity on a foundation of exclusion.

The words hit hard, made them all think.

Hawke was still chewing over the implications when he and the others left Riley and Mercy's home in the rugged SUV they'd driven down in together. Reaching SnowDancer territory, they decided to park the SUV in a lower area and run the last section home. It was such a clear night, the stars crystalline, that the wolf wanted to throw back its head and howl, but Hawke stayed in human form for now, as did the others.

It was easy enough for him to fall in beside Riaz, while Indigo and Judd ran ahead. "The idea of giving former enemies a way to prove their good intentions is never going to make sense to my wolf."

"It took a human to stop the Territorial Wars for a reason," was the lieutenant's answer. "I'm fucking impressed Lucas was able to fight his own instincts enough to put the proposal together."

Hawke was quiet for a while, the wind cool against his face as they ran. "Having a cub, being responsible for that vulnerable life, it changes a man." He'd seen it in Lucas, only now understood the depth of that change—to give Naya an undivided world, Lucas was willing to battle even his panther's most primal urges.

Because the cats? They were as possessive and as territorial as Hawke's wolves, and they did not forgive anyone who'd harmed their own. "Five years is a long time," he mused. "Plenty of room for people to fuck up if they're trying to game the system." Arrogant bastards like Ming LeBon would never have the patience to stay "clean" that long.

"And just because an asshole signs the accord doesn't mean we have to work with them." Riaz's voice was familiar in the night, as familiar as the dark woodsmoke edged with citrus that was his natural scent. "Open communication doesn't mean open access."

"Yeah." Hawke pushed his hair off his face, decided the adjunct proposal was one he'd have to sleep on. This would not be an easy or uncomplicated decision. "In other matters," he said to the man who ran beside him, "you're scaring people with your happy."

Riaz's laugh was all wolf, his eyes night-glow in the darkness when they met Hawke's. "You've figured it out, haven't you?"

"I've got some clue. You want to tell me if I'm right?"

"You know how I had that mating tug toward Lisette?" Riaz asked. "Like she was meant to be my mate?"

Hawke nodded, aware that lingering remnant of a relationship that had never been and never would be, had deeply frustrated Riaz. Wolf and man, both parts of Riaz had chosen Adria, loved the senior soldier with a furious passion.

"It's gone." Riaz's tone was jubilant. "Like it stretched so thin it just broke."

Hawke's wolf opened its jaws in a lupine grin. "I'm guessing this doesn't worry you."

"Are you kidding? It bugged the hell out of me. I *love* Adria, and that tug, it was like a splinter stuck under my skin."

Hawke could hear Riaz's scowl in his voice.

"Lisette and I had a chance once, sure," the lieutenant added, "but that chance passed. Adria's my woman, the only one I want. The suggestion that it might be otherwise pissed me off every fucking day."

"I get it." A predatory changeling who truly loved, loved all in. "People have always wondered what would happen if a changeling found his mate but chose to walk away."

"I don't know that my experience would apply to everyone," Riaz said after they'd navigated around a large rock in their path. "I mean, the whole situation was messed up. Lisette being human and madly in love with her husband, for one. That would've never happened if she'd been changeling. It was all off from the start."

"Yeah, you're right." If a changeling was in love, the mating bond couldn't come into play with anyone else—it was a law written in stone. Hawke knew of no exceptions. "You just did things backward," he said in realization. "Your love for Adria pushed the possibility of the mating bond with anyone else out."

"Damn straight." Riaz's tone held wolfish satisfaction.

"Hell, Riaz." Hawke whistled. "You're going to give the philosophers enough meat to chew over for years, if not decades. What, for example, happens to two changelings who try to walk away from a bond when neither is attached to anyone else?" Hawke couldn't imagine why anyone would walk away from the other half of their soul, but the philosopher types tended to think up ridiculous questions like that.

Riaz shrugged. "I don't think that would happen unless they were at war, like this couple Dalton told me about who were on opposite sides during the Territorial Wars. Even then, it'd be a two-way pull—I can't see how that'd give you enough breathing room to fall in love with anyone else. With me and Lisette, it was a dual repudiation."

A sudden grin as the lieutenant turned to run backward for a minute so he could face Hawke. "But really, I don't give a fuck about the philosophers. They can philosophize all they want. I just want to love the woman who owns my heart, the empress whose name is on my fucking soul."

Nothing more needed to be said.

. . .

RIAZ caught the scent of crushed berries and frost the instant he entered the den. Adria had passed by this way recently, as had several others. Skin aching with the need to touch her, he followed the scent—and realized Indigo and Drew were following along right behind him. SnowDancer's tracker had met his lieutenant mate at the waterfall, run the rest of the way back with them.

Riaz stopped. "Don't you two want to go to bed?" he asked pointedly.

Throwing one arm around Indigo's shoulders, Drew grinned. "Nope. Wide awake here."

Indigo's smile was less aggravating. "I wanted to ask Adria about one of the older pups under her authority and I keep forgetting. Promise it won't take more than a couple of minutes."

"Two minutes," Riaz said with a scowl. "Then scat."

"Gee whiz, Riaz, impatient m—oof." Rubbing at his abdomen, Drew made a pitiful face toward his mate. "Your elbow's really sharp, Lieutenant."

"I'll kiss it better." Indigo's tone was dry but she had her hand on Drew's back, was probably petting him under his T-shirt. "Now stop provoking Riaz. He hasn't seen Adria since this morning."

Drew's expression turned sympathetic, that of a man who understood what it was to adore a woman. Riley's younger brother might be the most irreverent wolf Riaz knew, but under the playfulness was a man who knew what it was to love, what it was to be loyal. "Best behavior," the tracker said. "I swear."

As it turned out, Drew hadn't needed to make that vow. Adria was up and awake and at an impromptu party thrown by the senior soldiers to celebrate the birthday of the man who held the leadership position among them. Elias was grinning and having a beer when Riaz walked in, his mate Yuki by his side. The hard-nosed lawyer had her hair down and was dressed in a white shift dress with wildflowers on it. Her eyes were only for Eli.

"Hey, how come we didn't rate an invite?" Drew groused while Riaz made a beeline for Adria.

"Riaz." Eyes of deepest blue-violet filled with delight. "Did—"

He cut off her question with a hot tangle of a kiss that made her claws dig into his nape as a moan formed in the back of her throat. A split-second later and his possessive lover was kissing him back with equal hunger as her scent heated up.

The others around them were predictably whistling like a feral pack of wolves when Riaz and Adria came up for air. A few had thrown back their heads to add a howl into the mix.

Ignoring the lunatics, he savored the taste of the strong woman who was his by taking another kiss, his heart thundering in his ears. "Drew's right," he said afterward. "Why no invite for us?"

Lips swollen and pupils dilated, Adria ran her hands down his body to the bottom of his T-shirt, so she could slip her hands underneath. He shivered.

"We threw it together after you'd all already left for Riley's," Adria told him with a smile that cut him off at the knees. "D'Arn found out it was Eli's birthday and sweet-talked Aisha into baking a quick cake."

"Sakura with friends?" Eli and Yuki's pup was a little slip of a girl.

"She's having a sleepover with Marlee." Leaning up, Adria nuzzled at his throat. "How was the meeting?"

"Good to see Riley and Mercy." He told her about the baby clothes Hawke had gifted the couple, drank in her pleasure. "Rest was business." A nip at her lower lip. "We can talk about it once we're in our quarters." No one expected mates or couples in committed long-term relationships to keep secrets from each other, and Adria was senior enough to have a right to the information he'd share regardless.

"You must be tired," Adria said with a soft, luscious brush of her lips over his. "Ready for bed?"

The golden-eyed black wolf that was Riaz's other half wanted to growl an assent. Wolf and man, Riaz's intent had been to steal Adria away, lick her up in the privacy of their quarters, but he could taste her own wolf's happiness in this gathering of those she worked with most often—the maternal cabal's lures notwithstanding.

And Adria's happiness was Riaz's.

"Let's stay," he said with a smile, his hunger sated enough to take the edge off. "I'll pet you later."

The gold streaks in her eyes going night-glow as her wolf rose to the surface of her skin, she grazed her claws teasingly over his neck. "Deal."

Indigo and Drew came over shortly afterward, and while the two women spoke about a teenager Adria was supervising as part of her secondary maternal dominant duties, Riaz and Drew went across to wish Eli a happy birthday.

Not surprisingly, Hawke, Judd, and their mates turned up bare minutes afterward, as did a number of others, word clearly having gotten around that a party was in progress.

Riaz was with Hawke a quarter of an hour later when his alpha's phone gave a sharp ping. "It's time?" he asked.

Hawke nodded, his husky blue eyes holding the wolf's hunger for the hunt. "BlackSea's going in."

PART 5

Chapter 39

AS PER THE plan he'd worked out with Miane's team, Vasic teleported in alone to the compound that might hold the vanished BlackSea woman. The location he arrived in proved to be as perfect as the neighboring lynx pack had stated: a corner of the property swathed in shadows because of large trees the owners had probably left up in order to further shield the back of the property.

There were lights on the fence but they didn't penetrate much deeper than a few feet. The house itself was only lit up in one discrete section. Between the house and this spot lay a large area of lawn and foliage. Teleporting right to the house would've been easier, but he had no way of knowing what security measures were in place; it was better to be patient than to set off a sensor.

Having pulled on his night-vision goggles, Vasic was calculating the best route to the house when he felt a telepathic scan pass over him.

Psy guards.

They wouldn't have picked up his presence. Arrow minds were too well shielded—but this wasn't a one-man operation. Miane hadn't been arrogant about BlackSea's involvement, had told him that if he could pull out Leila or any other captive on his own, then he was to do it. However, once Vasic did a scan of his own and realized the number of guards, he 'ported back to BlackSea's floating city.

Then, he, Miane, and Malachai overhauled the plan in light of his reconnaissance. It took precious time and he could feel the changelings straining inside their skin, but they forced themselves to remain calm and controlled. Every member of the team knew that this would be no empty substation in the wilderness but a heavily guarded fortress they'd have to breach with stealth.

"Close in," Vasic said after everyone in the team had been briefed on the updated plan; he then teleported without delay.

The first part was simple—to get to the house without alerting or harming the perimeter guards. It would slow their progress but give them longer to search the property before an alarm was raised—because the instant that happened, if Leila was here, she might either be harmed or moved.

Upon arrival, the team split up as agreed and each individual made his or her way to certain points. Four of the changelings would remain outside, ready to pick off guards should they come running in from the perimeter in response to an alarm. Vasic was already using his telepathic abilities to conceal their presence from a psychic sweep.

He, Miane, and Malachai would go inside.

The plan was to do it as quietly as possible, to confirm this was the right place and these were the right people, before they made any lethal calls. There was, after all, a chance that the house was, in fact, occupied by a celebrity or plain old drug dealer or another individual with a need and/or desire for extreme privacy.

Psy bodyguards were all the rage in certain quarters.

In the darkness, the BlackSea people became ripples of black against black. Vasic saw them, but he was highly trained at night ops, and from what he could tell, most of the property's guard complement was far from well trained. Good enough to guard an isolated home. Not good enough to spot men and women who knew how to move in the dark.

Part one went off without a hitch.

Meeting at the closest entrance, from beyond which Vasic could pick out no light, he and Malachai waited while Miane tried the old-fashioned door. It was locked. The BlackSea alpha pulled something out of a thigh pocket, used it on the door. The next time she twisted the handle, it opened. No audible alarms.

Instead of rushing inside, Vasic used a miniature low-beam flashlight to check for any electronic beams or signs the door was wired for a silent alarm.

Nothing.

The other two moved at his nod to clear the room; the three of them had worked out their responsibilities and tasks back on Lantia. Entering behind them, Vasic closed the door so it would remain a viable exit should Vasic be separated from the others and unable to 'port them to safety.

If no one knew they'd come this way, no one could lock it on them.

"It's an office," Malachai said in a near-subvocal whisper, his bulk behind the black wedge of a desk.

Flicking on a narrow-beam flashlight of his own, he ran it over the papers on the desk. "Shit, it's all decades old. Must've been left here when the property went into foreclosure."

That explained the leaves Vasic could feel underfoot, the damp in the air. "They didn't bother to clean up this section."

"Let's go," Miane said, already at the other door.

Vasic did a telepathic scan of the corridor beyond, indicated for them to go. He wouldn't have sensed someone as highly shielded as himself, but he doubted there was anyone with that level of mental discipline here. He was proved right. The corridor was lined with a moth-eaten carpet and empty of all life. They went quicker now, checking any rooms they passed but aiming for the section of the house that had been lit up when they arrived.

Vasic caught the first hint of voices almost five minutes later; the sounds were followed by whispers of light. He and the changelings crept right to the edge of the light, listened. Vasic knew that if BlackSea changelings had the same level of hearing as terrestrial changelings, then Miane and Malachai had to be picking up far more than him, but he picked up enough.

"... on the road. Barring any unexpected delays, she'll arrive at the drop-off point in twenty-four hours."

"You're sure she's broken?" A male voice. "The damn fish held out forever."

"Broken and ours," confirmed the second speaker, a female. "All she needs is time to regain full physical health, and she'll be primed and ready to hit whichever target we point her at."

Vasic knew the three of them could've backed off, allowed this place to continue existing so they could use it to track down the other vanished, but that wasn't the changeling way. They wouldn't sacrifice one for the many. The squad functioned the same way.

"Male speaker is Psy, female is human," he said in a tone so low he could barely hear himself. "First is protecting the mind of the second, and he's strong enough that I'd have to kill him to neutralize him psychically. The backlash might take out the female.

"A telekinetic hit could put them out of commission, but there's a slight risk the male will have a chance to blast a telepathic warning to his guards or to his superiors." Telepathic communication was near impossible to block. "Do you want me to strike?"

Miane's back was a furious line in front of him as she shook her head. "Mal."

"Be easier if one or both moved this way."

"Keep the human alive," Miane ordered. "Psy is too high a risk."

"I'll get them out into the corridor," Vasic warned before he teleported some distance back down the way they'd come and deliberately knocked over an old vase.

It didn't take long for the Psy male to start down toward the noise. He was being stealthy, but he was focused on the origin point of the noise, far down the hallway. Vasic 'ported back in time to watch Malachai rise up behind him and snap his neck. Miane was already moving toward the room from which the dead male had come.

By the time Vasic walked in, she had the human female facedown on the ground, her knee on the other woman's spine and the woman's arms wrenched behind her back. Miane's gun was pressed to the back of the woman's head, explaining the woman's silence.

A small communications unit lay on the ground. "She didn't get out an alert," Miane said in a voice as cold as the frigid darkness at the bottom of the ocean.

Vasic was already in the human female's mind, taking everything she knew about Leila Savea, the vanished, and the Consortium. It appeared the Psy male had bolstered her weak natural protections as well as extending his own shields over her, but with the latter gone, the former wasn't difficult to disassemble without causing brain damage. "I have it," he said quietly.

"Did she torture Leila?" Miane's eyes were chips of black ice when she glanced at Vasic.

Vasic thought of what he'd seen in this woman's mind, of how she'd taken pleasure in carving up Leila's face while the changeling screamed, and knew this was no time for mercy. "Yes."

The woman opened her mouth as if to beg or scream for help, but it was too late. Miane had slit her throat using a knife Vasic hadn't seen her pull out. "Are there any others here?" the BlackSea alpha asked after wiping the blood on the back of the woman's shirt and rising to her feet.

Vasic shook his head. "According to her memories, it was meant to be a long-term containment facility. Leila was the test subject. They moved her out this morning."

Jaw a hard line, Miane said, "Let's exit. Quietly as we entered. The longer the guards are in the dark, the longer we have to track down Leila without interference."

Vasic got the entire team out without incident, then told Miane what else he'd discovered in the woman's mind. "She was in charge of only Leila Savea." Another example of the fragmentation practiced so effectively by the Consortium. "Her job was to break Leila and train her to follow orders, even if those orders were to kill."

Interestingly, the torturer had believed herself equal to all others in the Consortium, which Vasic knew for a fact wasn't true. The CEO the squad had captured previously had been in the innermost circle, part of the decision makers who held power over the more disposable pawns below.

However, those details he'd share later. Currently, only one thing was important. "Leila was taken away in an SUV with the following number plate." He wrote it down for them. "Though the woman wasn't meant to and didn't know the final destination, one of the drivers slipped up and mentioned they were heading toward the Yukon."

"Can we hack into the traffic systems?" Miane asked Malachai.

The big male nodded. "I'm on it, but even though we're only searching a certain corridor, the country has a lot of uncharted roads that aren't used enough to justify traffic surveillance. If I was doing something illegal, I'd stay on those uncharted roads—and if I did take the main highways, I'd do it at night and make sure my plates were too muddy for the scanners."

Miane swore. "We need people looking for that SUV, but even if we alert all our people and the changeling packs our allies know, it won't be enough. There aren't enough of us."

Malachai paused, blew out a quiet breath. "There are a lot more humans on the roads, including truckers who travel at night and everyday individuals who drive back and forth to their homes and work."

Vasic could see Miane struggling with the decision she had to make. Send out a request across the Human Alliance network for information about the SUV and possibly find it—or have that information end up in the hands of the enemy, who'd either hide Leila once again . . . or eliminate her as too big a risk. The good news was that the latter would have to be a last resort: they'd put too much time and effort into her to discard her so quickly.

"I'll talk to Bowen Knight," Miane said at last, her hand fisted. "Request he ask his people to report any sightings of the vehicle."

"It's the best choice." Malachai held his alpha's gaze, his brown eyes appearing to glow as if backlit. "At least it gives Leila a shot before she's forced to kill, because once she does, we won't be able to bring her back. She isn't built for that."

"No, Leila is built for science and exploration and writing scholarly papers." All but vibrating with anger, Miane stalked to the comm. "Bowen

Knight doesn't need to know why I'm asking for this—I don't trust him enough yet. I'll bargain a favor for a BlackSea IOU."

"Actually, the Alliance owes us one," Malachai said. "I tipped Bowen off about an anti-human Psy cell we picked up on in Venice."

His alpha paused midstep. "Why didn't I know about this?"

"I was going to brief you, but then we heard about Leila's message and it didn't seem particularly important." Malachai shrugged. "It was only a fringe group of fanatics, nothing major, but they were apparently planning to storm the Alliance offices with weapons." He folded his arms. "Bowen confirmed our intel was right, thanked me. I told him one day, we'd call in the favor."

Miane's eyes narrowed slightly. "Sometimes, Mal, I think that brain of yours is a dangerous weapon. Good thing you're on my side." She input the call after Malachai moved out of the shot.

Vasic teleported home to Ivy before the call connected. His part was done. Leila Savea's life now depended on countless pairs of human eyes.

Letters to Nina

From the private diaries of Father Xavier Perez
November 3, 2076

Nina,

I've crossed many borders in the past year, somehow ended up making a home in San Francisco. I have a church, a congregation. They call me Father Xavier. It felt too big a thing at first, the respect inherent in it unearned, but I've come to accept my place here.

I may be but a humble man from a distant mountain village—but in this big city, there are many broken souls who need solace. I attempt to provide it, even as I fight my own demons, fight my own anger.

I'm no longer surprised when I find Psy sitting in the pews. They used to leave when they saw me, as if afraid I'd turn them in for believing, but now sometimes, they stay and we talk. I was such a fool before, Nina, thinking they weren't people but automatons. There is nothing that separates us but a twist of biology—they have psychic abilities and we don't. That is the only difference. Beneath the skin, they are as human as you or I.

My Psy friend though, he's as different from the parishioners as a rabbit is from a bird of prey. He is always in such control, so cold. Frigid as ice, until it would be easy to believe that he is an unfeeling robotic killer. Yet I've seen this man take a bullet to protect a child.

Heroes, I've learned, don't always wear white.

Sometimes they come from the darkness, shadows among shadows.

Your Xavier

Chapter 40

KALEB HAD BEEN searching for another area of the Net as healthy as Sophia Russo's ever since Sahara made the request. The NetMind and DarkMind had proven singularly unhelpful on that point. So much so that Kaleb was starting to become concerned at the twin neosentiences' behavior. Previously, even when the DarkMind turned erratic, the Net-Mind had remained unwavering and resolute in its duties.

The fact that the more stable neosentience was displaying erratic behavior of its own told him the problem with the PsyNet was far bigger than even the empaths realized, the flaw so fundamental that it was causing catastrophic damage to the "organs" of what was clearly a living system.

Given the lack of help, Kaleb had set up tightly defined search patterns that ran continuously. He'd devoted a significant percentage of his brain to the search. And after all that, he'd found only two other areas that appeared flawless in their health. It was possible there were more, since he'd basically run a manual search, but if so, it had to be a highly limited number.

The first new area was simple enough: it emanated from Clara Alvarez. Interestingly, she was an ex-Justice Psy like Sophia Russo. Coincidence?

It was the second clean area that proved problematic.

That small isolated region of the Net was pristine, beautiful, strong . . . and the mind behind the effect invisible. Not well shielded. *Invisible.* The only people Kaleb knew who had shields that effective were Arrows. He'd

only detected that there *was* a mind anchored in the area because one, he
was a dual cardinal with the attendant power, and two, because he'd made
it a point to learn how to spot Arrows back when the squad had been
under the command of Councilor Ming LeBon, who'd used them to mete
out death to his enemies.

It hadn't mattered if a particular assassination required an Arrow to
give up his or her own life; the ex-Councilor had treated the highly trained
and extremely intelligent men and women of the squad as replaceable.
Despite growing up in the "care" of a psychopath, Kaleb had never made
the same mistake when it came to his own people—and it was because of
Sahara. She'd taught him that people weren't disposable or replaceable by
being the unique, wild, extraordinary gift that she was . . . and by how
she'd seen the same in him.

"Don't get hurt, Kaleb! Who will I play with if you break your legs?"

*"You'll find other friends. There are lots of children in the NightStar com-
pound."*

*A reproachful look from the ten-year-old girl standing at the bottom of the
tree, the one with dark, dark blue eyes that always filled with light when he
stole away to see her. "But only you're you. Only you are my best friend."*

It was a fragment of memory that had reminded him to stay *Kaleb* no
matter how his psychopathic trainer tried to break him down over the
years. Because Sahara loved Kaleb, no one else. And he loved only her.

Sahara was also the one who'd made him see that, sometimes, it was
better to extend the hand of friendship than to force compliance by fear.
Santano Enrique had tortured him until Kaleb hated him with every
ounce of his being. Sahara had loved him, and for her, he'd do anything.

In line with that thought, he didn't attempt to break into the shielded
mind.

Instead, he dropped out of the PsyNet, made contact with Aden, and
asked the leader of the Arrows to meet him on the PsyNet, at the site.
"Do you see it?" he asked.

"You'll have to explain."

"The Net," Kaleb pointed out. "No rot, no disintegration, nothing but pure strength." He didn't need an empath to confirm it, could feel that strength like a crisp, fresh wind against his psychic senses.

Aden examined the psychic fabric with care. "You're right."

"The Es need to know who's causing the effect," Kaleb said. "It would give them a third data point for comparison."

"I'll check with the individual in question."

Kaleb let it go at that; pushing an Arrow was a useless endeavor.

Aden's message came in ten minutes later, while Kaleb was in a meeting with the alpha of the BlackEdge Wolves: *The Arrow is Stefan Berg, stationed on Alaris. He'll contact Ivy Jane personally.*

Kaleb knew he'd only been given that information because Sahara would share it anyway, once she learned of it from the empaths. Even Arrows, it seemed, didn't expect bonded pairs to keep secrets from one another. Excusing himself from the wolf alpha for a short period, he thanked Aden, then passed on all the information he'd discovered to Ivy Jane.

Stefan Berg, he mused as he returned to his meeting. As far as Kaleb knew, the powerful teleporter stationed on the deep-sea station had never officially been an Arrow. Clearly, however, Aden Kai considered the man one of his. Yes, it was never a good idea to take the Arrows for granted— or to assume you knew all their secrets.

IVY couldn't believe the identity of the third calm space in the Net . . . then she thought of Sophia and Clara, and suddenly the connection between the three was blindingly clear. Heart thumping, she sent a message to Stefan. The Alaris station commander had most recently visited the orchard two months earlier, during his mandatory leave "upside," as station folk termed it.

You don't need to teleport up to see me, she told him. *I think I know what's going on.* Though Stefan was a violently powerful telekinetic, he wasn't a born teleporter like Vasic. 'Porting took serious energy for him and he needed to maintain that strength to evacuate Alaris should the station ever suffer a serious incident.

Are you sure? Stefan messaged back. *I can meet you on the PsyNet without issue.*

Yes, I'm sure. I'll contact you if I need further information.

You know where I'll be.

Ivy laughed. These Arrows, they were definitely developing senses of humor.

When Rabbit barked and ran around her, she bent down to give him a rub that had his eyes rolling back in ecstasy. Goofy, wonderful dog. Leaving him with a smiling pat, she took a seat in one of the comfortable couches arranged just off her kitchen area, the nearest counter close enough that she could put drinks there, and people on this side could pick them up.

Almost the entire first level of her and Vasic's cabin was built this way—as open plan as possible and full of light. It was on purpose, so that any Arrows who visited would never feel isolated or alone. Ivy had decided that they'd had quite enough of that. And it seemed to be working; more than once, she'd had members of the squad drop by and just sit on a couch and work while she went about her own work nearby.

Today, Rabbit jumped up to sit beside her, his small body warm under her hand as she entered the PsyNet and went to the location of Clara Alvarez's mind, for which Kaleb had given her coordinates.

He was right: the area was clean of infection and vital in its strength. No disintegration, not even a single frayed thread.

Hope bloomed inside her.

Dropping out of the Net, she thought of what she'd learned at Zie Zen's funeral, knew she couldn't assume anything. The bond . . . that was the key.

She could call Clara, but that didn't feel right. She knew the other woman in Clara's capacity as Manager of Haven because that was where Samuel Rain continued to live, but Ivy and Clara weren't close enough for easy confidences—and Clara probably didn't want this information going out over a comm network. It would have to be a personal visit.

Clara was a good person and Ivy believed she would share what Ivy needed to know once she understood the gravity of the situation in the PsyNet.

Vasic was home, could teleport her if the former J-Psy agreed to a meeting.

Ivy hesitated, loathe to disturb him.

She'd finally gotten him to rest; he'd worked nonstop since the day after they scattered Zie Zen's ashes. She knew it was his method of coping but she'd had enough, had threatened to drug his food to knock him out if he didn't listen to reason.

He'd smiled that slow, quiet smile that melted her. "You'd never do that, Ivy."

"Ugh!" Glaring at him, she'd pointed to the bedroom. "Don't make me turn to the dark side, Vasic Zen!"

Smile deepening, he'd teleported them both into bed and been asleep less than a minute after she stripped off his clothes; that stripping had taken some time since he kept teleporting off her own clothes and stealing kisses when she gasped in surprise.

Ivy had zero willpower against Vasic in a playful mood.

After he fell asleep, she'd stayed in his embrace until there was no chance he'd wake, then left him with a caress through his hair. Her intent had been to finish up her own work before snuggling back against the heat of his body for a lazy nap till Tavish returned home from school. She'd known one of the other telekinetic Arrows would teleport the boy to the orchard if Vasic was still asleep, Tavish having been strictly warned not to attempt the 'port himself.

He was too young, didn't have the control.

That instruction might not have worked to stop him, but Vasic had quietly told the boy it was a matter of trust. "I'm not going to trap your mind so you can't teleport," he'd said. "I trust you to follow the rules."

Tavish's small face had filled with determination. "I won't let you down."

"I'm not waking him," Ivy said to Rabbit now, her voice decisive. "If the PsyNet's survived this long, it can survive another few hours while my Arrow rests."

The only reason she'd wake him early was if Miane Levèque called. Vasic wouldn't want Leila Savea to suffer any further if he had the power to help her. Despite her desire for Vasic to rest, Ivy hoped the BlackSea alpha *would* call, that there would be some news, especially of the SUV that had taken Leila from the compound Vasic had helped infiltrate, but when she slipped in to snuggle beside him, the comm was quiet.

As her powerful husband with his beautiful eyes of winter gray moved in his sleep to tug her tight against his body, Leila Savea remained among the vanished.

EIGHTEEN hours after the alert went out on the Alliance network, Miane got word that the SUV they were searching for had just been found, abandoned and torched in a gully. She'd made the wrong call. The Alliance clearly harbored one or more Consortium informants. That didn't surprise her—money talked, regardless of race.

Rage still burned ice-cold inside her.

At those who had taken her people, at the traitors within BlackSea itself, and at herself, for making the wrong choice. She knew rationally that all she'd had were bad choices, but that didn't matter. All that mattered was that this wrong call might've killed a vulnerable member of her pack who was counting on Miane to get it right.

"Emergency services found no body in the wreckage," she reminded herself.

That truth provided a slender reed of hope, but the anger that lived in her wouldn't ease until all her people were home and the ones who'd dared harm them had been brutally punished. There was strength in that anger, a cold-eyed and ruthless determination.

However, Miane knew no alpha could function as a true alpha if she ran on anger alone. That would poison her entire pack, leave it no place anyone wanted to be. Water-based changelings might not be like other changeling groups, might be *other* even amongst their own kind, but they *were* changeling and had a human side. As such, they were social enough to need a community on some level.

And even though the mammalian creatures in BlackSea often found it hard to understand those whose blood ran colder, they were one. The traitors didn't count, would be eliminated the instant Miane confirmed their identities. All the others . . . they were one, because water was life and they were united in protecting that precious resource.

As they were united by their very otherness.

When it came to BlackSea's alpha, she needed to function the same way as the alpha of any other changeling pack. Miane had to hold her people together, make sure they had what they needed for their souls to bloom and to stay strong. For Persephone, a little girl who'd been kept captive in a small room for months, torn away from her mother after having already lost her father, that meant a party to celebrate the birthday she'd spent alone and scared and far from home.

Persephone didn't know the date was wrong; she just knew it was her birthday party.

Miane scooped the still-thin child up into her arms while instinctively maintaining her balance on the gently rocking platform in the center of the floating city that was BlackSea's heart. There were a number scattered around the world, but Lantia was the biggest, and it was where they held the Conclave on alternate years.

To the world, the Conclave was the ruling group of BlackSea. In truth, it wasn't a thing but an event—a yearly gathering of as many of BlackSea's people as could make it. The reason for not always holding it at Lantia wasn't in fact the water temperature, as outsiders might assume. All healthy BlackSea changelings could survive and thrive in such waters—the ocean, after all, was deep and sweetly cold no matter where you were on Earth.

No, the reason the Conclave switched location between Lantia and Cifica in the tropics, was that it wasn't fair to always ask packmates from that side of the world to do the traveling.

Persephone and her mother had both missed the last Conclave, had been trapped and alone at that time. As Leila was now.

Forcing back her anger once again, Miane said, "You look like a princess," to the child in her arms.

Giggling, Persephone fluffed at the pink tulle that cascaded over Miane's arm. "Mama present." It was more than she usually said; her speech wasn't what it should be for her age, the trauma she'd suffered having left more than one mark, but the pack's healers assured Miane that Persephone was healing.

Children are far more resilient than we give them credit for, their strongest healer had said. *Surround her in love, keep her safe, give her the space and freedom to talk about what happened, and Persephone will overcome this, grow into the strong, unique individual she was always meant to be.*

Miane could do that, *was* doing that.

"Your mama gives good presents." Miane was so damn proud of Persephone's mother. Olivia had lost her mate at the hands of the murderous bastards who'd taken their small family, and for many changelings, that would've been a fatally crippling blow.

That didn't even factor in Olivia's torture and imprisonment.

But instead of curling up and dying, the other woman had pulled herself together with a fierce strength of will.

"For our baby," Olivia had said to Miane while still bruised and battered from her ordeal. "For the baby Cary and I created together in cool waters off the coast of New Zealand." Tears had been thick in her voice, tears she refused to shed. "I'll never allow her to feel lost and alone and scared again."

"I know." Miane had taken Olivia into her arms, held her close for a long time, until the dam had crashed open, until Olivia had cried brokenly for her lost mate. "I have not a single doubt that you'll be strong for Persephone," Miane had said afterward. "But you come to me when you need to grieve—and remember that she needs to grieve, too."

Persephone might be a baby, only two years old, but she'd been a daddy's girl. "Talk to her about her father," Miane had advised her wounded packmate the week after Persephone's rescue by the Arrows, "answer her questions, and if it gets too hard, you *come to me.*"

Miane had stayed awake with Olivia that entire night. They'd watched Persephone sleep and then, when Olivia was ready, she'd spoken about the day of the kidnapping, about how she and Persephone had been forcibly separated from Cary, who'd been strong, had fought hard to protect his mate and child . . . and about how Olivia had known when Cary was murdered.

"The mating bond tore in two." Olivia had slapped her palm flat against her heart. "It *tore*, like my heart was being ripped apart, and I was bleeding so much I couldn't breathe, couldn't think." Jagged gasps of air, the echo of the visceral, soul-shredding pain vivid in the brown of her eyes. "I wanted to give up, die right then and there, but I couldn't."

Her eyes had lingered on her sleeping child. "I found Cary after so long wandering alone. So *long*, Miane. He understood me like no one else ever has or ever will. He was me and I was him and we were whole together. Now . . . now I'm in pieces, but Persephone is whole and for her, I'll endure."

Miane knew full well Olivia wouldn't live to a ripe old age. The wound on her soul was too grievous. She'd fight the pain, live until Persephone reached adulthood, and then Olivia would simply not wake up one day— or quietly disappear into the deep, never to emerge.

When the time came, Miane wouldn't attempt to stop her.

Some wounds no healer could heal. Some pain no drug could soften. Olivia had courage enough to live until her baby was no longer a baby. It was all her alpha could ask of her.

Persephone clapped her hands on Miane's cheeks right then and smacked an exuberant kiss on her lips. "Happy birthday!"

"Yes," she said, lightly tickling the little girl, "happy birthday to Persephone. Let's go see your cake!" She carried the child to a table set up with birthday cake, tiny sandwiches, pretty finger food suitable for little hands and designed to delight young taste buds, cookies, and drinks.

Like all the furniture in Lantia, the table had been bolted down using

removable bolts that fit into otherwise concealed slots built into all the floors
and walls. It meant they could move things around as needed while still
securing them against rogue waves that caused the city to rock more than
usual every so often.

For the same reason, all the serving trays had a rubberized grip on the
bottom and the cutlery and plates were close to unbreakable while still
being biodegradable, should they fly off into the water. BlackSea people
were able to retrieve pretty much all such accidental debris, but they *never*
took the ocean for granted. Never took water for granted.

"Minni! Minni!"

Miane held out her hand to the other child running toward her. He
caught it easily, then as she pulled back her arm, he used his grip to climb
up her body and perch himself on her hip. At which point, she shifted
her arm to support his weight.

"Happy birthday, Sephnie!" His ebony-skinned face was bright with
good humor.

Persephone smiled and waved at her more vocal packmate.

Costas pointed at his black shorts and pressed blue shirt. "I got party
clothes, too." He patted Miane's black T-shirt, his next words a loud
whisper. "Didn't your mom get you party clothes?"

Biting the inside of her cheek at the solemn question, Miane managed
a sad face. "Yeah, she forgot." Her mom would forgive her the fib. "Do
you think I still get cake?"

Both children nodded firmly.

Snuggling them close for another few seconds, Miane then placed the
two gently on their feet. They immediately ran off to play together—
though she noticed that Persephone kept looking back to check that her
mother was in sight, as she'd done even when held safe in her alpha's arms.

It would take time for her to accept that Olivia wasn't going to leave
her again. A child that young didn't understand that her mother had been
separated from her under duress. She just knew that she'd been alone and
scared and her mom wasn't there.

Miane's jaw hurt, she'd clenched it so tight.

A big hand closed over her shoulder, squeezed. "Breathe," Malachai ordered. "She's home. We'll bring the others home, too."

Some, Miane knew, would return home in boxes.

The rage inside her threatened to flare again, but then Persephone's laughter lit the air and she remembered that sometimes, good won and evil lost. "Yes," she vowed. "We'll bring all our people home." Including Leila.

Alive or dead, none would be abandoned; none would be forgotten.

Chapter 41

MIDMORNING THE DAY after Ivy received the information about Clara Alvarez, her well-rested husband teleported her and Rabbit to Haven. It was a peaceful and sprawling green estate meant for F-Psy who were fractured—and it was also home to Samuel Rain. The robotics and bio-fusion expert who'd saved Vasic's life and who was now determined to build him a working prosthetic could've moved out, but he liked it here and had requested to stay.

"Do you have to go see Miane?" Ivy asked.

Vasic had received a message from BlackSea right before they teleported.

"No," he said into the gentle quiet, his body strong and warm as he stood partially behind her. "With the SUV lead having dead-ended, there's nothing I can do at this stage but wait until they have another location. The message had photos from Persephone's birthday celebration—we can look at them together after your meeting."

Ivy nodded, fiercely proud of the little girl who'd survived the monsters of the Consortium. Ivy wasn't the empath working with her, but she received regular updates from the young male E who was, and those reports told her Persephone had a defiant spirit that might be wounded but was in no way beaten.

"Do you want me with you?" Vasic asked, curving his hand over her hip. "Samuel asked me to come in for a deep-tissue scan."

"Go have the scan," she said. "I think this'll go better if it's just me."

When Vasic nodded, she tilted up her head and pressed a palm to his cheek. "Thank you for the ride." She was well aware she was ridiculously spoiled in how she could go anywhere in the world she wanted.

Just over three weeks ago, when she'd mentioned she wanted to try a pastry she'd heard about called *mille-feuille*, Vasic had taken her to a bakery in Paris. "I love you."

Vasic's expression didn't alter, but he turned his head to kiss her palm, while deep within, their bond vibrated with the potent strength of his own emotions. "That's one thing I never doubt." A faint smile that made her want to kiss him.

So she did.

Ivy. I'll teleport us back to bed if you're not careful.

Laughing at the cool warning that belied the sinful way he was kissing her back, his fingers stroking her hip, she stole another taste before pushing him away. "Stop distracting me."

His eyes glinted a promise of vengeance. "I'll see you soon, Mrs. Zen."

"You can count on it, Mr. Zen."

Lips curving, Vasic angled his head at Rabbit. "Come on, let's go see Samuel."

Rabbit padded off happily at his side.

Ivy took a few moments to watch her husband walk toward the main Haven building—he was so beautiful in motion—before she turned to head to the rose garden where she'd asked to meet Clara. The other woman was already there, seated on a familiar weathered wooden bench, her eyes on the colorful mass of blooms open to the sun and scenting the air.

"Ivy," she said as she rose, her smile warm.

The manager of Haven was dressed in a pale gray pantsuit paired with an aqua blue shirt, her golden brown hair parted in the center and rolled into a neat knot at the nape and her hands covered by thin black gloves.

"Clara." Ivy walked forward. "Thank you so much for agreeing to see me."

"Of course," Clara said as they both took seats on the bench. "Is it about Samuel? He's doing very well."

"No, it's something else." Deciding to dive straight into it, she told the other woman about the severe and deadly disintegration of the fabric of the PsyNet. Then she spoke about the two other healthy loci.

When she said, "You're the third," Clara's eyes widened.

"I see," the former Justice Psy said. "Do you know what sets apart the other two?"

"Not their abilities," Ivy said. "One is a teleport-capable Tk, the other a J like you." Then she added what she believed to be the critical factor. "Both are bonded to humans."

Clara didn't respond in any visible fashion, as Ivy continued. "I know you have a human husband," she said quietly. "I need to know if you're bonded on a psychic level—I swear I'll protect your privacy. The only people who know or need to know all have their own bonds." Each and every one understood that it was a gift, not to be harmed. "None of them would betray you."

Clara's brown eyes held hers for a long moment, as if she was judging Ivy's sincerity, before the manager of Haven reached down to quietly tug off the glove on her left hand . . . to reveal a golden band on her ring finger. "His name is Patrick," she said, her love for him a kiss against Ivy's senses. "And yes, we're connected on the psychic level. Mated."

"How do you keep the bond hidden?" Ivy whispered. "There's no hint of it in the Net."

"Anthony helped us," Clara said, and it wasn't as big a surprise as it should've been. Anthony Kyriakus, after all, was the man who'd created Haven.

"You see, he was already helping me," Clara continued. "Justice Psy don't last too long once our internal telepathic shields go." Shadows in her eyes, memories of all the evil she'd witnessed, evil that had acted like acid on her mind. "That was why he was able to react within microseconds when Patrick and I refused to follow orders and ended up mated."

A smile that made her entire face glow. "Then, when it became clear my ability to shield was starting to heal"—wonder touched her expression—"Anthony taught me how to take over, how to hide the bond and Patrick's mind."

"The only other J I know whose shields spontaneously regenerated is Sophia," Ivy murmured. "And she's unique."

"Sophie and I've talked this over," Clara said. "The only commonality between us is that we both love human men with unbreakable natural shields." She lifted her gaze from her wedding band. "And love can't be forced. If there's another answer . . . There are so many hurt Js in the world." Her hands fisted in her lap, pain drenching her voice. "You say the PsyNet is healthy around me—maybe that has something to do with the regeneration, too."

Ivy was beginning to realize that if her suspicions were true, then the single fact that connected Stefan, Sophia, and Clara had far more staggering implications than even she had guessed. "The shielding technique Anthony taught you," she said. "It must be phenomenal to hide your bond with Patrick so effectively."

A pause, before Clara said, "The shields are very strong, but the thing is . . . I always had the sense something was helping Patrick and me keep our secret."

"The NetMind protected Es for a century." A tremor of understanding ran through Ivy's bones. "I can see it doing that for a human mind in the PsyNet."

"Would you like to see?" Clara's question was whispered, secret.

Ivy nodded and joined Haven's manager in the PsyNet. The J-Psy slipped her own shields around Ivy's, with Ivy's permission—after Ivy warned Vasic what was about to happen. Only after Ivy was isolated did Clara drop a second layer of shields, and Ivy saw the autumnal warmth and cool blue rope of the other woman's psychic bond with another mind. That second mind wasn't Psy, though it shone as bright, in shades of icy blue. And it sat not in the PsyNet but not quite out of it.

No Psy mind could reach it, could hack it. Clara was the only point of contact.

Conscious she'd been given a gift, Ivy slipped back out of Clara's shields when the woman opened them. "Thank you," she said on the physical plane. "Why did you trust me?"

"J-Psy get good at judging people. I know your heart, Ivy Jane Zen, and I know it's good." Clara rose to her feet. "I have to go, but call me if you need anything else."

"I'd like to meet Patrick." Ivy had only glimpsed him at Zie Zen's funeral. "He seems fascinating."

"Oh, he is." A sudden smile. "Aggravating at times, but always wonderful."

Ivy sat in place long after Clara left, turning over the consequences of what she'd discovered. It all made sense—the NetMind's bloody images of loss and desecration, the fact that the PsyNet was barely maintaining coherence despite the number of active Es, why the Forgotten had a healthy network and the Psy didn't.

Because when the Forgotten left the Net, they took their human mates with them, while the Psy were told to sever those bonds or to suffocate them out of existence. Until in this generation, there were only *three* known human minds in the PsyNet.

Ivy understood now.

Until the dawn of Silence, the PsyNet had never been populated only by Psy. Changelings and humans had both been a presence—though, in the case of changelings, that presence would've been minor at most. From what Ivy knew as a result of her friendship with Sascha, changelings tended to pull their mates into their own psychic networks.

Not so with humans.

There were no records of humans being an *active* presence in the PsyNet, but even the old Councils hadn't succeeded in erasing eons of history that spoke of human-Psy marriages and relationships.

Such relationships had been unremarkable before Silence.

Ivy's own family history included multiple human ancestors.

The human race had therefore always been part of the PsyNet's psychic fabric, providing a mysterious and indefinable energy without which the Psy race's entire future hung in the balance.

And most humans hated most of the Psy.

Letters to Nina

From the private diaries of Father Xavier Perez
June 11, 2077

Nina,

I've acquired a second Psy friend. It turns out my two friends have known each other longer than I've known either one of them—but to induct me into their inner circle was a matter of trust that couldn't be rushed.

Having glimpsed the war they're fighting, the lies hidden beneath more lies that they seek to expose, I understand their caution. This second man, he's far more suspicious than my first friend and impossibly more dangerous.

Somehow, I have become the voice of reason. Don't laugh too hard. I find that the more I minister to my parishioners, the more I learn myself.

But nothing will ever change my heart. It bears only your name.

Love,
Xavier

Chapter 42

KALEB WAS AT home with Sahara when she got the comm call from Ivy Jane, with Sascha Duncan also looped into the discussion. He and Sahara had been on the deck of their home on the outskirts of Moscow, Kaleb running through a martial arts routine, while Sahara did the yoga that made her so graceful.

Darkness had fallen on their side of the world, and the stars had been bright overhead as they moved quietly on the deck lit only by the delicate metal lamps Sahara had set out. She'd bought those lamps in a market in Istanbul when he took her there for dinner one night, both of them in disguise.

"So we can act as young as we are," Sahara had said to him with a grin, wrapping her arms around his neck. "No one watching, no one expecting us to behave."

They'd eaten at a tiny café hidden deep inside the markets, surrounded by locals who'd looked at them sideways until Sahara pulled her favorite trick and spoke to them in their own language—right down to the sub-dialect used in the market area. By the time they left, she was fast friends with half the clientele and was well on the way to charming the other half. He'd just watched her laugh, watched her sparkle, and been happy.

She'd fallen in love with the metal lamps sold at what felt like half the shops in the markets, had scooped up four for their deck. Then she'd bought him a glass "genie" bottle for his study, the color of the finely blown glass a mix between red and cerise. He'd come home one day to find the bottle filled with blank "wishes" that he was permitted to write on and redeem at will, with Sahara acting as his genie.

And that bottle, it never ran out, no matter how many wishes he redeemed.

Dance for me, he'd written on more than one.

Watching Sahara create music with her body was a gift of which he never became tired. He'd been planning to ask if she'd dance a little tonight after she finished her yoga, but then had come the call from Ivy Jane.

He would've stayed outside while Sahara took it in privacy, but she popped her head back outside to say that Ivy and Sascha wanted him to listen in. Teleporting himself a towel, he rubbed the sweat off his face, then left the towel around his neck as he joined Sahara in front of the living room comm screen, on which she usually programmed images from her favorite dances.

"You might as well know." Lines of tiredness marked Ivy's face. "I've already told Vasic and Aden. At some point, we're going to have to go public."

When she began to speak, what she told them made too much sense. In particular, the near-total lack of human connections was the *one* thing that made the post-Silence PsyNet different from the Forgotten's ShadowNet.

Unfortunately, she was also right in her understanding of the current state of Psy-human relations. "The majority of humans will happily watch the Psy race collapse into oblivion," Kaleb said to Sahara once the other two women had signed off. "And the majority of Psy think humans are beneath them." The latter was pure stupidity, but Silence had fostered an arrogance that was going to take decades to ameliorate.

"I don't know," Sahara murmured, a look on her face that meant she was strategizing. "Maybe it's simply a case of giving humans and Psy reasons to interact. The heart will do the rest."

Kaleb raised his eyebrows. "All such situations will do is give them endless opportunities to ignore each other. That is, if they don't try to kill one another."

"Don't be so cynical." Scowling, Sahara tugged on the ends of the towel to hold him in place. "You know you believe in love."

"I believe in loving you." Always he would love her.

She rose on tiptoe. "I love you back more."

"Impossible." She was his life, his heart's blood.

Hands on her hips, he lifted her into his kiss. When she hooked her legs around him, it was instinct to move forward, press her back against the wall. Then his eyes landed on the wall that was his destination.

He stopped.

Following his gaze, Sahara smiled. "Our wall of memories is filling up."

"Yes." The photograph that had stopped him in his tracks was from a time when he'd teleported into DarkRiver territory to pick her up from Faith's and discovered Judd had come by to say hello.

Kaleb hadn't seen Sahara take the photograph, but it was of him and Judd in conversation, the rogue Arrow smiling faintly while Kaleb stood with his hands in the pockets of his suit pants, his head slightly angled in a listening position and his shoulders relaxed under the plain white of a long-sleeved business shirt.

He looked . . . open, unshielded against a man who was lethal should he want to be. But then, Judd was also the man who'd fought for Kaleb when even Kaleb didn't believe in his ability to hold firm against the darkness.

Some friendships were set in stone.

"I love that photo." Hugging her arms around his neck, Sahara kissed his jaw. "The backdrop of firs, your body language and his. It's obvious you're friends. Good friends."

"We need one with Xavier, too." The priest was the only other man Kaleb considered a friend. "When he's back." Father Xavier Perez was currently in a remote and mountainous part of South America searching for his Nina.

Kaleb and Judd had both offered to teleport him to the woman they believed to be the lover for whom he searched, but Xavier had made it clear he needed to fight this battle himself. In the interim, Kaleb had discovered it was difficult to practice patience while one of his closest friends walked alone in the wilderness. It made him understand why Judd and Xavier had been so concerned about him in the years before he broke Sahara free from her prison.

"You walk in aloneness, my friend," Xavier had said one day not long into their acquaintance, the other man's expression holding a peace that came from deep within the soul.

Kaleb could still remember his response. "There is strength in being without vulnerability." A false response even then, because he carried in his heart a vulnerability he would never give up, for to give it up would mean giving up Sahara.

She tried to lower her legs now, laughed and stayed in position when he refused to release her. "We'll get a photo with Xavier as soon as he returns with Nina."

Kaleb went silent.

"What is it? You're thinking deep thoughts." Dark blue eyes holding his as she reached up to brush strands of hair off his forehead, the charms on her bracelet catching the light.

"I'm wondering how so many people became entwined in my life." He was used to thinking of himself as a lone wolf but for Sahara. Only he had Judd and Xavier, too.

And then there was Leon.

Sahara's father continued to call him "son," continued to treat him with an absentminded paternal affection that Kaleb didn't know how to process. He'd been beaten and tormented by the only father figure he knew. He'd always understood that Leon was different, that the man loved his daughter, but Kaleb had never expected that paternal warmth to be turned in his direction.

"These people are in your life because you made the choice to be their friend." Sahara rubbed her nose gently against his. "You chose not to betray their loyalty even when it might have been expedient, and to stand with them when they needed your help."

"You make me sound good." He wasn't, she knew that.

"You know how to be loyal, Kaleb." A whisper, her breath kissing his lips. "How to love."

He had no rebuttal. He'd been hers since the moment they met. "Because of you."

"Being loved by you . . ." Her eyes shone like jewels as the psychic bond between them blazed with that glorious light that touched even the twisted heart of him.

He loved, *was* loved.

Kaleb needed nothing else.

"You still occasionally covet world domination, though," Sahara said with a grin after catching the edge of his thoughts.

"A small thing."

Shoulders shaking, she squeezed her legs around him. "If you can love that deeply, that passionately, why not humans and Psy?"

"A hundred years of hatred and distrust and arrogance."

Sahara waved a hand. "A small thing."

And though they were discussing the possible and catastrophic end of the Psy race, Kaleb felt his lips curve. "Of course. You believe the heart will conquer all."

She pushed at his shoulders. "I'm going to have the last laugh, Kaleb Krychek, just you wait." After which, she kissed him, the wrong thing to do if she wanted to condition him to change his opinion.

But Sahara didn't think that way. Neither did he. Not when he was with her.

"Let's shower," she said against his lips. "We're sticky from the exercise, and I've got to start plotting how to get humans and Psy to look at one another not as enemies, but as potential lovers."

Whatever their disagreements on racial politics, being naked with Sahara was one of Kaleb's favorite things. He loved sliding his hands over her skin, loved having her mind linked to his while he caressed her in different ways until he knew exactly what gave her the greatest pleasure. Of course, she did the same to him.

Kaleb didn't mind. He was hers to do with as she wished.

Tonight he pressed his hands to the tile above her head as she laughed and stole kisses and continued to argue with him as the water pounded down on his back. He met her arguments with his own even as he pressed more heavily into her, his rigid erection shoving impatiently against her abdomen. Shivering, she rubbed against him, and when she kissed him this time, her smile sank into him, her hand stroking up to curve over his nape.

He loved the way she held him, so possessive and demanding.

Kaleb. She closed her fingers over his stone-hard penis.

His body jerked but it wasn't in rejection. He was simply never ready for the jolt of pleasure that was Sahara's touch. *When am I going to be used to you?*

Maybe if we cause a few more earthquakes.

I think the seismologists are confused enough as it is. He could control his violent telekinetic power during sex, but only by punching it deep into the earth. It had certain repercussions.

Nibbling at his jaw, Sahara said, *Want to stop?*

Never. Kaleb moved one hand down to fondle her breast, cupping the warm silken roundness, then running the pad of his thumb over the hard nub of her nipple. Moaning in the back of her throat, Sahara released him, nuzzled her way down his neck. "I need you."

Lifting her with his hands under her thighs, he slid his erection through her delicate folds before pushing deep into her. She was so tight around him, but they fit; they fit perfectly. Gasping at his entry, she wrapped her arms around his neck, her legs already wrapped around his hips. "I love how you feel inside me."

Kaleb shuddered at her words, undone.

He rocked slowly into her, and when she tugged down his head and demanded a kiss, he opened his mouth over hers and they danced in love. Slow and gentle, skin sliding against skin and breaths mingling as the water ran down his back.

The earthquake was inevitable.

As was their solemn conversation after the shower, when they lay tangled in bed. All jokes aside, the PsyNet was in serious trouble. It wasn't critical, not yet, so they had a little breathing room, but that room wouldn't last forever. "You're never going to be at risk," he told Sahara. "If need be, I can haul the clean sections of the Net together, create a small but functional network."

Sahara rose up beside him on her elbow, her eyes troubled. "You made a promise."

One hand curving around her throat, he said, "I'll keep it. I'll fight to save the PsyNet and the Psy race." For her, he'd save instead of kill. And for her, he'd build instead of destroy. "But I won't flounder in a doomed network, and never will I leave you in danger."

Not even you, he telepathed, *can force me to watch you die when I can stop it.* He'd been made helpless to save her once. Never again.

Furious emotion filled her eyes. "I would never do that," she whispered, her voice raw. "I would never hurt you that way."

He realized he'd made her angry rather than desolate. "Then walk with me into this," he demanded. "Tell me you won't fight me if I ever make the call. Tell me we'll do it together."

Her eyes held his own and he knew his gaze was obsidian, devoid of stars. "I trust you with every tiny particle of my being and every corner of my soul," Sahara said. "If you ever say there's no hope, that it's time for the last throw of the dice, then I'll be right there beside you."

Shifting his hold to grip her jaw, he kissed her hard. "Now that we've settled that, let's figure out how to fix this so we never have to throw those particular dice." Because while he knew he'd save her, Kaleb also knew the loss of millions of other lives would devastate his Sahara.

To keep her whole, he'd have to ensure the PsyNet did not fall.

PART 6

Chapter 43

BOWEN KNIGHT, SECURITY chief of the Human Alliance, was not having a good week. In the past forty-eight hours, someone in the Alliance had betrayed a possible ally to the Consortium. Yes, there was a minimal chance that the leak had come from BlackSea, but Miane Levèque didn't think so and Bo agreed with her.

The timing pointed to an Alliance member.

Bo had realized from the first that there were apt to be Consortium stooges among the Alliance network—they had too many members and were too widely spread out for it to be otherwise—but having proof of it was a slap in the face to everything he wanted for his people.

That mess would've been bad enough, but almost on the heels of it had come a call from Ashaya Aleine that had dealt a catastrophic blow to the hopes he'd had that the human race could equalize the psychic playing field. "I've triple-checked every piece of data," the scientist had said, the blue-gray of her eyes unusually dark. "There's no mistake. The Alliance implants are beginning to degrade, with significant and likely fatal brain damage forecast as a secondary effect."

Those implants were meant to block Psy from rifling through human minds at will and they *worked*. Since the day the implant went in, Bowen hadn't had to worry about giving away secrets—private and of the Alliance—without realizing it. He hadn't had a constant knot in his gut from never knowing when a telepath would reach in and violate his mind, possibly force him to act against his will. For almost a year, he'd been free to be Bowen Knight, security chief of the Human Alliance and a man in charge of his own fucking destiny.

Now, the morning after he'd shared the devastating news with his senior people, all of whom had been implanted around the same time as Bo, he stood in the dawn-gilded splendor of Venice, on one of the sunken city's iconic bridges, and looked at the canal water below. All the while, he was viscerally aware that inside his brain, things were going catastrophically wrong.

The Alliance's internal medics and scientists had gone over Ashaya's work, but even before they came back to Bo with confirmations, he'd known Ashaya wasn't wrong. Ashaya Aleine wouldn't have passed on the data unless she—and her equally brilliant twin—were certain beyond any doubt of their conclusions.

He'd been the first implanted but wasn't yet showing any symptoms. One of the few Psy he trusted had confirmed the implant still functioned as intended, creating an impenetrable shield around his mind. As for the bad news, neither Ashaya nor the internal Alliance implant team knew when or if he—and the others from the first group—would begin to exhibit symptoms, whether it would be progressive or if it would go wrong all at once.

The one good thing was that because Bo and his senior people had been the first implanted and all but two were past the safe removal stage, they could act as the barometers. Everyone else who had the implant would be given the choice to keep it and risk death or brain damage, or have it removed and risk mental violation.

Hell of a choice.

Bo knew which one he would've made had he been offered it.

Irrespective of all that, he wasn't about to give up, wasn't about to accept that this was how it would end. He'd given Ashaya and the internal team carte blanche to run experiments, find a solution. If not in time for him, then in time for all those humans who'd make the choice to go to their deaths knowing they were safe from psychic rape.

Bo had authorized them to crack his skull and run whatever-the-fuck tests they wanted on his brain, should he die or even if he went into a vegetative state. But he refused to consider that future an inevitability.

He had countless more dreams to bring to fruition, the biggest and most important of which was to put the human race back on the political, social, and economic map. For centuries, they'd been thrust aside by the financial might of the Psy and the raw power of the changelings.

The changelings, at least, had never done it consciously. For the most part, they stayed within localized packs—but those packs were generally so cohesive that, despite their comparatively much smaller size and territorial focus, they were able to achieve things that disparate human families and individuals simply couldn't.

The only groups that bucked the curve were human families who acted as a single unit. The bonds between their generations were tight, elders teaching youths and those in the prime of their life working for the good of the family rather than for individual glory or advancement.

That structure mirrored what Bo knew of changeling packs—and unexpectedly, it also appeared to be how the strongest Psy families held on to their power.

Bo had watched and learned and realized that for the wider human population to compete with the Psy and changelings on any level, he'd have to restructure human society itself, weave a widespread global population into groups of tight-knit "villages." He also needed to find a way to overcome centuries of distrust and forge alliances with not just changelings, but with Psy, alliances his people would actually accept.

Signing the Trinity Accord had been a huge step on the road to his ultimate goal.

He didn't want the power for itself.

He wanted it because it would keep his people safe.

One of those people came up to him at that instant, sliding her arm through his as she leaned against his side. "Our Venezia is such a beautiful lady in the morning," his sister said, the evocative gray of her eyes on the glittering water through which a gondolier was slowly stroking his long, narrow craft.

Lily's fingers were slender and pale against the brown of his skin; the exact shade had been described as "caramel" by a long-ago lover. If he was caramel, Lily was warm cream mixed with sunshine, her birth parents both of Chinese descent where his had been Brazilian and Scottish. Her hair, too, was unlike his: slick straight and jet-black in contrast to the wave in the softer ebony of his when he let it grow out, and her body, it was so delicate that he had to stop his overprotective big brother response from going active any time he saw her with a man.

Their physical differences mattered nothing. They were blood by choice.

Soaking in her presence, he said, "Venice is Venice." A waterlogged and elegant matriarch of a city that had hung on despite all predictions to the contrary. "What are you doing here? I thought you had a date."

"I canceled it." Her fingers tightened on his biceps.

"Lily." Easing away his arm, he put it around her shoulders and half turned to tug her against his chest. "I'm not going to disappear overnight, and you know I'll fight to the bitter end. I've also got Ashaya and Amara Aleine onboard." The two women had minds terrifyingly beautiful in their genius. Bo interacted only with Ashaya, and she seemed grounded, stable, emotionally healthy. However, he'd heard vague rumors that said her twin was anything but—the price of genius?

"Hey, talk to me," he said to his own sister, the tiny girl his parents had brought home when she was a scared two-year-old orphan. According to his father, Bo had taken one look at her and loudly proclaimed he'd keep her safe. He'd done that, would continue to do it. Even if his implant went nova, what they found in his brain after death might finish what he'd begun. *"Lilybit."*

Lily's hand clutched at the back of his T-shirt at the sound of the childhood nickname. "You should've let me have the implant at the same time, too."

It had been a difficult decision for Bo to ask Lily to wait. He hadn't wanted his sister vulnerable to unscrupulous Psy, but the risk of the implant had been significant enough to sway him. "You know we had to do it in stages, iron out the bugs." So if the worst happened, the Alliance wouldn't lose all of its strongest.

Lily had received her implant eight weeks after his, was still in the safe removal zone should she choose to make that choice. He knew she wouldn't, but he hoped Ashaya and the others would find an answer before it was too late for her. Not only because Lily was his baby sister, but because while his sister was formed of delicate lines, she had a steely spirit that would carry the Alliance through if he fell. But even steel bent under unbearable pressure, and today his sister crumpled into him, sobs shaking her body.

He just held her, rocked her. "Shh." Stroking her hair when she finally went quiet, he said, "Tell me about this guy you canceled on. Will he pass the big brother test?"

Lily's voice was thick with emotion when she spoke. "He has tattoos and piercings and he rides a jetcycle when on the mainland."

Bo felt his eyebrows rise; steel will notwithstanding, Lily was about as ladylike as they came. She dated teachers and accountants and computronic techs. Men with soft hands and gentle voices. "You're having a late teenage rebellion phase?"

She elbowed him, and that was good, that was his little sister. "He's a doctor. A surgeon. He goes all over the world, wherever he's needed—and he donates his time and skills for free as often as he can. He just likes body art and fast vehicles."

Intrigued, Bo made a mental note to look up this tattooed doctor who'd put *that* tone in his sister's voice. "Why don't you call him? Reschedule your date?"

"I have a swollen nose and red eyes now." She blew her nose on a tissue she'd pulled out of the pocket of her capri pants. "And I want to hang out with you."

Tugging lightly at her hair when she went silent, he said, "You want to go on a gondola?"

"We're not tourists." A grumpy response.

"Who the hell says only tourists can play in the canals?" Snagging her hand to tug her down the bridge, he found them a gondola painted the standard sleek black and paid the gondolier extra to stay on shore while Bo took over his duties.

"Only for you, Bo," the man said, tipping his iconic straw boater at them. "I'm going to go have a coffee over there." He nodded at a nearby café whose owner was just putting out his outdoor tables. "Come grab me when you're done—and look after my lady. That's my livelihood you're borrowing."

Saluting the other man in a silent promise, Bo pushed off.

Lily finally started to smile again ten minutes later, calling his attention to interesting buildings as they moved through the water. "It looks different from this angle," she said from her seated position. "I love how quiet it is at this time of day and how you get to catch sight of things like that"—she pointed to a baker setting out wares hot from the oven—"see the city coming awake."

Bo, upright in the traditional position to pole the oar through the water, was keeping an eye out as he always did—side effect of being security chief. And he saw what Lily missed. "Look to the left. Early morning tourist about to get his pocket picked."

Putting two fingers to his lips, he whistled sharply. The would-be pickpocket's head spun around, as did the tourist's. Ignoring the latter, Bo met the eyes of the other. Shoulders slumping, the teenager glared at him . . . but turned and walked off in the direction he should've been heading. Toward school.

Lily chuckled. "Do you know everyone?"

"And their parents," Bo answered dryly and continued on down the canal.

He was hoping to see a sleek form under the water, as he'd done a couple of times after BlackSea first made contact by doing the Alliance an intel favor, but that water remained empty. Even though Bo should've been worrying about his brain, now that the first shock had passed, he was back to being pissed off at the traitor or traitors who might've ended the Alliance's chances of a friendship with the notoriously reclusive changeling group.

His muscles threatened to lock from the intensity of his reaction.

The fucking Consortium might be behind this, but each and every individual who'd signed up to join them bore his or her own responsibility. If Bo ever got his hands on them, they'd pay the price.

Chapter 44

NIKITA READ THROUGH the short and concise report Ivy Jane Zen had sent through to the Ruling Coalition about the serious deficiency in the Net.

Of humans.

No one, Nikita thought, had seen that coming, and not even the power and money at the disposal of the Ruling Council and their associates could fix it. Wanting to confirm that supposition, she contacted Sascha to ask if Psy could psychically coerce humans to bond with them.

The other Es would've been horrified and shocked at her question, but Nikita knew that while Sascha would be equally horrified, she wouldn't be shocked. Her daughter knew how Nikita's brain worked.

"No," Sascha responded, her cardinal eyes flecked with sparks of color from whatever she'd been doing prior to Nikita's call. "No one knows how humans are integrated into the Net without being an active part of it, but we do know coercion doesn't work." Her expression turned grim. "Otherwise, there would be other healthy sections."

Sascha didn't have to spell it out, not to Nikita: it was willful blindness to imagine that there weren't at least a few Psy around the world controlling humans through a telepathic link at any given point in time. Personally, Nikita had always preferred to use other methods—not out of any ethical considerations, but because mind control was a waste of time and energy.

After the call to Sascha, she made one to Anthony, using every tool at her disposal to keep the discussion strictly to Coalition business. It was more difficult than it should've been. Not only because Anthony had a razor-sharp intellect and a will as strong as her own, but because he'd somehow neutralized her defenses without doing a single aggressive act.

A man that powerful, that icily ruthless when the occasion called for it, who hadn't eliminated her from the chessboard while she'd been wounded and defenseless? One who'd actually *protected* her?

It did not fit with Nikita's worldview.

Neither did her reluctance to see his action as a weakness she could exploit.

Or her choice to call him when she could've sent an e-mail instead.

Ending the call before he saw too deep, as he had a habit of doing, she walked away from the wall-mounted comm to her desk and the black leather-synth of her executive chair. Since there was nothing she could do to assist the Es in their search for a solution to the human issue, she wouldn't waste her time on it. When and if they needed her skills and connections, they would contact her.

As she'd already cleared all Coalition business for the day, she'd spend the second half of the morning going over the financial standing of an airjet company she intended to acquire for—

Pain lanced through her abdomen before she reached her seat.

A knife stabbing into her over and over again.

Gripping the back of her chair, she breathed in and out until it passed. The surgeons and M-Psy had done a stellar job, but she'd suffered a critical injury, and there were some types of healing that simply couldn't be sped up.

Of course, according to certain parties, she was in this condition because of her impatience to get back to work.

Keeping a white-knuckled grip on the chair, she maneuvered around until she could take a seat. Tremors ran through her, disrupting her attempts to regulate her breathing. Weakness was not something she accepted in herself, but currently, she had no choice in the matter.

A knock on the door interrupted her only seconds later; it was accompanied by a telepathic touch that identified the person on the other side as her senior aide, Sophia Russo. *Come in,* she telepathed since her breathing was still too irregular for speech.

Sophia was one of the few people Nikita trusted to see her in this condition—the former J-Psy and her ex-cop husband wouldn't betray Nikita, so long as she didn't cross the moral lines they'd lain down. Many Psy in her position would see it as a bad bargain on her part, but Nikita valued loyalty—to know she wouldn't get a knife in the back was a price-less gift worth some readjustment of her methods and tactics.

Entering, Sophia crossed the carpet with a slim organizer in hand, but rather than speaking of work, she took one look at Nikita's face and shook her head. Her charcoal-black hair was in a soft knot at the back of her head, her skin pure cream in the midmorning sunlight that poured through the new and significantly reinforced glass. "You need to rest."

Nikita had her breath back. "I need to work."

Sophia didn't budge. Her body clad in a neat black skirt and sleeveless blue top, and her hands gloved in thin black material that protected her from accidentally sensing people's lives, their secret horrors and dreams, the former J was no pushover. "You can send me instructions from your suite."

Eyes of blue-violet took in the way Nikita's hand was pressed flat on her desk in an effort to control the trembling. "Collapsing after overex-tending yourself is why you're in such bad condition when you should've already been well on the way to a full recovery."

Sometimes Nikita wondered why she kept Sophia in her employ. Of course, it was partly because the other woman told her the truth, no matter what. "There are people watching me. Duncan stocks will start falling again should anyone realize the state of my health." It was why the medics always came to her, courtesy of a Tk in her employ. All were paid extremely well to keep their mouths shut. She'd also reminded them who she was and what she could do to their brains should they cross her.

Sophia's eyes went to the glass of the walls behind and to Nikita's left. "Even if someone is spying on your movements, they can't know what you're doing if you step out. I'll even make a note in your diary that you're in an internal conference room in the unlikely scenario that someone is able to hack into our systems."

The other woman placed her organizer on Nikita's desk, her stance resolute . . . and concern in her gaze. The J had a softer heart than she liked to pretend. Nikita knew; she recognized the signs after raising a daughter with an even softer heart.

"You've made enough of an appearance today," Sophia continued. "You also have a meeting at an external location tomorrow for which you need to be physically fit. I can juggle everything else so no one is the wiser about your health."

Nikita's abdomen was throbbing, but she couldn't risk using the pain-control mechanisms she'd been taught as a child, lest she unknowingly ignore a bleed or a tear because she couldn't feel it. "All right. I'll read the airjet data package upstairs." She'd get into bed first, try to sleep through the worst of the pain. "If the pain gets any worse, we'll get an M-Psy in to run a scan."

Sophia nodded. "I'll send the package to your organizer." The younger woman walked with Nikita to the door, stayed beside her as she got in the elevator.

Nikita didn't tell Sophia not to accompany her upstairs. She was weaker than she could remember being for weeks—it was possible she might collapse.

She trusted Sophia to catch her.

It wasn't until she'd changed into simple pajamas of navy blue and slipped into bed that she realized there was something she didn't trust Sophia to do: keep her silence about Nikita's condition when it came to two specific individuals. *Sophia,* she said telepathically. *Don't contact my daughter or Anthony about the current status of my health.*

I already did.

Nikita knew she should discipline her subordinate, but she simply didn't have the energy. *We'll discuss this after I rest.*

The voice that came into her mind seconds later was a male one. *Sleep. I'll make sure you're safe.*

I can keep myself safe, Nikita said . . . or tried to say. Except her eyes were heavy from the exhaustion of maintaining her front as a ruthless woman undaunted by what could've been a fatal wound, and she'd become used to that male voice.

Anthony Kyriakus hadn't yet let her down.

Sleep crashed over her in a black wave a heartbeat after that thought passed through her mind.

Letters to Nina

From the private diaries of Father Xavier Perez
August 10, 2079

Nina,

The world is changing in drastic and perilous ways. My two friends are unafraid of meting out death in their quest to erase evil and bring freedom to their people. It disturbs me and I argue often with them, but I can't sway them from their course—they believe the evil in the Psy race is too deeply rooted, that it must be excised with brutal force.

Only then can compassion have a chance to bud and bloom.

I've sat for hours in my church, praying for answers, for a way forward that won't stain the world in red, but I hear only silence from the heavens. I wish you were here. My friends think me wise, but you were always the one who could see through to the heart of the most complex questions.

I miss you each and every day.

Xavier

Chapter 45

SASCHA HUNG UP the phone and turned to Lucas, worry gnawing her gut. "That was Sophie. Nikita's still in pain, exhausted." It didn't surprise her that she hadn't picked up Nikita's exhaustion during their earlier comm call: her mother was a master at showing people only what she wanted them to see.

"Sophie says she barely rested for an hour before getting back to work." The only concession Nikita had made to her condition was to remain in her suite and in bed, rather than returning to her desk.

Lucas joined her on the aerie balcony, the two of them having decided to work from home today. They'd both spoken to Bastien first thing this morning about the other man's continued efforts to narrow down the individual who'd hired the captain to spirit away Naya.

"I'm getting close," Bastien had said, the passion of the hunt in the green of his eyes.

Sascha had spent the rest of the morning in discussions with Ivy and other Es, while Lucas played with and took care of Naya. Then they'd switched off and she'd happily taken cub duty while Lucas had conversation after conversation to do with the "adjunct signee" status he'd suggested. After intense discussion within their own pack, SnowDancer had agreed to back him, so he'd made the call to send the proposal out to a wider—though still limited—number of people.

Despite vociferous disagreement from several parties, he'd held his ground, panther and man both having made the decision that this was the only way Trinity could survive. Sascha had never been more proud of him. Because while her mate could act civilized, he was a dominant predatory changeling; to propose what he had meant fighting his most primal instincts.

Now, sliding an arm around her, he said, "The doctors warned that her recovery would take time, especially after her relapse." He kept his voice low, his eyes on the little black ball of fur playing on the forest floor below. Sascha, too, was keeping an eye on their baby, though she was doing it mostly through their telepathic link.

"I just . . . I want to be there for her, Lucas." Sascha leaned on the railing on this part of the balcony. "She shouldn't be alone." Taking a shaky breath, she tried to explain. "I've only recently realized how alone my mother has been her whole life. From the instant she learned she was carrying an empath—from the instant she decided to *protect* me, she's walked alone."

Sascha had thought her mother cold and heartless for most of her lifetime. As most recently demonstrated by the question Nikita had asked her about coercing humans into the PsyNet, her mother had a fluid concept of conscience at best.

Sascha was under no illusions about the woman who'd given birth to her.

What she hadn't understood was that everything Nikita had done while Sascha was growing up, *everything*, had been to protect her daughter. "She built an empire so I'd be shielded by a wall of sheer power, and if she had to murder to get that power, she murdered."

Sascha found that difficult to say, to admit, but she was fully cognizant of her mother's dual nature. Nikita had done terrible things, unforgivable things. Yet she'd done them all with the sole aim of protecting her child. "I can't accept the violence she did for me." She wet a throat gone bone-dry. "But I think of what I did to those mercenaries who wanted to hurt Naya, and I can see it's on the same continuum."

Lucas gripped her jaw, made her face him. "Your mother went far beyond that." His lips were a flat line. "I can't judge her for protecting her child, but at some point, it became about power. Don't take her actions on your shoulders. Got it?"

Sascha wished she could argue, but she couldn't. Yes, she'd defend Naya to the death, but she wouldn't massacre innocents in her daughter's name. "Got it."

"Good." Lucas rubbed the pad of his thumb over her chin. "But yes, for all her sins, Nikita did make sure you survived to adulthood."

"I think she did more," Sascha said as they both turned to look over the railing again. Naya couldn't go far, tiny as she was, but parental instinct was parental instinct. "I don't think it was chance that put you and me together on that project."

"I've had that thought myself." He growled down to Naya when she growled up in hello.

Sascha sent her a psychic kiss at the same time.

Happy, their baby continued her solitary game, leopard enough to enjoy alone time and changeling enough to not want it always.

Sliding his hand around to cup her nape, Lucas returned to their conversation. "Nikita made sure you had significant and daily contact with me and the pack."

"Do you think . . ." Sascha frowned. "But how could she know we were mates?"

Lucas shook his head. "I don't think she did. No way to predict that. My feeling is that your mother was playing the odds." He ran his thumb over her skin, petting her, loving her. Skin privileges between mates. Sascha slipped her own hand under his black T-shirt so she could touch the skin of his back.

That got her a feline smile and a lazy lick of a kiss that sent her heart thumping.

"She was Council," Lucas said afterward, "had access to the old records. She must've known that changeling packs had a way of pulling people from the PsyNet. Why not put you in connection with changelings in case it was still true?"

"That sounds like my mother." Sascha twisted her lips. "She did also probably want the deal. Two birds, one stone."

Lucas kissed her again, tender this time. Old hurts soothed by his love, Sascha glanced down at a bright mental touch. *Yes, you're a brave explorer,* she sent to Naya.

Naya growled in pride before continuing her exploring.

"Let's go see Nikita." Lucas's words had her attention snapping back to him. "Like I said, it's a good time for Naya to meet her—while your mother's defenses are down."

Her heart thumped. "I don't know if Vasic is free to do the teleport. I know he wasn't at home when Ivy and I spoke."

Lucas slid out his phone. "Let me give him a call."

SEATED on her bed with work spread out around her, Nikita wasn't expecting the telepathic page from Sophia. She began to respond . . . but then there was no need to ask why her aide was getting in touch with her.

It didn't matter how well Sascha shielded herself; Nikita always knew when her child was close. Before she could do much more than gather and put her work on the bedside table and push off the blanket, Sascha was walking into the room with her own child in her arms.

Nikita saw Sophia pull the door shut behind Sascha and her baby and then, for the first time, the three current generations of Duncans were alone in a room together.

"Don't get up, Mother." Not waiting for an invitation, Sascha pulled the blanket back up over Nikita's legs before taking a seat on the bed.

The girl child in her arms stared wide-eyed at Nikita.

"I told you it wasn't safe." Nikita was already calculating how to mitigate the danger.

"No one knows we're here," Sascha interrupted. "Vasic teleported us."

An Arrow. But an Arrow who'd previously worked with Anthony and who was mated to an empath as softhearted as Sascha. Since Nikita kept herself out of Arrow business, and the leader of the Arrows, Aden Kai, didn't appear to want to grab at power, Vasic had no reason to leak news of Nikita's physical condition.

Muscles easing, she allowed herself to look at the green-eyed child with a wild tumble of silky black curls who Sascha had just placed on the bed, atop the blanket. Instead of clinging to her mother, the child continued to stare at Nikita.

"Your mate's genes appear to have held sway."

"Do you think so?" Sascha ran her hand over her baby's back.

The child was clothed in a simple white sundress. She had tiny white sandals on her feet, the straps decorated with colorful designs.

"Look at the shape of her eyes."

Nikita did, saw what she'd missed at first glance. The intense richness of the green might be from Lucas Hunter, but the tilt at the corners, the gentle upward slope, came from Sascha . . . from Nikita.

Now that she was searching, she found other small pieces of the Duncan line in this child who was both Psy and changeling. The fine facial bones. The skin tone that was a shade or two lighter than Sascha's dark honey but still had enough brown in it to make it clear that Nadiya Hunter's heritage was a complex one.

"She'll be a striking adult." Nikita could see the promise of an extraordinary beauty that spoke to a wide cross-section of the world. "Teamed with her mixed-race heritage, it'll give her a useful advantage in business or politics."

Sascha's smile was affectionate, the hand she touched to Nadiya's hair loving. "She's going to grow up a good person. We'll make sure of it."

That, Nikita thought, was the difference between her and her daughter: Sascha thought in terms of goodness, Nikita in terms of advantages.

"Naya," Sascha said in a gentle tone. "This is your grandmother."

"Gram?" the child said with impressive enunciation for her age.

"Yes." Sascha's smile grew deeper. "Gram. She's my mother."

The baby stared at Nikita again for so long that Nikita felt the child was judging her, weighing up whether or not she was worth Nadiya Hunter's time. Yes, there was definitely some of Nikita Duncan in this Psy-Changeling child. It would stand her in good stead in a harsh world. She'd be far more able to protect herself than her empathic mother . . . though Sascha *had* acted impressively against the mercenaries who'd attempted to take Nadiya.

Maybe Nikita's child was finally growing claws of her own, now that she had a fragile new life to protect.

That was when the baby smiled, slapped its palms onto the blanket, and began to crawl up Nikita's legs. Nikita went still as deep, *deep* inside her, awakened a memory. "You did this," she found herself saying to the beautiful woman with cardinal eyes who'd once been her baby. "In the months after the birth, I was still . . . influenced by carrying an empathic child. I allowed you freedoms proscribed under Silence, allowed you to crawl where you wished when we were alone in my room."

The day the technicians had informed her that the eight-month-old fetus in her womb showed signs of the E gene, she'd felt the stirrings of something even more primal than the maternal protectiveness that had awakened the day she found out she was pregnant. At that time, most mothers carrying empaths were never told the truth, were instead fed lies while the machinery behind the Council ensured those E-designation children were funneled into special early-conditioning classes designed to suffocate the E ability.

Nikita, however, had been the scion of a strong family group and a woman who showed significant promise in her own right. She'd been given the findings—and in the eyes of the technicians who'd informed her, she'd seen death for her child, seen judgment. They'd wanted her to consign Sascha to an institution where she'd be raised as a broken cardinal, no doubt after enough damage was done to her brain to make her pliable, thus ensuring a cardinal E remained in a PsyNet that needed those Es but had abused them for so long.

Her mentor at the time had wanted her to try for a more "perfect" child. A woman of her strength and potential, he'd said, shouldn't be "saddled with the burden" of an E. Nikita hadn't been able to do anything but keep Sascha then; she'd done so by flexing what power she had—and by convincing those more powerful than her, including her own mother, that a cardinal child, even one considered flawed, would be a symbol of Nikita's strength.

She'd told them she would dispose of her child in an "accident" should Sascha prove problematic.

More than two decades on, Sascha lived and those technicians as well as Nikita's once-mentor were long dead.

Nikita didn't ever forgive those who threatened her family.

She hadn't had to kill her mother—Reina Duncan had died a natural death, but even before that, she hadn't interfered with Nikita's raising of Sascha. Reina had signed what Nikita asked her to sign, requested regular updates on Sascha's progress, and been content. Because, by then, everyone in the Duncan line knew it was Nikita who had the killer instinct, Nikita who'd take the family to *serious* power in the Net.

Nikita respected her mother for having understood that, for not getting in her way.

"I don't remember," Sascha whispered.

"Of course not. You were an infant." Nadiya had crawled up to Nikita's thighs.

Sascha reached out. "I'll get her. I know your injuries—"

"It's fine." Well able to handle a toddler, even in her weakened state, Nikita sat her grandchild against her, one arm around Nadiya's waist.

Content because she could see her mother, the child began to "talk." One out of every seven words was possibly comprehensible. "She has excellent vocal skills for her age."

"Yes, she's a chatterbox," Sascha said with a smile that exposed her heart.

Sascha's gaze met Nikita's when Nadiya fell silent, more interested in playing with the organizer Nikita had handed her. The child couldn't do any damage, and the logic puzzle Nikita had pulled up for her to solve was all bright-colored blocks, a program still in Nikita's archives from Sascha's childhood.

"I'd like to remember." There was a wistfulness to Sascha's tone that once more betrayed the softness inside her that Nikita had spent a lifetime trying to toughen up. "I'd like to remember a time when you and I . . . were just us. No Silence. No rules."

"It was never that way," Nikita said curtly. "I was born in Silence." And she'd been forged in a bloody battle for her child's survival.

But her grandchild would grow up in freedom, and her daughter no longer had to worry that someone would try to exterminate her for simply being herself. It was a victory. "Here," she said, and opened the telepathic channel that existed between mother and child, a channel no one else could access.

It didn't surprise her in the least that it was wide open on Sascha's end. Foolish, emotional child.

Bringing up memories of the times she and Sascha had spent in Nikita's bedroom when Sascha was still young enough that Nikita could enclose her in her own shields and hide Sascha's distinctive mental signature, she sent those memories to her daughter.

Sascha gasped, one hand rising to her mouth as tears filled her eyes, the white pinpricks disappearing to leave her eyes pure obsidian . . . but no, there were midnight-blue depths in Sascha's eyes now, as if the color that lived in an E's head was changing the very nature of her gaze.

"Mother," she whispered, the single word holding so much emotion that Nikita wondered how her daughter could bear it.

Then she remembered that Sascha was born to bear emotion.

Distressed by her mother's emotional state, Nadiya whimpered and, abandoning her game, began to crawl toward Sascha. Nikita released her grandchild's small, warm weight, watched as Sascha picked her up, nuzzled her, saying, "It's okay, Naya. Mama's okay."

Kisses followed, more touches and soft words, while Nadiya patted her mother's face as if to ensure there were no further signs of tears.

When Sascha put the child on the bed again, she crawled immediately back to Nikita. "Gram!"

"Yes, I'm your grandmother." Nikita allowed herself to take one small fist in her own hand, feel the vital life of this child who was of her blood.

"Nadiya will be at risk for years to come," she told her daughter. "It doesn't matter how many mixed-race children are born, whether they're Psy and human or Psy and changeling. She's the *first*. A symbol for those who want a new world order—and a target for those who'd rather go back to the old."

"I know." The resolute strength in Sascha's tone reminded Nikita that her softhearted child had annihilated an entire mercenary team. "We'll make sure she's protected but we won't cage her. She has to have the freedom to live her own life." She lifted her gaze from Nadiya to Nikita. "A parent can only do so much."

Nikita saw forgiveness in those eyes of midnight, saw understanding, saw an emotion she knew was love. Breaking the connection because she had to stay strong, had to remain the ice-cold bitch no one dared cross, she allowed Nadiya to "bite" at her knuckles. The child wasn't actually biting down, was more working her milk teeth gently over the bone, as if Nikita were a teething toy.

"I am . . . glad to meet my grandchild."

It was the closest she could come to betraying the emotions that lived so deep inside her that nothing might ever reach them again. It was the closest she could come to telling her daughter that she would murder and torture and die for her. As she would for the child of her child. The world might think she'd rejected Sascha, but Nikita had always played a chess game a hundred moves ahead.

"I'm happy she got to meet you, too." Sascha smiled. "We'll do this again."

Nikita inclined her head. "I'm surprised your mate let you in here alone." She knew Lucas Hunter was just outside the door, could feel his wild psychic energy.

"He says you'd liquefy the brains of anyone who threatened either me or Naya."

The DarkRiver alpha had always been a dangerous opponent. "Perceptive." She watched Nadiya wander off to the other side of the bed, saw Sascha restrain her instinctive protective urge in order to allow her child freedom to explore.

Then the child was no longer a child but a scatter of light . . . and a small panther cub was jumping off the bed. Nadiya turned to give her mother and grandmother a proudly satisfied look once she was on the floor.

Chapter 46

"CLEVER CHILD." NIKITA was impressed the toddler had figured out that to get to the ground, she'd be better off in her other form. "I've never witnessed a shift at such close proximity." Never been trusted with it.

"Extraordinary, isn't it?" Sascha said as Nadiya began to run around the room, curiously exploring everything she could. "Naya, be good."

A small growl, a mischievous look, but the cub eased up her pace.

"Did you intend for me to fall for Lucas?"

Nikita wasn't expecting the question. That didn't matter. Her self-conditioning was too ingrained. Her expression held. "No," she said, and it was the truth. "I knew your shields against emotion were failing and that you needed a way out. I also knew Psy had left the Net in the past to join changeling packs. It was meant to be a chance for you to find an exit route." Had Sascha not succeeded, Nikita's backup plan had involved a large amount of bloodshed.

"I would've rather you didn't mate with Hunter," she added. "As alpha, he's too much in the public eye. The idea was for you to disappear into DarkRiver." Instead, her daughter had become one of the key—and highly visible—members of the pack.

A soft laugh that made Nadiya utter what appeared to be a reciprocal growl. "You can't control everything, Mother."

"I learned that lesson when you came along." Until that moment, Nikita had been a perfect inmate of Silence. Cold and hard and determined to rise to the top with pitiless grace. "Carrying a cardinal empath of your violent strength had an undocumented effect on me." Which said something very interesting about all the women who'd come before Nikita—and about Nikita herself.

When Sascha opened her mouth as if to ask for details, Nikita shook her head. There were some things she'd never say aloud—never admit— even to her daughter. That was too slippery a slope, because the threat remained. In the world lived those who'd murder Sascha for being an E, for being the defector who'd brought a hidden revolution roaring into the light, and, unbeknownst to her, for being a poster child for happiness beyond Silence.

Not only that, to the fanatics, Sascha had committed a second and third transgression, both of which they deemed unforgivable: first, she had bonded with an "aggressive, unintelligent animal," and second, she'd given birth to a child with "tainted" blood. Idiocy and prejudice, all of it, but prejudiced idiots could be dangerous.

Especially to a small, vulnerable child.

Nikita looked at the panther cub currently chewing on the edge of the bedspread, out of sight of her mother's gaze. Nadiya's eyes caught Nikita's. She froze . . . then went back to her mischief when Nikita didn't give her away. It was so easy to win the trust of children, but this child would never be in a position where that trust could get her killed.

Her alpha father and empath mother would never permit it.

Neither would her deadly grandmother.

Attention back on Sascha, she said, "They told me you were flawed." Broken. Useless. "I told you the same because it was the only way to keep you safe."

Sascha shook her head and for the first time today, Nikita heard anger color her daughter's tone. "You could've found another way, a way that wasn't so brutal, that didn't make me question everything I knew about myself."

"No." Nikita would never second-guess the decisions that had kept her child alive. "You were too soft, Sascha. Always have been." A harsh truth. "I had to get you to protect yourself, make sure you weren't relying on me." If that had meant making her empathic child fear and despise her, so be it. "You had to trust only yourself."

"Is it what you believe? That I'm flawed?"

Nikita went to answer but decades of control kept her silent for long enough that Sascha turned away. She shoved past the control. "No," she said. "If I had, I would've never put you in a position of responsibility."

Looking back at her, Sascha smiled and it was a faint shadow of the expression. "I should've figured that out, shouldn't I?"

"Yes." One thing Nikita had always made clear—she didn't suffer fools.

Laughter from her daughter this time, which made her granddaughter want to know what was going on. Jumping back onto the bed with a helping boost from her mother, Nadiya shifted with the confidence of a changeling at home in either skin and allowed herself to be swept into Sascha's lap, making happy sounds when Sascha bent down to nuzzle her.

"There go another set of clothes." Sascha pretended to growl and bite her baby. "I should start dressing you in flour sacks."

Giggling, Nadiya kissed her mother's face, unrepentant joy in her expression.

Nikita took a mental snapshot of the moment, to be filed away in her most private memories. She'd never take an actual snapshot, because if it existed, there existed the chance that someone could find it, use it against her by harming Sascha and Nadiya.

The lack of an actual photograph didn't matter. Nikita's mental acuity was extremely high. She'd remember, just like she remembered that Sascha had made the same sounds as a child. Sascha had also smelled much the same as Nadiya did when Sascha held her out and Nikita took her into her arms. Perhaps all babies had that innocent scent.

A bright, curious mind glanced across hers. Nikita nudged the child back without causing harm or distress, accompanying the psychic action with a nonvocal suggestion that Nadiya protect her mind. "She needs to stop reaching indiscriminately for others using telepathy," Nikita told Sascha. "She's old enough."

"I haven't wanted to stifle her," Sascha replied. "And she's around friendly minds."

"She's Psy, Sascha. A powerful one." Nikita repeated her nudge when her grandchild reached out again. "*No*, Nadiya." A firm command that made the child go still, watchful.

"You must train her," Nikita told her frowning daughter. "You've taught her to shield and you've got your own shield over hers, but I can still send telepathic thoughts to her through the link *she* initiated. I could tell her anything I wanted, send her nightmare images, teach her to fear you, anything."

Sascha's face lost color, her eyes stark. There was a knock on the door a second later. Glancing over her shoulder, Sascha didn't speak, but Lucas Hunter didn't knock again or seek to enter the room. As Nikita had always suspected, the changeling mate-bond functioned on a psychic level in some fashion.

"You're right." Sascha's voice trembled. "I've been so focused on not crushing her or hurting her that I went too far in the opposite direction. It's like Lucas teaching her not to use her claws in play." Sascha snuggled her baby when Nadiya made her way back to her. "It's not hurting her to teach her psychic discipline; it's giving her the tools she needs to survive and thrive."

"Exactly."

There, in that moment, Nikita shared the first moment of pure and absolute understanding with her daughter. *Sascha, too*, she thought, *would do whatever was necessary to protect her child.*

ONCE, Lucas had thought he'd never voluntarily permit his mate and child to be alone in a room with Nikita Duncan, but here he was, holding up the wall outside Nikita's bedroom suite. Even when he'd sensed Sascha's sudden distress, he hadn't barged in. They'd been mated long enough that he could distinguish acute distress from a lesser emotional shock, and this had felt more akin to the latter.

Sascha's silent response through their mate-bond had eased his concern.

Lucas would never change his mind about Nikita Duncan, not after the things the woman had done as a Councilor, but as he'd told his empath, better a child who knew her powerful—and to a cat—intriguing grandmother, than that she be tempted to find out on her own.

That didn't mean he wasn't having to fight the urge to break down the door and get his mate and child out of there. A call from Mercy to do with the joint pack event distracted him for a few minutes, but even then, the majority of his attention remained hyperfocused on the door behind which had disappeared two pieces of his heart.

Sascha proved exactly how well she knew him when she exited. Immediately handing him Naya, she slipped her hand into his. His bristling protective instincts settled, his claws no longer in danger of breaking through his skin. They didn't speak until after Vasic had returned them home.

Lucas thanked the teleporter, who simply nodded.

Even after they were alone as a family, Lucas and Sascha waited until Naya was down for her nap before they opened up this particular box.

Lucas put on some soft music, drew his mate into his arms. As they swayed to the lazy beat, she told him about the meeting with her mother. "She meant it." Sascha's voice was raw. "That she never saw me as flawed."

Lucas knew others would never understand the import of Nikita's words, of how much they meant to Sascha. The hurt inside her that her mother had inflicted was no longer a scar, but neither could such pain be easily forgotten. "You've never been flawed." It still pissed him off each time she used that word in relation to herself.

"I know." She ran her hand over his back as she lifted her face to smile up at him. "I wouldn't dare argue with an alpha cat."

He nipped at her lower lip. "Smart-ass."

Eyes dancing, she kissed him all slow and sexy. Only when they were both breathless did she break the kiss to continue speaking. "Mother told me to start teaching Naya mental discipline."

His hackles rose. "Why do you sound like you're considering it?"

"Right now," Sascha said, "Naya is curious about everyone and anything, and I would never attempt to suppress that. But she's also dangerously *open*.

Not only have I not taught her to be careful who she connects with telepathically or to never connect to strange minds without my permission—"

"As we've taught her not to go with strangers." Lucas's bunched-up muscles began to relax.

Sascha nodded. "I was so intent on not suffocating her in any way, in giving her the psychic freedom I never had, that I went too far in the other direction."

"I understand, kitten." Lucas had to constantly fight his own overprotective urges. "If I could, I'd wrap you both in cotton wool." As well as every single vulnerable member of his pack. "You help me deal with that. I'll help you deal with this."

Lines of strain fading from her expression, Sascha said, "Mother gave me a number of tips about how to teach Naya what she needs, but I thought I'd speak to Shaya as well." A long pause, Sascha placing her head against his shoulder as they swayed to the music. "Nikita kept me safe, but it hurt. Ashaya is doing the same for Keenan without damaging him. He's a psychically strong and disciplined child who's lost none of his personality or joy."

Lucas dropped a kiss on her hair. "There's also the fact that she's guiding and teaching him while he's living in a changeling pack." Nikita had never had to deal with a child who was surrounded by primal and unrestrained emotion on a daily basis, rather than by the icy discipline of Psy under Silence.

"Yes, you're right. Several of Nikita's techniques would collapse under non-Silent conditions."

"You should talk to the Laurens, too." Walker Lauren, in particular, had been dealing with children outside the PsyNet and outside Silence, for longer than anyone else Lucas knew. Judd's brother had also been a teacher in the PsyNet.

Sascha nodded before leaning back to look at him once more, her arms hooked around his neck and her lips swollen from his kiss. "We have to write a whole new rule book, don't we?"

Lucas's panther rumbled awake deep in his chest. "That's what rebels do." And Sascha Duncan, cardinal empath, mate to an alpha, and mother to a Psy-Changeling child, was the rebel who'd blown the PsyNet wide open.

Letters to Nina

From the private diaries of Father Xavier Perez
June 1, 2080

Nina,

My first friend, the one I once tried to assassinate. His life changed drastically some time ago. He was ripped out of one world and had to learn to exist in another, and for a while, I feared he wouldn't adapt. But he did and here's how. This man I once saw as cold as ice now loves a woman as deeply and as passionately as I love you.

I feel such joy for him, Nina. To see the look in his eyes, that is hope. The same God that took you away from me has given him this chance. He doesn't agree with me, of course. He isn't a man of faith. He believes in honor and in fidelity and in standing behind your actions rather than putting faith in some "otherworldly entity."

The arguments and conversations we have, Nina. You would love it. He accepts me for who I am and I do the same for him and our other friend, and all three of us, we challenge one another. Your beautiful mind is all that's missing.

Even after so much time has passed, I still hope for you. But then I realize that if you're alive, you've chosen not to come to me and my heart shatters. Say you're not angry with me, Nina. Please. I could not bear it if you had forsaken me.

Xavier

Chapter 47

TEN IN THE evening in Venice and Bowen Knight was tapping his finger on his desk as he read through the latest report from the implant team when he received a message on his phone. He didn't immediately recognize the sender—not unusual, since everyone in the Human Alliance had access to his contact details. It sometimes made for a chaotic day, but most folks were good about only contacting him directly if it was a matter that needed to be brought to the attention of the Alliance's security chief.

The message was simple: We need to talk. Too sensitive to send over unsecured line.—Isaac

He did a quick search on the sender's number. It returned a listing for Beauclair Trucking based out of Vancouver, Canada. A little digging and he found the name of the owner: Isaac Beauclair.

Beauclair and his company had joined the Alliance a year earlier. According to the records kept by Bo's administrative staff, no one from the company had ever attended an Alliance meeting, but they paid their dues like clockwork and the owner had made two requests for Alliance assistance.

In both cases it had been a simple application for a business introduction.

Nothing unusual in that. Many Alliance members had joined for the same reason—to expand their network among other human companies. Of course, with the Alliance now part of Trinity, with far more streamlined access to Psy and changeling businesses, that element of their membership base had increased again by a significant percentage.

Bo also had access to certain security databases, and when he ran Isaac's name through those, he saw no red flags. The owner of the very successful company still drove a long-haul truck on occasion and he had a clean record. No smuggling allegations, nothing but a higher than average number of speeding tickets. The latter was a badge of honor with truckers—they always tried to push their trucks, the temptation of often otherwise empty highways too much.

Beauclair's company, however, was interesting: It had a reputation for security and reliability and, as a result, often carried high-value goods that couldn't be transported any other way. Teleporters didn't usually stoop to such pragmatic work, and even after all the technological advances to date, sometimes the best and most economically efficient way to move certain items from one place to the next was via the road.

Instead of messaging back, Bo called Lily in from where she was catching up on her own work nearby. His sister did a little hacking at his request, found the direct link to the comm system onboard Isaac's truck, and set up a secure call. According to Beauclair Trucking's records, Isaac was on the road today.

"Just tap this and you'll be set," Lily said, then left him to it.

The call went through without any difficulty, was answered audio-only on the other end.

"Who's this?" was the brusque question.

"Bowen Knight. You wanted to talk."

Audio-only turned into visual and audio, and Bowen found himself talking to a broad-shouldered man who looked remarkably like his official ID photo. Isaac Beauclair had white skin touched with enough sun that it was warm rather than cool, sandy red-brown hair cut fairly tidily but not ruthlessly, a neat beard that was more red than red-brown, and dark hazel eyes. From what Bo could see, the other man was wearing what looked like a band T-shirt in black, the print white.

"Didn't expect such a quick response," Isaac said. "Give me a second to put the truck on full auto-nav."

Bo waited while the other man did that, then Isaac came back onscreen.

"We have a few minutes before I have to retake manual control. The roads are a little iffy in this section of my route, couple of broken nav beacons that haven't been fixed."

"The line is secure," Bo told him. "I made certain of it."

"Figure you know your business." Isaac glanced over his shoulder, seemed to say something that wasn't picked up by the speakers.

When he turned back, his face held a grim look. "I might've done something that could blow back on the Alliance itself."

"Explain."

"I pulled into a truck stop couple of hours ago, went in to grab a coffee, use the restroom, usual stuff." Isaac shrugged. "When I came back out, there was this SUV parked next to my truck. Blacked-out windows, all-terrain tires."

"Anything unusual about that?"

"Not really. I see those vehicles now and then—mostly it's big CEOs or celebrities who want to travel incognito. They don't usually pull in at truck stops, but I figured maybe someone started jonesing for coffee or needed the restroom—but I still took a close look because of that alert about the other SUV that went out earlier." He paused and Bo had the sense he was ordering his thoughts.

Isaac Beauclair struck him as a very deliberate kind of man.

"So I jump up into the cab of my truck, and as I'm pulling the door shut, I glance down." His face turned grim. "SUV was all blacked-out, but it had a glass sunroof that wasn't and I could see right through it. I saw a man in the front passenger seat and a woman in back. She was covered with a blanket, but her face was all scarred-up and bruised and she looked fucking thin."

Bo could guess where this was going. "You intervened?"

"First I went and grabbed a couple of buddies who'd just brought in their trucks. Was a slight risk the driver of the SUV would return first and take off, but the dude in the car, he gave off a Psy vibe. I knew I needed backup."

Bo nodded; humans were very good at identifying Psy. They had to be.

It was a survival mechanism. Some family lines had developed an eerily accurate second sense about Psy in the vicinity, though they were all quick to state that it wasn't itself a psychic skill. Bo had never quite bought the latter. After all, Psy, changeling, and human came from the same original stock. And evolution, it never stopped. "Your buddies all human?"

"No," the trucker replied. "One of them was changeling—I figured he'd stay standing even if the Psy took me out." Isaac turned and spoke over his shoulder again, and once more, his voice was too quiet for the microphone to catch.

"I went up to the front passenger-side window, knocked," he continued after turning back to the comm. "Guy rolled it down, asked if he could help me. I asked what the hell was going on with the woman in back, and he said they were taking her to a hospital after finding her on the side of the road. Sounded plausible but that was when she woke up and said, 'Help me.'"

Isaac shrugged. "That was enough for us. I smashed in the back window to unlock the door while my changeling friend hauled the Psy half out of the window to hold his attention. Our other friend kept a lookout. I'd just got the woman out when a second Psy came running out, hit me with a telepathic blow."

The truck driver rubbed his temple. "It was hard as hell but not debilitating. I don't figure he was that strong, but he was strong enough to weaken us and that gave him a chance to help the other Psy fight off my changeling friend. I think they would've come for the woman but I pulled a gun."

Another shrug. "Got to have protection on these isolated routes, especially when I'm moving expensive high-tech equipment. So they hauled ass instead—one of my buddies got a partial plate. I'll send it through."

Bowen nodded. "The woman, you didn't take her to a hospital?" He'd figured out she had to be behind Isaac, in the cab of the truck.

Shaking his head, Isaac lowered his voice. "She was freaked out, begged for me to get her to the sea." He blew out a breath. "Her eyes . . . I never saw eyes like that. Like the blackest part of the ocean, no light, no shadow."

Bo felt the hairs rise on the back of his neck. He thought of BlackSea's request to track another black SUV, considered the plea made by Isaac's passenger, and he wondered . . . "Can you describe her to me?"

"Five four, black hair, light brown skin, heritage from the Pacific Islands maybe. She won't give me her name." He paused. "It looks like someone took a fucking hunting knife to her face."

Bo's hand clenched on the phone. "How long before you reach the ocean?" Isaac didn't seem like the kind of man who'd make the woman wait.

"Six hours," the trucker replied. "I was pretty inland when I found her."

That gave Bo plenty of time to get in touch with BlackSea. "I think I know who she belongs to—give me a little time to see if I can confirm." Hanging up to Isaac's curt nod, he pulled up the contact information of the man who'd tipped off the Alliance about that little cell of anti-human fanatics.

Malachai Rhys.

Beside the man's name was a title: BlackSea Security Chief.

Bo didn't expect his call to be immediately answered—the water changelings had a reputation for preferring their privacy and making it difficult for anyone to get hold of them. And right now, they were understandably pissed off at the Alliance.

However, Malachai picked up within the first two seconds. "Yes?"

"This is Bo Knight."

"Hold while I confirm."

Raising an eyebrow, Bowen leaned back in his chair. When Malachai came back on the line, he said, "How exactly do you confirm?"

"We have methods," the BlackSea male responded. "You didn't call to chat."

"No. One of my people has picked up a woman in bad physical shape who wants to go to the sea."

"Name?"

"She won't give it, but I have a description." He repeated it to Malachai. "She sound like one of yours?"

A pause, as if the BlackSea security chief was considering whether to confirm or deny. "Yes," he said at last. "We can take charge of her if you give us a location."

"Unless you call in a teleporter, you won't get her to the sea any faster than she's already going," Bo told the other man. "She's in a long-haul truck, safe and warm. You know how fast those truckers go." And there was nothing else on the road that could take down a truck that big.

"We need to know where she is, nevertheless," Malachai said.

It was Bowen's turn to pause. If he gave them Isaac's details, then he made the other man vulnerable. On the other hand, BlackSea had extended the hand of friendship, while the Alliance had let them down in return. Maybe it was time to even the scoreboard.

He sent the data. "You should have someone meet her at the beach. From the way she was described to me, I'm not sure she has the strength to take on the ocean."

"We'll organize that." Malachai's tone shifted slightly. "Pass on a message. Tell her to resist the temptation to shift. In her condition, the water near Canada is too cold for her—say her pack is on the way and promises to get her to warmer waters as fast as possible."

"Consider it done." Hanging up, Bowen passed on the message and alerted Isaac that he might end up with some company along the way. "Should be friendly, but if they give you problems, let me know. I'll call in a few favors, get you help."

"I'll make sure she stays safe," Isaac said before switching off.

Bo got another message an hour later: I've got an escort, front and back. Isaac had also sent through the vehicle ID numbers.

When Bowen checked with Malachai, the BlackSea male confirmed they were BlackSea vehicles. "They won't get in the trucker's way, but they need to be there for our packmate when she reaches the beach."

LEILA Savea didn't know why she trusted the man who'd rescued her— maybe *because* he'd rescued her or maybe it was because she'd seen the photograph tacked to his dashboard. It was of him laughing with a tall blonde woman who stood in his arms with no hint of fear on her face, though the man who'd introduced himself as Isaac was at least as big and as muscled as Malachai.

Whatever it was, she'd given in to her need to be clean of the ugliness of what had been done to her by showering far too long in the shower inside the living quarters of his cab. She'd probably emptied his water tank, but he hadn't knocked on the door to tell her to get out. Instead, when she finally came out, it was to see he'd left a pair of sweatpants and a T-shirt for her to change into.

His clothes would've fallen off her, but these kind of fit after she tucked the T-shirt into the sweatpants in a very unglamorous move and tightened the drawstring, then rolled up the bottoms of the pants.

Clearly, the clothes belonged to a taller, healthier woman. The laughing blonde? The idea made Leila happy, though both Isaac and the woman were strangers to her. And she needed to think thoughts of happiness right now. It was all that was keeping her from shattering, her psyche held together by a single fragile thread.

When she came to peek out at Isaac, he glanced back at her with a cheek-creasing smile. "You know," he said before turning his attention back to the road, "you're not the first girl I've rescued."

The part of Leila that had kept her sane in the darkness scowled. "I'm a woman, not a girl."

"Jessie was mouthy, too." So much emotion in his voice as he touched his fingers to the photograph. "She drives big rigs now. Drives me crazy, too."

"I'm a scientist," Leila found herself telling him, and in so doing, reclaimed a part of her lost self. "I study the creatures that call the ocean home."

Isaac whistled. "Smart." His tone changed on the next words, became rough. "Those assholes hurt you pretty bad." He nodded up ahead. "You need medical help from your people?"

She could see the gleaming white all-terrain vehicle through the windscreen, the landscape beyond painted by cloudy late-afternoon light. "Are you sure those people are mine?"

"Some guy called Malachai confirmed it."

Her eyes threatened to fill with tears.

Malachai wouldn't let anyone hurt her. He was Miane's and Miane protected her people, no matter how distant they were or how small their relative importance to the rest of the world. Each and every member of BlackSea was important to Miane.

Crawling up to sit in the passenger seat, she forced herself to say, "I could ride with them. They're going really fast." Only she didn't know them and Isaac was safe. Isaac had a beard like her father and he loved a woman with blonde hair and freckles scattered over her nose and across the tops of her cheeks.

"I could do with seeing the ocean," Isaac replied with a grin that reassured her he didn't mind this detour. "Been a while."

"My name is Leila." It seemed right to tell this good man who was taking her home.

"Pretty." Picking up something from the cup holder, he held it out. "You should eat a little more if you can."

Taking what proved to be a protein bar, she peeled it open with fingers that were swollen from how the driver of the SUV had wrenched her fingers back when she tried to run at a stop. He'd also punched her in the face.

"You have someone who'll look after you?" Isaac asked in that rough tone that was oddly comforting, like Malachai when he got gruff. "Once you reach home?"

The thought of home made her chest ache.

"I swim alone," she told him after swallowing a bite of the protein bar. "But I'll go to the city for a while, rest in my family's arms."

"You ever get lonely?" He grabbed an unopened water bottle from his side and handed it to her. "Swimming alone I mean? Ocean's a big place."

Laughter spilled out of her, unexpected and rusty. "Don't truckers drive alone for days at times?"

"Point to you." He chuckled and the sound was a warm blanket wrapping around her. "But I don't run alone much anymore." A glance at the photograph that said more than words. "The rare times I do, I still see people—at the truck stops for one. At the sleep stops, if we end up parking side by side to catch some shut-eye. No truck stops in the ocean."

"I have friends who swim by." She smiled at the memories of how her best friends would haul themselves up onto her boat and raid her galley shelves for cookies. One time, after the fiends had eaten her out of cookies until not a crumb remained, she'd come up from a swim to discover two large sacks of cookies left on deck, the supplies carried to her in waterproof bags.

"The gaps are longer than in your line of work," she told Isaac as her mouth watered for a taste of those chocolate-chip-raisin cookies. "Weeks rather than days, but we're social in our own way." Her smile faded under a sudden nausea, her skin chilled. "I don't know if I'll be able to swim in my waters anymore. The kidnappers might take me again."

Isaac shot her a dark look that didn't terrify—she already knew him well enough to understand his anger was directed at the people who'd tortured and imprisoned her. "You could swim with a group for a while," he suggested. "Fight your need for solitude to stay in your home waters."

Leila thought of how she'd fought so much already, of how she'd survived *unbroken* and felt a flicker of pride, an emotion she'd long thought dead inside her. "It might be nice to swim with my friends," she admitted, knowing those friends would welcome her despite their own normally solitary travels.

Her skin ached, hungry for the cool slide of water. At home, the water was so clear she could see beams of sunlight spearing through to scatter sparkles of light like a silent fireworks display. But right now, so far from home, the memory hurt. So she turned to something that didn't. "Will you tell me about your Jessie?"

Isaac grinned, and then he told her all about the tough, smart girl he'd picked up on a lonely road late one night, who he'd then chewed out for hitchhiking. That girl had grown up, grown even tougher and smarter, and become one of Isaac's best drivers. She'd also turned into a "tall gorgeous woman" who seemed to find pleasure in driving Isaac to distraction . . .

until one day, she stopped calling, stopped forwarding him funny e-mails, stopped being an integral and daily part of his life.

Leila's heart squeezed. "No," she whispered. "I don't want a sad ending." Couldn't deal with it. Not today. Maybe not for many days to come.

Isaac winked at her. "Jessie just got sick and tired of my thick head and decided to say to hell with me." His expression devolved into a dark scowl. "She started dating that pretty boy trooper Michel Benoit." Growling words that could've come from one of the big bull sea lion changelings. "I mean, really? A trooper?"

Leila's shoulders shook. "How did you win her back?" She knew he had, had just noticed the golden wedding band on his left ring finger. It was visible in the photograph, too, as was the glint of gold on Jessie's hand.

Shaking his head, the bearded trucker said, "That is one hell of a tale." He began to tell it, snarling every time he got to a part that involved his apparent mortal enemy Michel Benoit.

She was so caught up in his story that she didn't know when she fell asleep, but when she came awake, it was to a moonlit darkness and the salt-laced scent of the ocean. Eyes burning and heart thumping, she began to push at the heavy door. Isaac had already unlocked it, and by the time she pushed it open, he was there to catch her.

"Isaac"—tears rolled hot and wet down her face—"you brought me home."

He refused to release his grip on her. "I did, sweetheart, but you know what Malachai said. You won't survive a swim in your current condition."

Leila barely heard him, the music of the crashing waves a visceral pulse that pounded her name. Then a tall brunette with features that reminded Leila of another marine biologist she knew, a woman who hailed from the Lil'wat Nation, exited one of the escort vehicles and came over. She carried the scent of the ocean, too, deep in her skin.

Pack.

The realization was enough to pull Leila's attention from the sea, but not to separate her from Isaac. She didn't know this packmate, had never before seen her. Then the woman made a call, gave her the phone. Her entire body shook, because it was Miane on the other end, telling her she was safe, that this woman and her partner would bring her to her own waters.

"Canadian waters are too cold for you in your current condition," Miane said with command inherent in her every word. "It'll stop your heart even if you shift. Stay in human form a little longer."

Leila's entire self hurt with need for the sea, but she couldn't gainsay the first among them. "I won't shift." It came out a trembling promise.

"Only a short while longer, little dancer."

Little dancer.

No one had called her by the childhood nickname for an eon. Of course, Miane would remember—and in so doing, remind Leila of who she was under the scars and the pain. "I'll hold on," she promised in a stronger voice. "Until I'm home."

Taking the phone after Leila handed it back, the brunette pointed out a yacht moored in the distance, its sails glowing white under the silver kiss of the moon, then gestured toward a small jetboat in the shallows. "If you're ready?"

Leila swallowed, looked up at Isaac. "Thank you. Your Jessie is a lucky woman."

His smile was sunrise over an ocean. "Send me a postcard with palm trees on it someday. I've never made it to the tropics."

Throwing her arms around his big, sturdy form, she whispered, "Come visit me. Bring Jessie."

And then she couldn't fight the pull anymore, was heading down the beach so fast that her knees threatened to crumple out from under her. The brunette woman and a slender black man helped her onto the jetboat. She trailed her hand in the water and tried not to sob with need as they began to pull away.

Home, she was going home.

Letters to Nina

From the private diaries of Father Xavier Perez
July 14, 2081

Nina,

War has broken out. The streets of San Francisco crawl with soldiers. I'm writing this in the cellar of the church, in a stolen moment. Around me are refugees I and other able-bodied people have brought in.

There is no more time to write. I must go, must see if there are others I can help.

Xavier

Chapter 48

MIANE DIDN'T TAKE a real breath until Leila stepped onto Cifica, the city rocking gently under them in a rhythm that was the sea's pulse. The young woman had been ferried by yacht to the nearest large BlackSea city, then put on a high-speed plane home. That plane had landed two minutes ago on the water beside BlackSea's main city in the tropics.

"Leila." She took her packmate into her arms, held her while Leila cried.

"They made me ugly," Leila whispered against her chest. "I was never pretty but now I'm a monster."

"Never say that again." Miane fought her fury, squeezed Leila tight. "You are strong and beautiful and one of mine."

Leila's voice was thick when she answered, her fingers rising to her face. "The scars, Miane . . . I want them gone."

"We have an excellent surgeon." He was human but an angel with scars. "I'll get him to come out to the city." That Leila had spoken first of her scars didn't surprise Miane. All victims of trauma reacted differently, and she knew from Olivia Coletti that sometimes, a superficial statement or request wasn't superficial at all.

Each time I look in the mirror, Olivia had whispered to her, *I see them. This isn't my face. It's what they made me.*

"Will it work?" Leila asked shakily.

"Yes." Olivia's scars were already so fine that it was difficult to spot them under normal light. "He's very good."

A jerky nod. "I'm not vain. It's just . . ."

"I know." She kissed the shorter, slighter woman's temple, kept her warm and safe within her embrace. "We've missed you, Leila."

Sobs broke out of Leila's body anew, heartrending and painful and raw. But when it was over and Leila lifted tear-drenched eyes to Miane's, those eyes held a luminous light. "The world doesn't understand. They think because some of us swim alone and because the ocean is so vast, that we don't care."

Miane wiped away Leila's tears. "We know the truth and that's what matters." Miane would turn predator for her people, would fight any enemy to keep them safe. "We are BlackSea."

"We are one," Leila whispered, completing the motto that was written nowhere and yet that defined water-based changelings.

No matter how far they traveled or how deep, they were part of a bigger whole. Never forgotten. Never discarded. *One.*

PART 7

Chapter 49

TEN MINUTES AFTER receiving word that Leila Savea was home safe with her people, Riley walked with Mercy in the woods near their cabin, her arm hooked into his. He refused to let go of her—his tall, lithely muscled mate looked as if she'd topple over.

"Why didn't you put on weight anywhere else?" he growled at her. "At least you'd be more stable."

She bared her teeth at him. "Shut up. I can keep myself upright. And for your information, I ate like a bear before hibernation, but our children are voracious hooligans."

Riley waited when she stopped, caught her breath.

Wait, at no point in her pregnancy had Mercy *ever* had to catch her breath during a simple walk. "You're having a contraction," he accused.

"First one." A scowl directed at him. "Only tiny anyway. Probably be a few hours yet at least."

"Of course it will." Knowing that any children with Mercy's blood in their veins would be in no way predictable, he pulled out his phone and put in the call to Tamsyn.

"I'll be there in fifteen," the healer said, clearly already in the vicinity.

That was likely on purpose, with Mercy overdue. Not just in terms of a multiple changeling pregnancy but generally.

"Oh, crap!" Mercy almost bent over.

Heart thudding, Riley nonetheless kept his cool and began to stroke her back with the firm touch she liked. When she was ready, he helped her back up. They walked some more but stayed near the cabin.

Riley's instinct was to hustle her into a comfortable bed, but Mercy was a leopard sentinel and she knew her body. At one point, she pressed her hands palms-down against a tree and pushed out while he massaged her back, digging in his thumbs the way she demanded.

Even when she snarled at him, her eyes dark as a result of the increasing pain, he kissed her temple and petted her, and after the contraction passed, his wild, beautiful mate turned into him. "I'm sorry."

Riley kissed her cheeks, her lips in a caress that was all about comfort. "You can yell at me all you want. It makes me feel like I'm useful for something." Brushing back her damp hair, he held her as long as she wanted before they began to walk again.

Mercy's water broke a minute later.

The contractions were coming so close together by the time Tamsyn reached them that the gaps were measured in seconds rather than minutes. They didn't make it inside. The pupcubs were born in a rush on the soft grass outside the cabin, Mercy's hand gripping Riley's and her back braced against his as Tamsyn caught their impatient children.

Who all decided to come out pretty much on top of one another.

Wiping off their faces, the healer placed the children in Mercy's trembling arms. Riley slid his own under hers to help her hold them safe. "Hello," Mercy whispered, a softness to her that, until this instant, only Riley had ever seen.

She kissed each squalling face in turn before looking up at him. "You're a daddy now, wolf."

His smile felt as if it would crack his face. "Hell, yeah."

"Come around," she murmured as the pupcubs quieted under their mother's touch, at the skin-to-skin contact that was so important to newborn changelings. "They need to feel their daddy's touch, too."

Easing away his bracing hold, he came around to the side so he could support Mercy with one leg behind her back and still be able to hold their babies. He undid his shirt almost without thought and then Mercy was putting all three pupcubs in his arms. The "voracious hooligans" were strong and healthy but tiny. He nuzzled each soft face, drew in their scents, felt his heart expand again to make even more room for these three precious souls.

Tamsyn, who'd been taking care of Mercy, finally nudged them up and into the house. Only when all three pupcubs were snuggled up against Riley in the bed, skin-to-skin, did Mercy step into the shower for a minute.

Dressed in one of his T-shirts afterward, panties on underneath, she made a beeline for their babies. "Look at them. They're so perfect." She took a tiny foot, kissed each toe. Then did the same for the other two pupcubs as Tamsyn smiled and left them in privacy.

When Mercy took a pupcub and the baby whimpered at the touch of cotton, she tugged off the tee and snuggled their child to her heartbeat. The baby quieted at once. "Riley, we made three gorgeous babies," she whispered in open awe, her eyes shining.

With her hair cascading in red waves over skin of cream and gold, and her face luminous as she looked first at one babe, then leaned over to kiss the loosely fisted hand of another, the head of the third, Mercy made his heart stop. "We did," he managed to say, juggling the two pupcubs he held over onto one arm so he could close his free hand over Mercy's nape. "You're amazing."

A sparkling smile. "Never forget it, wolf." Leaning in, she nipped at his lower lip. "I want to hold them all again." She situated herself in a slightly leaning position against the headboard, pillows piled up behind her, then Riley placed the other two pupcubs against her.

Their tiny faces seemed to smile, their soft hands spreading on her skin.

Riley watched over them, feeling a joy so deep that neither part of him could articulate it. His mate was safe, as were their pupcubs.

Riley Aedan Kincaid could ask for nothing more.

Letters to Nina

From the private diaries of Father Xavier Perez
September 27, 2081

Nina,

Our city has been at peace for months.

The changelings won the battle that shattered that peace earlier this year, but both my friends believe this is only a temporary lull— change is building with ever-increasing momentum in the PsyNet, the network that connects every Psy in the world but for the rare few who have defected.

"An earthquake is coming, Xavier," one of my friends said to me just hours earlier. "Only the strong will be left standing when it's over."

I pray for the souls caught up in the turmoil, Psy, human, and changeling alike. I'm no longer full of hate toward an entire race. They are as good and bad, as perfect and flawed, as any one of us. In understanding that, I've found a kind of peace, too.

But my heart, it still hurts in the night from missing you. It's been so many years now and still I turn and look for your smile, still I reach for your hand. I know I always will.

Your Xavier

Chapter 50

LUCAS AND SASCHA arrived to welcome the pupcubs at the same time as Hawke and Sienna, a bare hour after the birth. Given the fact that Riley's alpha and his mate should've been far distant, Riley knew Hawke had made certain he was nearby this past week, as they waited for Mercy to give birth. Not just so he could greet the babies, but in case an alpha's strength was needed. Though Lucas was the one who had a direct link to Mercy, Hawke could share his strength through Riley.

Both alphas stopped in the doorway to the bedroom, their shoulders touching. It was an unusual stance for two such dominant predatory changelings—not only were they sharing space, they weren't pushing forward to assert who was more alpha. It revealed far more about their relationship—and the friendship and trust that tied them together—than either would ever admit.

"So," Hawke said, "I see nobody won the betting pool."

Lucas's smile was very feline. "Don't the rules say all the money then goes to your pupcubs?"

Beside Riley, his shirt-clad mate smirked. That shirt was his and it was unbuttoned enough that she could maintain skin-to-skin contact with the pupcubs while not showing her breasts—though as she'd pointed out, her breasts were "freaking amazing" right now.

Riley had zero arguments with that declaration.

She was sitting cross-legged under a sheet pulled up to her waist, two of their babies cuddled up against her, while Riley held the third one against

NALINI SINGH

his bare chest as he sprawled with his back to the headboard. Tamsyn had draped soft fleece throws over the pupcubs' backs, to help keep them warm.

Mercy said, "Yes and yes," in response to Hawke's and Lucas's statements.

Then she reached out and bumped Riley's raised fist with her own. "Here's to a plan well-executed."

Riley chuckled when Hawke shook his head and said, "Led astray by a cat."

"It was my idea." Riley dropped a kiss on the head of the baby in his arms. He and Mercy had been playing "pass the pupcubs" the entire hour since the birth, ensuring each child received equal time with both parents. Not that the sleepy hooligans seemed to care, curling up happily against either father or mother.

"Lara helped," he added.

The SnowDancer healer had "accidentally" left up a doctored scan on her view screen for a short period. A packmate had seen the four distinct outlines in the image and rumors being what they were, suddenly all the betting had skewed toward quadruplets.

"Tammy, too." Mercy nuzzled the pupcubs in her arms, then reached over to touch her fingers to the back of the baby Riley held. "She confirmed the rumor by refusing to confirm it while making it obvious it was true."

Both alphas grinned, then flowed into the room. Riley didn't know how they did it, but somehow, they got in at the same time without jostling or pushing. As if they'd coordinated it subconsciously. And yeah, he'd keep that thought to himself—Luc and Hawke might be friends, but they hated it if anyone pointed that out.

Lucas sat on the bed on Mercy's side, while Hawke stood beside Riley. No words needed to be spoken. He and Mercy handed over their precious burdens to their alphas, to be accepted as pack, to be welcomed. All three babies remained calm and quiescent, as was normal for a young child in the presence of their alpha—the interesting thing was that they stayed calm for *both* alphas.

Hawke and Lucas didn't hand back the children until both had handled each child. That was when Sienna and Sascha peeked in and asked if they could cuddle the pupcubs. Both women tumbled onto the end of the bed when Mercy waved them in and there was smiling and cooing and snuggling.

Mercy, meanwhile, just looked smug and happy.

Which made Riley very smug and happy.

Arm around her, he glanced from Hawke to Lucas, then back to his own alpha. "So?" Their babies wouldn't shift for approximately a year, but the alphas would know which pupcub belonged to which pack. A good alpha—and both these men were extraordinary alphas—knew his pack.

Lucas's eyes met Hawke's.

Panther-green and wolf-blue, both sets glinted.

Lucas was the one who spoke. "We figured we'd keep you in suspense like you've kept everyone else the entire pregnancy."

Mercy threw a pillow at her laughing alpha's head. "I'll kill you, I swear to God." A pause before she released her claws and looked consideringly at Hawke. "I'd kill you first though."

"Never doubted it." With that, Hawke reached out and plucked the two boys out of Sascha's arms, while Lucas took their little girl from Sienna.

Sascha's eyes widened. "Two wolf pups to one leopard cub. I guess this answers the question of which one of you is more dominant."

"No, it doesn't," Riley said. "Isabella was born first, led the charge." Riley nuzzled a kiss to Mercy's hair. "I'd say we came out even."

"Good answer, wolf." A kiss that held sunshine, his mate's delight open.

"I thought so," he murmured. "I bet Isabella runs the boys ragged."

"I love that name." Sascha smiled down at the pupcub she'd stolen from Lucas. "Is she named after your grandmother?"

Mercy nodded. "I figure an alpha is a good namesake for our girl. Her middle name is Maeve, after Riley's mom." She twined her fingers with Riley's. "Acton is for Riley's father and Michael for mine." Her smile grew deeper. "Belle, Ace, and Micah."

Grinning, she added, "We decided we'd better come up with nicknames before my brothers did it first. God knows what Shadow, Herb, and Frenchie would've chosen." As everyone laughed, she kissed Ace's cheek after Hawke returned their youngest son to her arms and Micah to Riley's.

Riley and Mercy had chosen the family names because they wanted their children to feel firmly rooted despite the fact that all three were unique and would be forging their own path. It was for the same reason that they'd had a long discussion before settling on Smith-Kincaid as the pupcubs' surname. A bit of a mouthful yes, especially since all three had middle names, but it meant their babies, regardless of their changeling animal, would never wonder if they belonged more to one parent than to the other.

"Michael's middle name is Hawke," Riley told his best friend.

Hawke froze, then said, "Hell." The single word held a storm of emotion, his wolf prowling in his eyes.

"And Acton's is Lucas," Mercy told her alpha, to the same intense reaction. "Wolf or leopard, we wanted our babies to know they are cherished by both packs."

That, Riley thought, was the purest truth.

TEN minutes later, Riley saw Mercy's eyes follow Hawke as he handed Ace over to Lucas, before taking Belle and Micah from the leopard alpha. He knew why she was so intrigued—both alphas were treating the children as their own. That wasn't usually a choice. Alphas were as territorial about children in their pack as parents were about their pups or cubs.

Lucas caught their glances. "In terms of pack hierarchy and for any disciplinary needs, Belle is mine, while Micah and Ace are Hawke's, but they're all ours."

It was an extraordinary thing for a predatory changeling alpha to say . . . yet it resonated with Riley. He was Hawke's, but he'd fight to the death for Lucas, too, because DarkRiver needed Lucas, and Mercy needed DarkRiver. He knew his mate would do the same for Hawke, no matter how often she might threaten to kill him.

Now, she stole back Belle, nuzzled her sweet face. "You hear that, kiddo? You're going to have to deal with *two* of them."

"She can handle it." Lucas touched Mercy's cheek with the affection of alpha to packmate. "Belle's your kid—with a bit of wolf thrown in, but we won't hold that against her."

Hawke growled at the other alpha, but it was hard to take his "threat" seriously when he was cradling Ace against his chest, his hands covering the pupcub's tiny body as he rubbed his jaw gently against Ace's face. Ace's hand opened then fisted against Hawke's chest, though his eyes stayed closed.

At the other end of the bed, Micah was yawning in Sascha's arms while Sienna gently brushed the dark auburn hair on his head. All the children had that dark shade that would probably become a deep brown with auburn highlights as they grew.

A blend of their parents.

It made Riley smile just as he caught the first hint of animated voices arrowing in their direction.

His and Mercy's siblings, as well as Mercy's parents, tumbled inside minutes later, all joy and excitement and love. So much love. Their children would never lack for either playmates or care. And when they came home, they'd do so to parents who adored one another and their babies.

Mercy looked up right then, her eyes shimmering with emotion. "I love you, Riley."

"Ditto, kitty cat," he whispered, stealing a kiss while their babies held court, and for the first time in known history, wolf and leopard adults mingled with newborns in their arms, no protective aggression in either party.

Family, Riley thought, SnowDancer and DarkRiver had been becoming family for a long time. Belle, Micah, and Ace had added the final seal on that bond.

BASTIEN bared his teeth at his brother, Sage, when Sage dared try to take Micah from him after Bastien had just claimed his nephew from Drew. Sage pushed in anyway, putting a friendly arm around the waist of Bastien's mate, Kirby, as he pressed up against her back and peered over her head at the baby in Bastien's arms.

"Hey, peanut," he said, touching a finger to the sleeping baby's nose.

That nose wrinkled up but the baby slept on.

"Bastien, I want to hold him." Kirby held out her arms on that whisper, and he put Micah into her gentle embrace.

Face lighting up, she cuddled the baby close. "Hey, you." A gentle kiss to one velvet-soft cheek . . . and the baby made a tiny sound that could've been a happy growl.

"Did you hear that?" Bright lynx eyes, Kirby's cat as curious about this new packmate as the human side of her. "He likes me."

"Of course he likes you. He knows family." Bastien's heart was a huge thing inside his chest. "Look after them both," he ordered his brother before going to find Mercy.

His sister was still sitting in bed, more because so many people were piled on it, talking and laughing, than because she looked in any way weak. Bulling his way through the crowd, he scooped her up in his arms to her laughing admonitions and smacked a kiss to her cheek. "You did good, Carrot."

"Grr." Claws dug into his shoulders but she kissed him back. "It hurt like a bitch." A thoughtful pause. "I think men should have to give birth, too."

Bastien winced. "Yeah, no." Kissing her again, he put her back on the bed before her mate decided he was manhandling her too roughly and came after him—Bastien was confident of his own skills, but he wasn't about to go up against a new dad who happened to be a SnowDancer lieutenant known as The Wall for his hardheaded stubbornness and refusal to surrender.

He caught Lucas's eye as he was weaving his way out of the room, shook his head. He hadn't yet zeroed in on the individual who'd paid the captain of the ship meant to be Naya's prison. But he was close, so close he could almost smell it, almost reach out and grab that person by the throat, claws extended to bloody damage.

Lucas nodded, the alpha's expression stating he had trust in Bastien's abilities.

Leopard padding inside his skin, Bastien returned to Kirby to find

Sage cradling the baby under Kirby's own hold. It meant his brother was pretty much cuddling Bastien's very cuddleable mate.

Bastien shook his head. "You can't steal either one of them, Herb."

Sage managed to give him the finger while continuing to smile at the baby. Kirby, meanwhile, turned very carefully in Sage's hold and handed the baby to him. "Support his head," she instructed, as Bastien's brother took Micah with utmost care.

"Hey, kid." Sage's grin split his face. "I'm your uncle Sage. Your *favorite* uncle."

As Sage wandered off to Grey, who'd just claimed Belle from her aunt Brenna, Bastien wrapped his arms around Kirby from behind. "Cute, huh?"

"Gorgeous," Kirby agreed. "I want one."

Bastien chuckled. "Let's get you used to shifting first." Kirby was still settling into her skin as a lynx; she was also spending time with the family she'd never had a chance to know as a child—and she was becoming an integral part of his. The latter wasn't much of a choice. The Smiths and DarkRiver had embraced her as one of their own; Kirby fit like a missing piece.

The cubs, especially, loved playing with Kirby. She was an adult, but her lynx form made her smaller than adult leopards, and so to the cubs, she seemed a perfect-sized playmate. The fact that she happened to be a kindergarten teacher and had the patience to both play with and handle spirited cubs made her even more of a favorite.

Now she laughed. "You might possibly be right—plus, I think we'll be babysitting the pupcubs often."

"Hopefully after they're a little bigger. I'm kinda freaked out by their tininess," he admitted in a subvocal whisper. "So fragile."

Kirby patted one of his hands. "You'll be fine. You have the gentlest hands." Lifting one of those hands, she pressed a row of kisses to his fingertips.

And there went his heart going boom all over again.

Letters to Nina

From the private diaries of Father Xavier Perez
June 23, 2082

Nina,

I am in the mountains near—

XAVIER lifted his hand from the page and stared out over the mountains of his homeland. The sounds of children's voices rose up from the village below, where the little ones learned under a woven canopy held up by six poles pushed into the earth. The weave was treated to be waterproof, and on the ground was a thick rug on which about half the children sat and recited their mathematical tables.

At the back were the older children. Instead of facing the teacher, they sat in small groups, their heads bent together as they worked on a project. This far into the mountains, there were no separate classrooms. The children all had large-size organizers developed especially for such usage, plus access to a remote teacher for different subjects.

However, as well as eating lunch together, they gathered together for an hour at the start of the day and an hour at the end to learn communally and to discuss their learning across age groups. It wasn't only humans who sat under the canopy—several changeling children attended lessons in this village, since their pack had too few children to justify a separate classroom.

It gave Xavier's heart solace to see their happy faces, their bright smiles, their innocent friendships.

But his own smile was long lost, for he'd finally reached his destination . . . only to discover that Nina wasn't here. Judd and Kaleb hadn't been wrong—a woman who could well be his Nina had been in this village less than a month earlier. She'd been standing in for the village medic who'd gone away for training, had moved on to her next post once the medic returned.

He swallowed, looked down at the letter he was writing, started again.

> *In my fantasies, I used to imagine that perhaps you'd lost your memories and that was why you hadn't searched for me, but if this is you, then you remember your training, you remember being a nurse. You've chosen to stay here, far from me. You've chosen to change your name so I won't find you.*
>
> *My heart breaks at the thought of it but I won't turn back now. I must know if it's you and if there is any hope of begging your forgiveness. The villagers tell me you don't have a lover that they know of—they are loyal to you, but an elder here recognized me as the man of God who had helped a friend in another village once. She was willing to trust me.*
>
> *I must believe her. For the idea that you now belong to another—*

Xavier's hand shook.

Leaning his head back against the tree trunk, he blinked away the heat in his eyes, then put away the notebook and his pen. It took but a moment to pull on his backpack. Seconds later he was heading away from this village and toward where the elder had told him the woman named Ani had gone.

TWO days of trekking through the mountains and Xavier was a bare fifteen minutes from his new destination. Instead of carrying on, he forced himself to stop by a small waterfall. If this was to be his last meeting with Nina, he'd show her his best self. Stripping, he took out the biodegradable soap in his pack—thanks to a small care package that had been gifted to him by Judd's mate—and washed himself.

Drying off afterward, he pulled on underwear and a pair of khaki-colored cargo pants before using his phone camera as a mirror while he scraped off the ink-black beard that had grown in during his journey.

Nina had always liked him clean-shaven, though she didn't mind stubble.

Especially when they kissed.

Gripping the memory of her touch, her kiss, in a tight fist, he finished shaving, then splashed on aftershave from the same care pack. His hair, tightly curled as it was, needed no brushing. Reaching to the bottom of his pack, he pulled out a pristine white T-shirt, shrugged into it. The color was stark against the teak shade of his skin, the fabric a little stiff because it was so new. Beneath it lay a necklace he'd worn for years.

Socks and boots on, and he was as ready as he'd ever be.

His pack felt heavier this time, but perhaps that was his heart weighing him down. No matter. He had to go forward, had to know.

Stepping back onto the path, he made his way to the village.

Children saw him first; they always did. Pelting away at light speed on bare feet, they called out to their parents and other elders in a language that wasn't identical to his native tongue but that was close enough for him to understand.

Making his way to the edge of the village, he waited with screaming patience until an elder, his brown-skinned face gnarled with life, came to him, asked him his business.

"I've come to see Ani," he said.

The elder's wary welcome turned into a scowl. "Who are you to look for our Ani?"

"I've been searching for my Nina for many years," he said softly. "Since the day the Psy destroyed our village. My friends tell me Ani is Nina."

A snort. "If she is? She's changed her name. Seems to me she wants to escape you."

A dagger to the heart, those words made him stagger within. "Yes," he accepted even as he bled. "But I need to hear that from her." He met the elder's dark eyes. "You have no need to fear me. All I want is a moment with her."

Then he heard it: Nina's laughter.

Head jerking up, he dropped his pack and walked past the elder without looking back. He was conscious of further scowls and grumbling around him, conscious of people following, but he didn't care. He had to see her, had to beg her forgiveness.

Then there she was, dressed in a simple dress of pale yellow that swirled around her calves as she spun and spun with her hands locked to those of a child of about seven or eight. Other children danced around them, laughing and calling out for their turn.

"Ani! Ani! Me! I want to have a go!"

His heart, it was a massive drum whose beat thundered in his ears. He would've gone to his knees except that he wanted to see Nina's eyes . . . and then the spin stopped and she turned laughingly toward him . . . and there was no recognition in her eyes.

She looked straight through him.

Xavier's breath turned into jagged shards in his lungs before his mind caught up with his heart. Regardless of how angry she was with him, Nina would never be able to coldly ignore him. They'd been too much to each other for such distance.

Yet though her face was turned toward him, she didn't meet his eyes. Then he knew.

Walking toward her, he watched her head angle a little to the left, her awareness of his approach clear. "It's Xavier," he said when he was only a foot away from her.

Her lips parted in a whisper. "Xavier . . ." A hand rose, trembling.

He bent so she could touch her fingers to his face, so she could trace the lines of him. His beautiful Nina with her dark, dark eyes that were so much paler now, the hue watery blue. The color of someone undergoing regeneration after catastrophic damage to the eyes.

It took up to a year for the regeneration to work, and if Nina had been hurt during her jump into the water and remained up in the mountains all this time, the delay was understandable—regeneration was highly specialized and came with the attendant cost. Nina would've had to qualify for a grant or be given the treatment by a sympathetic clinic. Even then, if an attempt failed, she'd have had to wait the mandatory three years before a second attempt.

Today, those sightless eyes seemed to meet his as she shaped her fingers over his face. A tear rolled down her cheek. "Xavier," she whispered again. *"Xavier."*

He took her into his arms even though he knew he should wait, should be sure she wanted him to do so. But he couldn't stand by while Nina cried. "Shh," he whispered, the sound rough because his own throat was thick, his eyes hot. "Hush, my love." He spoke in their shared dialect, a dialect that had only been spoken in a village long destroyed. "Nina, please don't cry."

But she continued to sob and then he realized he was crying, too, and they were holding on bruisingly tight to one another. He was vaguely aware of children being drawn away, of the adults leaving, until he was alone with his Nina and she wasn't pushing him away but holding him close.

". . . you were dead," she said in a shaky voice. "They told me you were dead." Again and again, she repeated that.

Stroking his hand over her mass of curling black hair, he kissed her temple, her cheek, the taste of hot salt in his mouth. "I searched," he said. "I searched for so long. Where were you?"

Their words merged together until they weren't words any longer. They'd been apart too long to do anything but hold on to each other, rocking. The world was quiet around them, the villagers' voices some distance away, when he and Nina were finally able to breathe enough for more words.

Pressing a kiss to her hair, he reached down for her hand, her bones slender and her skin a lusher brown than his. "Walk with me?"

Her fingers wove into his in a silent answer, and the two of them walked into the verdant greenery around the village, until they were private, alone. Then, his hands cupping her face, Xavier admitted his guilt. "I should've never made you jump."

Her hands found his face again, held him with sweet tenderness. "Then I would be dead." Her voice was raw from her tears but resolute. "*Everyone* died. That's what they said."

"Who?"

"All the people I asked, and I asked so many." Jagged rasps of breath. "The water was so fast, so hard. It swept me far from our village and at some point, I hit my head and I can't remember what happened next—I know I was taken in by other villagers, but they didn't find me until four days after the attack."

Her hands kept touching him, as his kept touching her. "My rescuers took me to an off-the-grid local clinic and the doctor there did what he could, but I was in bad shape, barely coherent for over two months."

"Why didn't they take you to a bigger hospital?" Even as he asked the question, Xavier knew the answer—the Psy had been doing fatal damage throughout the region at that time, until the people who called these mountains home no longer trusted the cities or the big hospitals staffed by Psy.

Nina said the same, then added, "Even after those two months, I wasn't quite right. I had broken bones and other injuries that were still healing, but my head was the worst. I couldn't hold on to thoughts, on to memories." She trembled. "For a while I thought I'd never find myself, always be lost, but it came back over the next eight months."

She slid her arms around him once more. Locking his own around her, he said, "You began to ask questions the instant you were yourself again," he said, knowing his Nina. "And people told you everyone had died."

A jerky nod. "I didn't believe them. I went back home but there was no village there, nothing but an empty landscape cleared of all signs of our families, our friends."

"The Psy did that," he told her. "The same Psy whose soldiers murdered everyone we knew." It was important to him to differentiate the one from the group; the years since the attack had taught him that the Psy race wasn't one big entity but millions of separate individuals.

Just like him. Just like his Nina.

She thumped fisted hands against his chest. "Why didn't you leave me any signs? Why didn't you tell people you were alive?"

He wanted to shield her, couldn't. "I took a telepathic hit," he said and felt her flinch. "When I came to, everyone was dead and I knew the Psy would be back to clean up." He swallowed. "I couldn't bury anyone, or it would've alerted them to possible survivors. God forgive me for that choice."

"You could've never buried so many, Xavier," Nina said softly. "God knows your heart."

Holding on tight to her words, he said, "I haunted the mountains searching for you and eventually joined up with a small group of rebels who'd made it their life's work to sabotage or destroy all Psy operations in the area." Those men and women had been driven by the same need for vengeance that had kept Xavier alive at the start, even through the worst despair.

"I stayed nearby for three months, but my work with the rebels eventually took me some distance away in the opposite direction to this village." Unknowingly separating him from his heart. "When I was shot in an operation, they doctored me until I could take care of my own wounds, then left me in a cave with enough supplies to see me through." Injured as he was, the rebels had considered him dead weight.

"I couldn't move more than a few meters for over a month." He'd tried to crawl to his devastated village at one point, wanting to die on home ground, only to be forced to turn back after he came dangerously close to unconsciousness. No one in his condition could survive a night in the cold of the mountains without some kind of shelter.

Even knowing he'd never have made it, Xavier wanted to tell his younger self to keep crawling, to find his way back to the village and to Nina. "By the time I returned, the nearby villages had been long deserted and people farther out knew nothing."

His shoulder muscles knotted, his fist clenching in her hair. "I asked over and over." Yet the mountains were big, and back then the people who called it home often moved because of fear or need or environmental factors, a multitude of reasons. It wasn't improbable that Nina hadn't spoken to any of those same people when she came to look for him. Especially since she'd returned long after him.

"Why do they call you Ani?" he asked, his heart in a painful vise.

"It's what my rescuers named me at the time when I wasn't myself . . . and after . . . when I thought everyone was dead, that you were dead, I didn't want to be Nina again."

A heartbreaking answer that betrayed the depth of her pain.

"I searched for you," he said, needing her to know, to believe. "I've been true, loved no other." Falling to his knees as her tears began to flow again, he dared say the words he'd held inside for so long. "Say you'll forgive me, Nina."

"Xavier." Going to her knees in front of him, she shook her head and his heart sank, his world narrowing to only her face and to this instant that might forever break him.

"There is no need for forgiveness."

He took a harsh breath, another.

"I know you did what you did out of love." Her kiss was a benediction. "I love you, Xavier. I've listened for your voice even after the world convinced me you were dead." Her fingers shaped his lips. "I've loved no one but you."

Shaking, he was the one who fell into her embrace this time. She held him with love in every breath. "My Xavier."

"THE regeneration might not work," she said to him a long time later, as she sat cradled against his chest while he leaned his back up against a sturdy tree with dark green leaves. "This is the second and final attempt."

He was happy to hear no worry in her tone that he'd feel differently about her. She knew he loved *her*, regardless of her physical appearance or health. "You're revered as a nurse."

"I have an apprentice who acts as my eyes, and together, we manage."

She was more than managing, he thought, considering the fidelity she'd engendered in people used to being loyal only to those they'd known all their lives. "I have connections now, Nina. I can get you to better doctors if you want."

"I've learned to live how I am, even thrive, but I could do my work better with both eyes or at least some vision." Her fingers grazed his jaw. "I'm selfish, too. I want to see you again."

Joy was a sweet pain through his veins. "Then we'll find the best specialists." He knew Judd and Kaleb would both help him without question; family, he'd learned, had many different faces. His now included two Psy with deadly abilities.

"There are others here," Nina said. "So many people still isolated, disbelieving of the changes within the Psy and unwilling to return to the lives they abandoned in order to survive. Many need proof they won't be murdered should they return to their lands. Others need medical help, access to wider education—"

"I'm with you." Xavier had fought beside his friends for years. Now it was his time to walk beside Nina. He'd said good-bye to his parishioners at the outset of this journey, wanting to go into it with his whole heart and soul. But he hadn't abandoned them. Never would he do that to people who had given him as much succor as he had them.

He'd left them in the gentle, capable hands of a young woman of God who was ready for her own congregation. She had strength enough to offer a shoulder to those in need and heart enough to open it to any soul that walked through the door.

He was at peace with his decision to leave San Francisco, could think of no better life than to live it beside Nina. "I'll call on every favor I have to help the people who kept you safe until I could find you again." Until he could hold her close again, his heart beating in time with her own.

"Will you ever ask me?" Nina chided an hour later. "Really, Xavier, you're taking the concept of becoming your own man first too far."

His smile was startled joy on his face, memories cascading through him of a young Nina rolling her dark eyes when he proudly told her he'd ask for her hand only when he could build her a home worthy of her spirit. "I think we've both waited long enough."

Reaching for his necklace, he tore it off to drop a ring formed of gold, and set with sapphires and diamonds, onto his palm. He'd bought it years earlier, after he came to San Francisco and found a steady position. Being a Second Reformation priest didn't pay much, but Xavier hadn't needed to spend much, either. He'd saved it all for Nina's ring. The stones were small but the delicate beauty of them perfectly fit her bone structure.

He reached from behind to lift her hand. "Will you marry me, Nina?"

"Today, if you arrange it," was her answer, her smile as radiant as the moon.

TWO days later, when Xavier called Judd to ask for assistance in getting specialist help for the woman who would soon be his wife, he got far more than he'd bargained for. Judd not only put him directly on the phone with the SnowDancer healer—who was then able to get Nina into treatment at the best facility in the world—the other man spoke to his alpha, and Xavier was suddenly in touch with the AzureSun Leopards.

The leopards' connection to SnowDancer came through the SnowDancer-DarkRiver pact, with the AzureSun alpha, Isabella, the grandmother of a DarkRiver sentinel. And, he was proudly told by said alpha, the namesake of one of three newborn members of DarkRiver.

"My great-grandchildren," the alpha had said, while appearing not the least like a great-grandmother.

Isabella Garcia was a powerful alpha who held the loyalty of her people, despite being in her eighth decade. Even Xavier hadn't realized changelings didn't always go for physical strength in an alpha. Wisdom was also treasured, with the sentinels acting as the alpha's physical arm.

While AzureSun's power base was in another part of South America, they had contacts in Xavier's region on whom he could call should he have the need. They also gave him permission to access certain resources that would help ease his and Nina's journey as they fought to undo the damage that had been done to the people of these mountains.

"My granddaughter's alpha, young cub though he is," Isabella had said, "has taught me the value of relationships beyond the pack, of treating neighbors like family."

It had taken Xavier a minute to realize the "young cub" was Lucas Hunter. One of the most visible and powerful men in the world, thanks not only to his pack's strength, but also because of who and what he represented in the Trinity Accord.

And Xavier was connected into that network.

All because of a friendship formed with a soldier he'd first seen in a nameless bar.

Then Kaleb called him, having been alerted by Judd, and Xavier had access to a teleport anytime he needed one to take Nina to the physicians. That wasn't the only thing.

"I have wealth no one could spend in a single lifetime or even ten lifetimes," the cardinal said. "I've created a charitable foundation with a significant endowment that you can use at will for your humanitarian work."

"Thank you, my friend." Xavier accepted the generosity without argument because he understood how big a step this was for Kaleb—this friend of Xavier's didn't trust easily, much less allow people into his life.

For him to offer such a gift was a precious thing. "Is your Sahara well?"

"Yes." Kaleb's tone didn't soften as another man's might have when he spoke of his lover, but Xavier understood this friend of his, knew Sahara Kyriakus was his heart.

"And your Nina?" Kaleb asked.

Xavier smiled. "Yes."

LATER, as he walked under a carpet of stars with Nina, their hands linked and her warm, earthy scent so sweetly familiar, he said, "I wrote you letters."

Soft laughter. "Finally." Her teasing made him feel young, wild, free. "I'll read them all once I can see."

He couldn't help but clasp her hand tighter. "I'd like to read you some now." Before they wed, before it was too late for Nina to back away. "I want you to know what I've done . . . who I've become."

Gentle reproof in her expression. "My love for you will never fade."

Xavier had no doubts of the truth of her vow, but he still needed her to understand how much he'd altered from the laughing young man she'd known, didn't want to steal her with false promises. So he read out the letters that spoke of battle, of violence, of his friendship with Judd and Kaleb.

"I'd like to meet your friends." Nina's hand remained firm in his. "We've both been marked by life, Xavier, but we haven't changed where it matters." She lifted their clasped hands to his heart, then to hers.

Yes.

They continued to walk together, content to simply be with each other. He spoke at times, Nina at others. At one point, he said, "I once told one of my friends that love is the greatest form of loyalty. But I think from loyalty can come love."

"Of course." Turning into him, she laid her head against his chest.

Listening to his heartbeat, as he so often found himself simply watching her breathe.

"So many bonds," he murmured as the two of them stood under a night sky that reminded him of Kaleb's cardinal eyes. "So many connections. Our world is becoming the interlinked entity it was always meant to be."

The majority of those connections were fragile, breakable, or barely budded, but a rare few had passed the Rubicon, would endure. Such as the bonds that linked him to Judd and to Kaleb, the bonds that linked Judd to his mate and his pack, the bond that linked Kaleb to Sahara, and through her, to another pack.

Such was the bond that tied Xavier to his Nina, and through her, to all the villagers she knew. In return, he could link her to so many others. Together their family spanned continents . . . and it existed right here in this moment when he held Nina.

PART 8

Chapter 51

BO WAS UNSURPRISED when he received a visit from Malachai Rhys as the sun was setting over Venice in a splashy display. What he was surprised about was the public nature of it. "I had the feeling you wanted to keep the Alliance-BlackSea relationship on the down low," he said as he held out his hand.

Malachai shook it after stepping out of the water taxi that had ferried him from the mainland. Then he removed his mirrored sunglasses in what seemed a conscious act. Realizing it was, that to see the eyes was to know the man, Bo removed his own and tucked them into the pocket of the short-sleeved shirt of chocolate brown detailed with bronze studs that he wore over jeans.

"We've had a change of heart." Malachai slid his hands into his pockets on those words, a big man in a flawlessly tailored black suit teamed with a crisp white shirt. "Some people only believe in power they can see."

Humans knew that better than any other race on the planet. "It certainly does us no harm to be linked to BlackSea." Bo wasn't about to turn down a potential ally when the world remained a turbulent place—and when the Consortium had only gone quiet. Everyone who knew of the group also knew the vipers would rise again, that they were probably plotting their next move at this very instant.

Then there were the smaller fanatical groups, and they weren't all Psy.

"You've suffered no blowback as a result of rescuing Leila?" the Black-Sea security chief asked as they began to walk along the edge of the canal.

"Isaac can take care of himself." Though Bo had offered him Alliance assistance should he need it. "Whoever kidnapped your packmate—" He paused. "Is that the right word?"

Malachai gave him a sidelong glance that was at once penetrating and quiet. "We've adapted to use the common terms."

Bo read the subtext: to be too different made it difficult to be part of the world.

"Like I was saying," he continued, "whoever kidnapped your packmate would do better to just let it go. No point hunting Isaac and his friends and giving us more clues to follow."

"I agree." The other man said nothing further until they'd passed a group of tourists taking pictures of a balcony that was a delicacy of froth and curves. "What's your price for assisting Leila? It was a far bigger favor than the one we did you."

Bowen had considered leveraging the rescue. Despite the projected degradation of his implant, he'd so far felt no ill effects. His mind was as sharp as ever, and it constantly sought angles to bring more power to the Alliance. Humans had been forgotten and crushed into the earth for far too long. It was Lily who'd talked him out of any mercenary demands.

"Some things we do," she'd said, "define our very humanity. Lose that and we may as well be Psy under Silence."

Her words had cut through the increasingly ruthless nature of Bo's thinking processes. He didn't want to save his people by turning them into the very race that had for so long been their enemy. Oh, the war had never been obvious, but Psy had raped human minds for centuries, stealing their ideas, stealing their will.

Gritting his jaw against the fury of his emotions, he didn't speak until he could temper his tone. "We don't want anything." An alliance, a true alliance, couldn't be bought or demanded. "I spoke to Isaac since he's out of pocket after delaying his delivery to take Leila to the ocean, but he says it was worth it to get her home."

Malachai paused on the edge of a quiet canal, the two of them standing side by side. "Somehow I doubt the security chief of the Human Alliance has such a magnanimous heart."

Bo folded his arms. "He doesn't, but he also doesn't do deals using the lives of innocents as collateral." His hair, which had grown out from the no-fuss-no-muss shave he'd sported for so long, was cool under his fingers as he thrust them through the wavy strands. "If you need to put a name on it, consider it a sign of friendship on our part."

When Malachai turned to look at Bowen, his brown eyes appeared lighter, closer to a pale gold, as if something else lived beyond. And from the unblinking way Malachai watched him, his expression so indefinably *other*, that something truly did not think like a human in any way, shape, or form.

The hairs rose at his nape.

Bo, like most terrestrial beings, often wondered at the makeup of the water changelings. Dolphins were a known form, sharks were rumored, large water snakes confirmed and whales whispered about, but other than that, no one really knew for certain.

One of Bo's friends, a lifelong sailor who'd circumnavigated the globe more than once, swore up and down that he'd been rescued by an "honest to God" mermaid after he fell overboard during a massive storm. Get him drunk and he'd tell you that her eyes had been glowing blue, her skin luminous white, and her hair like a million streamers of light. He'd admit he hadn't seen her legs, but she "swam as if she had a great big tail and I *definitely* saw her gills!"

Bo wasn't sure he believed the other man, but there was no question that something had saved his life. His crewmates verified he'd fallen overboard and disappeared from view before they could throw out a life preserver. They'd got the shock of their lives when he clambered back onboard—especially since by then, the storm had carried them over fifty nautical miles from where he'd fallen overboard.

Clearly, the ocean kept many secrets.

Malachai . . . No, Bo couldn't figure him out, but one thing was for certain: he couldn't be a small creature. Changeling shifting physics might be weird, with mass never equal from one form to the other—or that was how it appeared to Bo's eyes—but Malachai had an innate sense of bigness about him.

Bo simply couldn't visualize him as a small creature. Like a turtle.

"Are there changeling turtles?" he asked on a whim.

The security chief's lips curved up at the edges. "Do you know one of the oldest creatures on earth is a tortoise?" he asked, instead of answering Bo's question. "Two hundred years at last count. If a changeling were that, do you think he or she might live hundreds of years?"

Bo blew out a breath at the idea of it. "To see all those centuries pass, all the upheaval and change . . ."

"An incredible thought, isn't it? But maybe a being so old wouldn't care that much about the world, would be happy living on a distant island far from Psy, humans, and changelings alike."

Hard as he tried to read the other man, Bo couldn't work out if Malachai was making idle conversation or actually giving him an answer. "I figure someone that old, they wouldn't be like you or me anymore," he said at last. "I don't mean that in a pejorative sense. I guess I'd see such a being as having changed into something other, a new entity with which we'd no longer have much in common."

Again, Malachai looked at him with those eyes that weren't quite right, the color having faded even further. "An interesting idea for a security chief. Profoundly philosophical."

Bo shrugged. "I can even read without moving my lips."

The BlackSea male's chuckle was deep. "So can I. Though it's difficult when the sea is turbulent." Amusement alive on his face, he said, "How about a drink?"

"I know a place."

They fell into step again as Bo led Malachai to Bo's favorite hole-in-the-wall bar. They didn't speak about politics or alliances or whether Malachai had been messing with his head with that talk of two-hundred-year-old changeling tortoises, but the fact that the BlackSea security chief was having a beer with the Human Alliance security chief was notable in itself.

And it *was* noted by those who knew what and who Malachai was.

Some saw it as a sign of Trinity's success. Others saw it as a possible problem. Still others saw it and decided that any pact or union between the two groups could *not* be permitted to succeed. Humans and water changelings covered every part of the planet. Should they unite, they could become an unstoppable power.

But no one did anything on that hazy Venetian day as the sun dropped into the ocean and the stars started to glitter.

That day, two dangerous men sat, had a beer, and discussed the latest football scores.

THE next day on the other side of the world, in a valley drenched in sunshine, the most lethal Psy men and women in the world came together with their young. Aden hadn't been sure the event would work, that his people would understand what it was to celebrate, but he'd forgotten to factor in a new data point.

Arrow children had been playing and meeting with their changeling and human friends for some time now, had picked up far more than Aden realized. All the adults had to do was mention an upcoming celebration and they'd gone into creative mode, making decorations to hang around the central gathering area and suggesting suitable foods.

A few had shyly asked if they could have colorful new clothes.

The event was undoubtedly far more structured than a comparative gathering of humans or changelings, but . . . "I sense no discomfort," Aden said to Zaira. "People are glad to be here, to acknowledge those of us who have bonded."

His commander nodded, her curls blue-black in the sunshine. "To see us gives others hope." With that, she turned and hauled down his head for a kiss intimate and possessive and as full of wildfire as Zaira.

His head was still spinning when they broke apart, and though he knew others watched, he was interested only in the woman who was his. "An attempt to engender even more hope?"

"Arrows are practical." She ran possessive hands over his shoulders. "It's good for them to see what lies ahead if they take a chance and step outside the cold black box of Silence."

Aden was about to answer when he noticed something. "Look at the picnic table to the left."

Carolina, long green ribbons in her pale blonde hair, was trying to pick up a cupcake that kept disappearing out from under her fingers, only to reappear on another part of the table. Her cheeks got hot red, her eyes narrowed, her breath puffing out as she tried to beat the switch. Finally, the infuriated six-year-old spun around and, scowling, ran straight to where an innocent-faced Tavish sat on the grass with a friend.

As Aden watched, she snatched the cupcake from his plate and took a big bite.

"Hey!" Tavish cried.

Chewing the bite and swallowing, Carolina said, "I know it was you!" She defiantly stuffed the rest of the cupcake into her mouth, then hands on her hips, glared at him while her cheeks puffed up like a chipmunk's.

Tavish started to protest his innocence but only lasted half a minute before he collapsed into laughter with his friend. "It was so funny!"

Having swallowed the cupcake by now, Carolina glared at the two boys for another minute before the first giggle escaped her.

Zaira's lips curved. "Tavish is right, it was funny." Reaching up to push back a lock of Aden's hair that had fallen on his forehead, she said, "Psychically gifted children are going to find unique ways of getting into trouble." In her expression, he read memories of how she'd been beaten and caged, her telepathic strength seen not as a gift but as a tool to be broken to her parents' use.

Shaking his head against the rise of his own rage, he cupped her cheek. "We'll never harm them." It was a reiteration of a promise he'd made the day the squad became his, and he could set the rules. "Each and every Arrow child will grow up in freedom."

Zaira's hand closed over his. "Freedom."

It was all that needed to be said.

PART 9

Chapter 52

LUCAS WAS PLAYING outside with his cub the afternoon of the joint celebration when Sascha called down to say he had an urgent call from Bastien. Shifting back into human form, he caught the phone she dropped down—along with his jeans—then kept an eye on Naya while Sascha climbed the rope ladder to the ground.

"Come on, Naya," she said with a loving smile, her voice drenched with the happiness she found in being with their child. "You get to teach your mama how to stalk like a cat."

Excited, Naya began to pace deliberately, showing Sascha what Lucas had been showing her. She was gorgeous and so was his mate, but Lucas knew Bas wouldn't have interrupted him during his rare time off unless it was important, so he moved a short distance away to take the call. "Bas, what is it?"

"I've found the end of the money trail," the other man said. "To the captain who was going to take Naya to Australia. You know that. Shit. I'm punch-drunk from the success and slightly sleep-deprived."

Lucas's panther had gone hunting-still inside him at Bastien's first words. "Who?" he asked quietly.

"Psy named Pax Marshall."

The fingers of Lucas's free hand curled into his palm. "You're dead certain?"

"Without a shadow of a doubt. Money came from what looks like a personal slush fund used for various off-the-books activities."

Lucas consciously stopped himself from growling, held his claws in. He had to think with crystal clarity right now, couldn't be blinded by the primal instincts of his panther. "Could anyone else have accessed that account?"

"Sure, but they'd need to know every single one of Pax's passwords. I couldn't get into the account itself, that's how secure it is, but the trail definitely dead-ends there."

"Send your report through to me." He knew Bastien would've been adding to that report as he went, setting out the complicated financial maze in a way Lucas could easily process.

"Give me one second. And . . . done."

"Thanks, Bas. Now get some rest before the party or your mate will have my head."

Chuckling, Mercy's brother signed off. Lucas stood in silence for a minute, thinking through Bastien's information. Then he thought of everything he knew about Pax Marshall and made another call, asking Aden a single question when the leader of the Arrows answered. "Has Pax Marshall ever been categorically fingered for even one of his rumored illicit activities? Any proof at all?"

"No," Aden answered without asking why Lucas wanted to know. "That's part of why he's considered so brilliant. Everyone knows he's crossed lines, but no one can prove it. Not even the squad."

"Thank you, Aden." Hanging up, he put away his phone and went to join his mate and child. It was only after Naya curled up for a nap in the sun that he told Sascha what Bastien had discovered *and* what Aden had said.

His mate's gaze was intent. "You think it's too easy?"

"But that's just it—it *wasn't* easy. It was brutally hard from Bastien's perspective, and he's a genius at this stuff." Lucas leaned back against the aerie tree, Sascha in front of him and Naya napping a few feet away. "When I say Bastien's a genius, I mean it. Other companies, including major Psy ones, have tried to poach him from us over and over."

Sascha chewed on her lower lip as her eyebrows drew together in thought. "If it took Bas days to track this transaction, then it was well hidden. So well hidden that most people would've never found it."

Another long pause. "On the flip side, if DarkRiver was *meant* to find it, then knowing Bas was on our side would've been a guarantee of eventual exposure." She blew out a breath. "And why would Pax pay the ship's captain directly when he's rerouted all other payments through patsies?"

"Exactly—but on the other hand, if he wanted control of Naya, he might not have wanted to involve anyone beyond a not-particularly-intelligent captain who could be disappeared with no one the wiser."

"Proof on both sides of the line."

"Yes." Lucas's panther didn't like that. It liked black and white, enemies and friends. It also wanted the threat to its cub eliminated once and for all.

He saw the same frustration on Sascha's face.

"If DarkRiver moves against Pax and it's not him," she said, "we'll have done someone's dirty work for them, removed a power who might be standing in their way."

"But if we don't move and he *was* behind the kidnapping attempt," Lucas said on a growl, "then he remains a deadly threat."

Thrusting her hands through her hair, Sascha spun away to stomp to a tree on the other side of the clearing below their aerie and back. "I wish I wasn't an E sometimes, that I didn't have a conscience! I'd go to Pax and torture him until he broke."

Lucas let Sascha blow off steam. His mate would never do any such thing, but he understood the raw edge to her emotions. He wanted to tear Pax Marshall apart right now, but the human side of his mind was still thinking. "Pax has also embraced Trinity," he said. "Eliminate him and suddenly, there's a power vacuum, a powerful family left anchorless. Major disruption in the Net and Psy turning away from changelings because of our violent tendencies." That's exactly how a DarkRiver attack would be spun.

Eyes starless, Sascha walked into the arms he'd opened and hugged him with passionate strength. He held her close, giving her the skin privileges she needed to find her center again, even as she stabilized him in turn.

He knew the answer long before he could trust himself to vocalize it. "We can't move." It was a bitter conclusion, but Lucas wasn't about to be played, not by Marshall or anyone else. "We watch him through every method available to us, including the deal he's doing with SnowDancer. The Arrows will help us, if only to protect Trinity, so we'll have eyes in the PsyNet."

"We can't tell Nikita." Sascha took a deep breath, exhaled, her eyes midnight-still when she looked up. "She'll kill him or insert a virus into his mind."

"Your mother is cold, calculated, rational," Lucas pointed out. "Killing Pax Marshall right now would be a mistake."

"Lucas, my mother is all those things, but she only has one response when Naya or I come under threat."

Lucas thought about it, nodded. "We don't tell Nikita."

Walking over to Naya's sleeping body, Sascha took a cross-legged seat on the forest floor and carefully transferred Naya into her lap. Their cub purred at her mother's touch but remained fast asleep, adorable little snores occasionally breaking up the sound of her steady breathing.

Watching the two of them was a forcible reminder to Lucas not to let the evil and darkness in the world taint the happiness he'd been given. He went to join them, sliding in to sit behind Sascha with his legs out on either side of her and his chin on her shoulder. If he kept turning to caress her neck with licks and kisses until she melted into him, well, he *was* a cat.

"I've got it," Sascha said suddenly, while he was kissing his way along her jaw. "The silver lining."

He bit her earlobe gently, tugged.

Shivering, she ran her hand along one of his thighs, her other hand on Naya's back.

"Trust an empath to find a silver lining." The joke was an old one between them. "Hit me with it."

"If this was a setup"—she angled her head to kiss his jaw—"then the work is done and the people behind the attempt have no more reason to come after Naya. And if it wasn't a setup and Pax Marshall tries again, we'll have eyes on him the entire time."

Lucas's growl was one of satisfaction. "Here's another silver lining—we have a lot of friends now, people we can trust to watch him for us, people who'll work with us to protect our children as we'll protect theirs." No more would they be isolated targets.

"That's a good silver lining," Sascha murmured just as Naya lifted her head on a feline yawn that had Lucas tugging playfully at his cub's ears.

Grumbling sleepily, she butted his hand until he scratched her behind those ears.

Her purr was that of a cat five times bigger.

Lucas's panther purred deep in his chest in response. "That's my girl."

Smile carved into her cheeks and Naya's tail wrapped around her wrist, Sascha lifted her free hand to his jaw. "Enough of Pax Marshall or the shadow behind a power play. They'll still be there tomorrow." It was an order. "Tonight is a time for pack and for family, whether of blood or of the heart."

Chapter 53

TEIJAN AND HIS people weren't used to walking so blatantly into a predator's territory. Yes, the Rats had a business agreement with Dark-River, and DarkRiver had stepped in more than once to save the lives of those who lived Below, while Teijan and his people had stayed and fought rather than run when war rained bullets on the city.

However, when it came down to it, Teijan's Rats simply did not and could not play at the power levels held by the leopards and wolves.

He was proud of his people and all they'd achieved, but he also understood that their lives would always be at the margins of normal society. Only in their world in the disused tunnels below San Francisco did they feel free to laugh, to live. But this, tonight . . .

"You sure about this?" Zane asked as they got off their jetcycles after parking the vehicles at the mandated spot in DarkRiver territory.

"No," Teijan said to his friend and second in command. "That's why everyone else is forty-five minutes behind us." If this invitation to a joint DarkRiver-SnowDancer event was a true gesture of alliance, friendship, and respect, then Teijan couldn't afford to reject it. If it was something else . . . then as alpha, he'd take the first blow.

His people knew not to come in any closer until and unless they heard from him.

"Well, at least Clay delivered the invite." Zane fixed the cuff of his tailored white shirt, which he wore over black pants and under a black jacket. "He's always been straight with us."

"Yes." That relationship was why Teijan was here.

"Teijan." As if summoned by the mention of his name, Clay walked out of the trees.

Unlike Teijan and Zane, the leopard sentinel wasn't wearing a suit, but his clothing was just as crisply formal—a collarless dark green shirt worn over black pants and glossy black boots. The only thing that didn't fit was the pink beaded bracelet around his wrist with his name spelled out in square white blocks.

But of course it did fit. Zane was currently rocking a temporary princess tattoo on the back of his left hand, complete with a glittering crown. Daughters had a way of getting their fathers to stand still for things they'd allow no one else.

"Just you two?" Clay asked after a quick scan.

Shaking the leopard's hand, Teijan said, "The others are following."

Clay's slight smile held no insult. "I'm your guide. Come on."

Fighting primal instincts that told him to get the fuck out of danger, Teijan followed. A number of his people had advised him against this, fought bitterly against his decision, but Teijan had been resolute. "If we hide and stagnate, we *will* eventually die," he'd said. "The last time we took a risk, we earned the official right to claim these tunnels, and we ended up in a business partnership that's brought the pack countless opportunities and given our youths the funds to study Above in specialties we could've never before afforded."

His words hadn't swayed the doubters, but they were in the vehicles following—because disagreement or not, Teijan's Rats were loyal. That most of them were technically human, the flotsam and jetsam of society, made no difference. Together with the three adult rat changelings and one child, those discarded and abandoned bits of humanity had become a powerful intelligence network that made Teijan proud each and every day—and that had given all his people back their own pride.

"Where's everyone else?" he asked Clay, because while he could hear faint sounds in the distance, there'd been no other vehicles where he and Zane had parked. No wonder Zane's eyes were darting around waiting for an ambush at any instant. Teijan's own vigilance was at fever pitch.

"That's the designated parking area for your pack," Clay said without missing a beat. "We had to spread around the projected number of incoming vehicles to protect the forest."

It all made sense, but Teijan couldn't silence the wary voice of caution . . . until a leopard cub pounced on him from a tree. Teijan caught the small body instinctively, for a child was a child. Even when that child growled at him, green-gold eyes glinting in challenge.

Catching Clay's amused look, Teijan bared his own teeth, let them elongate. And suddenly, the child was shifting in a shower of light.

Teijan heard Zane catch his breath, felt his own heart kick.

A small boy with dark blue eyes and tumbled black hair was staring wide-eyed at him heartbeats later. Lifting a finger, he touched one of Teijan's incisors. "I can't do that!" It was a disgruntled statement.

Teijan returned his teeth to their human state. "What can you do?"

The boy showed him claws and growled again. "See?"

"My claws aren't that big," Teijan said.

A satisfied grin before the child shifted back to leopard form and lunged at Clay. Grabbing the cub, Clay rubbed the boy's head. "Where's your twin troublemaker?"

The cub pressed his face affectionately against Clay's in answer before jumping to the forest floor. Padding in front of them—with glances back to ensure they were following—he led them to a space humming with people and redolent with food. Musicians were still setting up in one corner, but children ran this way and that and people had begun to gather and talk in small groups.

"You okay to guide in the rest of your people?" Clay asked. "I have to help finish putting up the lights—last-minute fix when the old set gave out."

"Yes." Teijan waited until Clay had walked away to glance at Zane.

His second in command's face was as close to tears as Teijan had ever seen it. "It's real," Zane said, voice husky. "Cats would've never permitted their children anywhere near an ambush."

Teijan knew why Zane was so overcome. Because he had a child. A daughter who might one day choose to—and be welcome to—live Above. A daughter who might even come to call the cub who'd met them not just a far more powerful ally, but also a friend.

Bringing out his phone, he made a call to his third in command. "Come," he said, his own chest tight. "It's safe. We are welcome."

Chapter 54

IT WASN'T UNTIL all their guests had arrived and Lucas and Hawke were standing in the center of the empathic training area about to officially open celebrations that Lucas realized he and Hawke hadn't discussed one crucial aspect of the event: which one of them would open it?

That might seem a specious detail to those who didn't understand changeling culture, but it wasn't. It had to do with dominance and with respect. If Lucas opened the celebration, it would be taken as an insult to their alpha by the wolves. If Hawke did it, the leopards would be pissed.

Wrecking the entire idea behind this event.

"Shit," Lucas muttered under his breath at the same time that Hawke said, "Fuck."

They glanced at one another. "Shall we try to time it so we both speak at the same instant?" Lucas asked in a subvocal murmur.

"You think we can pull it off?" Hawke scowled.

To anyone looking at the two of them, it would appear they were arguing. That was acceptable. Everyone knew he and Hawke weren't friends, even if their mates thought otherwise. "I don't know, but if we don't do something soon, we'll mess this up before it begins."

Hawke rubbed his clean-shaven jaw and went to say something when a voice rose up from the crowd that had gone silent around them. "I say you flip for it."

They turned as one to see that the speaker was Max Shannon.

Grinning, the ex-cop walked up to them and flipped a coin high in the air before catching it on the back of his hand, his other hand coming down over the top to obscure which side it had landed on. "Anyone disagree?"

Groans filtered out from the crowd, mingled with laughter.

The tension broke.

Max was a neutral party, his idea genius. No one could argue against chance.

Humans, Lucas suddenly thought, had been making peace among changelings for generations.

He looked at Hawke, caught the glint in the wolf's eye before Hawke said, "Heads."

"Tails then." Folding his arms, Lucas waited as Max stepped back and, with great ceremony, lifted his hand from atop the coin.

Lucas's snarl announced the results even before Max said, "Heads!"

There was cheering and booing in the audience but it was good-natured.

Clapping him on the back, Hawke said, "Next time, cat."

That quickly, Lucas realized they'd settled the issue for all future events that involved both packs. They'd switch off now that the pattern had been set. No issues of dominance or insult, just two powerful predators being careful to respect each other's space. "You better believe it." He moved to stand next to Hawke as the wolf officially opened festivities.

But Hawke had more to say, his words ones Lucas would've spoken, too, had he won the toss. They'd talked about this, come to an agreement. "You're here because we consider you family." His eyes scanned the audience before he glanced at Lucas.

"Each and every one," Lucas said, because these words needed to be spoken by both of them. "We expect you to treat each other as family, too." He wondered what Kaleb Krychek would think about that, but the cardinal Tk was now deeply connected to DarkRiver whether he liked it or not.

"As for the guests of honor . . ." Hawke and Lucas stepped aside to reveal Mercy and Riley behind them, their arms full of tiny wrapped bundles.

Who started squalling in red-faced fury right on cue.

Laughter rippled through the clearing and suddenly everyone was moving, talking. A special area had been set aside and prepared for the babies and toddlers to play and tumble in without worry, while Ben, Sakura, Keenan, Noor, Roman, and Julian led the charge in the under-ten department, racing off to play some game that involved climbing trees. A little girl of maybe seven or eight who was with the Rats watched big-eyed after them, but stuck to her family.

Then Julian turned back and came over to her.

She remained hesitant until her father and Teijan both said something that made her smile and bare teeth that turned sharp and pointed as Lucas watched. Julian showed her his claws in response and suddenly, both children laughed before running off to join the others.

The slightly older children, including Marlee, were soon gathering to chatter among themselves.

When it came to the leopards and wolves, those at the end of their teen years and in their early twenties had pretty much made their peace at a New Year's event organized by three of their own, and they drifted into small groups to talk and to flirt.

The adults weren't all used to working together, but they were being shown the way by the ones who were and conversations soon began to flow naturally.

It was the preteens and younger teenagers who remained in their own pack clusters. Not unexpected since kids that age tended to be awkward anyway. It would take them time to adapt, but Lucas could see them watching the older teens interacting, knew they'd grow up seeing such interactions as normal.

Right then, he glimpsed Jon slouch in his teenage-boy way to the food table groaning with dishes brought in by cats and wolves, their other guests asked to simply bring themselves. So of course they'd all brought gifts, not just for the pupcubs, but others that could be shared out among the children here tonight.

As Lucas watched, Jon reached for a sandwich half . . . right as two female wolf teens sidled over and beamed at him. Both were wearing dresses so short and skimpy that he was certain they'd sneaked those dresses out of the den by putting on something much more parentally acceptable over it.

Jon looked taken aback.

Abandoning his sandwich, he began to back away. The girls followed.

Shoulders shaking at the evidence that maybe it wouldn't take long for the younger teens to adapt after all, Lucas nudged Hawke's shoulder.

The wolf alpha was holding a pupcub but followed Lucas's gaze. "Oh, for Christ's sake," he muttered. "Yo, Heather and Dani!"

Spinning around to look at their alpha, the two girls gulped and scuttled over. Jon took off into the trees the instant they were no longer holding him captive. Meanwhile, Lucas tried to keep a straight face while Hawke disciplined the two girls. "I seem to remember you wearing clothes when you left the den."

"We are wearing clothes," one of the girls protested.

"*Oh?*"

The single word was enough to make them turn bright red and duck their heads as they twisted their hands together. Neither pack was prudish in the least, but adults and children both were expected to dress suitably for formal events. It was about discipline and respect—and in this case about being age-appropriate.

No one would've batted an eye had an eighteen-year-old worn one of these dresses to go clubbing. But barely thirteen-year-olds, if Lucas was guessing their ages right, at a family celebration? It was a wonder they'd stayed under the radar this long.

"And what did I tell you about stalking DarkRiver boys?" Hawke asked the two chastened wolves.

"That cats are shy and we should be nice."

Lucas almost choked, had to cover it with a fit of coughing. *Shy?* For cats? Hawke shot him a glare, as if to say, *What the hell did you come up with?* Lucas didn't admit he'd told DarkRiver kids that the wolves were far shyer than cats and they had to take care.

"But Jon isn't a cat," one of the girls pointed out, looking up through her eyelashes. "He's human."

"And he's soooooo pretty!" Her friend all but melted into the earth.

A single growl from Hawke and they froze, spines dead straight.

Holding their gazes, their alpha said, "Go change, then you're in charge of making sure Ben doesn't get into trouble."

Two faces fell, their looks of despair so comical that Hawke's lips twitched. "For an hour," he amended. "After that, I'm sure someone else will need to be punished." He reached out to hug the girls to him one-armed. "You can sashay all you want when you're a little more grown. Right now, you're still pups. Now go put on your proper clothes."

Feet dragging, the two disappeared off into the trees, where they'd no doubt stashed the clothes with which they'd fooled their parents. Hawke looked down at the pupcub in his arms as the child grumbled in her sleep before her expression turned beatific. "Yep, you're going to be trouble, too."

"Of course she is." Lucas tapped Belle on the nose. "We wouldn't have our cubs or pups any other way."

"No," Hawke said with a smile as the two girls he'd sent off returned in skirts and pretty tops. The pair went straight to Ben—who was currently hanging upside down from a tree branch while trying to stuff cake into his mouth. It appeared to be a competition, with Roman hanging in the same position beside him.

It was pack. It was life. It was family.

WALKER Lauren stepped onto the dance floor with his partner. Who beamed up at him, the lightest touch of pink lip gloss on her mouth. He wasn't ready for his baby girl to grow up, and at a few months past ten years of age, she wasn't quite there yet, but she was close enough that things that hadn't interested her at all a year earlier now intrigued and fascinated.

Such as lip gloss she'd told him tasted like strawberries.

"Come on, Daddy." Marlee held out her arms in perfect position for a slow dance.

Walker bit back a smile, because at this instant, she was his baby again, that small warm bundle he'd cradled and rocked in the darkness of the night when no one could see how much he loved her. In the PsyNet under Silence, such things had been forbidden, a father's love for his child verboten.

No more.

"Just a second." Reaching down, he picked up her much shorter form and, holding her easily with one arm around her waist, engulfed her raised hand with his other, their arms at a ninety-degree angle. "Place your free hand on my shoulder."

Marlee obeyed his quiet instruction, but her mind was on other matters. "Don't wrinkle my dress."

"I won't." That dress was one Marlee had bought on a shopping trip with Lara. A vibrant blue that brought out the light green shade of Marlee's eyes, it had a sparkling neckline studded with what Marlee called "jewels" and no sleeves. The skirt went to her ankles, with tulle underneath. It was the dress of a little girl turning into a big girl. Marlee adored it.

As Walker adored her.

Pressing a kiss to her forehead, he said, "Your hair looks beautiful."

An incandescent smile. "Lara did it!" Marlee lifted her hand off his shoulder to pat the updo into which Walker's healer mate had combed Marlee's strawberry blonde locks. "You really like it?"

"I love it." As a teacher and a father, Walker had always tried to encourage any child in his care, but it was only after leaving the PsyNet that he'd finally had the freedom to say such sweet words to his little girl.

And to the bigger girl who danced in her mate's arms not far away.

Sienna sparkled tonight, her ankle-length black dress made of some fabric that caught the light in a hundred different ways. Unlike Marlee's dress, Sienna's hugged her form, the long sleeves tight to her arms and the neckline jaggedly asymmetrical. The dark ruby red of her hair fell down her back, hiding it, but he'd seen the deep vee there.

"Uncle Walker," she'd said with a scowl when he'd warned her she'd get cold. Then she'd thrown her arms around him. "I love you, too."

That his dangerous niece could say that to him was a gift. That she *wanted* to say it to him was an even greater one. Sienna's eyes caught his right then as Hawke spun her out, and her cardinal gaze was full of delight. Hawke spun her back into his chest a second later. Landing with her hands flat on her mate's body, she tilted up her head just as the wolf alpha bent his.

Walker looked away from the kiss that said a thousand things without a word being spoken, and down into the glowing face of his daughter. One day, she, too, would have a mate to love, a mate who loved her in turn. When that time came, he'd let her go with his blessing to live a life extraordinary and beautiful and full of freedom, but until then, he'd watch over her.

Now, catching her wide-eyed interest in something Drew was doing to Indigo, he copied the move and dipped Marlee over his arm. She giggled in girlish delight, saying, "Again, Daddy!" when he lifted her up.

So he did it again.

Marlee was flushed and happy when the song ended.

"Come on Marlee-Barley, time to dance with me." Toby held out his hand.

Walker's nephew was in the awkward gangly phase, but he'd scrubbed up for today in black pants and a short-sleeved shirt in dark blue that had epaulets and visible stitching as detailing. His hair, as ruby red as Sienna's and as striking, was neatly brushed but already falling forward. It was his eyes that made Toby though—cardinal starlight, they held a sweetness it was rare to see in a boy his age.

Walker worried about Toby, but sweet as he was, his nephew seemed to be holding his own, even in the midst of a wolf pack. According to Lara, he seemed to have the same effect on his packmates as a fledgling healer, engendering trust and making people feel better with his simple presence.

Perhaps it was because Toby had an empathic gift or maybe it was simply that Toby had been born with a deep gentleness of spirit. He'd have been crushed into line under Silence, but here, he was free to grow into his personality.

Tonight, he took a delighted Marlee as his dance partner and they spun into a fast dance, both of them stamping their feet and moving their arms with the beat. When Ben, dressed in a tiny tuxedo Lara had pronounced "deathly adorable," ran over to join them, they laughed and made a space for his small body.

"What's my Benny going to do when Marlee matures before him?" Ava asked, having come to stand beside Walker at the edge of the temporary dance floor. Her glossy dark locks were streaked with metallic blue and glittering silver and swept up in a complicated braid. "It's already happening."

"He's tough. He'll handle it." Ben and Marlee had long been firm best friends despite the age difference between them, some indefinable aspect of each speaking to the other. However, like Ava, Walker could see that relationship altering shape in front of his eyes. Their interests were diverging, would take them in different directions in the coming years.

"But," Walker said as they watched their children dance, "whatever happens, I can't see them ever drifting totally apart." Their relationship was too strong, too rooted, and for all his childish antics, Ben was oddly astute. As if he saw people for exactly who they were.

A boy like that would grow up into an extraordinary man.

Ava sighed. "She's still going to break my poor boy's heart in a few years. No girl of fourteen is ever interested in a boy of ten."

Wrapping his arm gently around Ava's shoulders, Walker held her to his side with the affectionate skin privileges that had developed between them over the time Walker had been mated to Lara. The two women were best friends, Ava in and out of their home, as Lara was Ava's. Walker also liked Ava's mate, Spencer, a great deal and they often had dinner with the other couple, while Marlee loved spending time with both Ben and his baby sister, Elodie.

The toddler was currently laughing uproariously with Naya Hunter, both of them seated on an outdoor play mat.

Their baby laughter was making several nearby adults grin. Walker couldn't resist his smile, either. "I don't think a small thing like a broken heart would stop Ben from pursuing Marlee as soon as he's old enough," he said.

Ava chuckled. "You're right. My boy has stubborn determination down to an art." Rising on tiptoe, arm around his back, she tried to look out over the dancers. "Where's Lara?"

"Chatting with Tamsyn about the pupcubs."

Looking over to where the two healers stood, Walker saw them move apart after a quick hug. Lara turned to head toward him at the same instant that Ava said, "There's my sweetheart. I'm going to haul him into a dance before he gets too caught up in photographing the event."

Walker let Ava slip away and moved to meet his mate halfway. She'd tamed the corkscrew curls of her black hair into a fancy twist tonight and the red glints within shimmered when she passed under a cascade of tiny lights, but nothing shimmered as bright as her smile when she met his gaze. Her dress was ankle-length, the color a deep blood orange that looked exquisite against the natural dark tan of her skin.

It caressed her form as she moved, the simple lines of it graceful and elegant both.

"Are the children happy and busy?" she asked as she reached him.

"Yes." It hadn't always been easy for Walker to trust the bonds of pack, especially when it came to the children, but he was a true SnowDancer now, understood that in a healthy pack, a child need never look far for affection or assistance.

Biting down on her lower lip, Lara tugged on his hands. "Let's sneak away for a bit."

Walker had never played, not as a child, not as a young man. But he was mated to a wolf now, and to a wolf, play was as necessary a part of life as breathing. Releasing his mate's hands, he slid one of his around to lie against her lower back. "This way." His height made it easy for him to see through the mingled guests.

It still took them several minutes to navigate their way out, as pack-mates and friends wanted to say hello, but he finally got them to a spot in the shadow of a cabin. Far enough away from the party that they could speak in private, but close enough that they could still see the festivities. "Do you want to go into the forest?" Stroking his hands down her back, he rested them on the curve of her buttocks. "I want to."

Lara looked at him through the thick fan of her lashes. "Bad man." Her smile belied her words. "Leading me off the straight and narrow."

Walker went to say that was his responsibility as her mate when some-thing altered in the air between them . . . or perhaps something altered inside him. He didn't know how to describe it, but he knew for certain that Lara's body was no longer the same as it had been yesterday. Leaning down, he looked into her eyes.

"Walker?" Lara raised one hand to his cheek. "What's the matter?"

Shaking his head, he tried to put a finger on what was bothering him . . . and *oh*. "Did you do a pregnancy test today?"

"No, I was going to wait till—" Lara's eyes widened, one hand going to her abdomen. "Are you *sure*?"

He nodded. He couldn't explain how, but he was sure. It was as if the mating bond had sent him a little pulse of knowledge, a warning that he'd have to take extra care of his mate in the months to come. "Yes, I'm sure."

Tears filled her eyes. "Walker, oh. A baby."

He gathered her in his arms, his own heart thudding so brutally inside his chest it almost hurt. "I love Marlee until it's hard to breathe at times," he told her. "But I never had the chance to experience all the stages of her development. I had to steal time with her." The times she wasn't in day care and her mother, Silent and without rebellion, wasn't around to see how Walker treated his child—as if she was precious. As if she was his heartbeat.

"You won't miss out on anything this time around." She lifted her tear-wet face to his. "We're going to go through this together, all of us. The whole family." Her face glowed. "I can't wait to tell the children."

He loved her even more for loving Marlee and Toby as her own, for treating them like a mother would her babies. "Together," he echoed, and holding her close, looked out at where Marlee was now sitting on the ground eating cake with a similarly occupied Ben next to her.

As he watched, Ben offered her what might've been a chocolate decoration from his piece. She accepted it, giving him something from hers in return. When Spencer moved into view to take a snapshot of the two, Walker knew he'd be asking for a copy.

"Do you think she remembers?" he asked Lara. "The times I had to be cold with her? The times I couldn't pick her up when she cried?"

"Marlee is one of the most well-adjusted children I know." Lara brushed his jaw with her fingers. "Whatever she might've missed out on in her childhood, she always knew that you loved her."

Emotion rising in a tide inside him, Walker spread his hand over her hip. "When shall we tell the family?"

"After I do the test, double confirm." Lara's voice was shaky. "I feel like I'm made of champagne, bubbles of happiness fizzing up my brain."

Walker could've never come up with that description, but it was exactly right. "Me, too," he admitted, bending until their breaths kissed and he could drink in her sheer joy. "Me, too."

Chapter 55

JUDD DIDN'T KNOW quite how he'd ended up with an armful of baby, but someone had handed the child to him, and so he now found himself looking into big brown eyes that looked back at him with just as much curiosity. She wasn't one of the newborn pupcubs. He was fairly sure this child belonged to a leopard soldier named Emmett and his human mate, Ria.

Baby stealing was rampant at the party, the children passed around to be adored and kissed and spoiled. The pups and cubs and pupcubs seemed to take it in their stride, pack creatures that they were. But since no one seemed to realize that Judd had a baby, he stepped a little farther away from the main lights so he could spend more time with this tiny brown-eyed creature.

"Hello," he said, though he knew the baby was too young for verbal communication.

She waved a fist at him.

Cradling her in one arm, he took the offered fist in his free hand. Her skin was so fragile, her bones so soft, and her grip delicate but determined when she tugged at his finger. He found himself smiling, fascinated by her small movements, the way she clearly wanted to bite down on his finger though she had only the merest suggestion of her first two teeth.

"Gorgeous man, you just melted my heart into a puddle."

He'd known Brenna was coming nearer. He could feel her always. When she stopped at the other side of the baby and sighed, he glanced over to meet the extraordinary beauty of her gaze. "Why are you melted?"

"Seriously hot, seriously dangerous man with a tiny, adorable baby in his arms, both of them fascinated with one another?" Uncaring of her stunning ankle-length gown in poppy red, Brenna fell dramatically onto the ground, arms flung out. "Dead." Pushing up onto her elbows, she said, "Especially since it's my hot man holding a baby."

He helped her up using his telekinesis. "You want to hold her?" he asked, strangely reluctant to pass over the soft, warm weight.

"No, it's okay. You keep holding her." Brenna smiled, obviously able to read his emotions. "Her name is Mialin Corrina." Kissing the baby's cheek, Brenna whispered, "Pretty, just like this tiny kitten."

That kitten smiled and made happy sounds that did things inside Judd.

"Did you ever hold Marlee or Sienna?" Brenna asked.

"Marlee." Not often, only when he'd been able to slip the leash of his trainers, and then only when his brother was alone except for the baby. "She used to do this, too." Grip at his finger and later, at his hair. "I always found it so peaceful to hold her." Feel the beat of her heart, the warm puff of her breath. "I never had the chance with Sienna."

Brenna stroked his forearm. "If I'm right, you'll be holding another baby very soon."

Judd began to ask what she meant when he caught the line of her sight. His brother Walker was standing in the shadows thrown by a distant cabin, but there was no mistaking the joy on his face, or the protective way he had his hand over a beaming Lara's stomach.

Judd's heart gave this great big kick of a beat. "If anyone deserves to be a father again, it's Walker." His brother was the best father, the best man, that Judd had ever known.

Brenna tucked herself under his arm when he held it out. "Do you want kids?"

Judd looked down at the now sleepy-eyed baby in his arms, found himself nodding. "One day. When we're a little older and more . . . like Walker and Lara. More steady. Do you know what I mean?"

"I know exactly. They're rooted and solid, anchored." She slipped her arm around his waist. "We're still finding our way, discovering who we are. But one thing I know—you're mine and I'm yours and any growing we do will be together."

"Always." Judd couldn't imagine life without Brenna. It simply didn't make sense to him. "Do you think I should give her back?"

"Finders keepers, I say."

So they kept the baby for an hour, watching her sleep and touching her upturned nose every so often, or brushing their fingers over her little fists. It was Emmett who finally came to claim his daughter. "Come on, baby girl," he murmured, taking her from Judd.

His hands were big and a little scarred, his face rough-edged despite the fact that he'd shaved, but the tenderness in his hold was endless. The baby's face lit up even in sleep at the sound of her father's voice.

"Thank you for letting us hold her." He knew Emmett must've been aware of his daughter's location every instant that she hadn't been in his arms.

"I figured she couldn't be more safe than with an Arrow. You protect the innocent after all." Emmett kissed his daughter's forehead. "But now this kitten's great-grandmother wants to see her and she has first rights."

As the other man turned and walked away, Judd felt his heart give another kick. Because for the longest time, the Arrows had been the nightmares, the bogeymen. They'd protected, too, but no one had seen it. Now, at last, the world was starting to understand. It no longer mattered so much to Judd, but for his brethren . . .

He searched for and found Vasic in the crowd. The teleporter was standing quietly beside his mate while she chatted to Sascha, but he was engaged. He was present. As was a man who wasn't an Arrow but who walked the same dangerous roads. Catching his gaze, Kaleb nodded. Judd nodded back before returning his attention to the wolf who'd hauled him into her arms and taught him to live.

"Let's dance," he said. "I want to celebrate this night."

ANNIE'S leg ached but it was nothing major, not now that she was using the anti-inflammatories Tamsyn had prescribed. The relative lack of pain left her free to enjoy the festivities. She'd become used to changeling events in the time she'd been mated to Zach, but this one was unusual in more than one way. Not just because of the wolves but all the others here tonight.

That was when she saw him across the clearing. He was standing by the trees, separate from everyone while his eyes tracked the woman with dark blue eyes who was Faith's cousin. Annie knew who he was of course—hard for anyone not to recognize the man rumored to be the most powerful Psy in the Net.

But seeing Kaleb Krychek on the comm screen was different from seeing him in person. The power that pulsed off him . . . It was strangely familiar, but perhaps she was fooling herself. Still, she had to know.

Moving carefully and using her cane for support, she made her way across the clearing after checking to see that Rowan was happy in the arms of one of his young aunts. *There he was, her beautiful boy.*

She felt as if she was smiling with her entire body.

The constant use of the cane, the problems with her leg that had resulted from the change in her balance during pregnancy, it was all worth it.

Of course, Zach was a growly overprotective leopard who hated seeing her in any pain. If he had his way, she'd be sitting in bed drinking tea and eating crumpets every day. Smile growing impossibly deeper, she looked around, found her mate.

He was hunkered on the ground with his nephew Bryan standing behind him. Bryan had his hands over Zach's eyes as he asked his uncle to guess something. *Ah,* that explained why Zach hadn't zeroed over to her as soon as she left her comfortable seat. She liked that seat, loved how people constantly came over to socialize and how the cubs squeezed their warm, squirmy bodies in beside her when they wanted a rest.

Annie wasn't stubborn without reason, and there was no reason to put unnecessary pressure on her leg when she could sit now and save up her energy for later.

Like for petting her mate.

But she couldn't sit. Not tonight. Not at this moment.

Kaleb's eyes connected with hers when she was still several feet away. He scanned away an instant later, likely believing she was moving to join a group a little way to his left. When she stayed on course, however, he returned his attention to her; she was close enough now to truly see those extraordinary eyes, see the white stars on black that was a cardinal's gaze.

After coming to know Sascha and Faith, she'd realized cardinal eyes weren't all the same. Each was distinctive . . . and this pair, she would never, *ever* forget. Throat thick, she came to a halt about two feet from him, the two of them far enough away from everyone else that they had privacy. It was clear he didn't recognize her. Why should he? She'd been a small, skinny girl of seven at the time he last saw her.

He'd been a child, too, but those eyes. Those *eyes*.

"May I be of assistance?" he asked when she stayed silent. "I can teleport you back to your seat if you're in pain."

Annie shook her head, her eyes burning. "It's you," she whispered.

He stared at her for several seconds before his gaze went slowly to her leg, then to the cane on which she rested her hand and her weight. When he lifted that starlit gaze to meet hers once more, she knew he remembered. Remembered the freak bullet train derailment, remembered the small girl trapped under a crushing weight of metal, remembered lifting that metal so she could be pulled out.

"They saved your leg."

Swallowing, she nodded. "Plassteel that grew as I grew," she told him. "It was the most advanced operation at the time." There had been progress since then, and Annie had been considering one more operation that would fix the remaining issues, but then she'd fallen pregnant and decided the operation could wait. "My name is Annie Quinn."

"I saw you with an infant." Kaleb's voice was as midnight as the sense of power that swirled around him.

"Yes, he's mine. Mine and Zach's." A tear rolled down her face. "Thanks to you, I'm here and I'm—"

"Angel." Zach's voice, holding a hard edge. "Why are you crying?" He placed a hand on her lower back, Rowan cradled in his other arm.

Looking into his beloved face, she said, "Zach, it was Kaleb." More tears rolled down her face. "All those years ago, it was him."

Her mate's grim expression changed into one of quiet respect. Sliding his hand out from behind Annie, he held it out to Kaleb. "It's an honor."

Kaleb shook Zach's hand, though Annie could guess he wasn't a man at ease with skin privileges on any level—except with Sahara.

"I did what was necessary," he said with no change in his intonation or expression.

"You did what was right." Annie refused to allow him to brush aside his heroism. He'd been a boy with such old eyes, and he'd done what was *right*. From what she'd learned of the Psy since becoming part of Dark-River, she knew that choice would've cost him.

Under Silence, a telekinetic child would've been strictly supervised . . . and likely tortured in an effort to teach him control. "You were a hero that day," she said through a throat gone raw. "I will never ever forget what you did."

Zach pressed a kiss to her temple. "Thank you for saving my mate," he said to Kaleb afterward. "I've wanted to say that to Annie's 'boy with the cardinal eyes' for a long time."

Kaleb inclined his head very slightly. "There is no debt," he said, as if he'd tried to work out why she'd approached him and come up with that answer.

Smiling, she wiped away her tears. "I know. You're a good person."

"I believe you'd be one of two people on the planet who'd say that. The other one is the woman changelings would describe as my mate, so she's understandably biased."

That made her laugh wetly while Zach grinned. "Can't say the man's not honest." He rubbed her lower back. "You want to tell him or shall I?"

"I want to." Touching her fingers to her baby's, she said, "This is our son, Rowan." She looked up to hold Kaleb's eyes. "I'd like to use your name as his middle name." Without Kaleb, she wouldn't be here, wouldn't have a mate and a son. It was important to her to honor the act of courage of the boy he'd been in a way that made him part of her family.

Kaleb took several seconds to reply. "Are you sure you want him linked to me?" he asked at last.

"Yes." She knew what the world saw when they looked at Kaleb Krychek, but she saw the hurt boy who'd nonetheless thought of others. She was glad, so glad that he'd found joy, that he'd found love. "You will always be a part of our family, and I hope you'll accept that invitation in the spirit it's given."

Kaleb's eyes left hers, found his mate's, and Annie had the sense he was talking to her. When he looked back at her, he said, "Thank you."

"We'll send you our details, in case you'd like to visit." She didn't think Kaleb Krychek was the visiting-babies-and-friends kind of man, but he was family now and would be treated as such. "I hope you come."

"Yes," Zach added. "You'll be welcome."

AFTER Kaleb inclined his head in acknowledgment of the DarkRiver couple's offer, the male—Zach—began to coax his mate to head back to her seat. Having noticed how heavily Annie leaned on the cane and was now leaning against her mate, Kaleb said, "Would you like a lift?"

They both stared at him before grinning in concert. It was Zach who said, "Why the hell not?"

It took less than a heartbeat. He could see the destination and they were standing in front of him. Even as Annie opened her mouth to speak, the couple and their baby found themselves by the comfortably cushioned wicker chair from where Annie had walked over. Laughing, the couple waved at him before Zach helped Annie into her seat, then handed the infant to her.

An infant named Rowan Kaleb Quinn.

That was the first time I exercised my own free will, he said to Sahara as his heart walked toward him, a woman of about five two in a strapless gown the color of ripe cherries that set off the warm shade of her skin. She'd chosen the black-on-black suit he wore, caressing her fingers over his pectoral muscles before she buttoned up his shirt.

I glimpsed news of the train derailment on the comm screen, he told her, *saw that a small girl was trapped underneath all that twisted metal.* A child just like him, hurt and broken. *So I snapped the chains on my mind and for a small fraction of time, I was free and I was doing something good.*

Flowing into his arms, Sahara looked up at him with eyes that had always seen him for exactly who he was—a man who lived in the gray but who loved her with every dark corner of his soul. "You were being true to yourself." She spread her hand over his heart. "Even in the horror, you found the will and had the courage to fight for what was right."

He brushed his hand over her hair. Here, with the changelings, such contact between mates was accepted—expected even. They were a highly tactile race, and while Kaleb would've found that strange before Sahara came into his life, she'd long ago taught him the value of a touch given in affection and love.

Let's be young and happy today, Kaleb. Sahara's mind speaking to his, her telepathic voice poignant with memories of all the celebrations they'd missed, all the pain they'd survived. *Like we were in that market in Istanbul. Forget about everything else for one night.*

Kaleb was always on alert for threats, but that didn't mean he'd deny Sahara. If she asked for the moon, he'd find a way to lay it at her feet. *Anything you want.*

The catastrophic problem with the Net would still be there tomorrow, as would the Consortium's machinations and the politics of the powerful and dangerous.

Will you dance with me? The charms on Sahara's bracelet clinked against one another as she lifted her arms to link them around his neck, her love for him proud and open.

Deep inside, even the part of him that was the void, merciless and dark and broken, knew happiness, knew joy. *You're the dancer.* But he took her into his arms and they moved to the rhythm of the slow, romantic song the band was playing. Kaleb knew it was romantic because Sahara whispered that to him while stealing a kiss.

Her hair was soft, carrying the fresh scent of her shampoo. He'd washed her hair for her in the shower earlier that day, after which he'd demanded payment for his work in kisses. With her, he could be young, could be the boy with whom she'd fallen in love before the world tore them apart.

No one interrupted them for that song or the next. But on the third . . .

"Hi, Mr. Krychek!"

Kaleb glanced down to find himself looking into the face of a child of about five or six, the boy's dark hair messy silk. "Hello."

"Zach said you teleported him!" The boy was all but jumping up and down. "Can you teleport me?"

Do you think he has any idea I'm considered a deadly threat by most individuals on the planet?

Nope. Sahara's eyes laughed at him. *He thinks you're a new toy.*

It cost Kaleb nothing to teleport the child to the far side of the compound. He could hear the boy's excited cry from here. "Perhaps we should leave before he tells all his small friends."

Weaving her fingers through his, Sahara tugged him forward. "Come speak to the adults. They'll make sure the children behave."

Kaleb found himself next to Judd not long afterward, Sahara having led him to the man who was his friend. "You two talk," she said. "I haven't had a chance to catch up with Faith yet."

"Do you get asked to be a personal teleporter?" Kaleb asked Judd after Sahara blew him a kiss and began to weave her way through the crowd to find her cousin.

"Yes." A slight smile from the former Arrow. "Even though I occasionally dump them in the lake."

"I probably shouldn't do the same as I'm a guest, and over half the people here are still certain I'm going to kill them at any moment."

"True." Judd nodded toward Annie and Zach. "Saw you talking. You know them?"

"Yes. From a lifetime ago." He realized he'd never told Judd of the childhood incident, did so now. "She's going to give her child Kaleb as a middle name." He still wasn't sure how he felt about that.

Judd's expression turned solemn. "An honor and an invitation."

"Yes." Kaleb saw a child running toward them, teleported the girl right next to her elders—who grabbed her by the shoulders and made her sit down to eat at a picnic table. "It appears I'm gathering even more . . . people."

"People?" Judd shook his head. "I think you mean family."

"Sahara is my family."

"She's the center, yes, but a family is a living organism. It grows in many directions. Like Xavier's Nina—she's now part of our family, too." Judd's eyes followed a pair of leopard cubs who'd snuck under the food table and were attempting to pull down the tablecloth. A tiny panther cub stood on this side of the table and looked at them with an inquisitive expression on its face.

A second later, the leopard cubs found themselves in front of a tall brunette dressed in a fitted gown of shimmering bronze. She looked down at their startled faces, then located Judd in the clearing and called out, "What did they do?"

Judd pointed to the tablecloth they hadn't quite managed to dislodge.

Hands on her hips, the brunette scowled down at the cubs who were now both sitting up in an attentive pose. "You do realize I could punish you by saying no more dessert this entire party?"

Flopping onto their fronts, the cubs hid their eyes using their paws.

Kaleb could see the brunette struggling not to smile.

Going down on her haunches, she lifted the cubs by the scruffs of their necks. "That was a very naughty thing to do," she said sternly. "I'm going to give you a pass because it's a celebration but any more naughtiness and I'm taking you home and making you Brussels sprouts for dinner."

The cubs' mouths fell open.

"Yes," she said in that same stern tone. "Brussels sprouts, with spinach for dessert. Now, will you be good?"

Two quick nods.

"Hmm. I'll be watching." Setting down the chastened cubs, she managed to keep a straight face until they were far enough away that they didn't see her grin as she came over to Judd and Kaleb. "People keep telling me they'll get into less mischief as they get older, but I swear they're just getting smarter about their naughtiness."

"They know they're safe," Kaleb found himself saying. "It gives them the freedom to push boundaries."

The brunette, who he'd identified as the DarkRiver healer, Tamsyn Ryder, nodded. "I know, but I'm already starting to dread their teenage years. I have visions of jetcycles and climbing up girls' walls at night." Affection colored every word. "Knowing the two of them, they'll work together to steal ladders to scale those walls."

Kaleb didn't understand children, especially not children like this. He understood Arrow children the best. But he could also see why Aden was working so hard to reform the very foundation of Arrow society. It had to do with love and with trust.

The kind of love and trust that had him teleporting his mate away from Faith without warning ten minutes later.

"Kaleb!" His name had barely cleared her lips when he teleported them into the forest.

"Are you kidnapping me?" Sahara scowled at him but stayed flush against his body.

"We never finished our dance."

Sahara's response was soft, her eyes holding a thousand dreams. "We never will. This dance we're in, it's forever."

Good.

Chapter 56

SPOTTING KIT ON the far edge of the celebration, Lucas pressed a kiss to the temple of the sleeping pupcub in his arms before passing the child's small, warm weight to his doting grandfather. He then made his way directly to the young soldier. There was a look in Kit's eyes that the panther in him well understood.

"When are you leaving?" he asked the man he'd watched grow from babe to youth to this soldier who had earned his deepest trust.

Kit blew out a breath. "I thought, tonight." A half smile. "Hopefully no one will notice with all the excitement, and I'll be long gone by then."

Lucas knew why Kit wanted to go without telling anyone—leopards understood the need to roam, but Kit was a child of the pack and many would miss him desperately. Especially the cubs. "You've spoken to the children?" Julian and Roman, in particular, considered Kit a big brother.

"I told them I'm going on an adventure." Kit shoved a hand through his hair, his eyes holding a deeply feline curiosity. "How did you know?"

Lucas just shook his head. He was alpha—a good alpha always knew the heartbeat of his pack, and he'd known for a while that Kit was restless and straining at his skin. He needed to stretch himself, explore the wider world, even more so than most leopards because Kit had the scent of a future alpha.

That wasn't, however, what made a true alpha. Being alpha took an ability to love with a depth that included each and every person under the alpha's care; it also required a temperament that fostered trust in the bonds of pack. Rough or sophisticated, growly or warm, each alpha was unique, but the best alphas had both those qualities.

So did Kit.

Any pack he founded would be strong, would endure. Lucas had seen the young male come into himself over the past year. Already, his peers looked to him for leadership; when it came time for him to strike out on his own, he'd have sentinels ready to back him and build a pack with him.

That time, however, was in the future. For now, Kit remained a child of DarkRiver heading out into the world, to roam as his leopard demanded. "Be wild," Lucas said with a smile. "Explore everything you want to explore. Run hard, play hard, find your skin." Tugging the boy close, Lucas hugged him tight.

Kit hugged him back as fiercely. "I need to roam," he whispered, "but I'll miss everyone."

"Roaming doesn't mean disappearing," Lucas reminded him when they drew apart. "Stay in touch and meet up with packmates who are roaming in the same areas. You can discover who you are without turning loner. I have a feeling Cory and Nico are nearly ready to roam, too, so you might run into them sooner rather than later."

Relief colored Kit's features. Lucas understood. Their nature was dual—the solitary leopard and the social human. It was at this stage of life, a point that came at a different time for each one of them, that the leopard became more ascendant than the human. However, they remained changeling. Being totally solitary wasn't a natural choice.

"Look after Rina," Kit said, then laughed and closed his hand over the dog tags that hung from his neck. "She'd kill me if she heard me say that, but—"

"I get it." Rina and Kit had become a tight unit after the deaths of both their parents. "I'll make sure she doesn't get into too much trouble." Rina had done her roaming and though her edgy tendencies remained, that was part of her personality and nothing Lucas would try to crush. All he'd asked from her was discipline. "Go. Roam."

Kit's grin was wild, his eyes turning leopard. Shifting on his heel without further words, he faded into the trees, a young leopard heading out to explore the world.

"I'll miss him," said a familiar female voice from behind Lucas, slender arms sliding around his body as she pressed her cheek to his back.

He closed his hand over one of Sascha's. "I know, kitten, but it's how we grow." Sascha found it hard each time one of their young adults left the pack; her instinct as an E was to hold her family together, keep them safe and happy. Consciously, she knew the majority of leopards needed to roam to settle into their adult skins, to be truly happy, but that didn't lessen her worry at watching them go. "He'll come back."

"But he might leave again one day, more permanently."

"Yes." There was a high chance that, bonded as closely as he was to DarkRiver and Lucas, Kit would offer to remain in the pack as one of Lucas's sentinels. But should Kit make that offer, Lucas would decline it. Not because he didn't want Kit's strength and loyalty beside him, but because he knew Kit was meant to lead his own pack—he was one of the most promising young alphas Lucas had ever known.

Lucas would do him a disservice if he didn't push him to be all that he could be.

"Often," he said to his mate, "our chicks have to leave the nest to find their wings." Turning, he wrapped his arms around her. "That doesn't mean they aren't still ours. Even when Kit leaves DarkRiver, he'll still be one of us."

Sascha nodded, took a breath. "I'm trying not to think of Naya going off on her own one day in the future."

Chuckling, Lucas nuzzled her. "Kitten, our cub isn't going anywhere anytime soon." Not to roam and not because she'd been stolen away by enemies.

Lucas would protect his child to the death. If Pax Marshall proved to have been the mastermind behind Naya's planned abduction, Lucas would take vengeance against the Psy male. And if it turned out that Pax had been set up, then Lucas would go after the shadowy figures pulling the strings of what could've been a deadly game.

"But Naya will eventually go off roaming," Sascha insisted and, a scowl on her features, said, "Do you know what Jamie did while he was away? *Race cars* at dangerously high speeds, make friends with bears who got him drunk every day of the week—"

"You gotta watch bears. They can drink anyone under the table."

"Stop laughing." She pushed at his shoulders. "I'm not sure how he made it back in one piece, especially after he decided to go deep-sea diving. What cat does that?"

"Jamie's always been a law unto himself." Lucas shuddered at the idea of being submerged that far in the deep. "Did you notice the weirdest change?"

When Sascha frowned and looked around for the male Lucas had just promoted to sentinel alongside fellow former senior soldier, Desiree, Lucas said, "His hair's the color he was born with." It happened to be a rich chocolate brown.

Sascha's eyes widened. "I didn't realize. But he feels all right."

He knew she meant that in the empathic sense. "Well," he said, nipping and sucking at her lips in a teasing kiss, "when a cat takes up deep-sea diving, changing hair colors probably isn't very exciting anymore."

Sascha's laughter drew the attention of one of the cubs who hadn't yet given in to exhaustion. Normally, they'd all be down by now, but since it was a special occasion, he and Hawke had relaxed the rules. Catching Roman in her arms, the boy in human form and miraculously dressed in the same clothes he'd arrived in—which meant he'd actually cached his clothes pre-shift—Sascha hefted him up.

"Oof," she said as she settled him on her hip. "Did you eat an entire cake?"

Roman's eyes widened. "I shared with Jules and Issy and Dai and Naya."

"Well, that's all right then." Sascha kissed him on the cheek, and Roman put his head on her shoulder.

He was asleep by the time they reached the other side of the pack circle. Seeing them, Nathan reached out to take his son into his arms.

Rome didn't wake, sleeping with the carefree abandon of a child who knew he was safe and loved.

After pressing a kiss to his son's silky black hair, Nathan caught Lucas's gaze and angled his head to the left. Lucas looked in that direction to see a pile of cubs and pups, Naya included, fast asleep on a soft blanket someone had laid out. Two little girls lay in human form amongst the furry bodies: Noor, and Aneca, one of Teijan's pack.

Nathan walked over to place Rome with his playmates, including Jules. The boy stayed in human form but curled around the others. They, in turn, moved in their sleep to snuggle around him, and he was soon blanketed in golden fur spotted with black as well as the soft brown fur of wolf pups. Naya slept in the protective circle of his arm, Jules's furred body on her other side.

Sascha was right.

One day, these children, too, would head out to roam.

Lucas looked back toward the place where Kit had disappeared and wished that cub well. The pack would be waiting for him when he was ready to come home, whether that was a month from now or ten years. Each leopard's journey was his own. Knowing adventure and discovery awaited Kit, Lucas and his mate rejoined the party that celebrated a bond signed in blood and welded together by loyalty—and now, by three newborn lives.

The parents of those newborns, a wolf lieutenant and a leopard sentinel, danced to a soft, slow ballad with the unconscious grace of a couple in sync on the deepest level. And though they appeared lost in one another, Lucas was fully conscious that Mercy Smith and Riley Kincaid knew the *exact* whereabouts of each of their three babies. The new parents tended to only be able to bear the separation from their pupcubs for about five minutes at most.

Then they'd reclaim Belle, Ace, and Micah, cuddle them close.

Smiling within, he took in the others here: lethal and dangerous Kaleb Krychek who'd just emerged from the forest with his laughing mate; easy-humored Max Shannon and his wife, Sophia Russo; ex-Psy Councilor and current member of the Ruling Coalition, Anthony Kyriakus. Then there was Teijan's sharply dressed presence near Ivy Jane, the empath currently chatting to Tally—who gently cradled a pupcub, while Ivy's Arrow mate spoke with the Rat alpha.

Nearby, Forgotten leader Devraj Santos chatted to Jon and Clay, and not far from them, Katya Haas was deep in conversation with Ashaya Aleine and Alice Eldridge. Ashaya's twin had turned down an invitation to attend, having no desire to be part of any kind of a social gathering, but Lucas knew she was present in some sense through her unbreakable tie with Ashaya.

Myriad bonds connected the people here.

It was a tangled kaleidoscope. One he could've never imagined the day he first sat across the table from a beautiful woman with eyes of cardinal starlight. Those eyes met his at that instant, her body warm at his side. He went to draw her into a kiss when he felt a tug on his pant leg.

Leaning down, he scooped Naya into his arms. "I couldn't have imagined you, either," he said to their mischievous cub, who'd padded away from her sleeping friends and now growled happily at him.

Sascha's laugh was soft, her kiss passionate against his lips. Held between them, her mother's hand on her back, Naya purred, happy and safe and with no awareness that she was the embodiment of change.

Nadiya Shayla Hunter would never have an ordinary life.

And perhaps, if the adults here and around the world got it right, she'd never know anything but friendship and family and hope. Not war. Not racial discord. Not anger and distrust.

"I like to imagine a future," he said to Sascha, "where one day, our daughter stands in the center of the United Earth Federation and when she speaks, the ears that hear her voice are Psy and human and changeling and Forgotten and every possible blend."

Eyes shining wet, Sascha whispered, "No divisions, no artificial lines."

"Yes." He tapped Naya on the nose when she tried to bite his jaw. "Just a vibrant peace."

"Well," his mate said slowly, "not quite three-and-a-half years ago, when we mated, you punched Hawke hard enough to knock him down. Tonight, he's rocking a pupcub who technically belongs to you. Roughly three years for wolf and leopard to become family." A deep smile. "It's not a bad start."

She took their baby when Naya jumped over, nuzzling and cuddling their cub with sweet maternal affection. "I believe in us." Her eyes met his, streamers of color in their depths. "All of us. I believe we'll find a way out of the darkness. The Consortium won't win—and in defeating it, we'll forge bonds no one will be able to break."

Lucas ran his knuckles over her cheek. "Trust an empath to find a silver lining."

Turning her head, Sascha kissed the skin above the pulse in his wrist. "Our daughter *will* stand in the United Earth Federation and when she does, we'll proudly tell everyone we know that that's our baby."

Panther prowling to the surface of his skin, Lucas gathered his mate and their child in his arms. "Hold Trinity together, defeat the Consortium, help the Psy save the PsyNet, and help the humans figure out a way to block psychic intrusion, and finally, set up the UEF." He nodded. "Let's do it."